"I was hoping ⟨⟩ W9-AOR-558 about Corey," Beth said.

"Everything okay?" Nick asked.

"I'm not sure. Corey's afraid you'll send him back to his grandparents if he doesn't read well."

The woman didn't beat around the bush. "Where would he get that idea?"

Beth shrugged. "Your son told me in confidence, but I thought you should know because he's stressing about reading."

Nick nodded, but his gut felt like it'd been shredded. He'd left Corey behind before so it only stood to reason that his son didn't trust him not to do it again.

"You okay?" Beth's voice was soft.

His little guy had so much riding on those seven-year-old shoulders.

"I think Corey wanted you to come today because he's not easy around me anymore," Nick said. "He thinks I'll leave him. I don't know what to do about it."

"Maybe what you need is something fun to do together. Find some interests in common."

Right now, that interest was Beth Ryken. Corey liked her, and so did Nick.

Maybe too much.

Books by Jenna Mindel

Love Inspired

Mending Fences
Season of Dreams
Courting Hope
Season of Redemption
The Deputy's New Family

JENNA MINDEL

lives in northwest Michigan with her husband and their three dogs. She enjoys a career in banking that has spanned twenty-five years and several positions, but writing is her passion. A 2006 Romance Writers of America RITA® Award finalist, Jenna has answered her heart's call to write inspirational romances set near the Great Lakes.

The Deputy's
New Family

Jenna Mindel

HARLEQUIN® LOVE INSPIRED®

Recycling programs for this product may not exist in your area.

LOVE INSPIRED BOOKS

ISBN-13: 978-0-373-87910-6

THE DEPUTY'S NEW FAMILY

Copyright © 2014 by Jenna Mindel

www.Harlequin.com

Printed in U.S.A.

But now the Lord who created you, O Israel, says:
Don't be afraid, for I have ransomed you;
I have called you by name; you are mine.
When you go through deep waters and great trouble,
I will be with you. When you go through rivers of
difficulty, you will not drown!
—*Isaiah* 43:1–2

To my sister, Lisa.

Although I was a pesky baby sister
who wouldn't stay out of your stuff,
you inspired me to love words—reading them (yours)
and then eventually writing them (mine).

You also taught me the real joy of haiku.
Thank you…for everything. I love you!

Acknowledgments

To Julie Mindel, Abby Carter and Tracey Miller:
Thank you for your rich examples and answers to
my many questions about reading levels, classroom
activities and standards. I applaud what you ladies
do! And I really appreciate your time as well as
giving me a glimpse into your worlds. Thank you!

To Kyle Sitzema: Thank you for your firearm
expertise. See, I finally wrote a red-headed hero!

To Christine Johnson: Thank you for sharing your
sailing knowledge. I couldn't have written that
exhausting scene without you!

Chapter One

"Miss Ryken, you've got a new student." The familiar voice of her school principal was warm but bore unwelcome news.

Beth Ryken didn't like surprises and a new student when the school year was two months from over wasn't good news at all. Core standard evaluations still had to be met and time at the end of the year was always fleeting.

Gathering her thoughts into a quick prayer for patience, Beth looked up but her gaze snagged on the tall man standing beside the principal. He was lean and mean looking in spite of the boyishness in his face. And he had short red hair. Not exactly a common combination. He also had an angular jaw and a strong nose that looked as if it might have been broken a time or two. Put him in a kilt and he'd be devastating to females everywhere.

Cool gray eyes assessed her. The man didn't look pleased by her perusal. Annoyed, maybe. Cynical, definitely, but not at all happy.

Beth ignored those itchy fingers of attraction that scratched up her spine. Tossing her hair over her shoulder, she focused on the boy standing in front of the man.

Red hair like his father and the same colored eyes, which looked lost instead of cold.

Beth melted. "Hello."

The boy gave her a hint of a smile aimed straight into her heart.

"This is Nick Grey and his son, Corey. They just moved to the area," her principal explained. "Beth Ryken is one of two second-grade teachers here."

"Welcome to LeNaro." Beth held out her hand to the youngster. "Corey, I have the perfect spot for you next to Thomas. His table could use one more boy to make it even. We're coloring tall ships right now and I'll have Gracie get an extra page for you."

Corey looked up at his father for direction.

He gave his approval with a quick nod while he released the hold he had on his son's shoulders.

Nick Grey did not wear a wedding ring. There wasn't an indentation or even a white mark left behind by a ring. If he'd been married, it must have been a long time ago. The only jewelry the man wore was a bulky watch clamped on to his wrist.

Typically, when dads dropped off their kids at a new school, it was safe to assume they were single, but something in Corey's eyes hinted at sadness. Was there a custody battle going on?

"Everyone, I'd like you to say hello to Corey Grey. He's new to our school."

The kids mumbled their hellos and then quieted when they spotted Corey's dad. Her students stared openly with awe, too. Mr. Grey's hair wasn't *that* red, so it had to be something else about the man. Like maybe how his pushed-up shirtsleeves revealed arms that were taut and whipcord lean. He reminded her of a power line that shot deadly sparks when snapped. Yeah, the guy looked a little dangerous.

Corey slipped his hand into hers.

Beth gave it a quick squeeze and led the boy toward the table and Thomas. "No backpack?"

Corey shook his head.

Beth glanced at his father before giving Corey a friendly wink. There was still a black one in the lost and found in the school's office. He'd need something to carry his books and papers home. "We'll get you set up."

Once the boy had been seated and introduced to his tablemates, Beth turned her attention back to Nick Grey. Not hard to do. Something about the man invited long looks.

But Nick watched his son with steely concentration before resting his unsettling gaze upon her. "I'll be back to pick him up after school."

"Whoa, wait." Beth held up her hand. "A little more information would be good."

Nick cocked his head toward Tammy, her principal. "She can fill you in." Then one more glance at his son. "I have to leave for an appointment."

Not quite rude, but terse came to mind, and authoritative. Was he military? The only military base nearby was a Coast Guard air station in Traverse City twenty miles south. Long commute, but maybe he wanted his son in a small school setting.

Beth reached a hand out to Nick. He was a good few inches taller than her, a rarity since she hovered near the six-foot mark. "Okay, well, nice to meet you, Mr. Grey. I'm sure we'll talk more once your son settles in."

Nick looked at her offered hand a moment before accepting it. "Sounds good."

First Beth registered his strength and then the warmth

of his skin as his hand gripped hers for a firm shake. But looking into the man's eyes was what made her breath hitch. He really looked at her, as if delving down deep to see who she was. Not that he could possibly know with only one look but Beth still shivered.

And then he gave her a nod, let go and left.

Beth blew out her breath with a whoosh. "What was that?"

Tammy laughed. "Odd man."

Odd didn't quite cover it. Beth's heart still raced. "So what's the deal here?"

Tammy shrugged and lowered her voice. "Pretty vague, really. Mr. Grey showed up early this morning with his son and his medical records and filled out the paperwork for admission. There's no Mrs. Grey—she died a year ago. The boy's maternal grandparents are listed as the second emergency contact."

Beth's heart twisted. Corey Grey lost his mom at a tender age. Yup, sad story. Poor kid. She watched as he quietly colored his paper. So far the boy kept to himself with little interaction with his tablemates. Even bubbly little Grace Cavanaugh couldn't pull Corey into conversation. Was he shy? Or something else?

Beth continued to stare. Corey wanted a crayon, but he waited for Thomas to put it down before reaching for it. "What about testing?"

"Let's see how he does over the next couple of weeks, and then we'll meet and discuss a plan of action with the school counselor."

Beth nodded. Tammy was an excellent principal with an elementary teaching background. LeNaro Elementary School prided itself on meeting its students' educational needs first and foremost. They didn't push kids through the lower grades if they weren't ready to move on. If extra attention didn't work, they often recommended a student be held back. Not a popular approach, but the bridge between first and second was a big one. Preparation for third grade with its state standards testing was bigger still.

Beth had a bad feeling about Corey Grey. Loss of his mother plus a tight-lipped father and a new school usually added up to trouble for a seven-year-old. She'd have to keep a close eye on the boy. It wouldn't be hard to do. The kid had already stolen her heart.

Still, Beth needed to review the previous school's assessments before making any assumptions, but her gut feelings usually turned out correct. In Corey's case, that wasn't a good thing. Her guess was Nick Grey wasn't the kind of man who'd take bad news about his son very well.

She rubbed her arms as if a cold breeze had blown into the room. Nick Grey might be a difficult parent to deal with, but she'd find a way to figure it out. She always did.

At the end of the school day, Nick climbed into the driver's seat as Corey buckled up in his booster seat in the back. "How was your first day?"

The kid shrugged.

Nick gripped the steering wheel a little tighter and tried a more specific question. "What about your teacher? Is she nice?"

"Yeah, she's nice." Corey stared straight ahead.

"Good." Nick was beginning to think maybe he'd been wrong in taking Corey from his grandparents.

He'd been wrong about so many things, but Nick believed a boy belonged with his father. Was it selfish to uproot Corey yet again, so soon after losing Susan? Or was all this the price of leaving his kid behind while he finished up a tough case?

Lord, help me out here, please.

Waiting in the line of cars belonging to parents picking up kids, Nick drummed his fingers along the base of the steering wheel. This sort of thing was all new to him, but he'd get used to it. After this morning's appointment with the county sheriff to complete paperwork before he officially started as a deputy, Nick had finished unpacking their belongings. He had purchased a small house complete with a picket fence situated on two pretty acres a couple miles north of town. It was a start. A new start. One he prayed he'd get right.

"Hey, there's Miss Ryken!" Corey had suddenly come to life and waved out the open window. "Beep the horn."

"I'm not beeping the horn."

No way did Nick want to invite her attention. She was everything he liked in a woman on the outside, but she looked a little bit like his dead wife. Only taller and fuller, which, he had to admit, he liked even better. Susan had been obsessed with losing weight when she didn't need to. She constantly fussed over food, measuring and counting calories.

"Come on, Dad."

"The line is moving." Too late—Beth Ryken noticed them and walked toward their idling car. Nick swallowed hard.

"Hi, Corey. Mr. Grey. How was your first day?" She leaned down near the open window on Corey's side and her blond hair fell forward in long waves.

Nick watched the two cars ahead of him creep and then stop. He wasn't going anywhere anytime soon. "He's pretty stiff-lipped about today."

Beth gave him an amused smile. "Like father, like son."

Corey glanced at him and Nick thought he might have seen a glimmer of pride in his son's eyes, but it came and went so fast, Nick couldn't be sure.

"It was fun," Corey finally said.

Beth's perfectly shaped eyebrows rose. "Fun is good. That means you'll come back tomorrow."

Corey nodded.

"Miss Ryken." Nick tried not to stare at her. "Do you know of any after-school programs or good caretakers in the area?"

Her brow furrowed as the cars in front of him started to move. "Why don't you pull around so we don't clog up the line?"

Nick nodded and nearly kicked himself for asking her instead of the principal, but he needed the information. Should have gotten the leads before he'd moved here, but he believed face-to-face was always better than over-the-phone conversations. He was a pretty good judge of character.

Most times.

He'd never been wise when it came to women, though. He fell too hard too fast.

He pulled out of line and parked and then got out. "Corey, stay in the car."

His son stayed put.

Beth jogged toward him. Tall and strong. Confident.

Nick clenched his jaw. She was a sight to be savored.

"Are you looking for a structured program for Corey?"

"I start work soon, and I don't want Corey home alone after school. Any recommendations?"

"I can send a list of care providers with Corey tomorrow. We have an art-and-crafts-focused program after school, but it's only on Thursdays. I'm one of the teachers who staff it."

Nick looked at his car. Corey hung on their every word as he looked out the window. "That sounds good. Sign him up."

"I'll send a release form for that, as well." Her attention was caught by something across the street and then she waved.

Nick turned to see who it was and spotted an older woman dressed for yard work. Raking that lawn was bound to be a challenge considering all the flowers and statues that littered the grass.

"My mother," she explained.

"So your folks live right there?"

Beth's deep blue eyes clouded over. "Just my mom and me. My dad died when I was fourteen."

"Sorry to hear that." Nick tucked the knowledge away. He'd patrol this area soon and he'd pay special attention to that house with two women alone.

"Thank you. I understand that you're widowed."

"Yeah." Nick narrowed his gaze. He knew the kind of offers that usually came after that information. He was in no place to get involved with anyone, let alone someone like Miss Ryken, whose sunny nature seemed too good to be real.

"That must be difficult for you both." Her expression was open and honest. Sweet, even.

"It can be." Nick braced for an invitation he might want but wouldn't accept. He hadn't missed the blatant interest in her eyes when she'd checked him out this morning.

"We have a really good school counselor." Beth fished in her mammoth-sized purse. "Here's her card. She meets with all the students, but it would be wise for you to make an appointment to talk with her right away."

Nick swallowed his surprise and nodded. "Thank you."

"You're welcome. Gotta run." She smiled brighter than sunshine and headed toward the back of his car. "See you tomorrow, Corey."

"See you tomorrow." His son sounded eager.

Nick flipped the card for their school counselor/social worker into his wallet. He'd call the woman in the morning. This school stuff was all new to him. His wife had taken care of that. After Susan's death, Nick's mother had stepped in to finish out first grade and get the boy started with second grade until she got bogged down with his sister's issues.

The past six months, Susan's parents had kept Corey safe and sound with them while Nick finished a delicate undercover case that took him out of town most nights. He'd had few days off and they were erratic at best.

He watched Beth cross the street and slip inside the modest home where she lived while her mother made a feeble attempt to rake up dead leaves from last fall.

Nick needed to step up. He wanted to be the kind of father his boy deserved, only he wasn't exactly sure how. He slipped behind the wheel and looked at his son. "Hungry? There's a café in town or the mini-mart and then we have to hit the grocery store."

Corey wasn't listening. He watched where his second-grade teacher had gone like a hawk. "Is that where Miss Ryken lives?"

"It is."

Corey looked at him. "Why can't I go there after school?"

Nick coughed. Not exactly something he could ask his son's teacher and she certainly hadn't offered, but that sure would make things convenient. "You really like your new teacher."

Corey nodded, looking deadly serious. "She's kinda like Mom, on her good days."

"I know." Nick felt as if he'd been punched in the gut. Corey had noticed the resemblance, too.

How did he handle that one? Ignore it, as he'd tried to

do with his wife? She'd had too many bad days, and some days Susan barely bothered to get out of bed. Nick and Corey had been a team then. A silent partnership of protection against Susan's mood swings.

Nick hoped Miss Ryken's blond hair and blue eyes were as far as the similarity to Susan went. Corey's teacher had a sunny demeanor as well as good looks, but the instant attraction that had sliced sharp through him made him nervous. He'd fallen hard before, before he saw the darkness that lay underneath Susan's cheerful facade.

If love was blind, then Nick had been deaf, too.

"Who was that you were talking to earlier?"

Beth picked through her mother's latest shopping bag on the kitchen table, sorting out things to keep and return. "Do you have the receipt for these?"

"In my purse."

"Mom, you really need to stop buying stuff you don't need."

"But they were on sale."

Beth rubbed her eyes. Everything on sale ended up in her mother's tiny house. "We've got to stick to your budget."

Her mother gave her that look of tried patience. They'd been over this before. Several times in fact. "You didn't answer my question."

"What question?"

"Who was that tall man you were talking to?" Keen interest sparkled from her mom's eyes. Her dishwater-blond hair was covered with a flamboyantly patterned silk scarf, another "on sale" purchase. Who did yard work wearing *Ann Taylor*?

Beth waved her hand in dismissal, but her heart skipped

a few beats at the mere mention of Nick Grey. "Oh, he's the dad of a new student in my class."

"Married?"

Okay, so every one of her friends was either married or getting married and her mom hoped the same for her. At twenty-six, it wasn't as if Beth was beyond hope, but she'd always been the proverbial bridesmaid. In a couple weeks, she'd repeat that role for her best bud and ex-roomie, Eva Marsh. Beth didn't need a reminder of her very single status, nor did she need her mother ferreting out prospects. Not that Beth had much success on her own.

She let loose a sigh. "Mom…"

"Well, is he?"

"No. He's widowed."

Her mother's smile grew even wider. "Interesting."

Yeah, very. Who wouldn't be moved by a handsome widowed man and his adorable son? "Can I have that receipt?"

"You're awfully bossy since you moved back home." Her mother bustled for her purse and then handed over the offensive slip of paper totaling the merchandise from a department store in Traverse City.

"Just trying to keep you out of bankruptcy." Beth smiled sweetly. She'd moved home over Christmas after she'd gotten wind of her mother's dwindling bank account. Something had to be done.

"You've got a smart mouth just like your father, God rest his soul." Her mom stripped off her work gloves and washed her hands. "What do you want for dinner?"

Beth shrugged.

Her mother used to get in hot water with her father over spending habits, too. On a cop's salary, they could afford only so much and her mother had expensive tastes. But she'd never been this bad with her shopping sprees before, had she? Maybe now that Beth saved every penny, her mother's spending glared brighter.

Beth's dad used to say the key to happiness was being content with what you had. He used to tell Beth to do whatever she loved and be grateful to God for everything. God had given her a passion. It was teaching. Her dad's had been for police work. It got him killed.

"Beth?"

She shook off her thoughts. "What?"

"Dinner?" Her mom cocked her head. "My, my, that man really got to you, huh? What's his name, this father of your new student?"

Nick. Nicholas Grey. The name kind of rolled easily around in her brain. "What about the leftovers from last night? Let's eat those and I'll make a salad."

Her mother made a face. "I suppose."

Beth chuckled. She'd called a halt to throwing out food, too. Her mother was a wonderful cook who loved to create masterpieces in the kitchen, but she made too much and then left it in the fridge too long. Since moving in, Beth never had to worry about packing something good for lunch.

Beth got up to make that salad while her mom reheated the chicken carbonara from Sunday's dinner. Beth glanced at the woman who worried her. Ever since her mom's work hours had been severely cut back at the airport in Traverse City, her mom's handle on her finances had slipped. Even with Beth's rent payments for living here. The shopping trips increased. Was she bored? Or was something else going on?

Nick Grey's question about after-school day-care providers filtered through Beth's mind. Could watching Corey bring meaning back to her mother's daily routine? Something about that little boy's reserve made Beth think her mom's flamboyant style might be good for him. It didn't get any more convenient than walking across the street from school.

The fact that Beth would get to see more of Nick Grey when he picked up his son brought a heady flip in her belly. Followed by guilt. This couldn't be about exploring the immediate attraction she'd felt for Corey's dad. Although it might be a nice side benefit.

Beth stopped cutting a carrot and looked at her mom. "Would you be interested in watching a seven-year-old boy after school?"

"Is he a good kid?"

"I think so." Another gut feeling.

Her mom's gaze narrowed. "Who?"

"Corey Grey, my new student. His mom died a year ago, and he seems a little lost."

Her mom's face fell. "How awful for him."

"That's why I was talking with his father. He asked about after-school care providers. If you're interested, I can let him know. If not, no problem."

"Let me think about it." But her mother looked interested.

Her mom could use the extra money, but Beth knew that wouldn't be the reason if she agreed. A softy at heart, Mary Ryken would be all over a child in need.

When they were done with dinner and cleanup in the kitchen, Beth headed for her usual spot at the dining room table to grade papers. After that she'd walk to the LeNaro community pool for her daily swim. Ever since moving back home, Beth found that several laps in the pool not only helped her relax, but it helped fight the extra calories from her mom's cooking.

Beth was no skinny mini. She'd always been tall and full figured. She tried to whittle her hips with swimming, but her body refused to cooperate. Her mother said size fourteen was not fat but normal. Still, standing six foot in bare feet wasn't exactly common for a woman. Not too many men were knocking down her door for a date.

She sighed and got back to work but the memory of looking up at Nick Grey invaded her concentration. He was certainly tall enough.

Later when Beth skipped down the stairs with her duffel bag ready for the pool, her mom stopped her with a raised hand.

"I think I will watch that boy after school. You can tell your Mr. Grey that I'll do it until school's out and then we'll see. What's he going to do for the summer?"

Beth shrugged. "I don't know, but I'm sure he'll figure something out. We've got a couple of months yet. I'll let him know tomorrow. Maybe we could do a trial run, you know, make sure you and Corey click."

Her mother nodded. "Yes, do that."

Beth hesitated to leave. "You're sure about this?"

Her face broke into a wide smile. "Very sure. Have a nice swim."

"Thanks."

Walking down the sidewalk, Beth didn't bother to enjoy the sight of spring flowers blooming along the way or the mild warm night air. Her mind whirled. Would Nick agree to Corey staying with her mom after school? It might be good for both of them. And Beth couldn't help feeling a shiver of excitement at the thought of seeing Nick Grey more often.

She'd have to be careful, though. It wasn't smart to get involved with a student's parent when there might be issues. Could get messy real quick.

Chapter Two

Nick made breakfast. The eggs were too hard and the bacon a little too crisp. He wasn't a whiz in the kitchen, but he knew enough to get by. Knowing how to get by was what made him good at undercover work. God's grace had kept him alive during his last assignment, which had taken him away from home most nights. But that line of work was over. For his son's sake, he couldn't take those risks anymore. So he'd kissed the adrenaline rush goodbye and transferred into a rural county sheriff's department. About time, too.

Nick would never understand why that same grace hadn't covered his wife when she'd wrapped her car around a tree. But then, Susan might have made her own decisions about that. It wasn't *that* rainy the night she'd wrecked. He'd never know for sure. He'd make sure Corey never knew, either. He'd rather his son remember his mom's good days.

He turned away from the stove to holler down the hall at his son, but the kid was already dressed and seated at the kitchen table.

Nick slipped a plate in front of his son.

Corey stared at it for a few seconds before digging in.

Susan's mom made picture-perfect eggs. Susan had, too. When things were good, they were great, but then she'd hit a dark stretch and nothing worked well. If only they'd dated longer before they married, if they'd waited to have Corey, maybe…

Maybe he would have known, but then again, maybe not. Her wild bouts had come well after Corey was born.

"You're ready early." Nick sat across from his son and sprinkled his eggs with hot sauce before digging in.

Corey nodded.

Nick racked his brain for something else to ask. Getting his kid to talk to him was worse than questioning a perp. They went nowhere fast. "I'll pick you up after school."

Again the boy nodded.

They ate the rest of their meal in silence.

Nick grappled with frustration. He had a lot of ground to make up for leaving his boy behind for the past six months. Pretty hard to make a seven-year-old understand that he was safer with grandparents who lived an hour north of the city.

Another reason to transfer. Nick wanted to sleep better. He'd never grown used to worrying about some thug finding out where he lived. That had been the sole reason he'd refused to buy a house despite Susan's prodding that she and Corey deserved better than their Grand Rapids apartment.

The quick drive to LeNaro Elementary School was a quiet one, but the closer they got, the more Corey came to life. He'd lean forward, look out his window and clutch the backpack given to him by his lovely teacher.

Nick parked and unbuckled his seat belt.

"I can walk in by myself."

Nick looked at his son, careful not to bruise that seven-year-old ego. "I know you can."

"Then why are you getting out?" Corey's eyes narrowed.

"I'm going to talk to the school counselor. You being new and all, it's probably a good idea, don't you think?"

Corey shrugged. "I dunno."

Nick didn't, either. Beth Ryken had suggested it and since she probably knew more about kids than him, he was taking her advice. He didn't start work for a few days yet, so now was as good a time as any to see what this school counselor was all about and let her know Corey's background. He only prayed they wouldn't label him as troubled like the last school.

Entering the elementary school, Nick was struck by the noise of kids banging their lockers shut and chattering as well as the smell of breakfast wafting from the cafeteria. Maybe Corey would have eaten better here? Once he started his morning shift, Corey probably would. The principal had informed him about the school's breakfast program for kids dropped off early.

He looked down at his son with a mop of red hair and scattering of light freckles. The kid was the spitting image of himself as a boy. Sad, too. Nick's parents had divorced the summer he had turned ten. As the oldest, Nick had always felt as if it was somehow his fault. His and his sister's for fighting, for not being quiet when his dad came home exhausted from his shift as a Grand Rapids city cop.

A sharp tug at his heart kept him walking alongside Corey instead of turning into the school office. Crazy maybe, but he didn't want to say goodbye to his son. If he had kept his boy out today, they could have spent more time together. Doing what, he didn't know. Nick hadn't spent enough time with Corey ever since Susan had died. He'd always regret that.

Nick let work come first too many times. Needing to get

the bad guys never flew with Corey. Those big eyes of his son's saw through his excuse for what it was. An excuse.

Nick was scared of raising a little boy on his own.

"What are you doing?"

"Thought since I'm here, I might as well walk you to class."

"I'm not a baby."

"I know." Nick caught a glimpse of a flowered skirt attached to the pretty second-grade teacher standing in the doorway.

Beth Ryken gave them a sunny smile that nearly knocked him on his backside. The woman was that beautiful.

"Good morning, Corey and Mr. Grey."

He gave her a nod. "Miss Ryken."

"I got my backpack, see?" Corey stepped into class without a glance backward.

"That's good. I'm going to talk to your dad a minute."

Corey actually smiled at her. The woman had charmed his son, as well.

She stepped out of the doorway into the hall. "He's a great kid. A little serious."

Nick sighed. "It's been tough on him since his mom died."

Her blue eyes softened. "And on you, too, I imagine."

Not as it should have been. He'd stayed undercover and sloughed off his kid first to his mom, then to Susan's parents. Not fair to them, even though they'd welcomed Corey with open arms. He cleared his throat. "Yeah."

"I wanted to tell you that I might have found an option for Corey after school."

"Really? Where?"

She took a deep breath and smiled. "My mother."

"Across the street?"

"Yes. She could use the extra income. I think she'd be great with Corey, but you'll want to meet her and find that out for yourself."

Nick couldn't believe his ears. Corey had requested the same only yesterday. "And you'll be there."

She looked confused. "Ah, yeah, after I finish up my day here. But you'll have to talk nuts and bolts with my mom. Pickup times, that sort of thing. I can introduce you after school today if that works."

"That definitely works. I'll pick up Corey here and then walk over with you." It was nice to talk to a woman at eye level. Corey's teacher smelled like spring and new beginnings. *Like kissing in the rain.* Whoa. Not a place his mind should go.

"And your mom's name?"

"It's Mary Ryken. She works part-time at the Cherry Capital Airport in Traverse City." Beth Ryken sounded breathless.

Nick stepped back, away from the allure of the woman in front of him. Her mother needed the money, she'd said. With gas prices the way they were, her twenty-mile one-way commute would be expensive. "I look forward to meeting her, and then we'll see."

"Great." That sunny smile again.

Nick couldn't look away.

"I better get started with class." Her cheeks went rosy pink.

"Oh. Yeah." He extended his hand. "Hey, thanks for this."

"You're welcome." She accepted his handshake and her skin felt soft.

He didn't want to let go but had to before he made a fool of himself. "I'll see you later, then."

She nodded and slipped back into her classroom.

Nick walked down the hall and checked his watch. He'd see the school counselor and then head for the sheriff's department. He'd run a background check on Mary Ryken before making any decisions.

Beth checked the clock on the wall. Just a couple minutes until the bell would ring, ending the school day. She glanced at her students working on their homework for tomorrow—a short reading passage with questions next to it.

Beth spotted Corey with his head down and wandered over. "Everything okay?"

He shrugged and sniffed.

Beth's midsection tightened as she knelt down. "What's up, Corey?"

"I don't want to do this." His eyes were red, but so far no tears had leaked out.

The bell rang and kids clamored for their jackets and backpacks. Corey stayed put and stared at his work sheet; he hadn't answered any of the questions.

Beth directed the kids as they left, all while keeping a close eye on Corey, who looked devastated. She gathered his things from the cubby locker and dropped them on the seat next to him. Beth was about to sit down and have a chat with him when Nick Grey popped into the classroom.

"Hey, bud, why the long face?"

Corey quickly shoved the work sheet into his backpack and shrugged.

Nick looked at her for direction. For the meaning behind his son's sulk.

She smiled, but her mind churned. "If you both don't mind waiting a few minutes while I clean off my desk, we'll head over to my mom's."

Corey's head jerked up, his demeanor totally changed. "We're going to your house?"

"Yes. To meet my mother." That was all Beth would say, in case Nick chose another option for Corey's after-school care.

"Cool." Corey slipped into a navy windbreaker.

"Do you want us to wait in the car?" Nick's worried gaze lingered on his son.

"Oh, no. I'll only be a minute." Beth kept her voice up-beat, but her initial worries about Corey returned.

Why had he been upset over a short reading assignment? The subject matter had been harmless enough. Tall ships and their sails. She'd have to talk to his father about that.

By the time they crossed the street, Beth had decided on discretion when she talked to Nick Grey. This was only Corey's second day in her class. New school, new home, no friends yet—it all added up to stress. Her principal hadn't received Corey's transcripts from his old school yet, so she shouldn't jump to conclusions.

Beth opened the front door and sniffed. Her mom had been baking. Nice. She gestured for Nick and Corey to come in and then kicked off her shoes. "Mom? I'm home and I brought guests as promised."

Her mother came toward them and looked right at Corey. "You must be hungry for a snack. I've got chocolate chip cookies straight from the oven."

Corey nodded and then looked at his dad.

"Thank you, Mrs. Ryken, that sounds wonderful." Nick held out his hand. "My name's Nick Grey and this is my boy, Corey."

Her mom gave her a quick wink. "Yes, Beth told me about you both. Come on into the kitchen."

The kitchen smelled like melted butter and chocolate,

and Beth got busy pouring glasses of milk while her mom passed around a plate of warm cookies. Corey appeared to be on his best behavior. He took a napkin and carefully spread it on his lap before eating. That was definitely not a trick he'd learned from his father. Nick wolfed down a cookie with one bite while reaching for another.

Beth quietly slipped into a seat and grabbed a cookie, giving Corey a smile.

"I see you like flowers," Nick said. "There's quite a few in your yard."

Her mom nodded. "I love having them pop up willy-nilly every spring. They keep spreading and I love the surprise of where they'll go next. I won't mow my lawn until after they've bloomed. But my annuals are a little more organized."

That answer seemed to please him, and Beth nearly laughed. Nick was using her mother's erratic gardening as some sort of test, and evidently, she'd passed the first question.

"Beth, why don't you take Corey to fill up the bird-feeders while I talk to his father?" Her mom peeked at Nick over her designer-brand reading glasses. "If that's okay with you."

"It is." Nick smiled. It was an awkward smile, as if he wasn't used to doing it.

Beth let her gaze linger. Smiling was definitely something Nick should do more of.

Turning to the man's son, Beth slapped her hands on her lap. "What do you think, Corey? Do you mind going outside with me?"

The boy had finished his second cookie and had chocolate smeared in the corners of his mouth. He gave her a heart-stealing grin. "Okay."

Beth held out her hand to the boy. "Let's go. I'm going to need your help."

They stepped out of the kitchen onto the back deck. She knew they were in full view of Nick and her mom. A year before Beth's father died, he had installed big windows and a sliding glass door along the back wall of the kitchen as a Mother's Day present. Their backyard was large and her mother had birdfeeders scattered everywhere. Didn't matter where a person sat in the kitchen or living room, they'd have a clear view of birds scattering seeds.

Beth opened the door to the shed and grabbed a bucket. "So what happened today, Corey? Why don't you want to do the homework assignment?"

The boy shrugged. "I just don't."

She filled the bucket with birdseed and handed it to him. "Did you have homework at your old school?"

He shook his head.

"Did you get it done in school, then?"

He shrugged. "Grandma didn't give homework."

Beth frowned. "Tell me about your grandma."

"She used to read to me a lot and show me how to count."

"What about your teacher? Did she read to you, too? Or did she have you read the stories on your own?"

Corey stopped filling a low birdfeeder and looked at her as if she'd missed the obvious. "Grandma was my teacher."

"Oh." Beth closed her eyes. She definitely needed more information. She needed to talk to Nick.

Nick watched his son with Beth. He could tell that Corey talked to her. As they filled birdfeeders, Corey chatted easily.

He glanced at Beth's mom, who'd been watching him.

She was a nice lady, if a little scattered. "I think Corey will do well here after school."

"I'd love to have him, and this works well with my weekday shift of seven till noon at the airport. Plenty of time for me to run errands and get home to meet Corey."

"Some weeks I'll have midweek days off and work the weekend. Would you mind Corey hanging out during the day on a weekend?"

Mary's brow furrowed. "What is it that you do?"

"I start with the sheriff's department in a few days."

Mary Ryken's eyebrow lifted, but the expression on her face had fallen into disappointment. "You're in law enforcement."

"Yes, ma'am. A deputy." Nick drained his glass of milk. Mary had offered him cookies until he'd stuffed himself.

"My husband worked for the same but was killed on duty."

"Yes, ma'am. I'm sorry for your loss." He'd looked it up. It was what made her a good choice. Mary understood a cop's life. She'd lived it. She'd understand if his shift ran late.

Her eyes grew stern. "Don't let it happen to you. That boy needs you."

Nick nodded. It was why he was here. Why he'd transferred out of undercover work. "I don't plan on it."

"No one ever plans on it, but it happens. And it happens to the best of them." Mary's tone hardened.

He waited for her to pass on watching Corey but she didn't say a word, only looked at him expectantly.

"The job's yours if you want it."

"I do." She smiled. "And weekends are no trouble. I'm a homebody on weekends, and Corey can go with me to church if that's okay with you. Our church has a good children's program."

"That would be great. We need to find one anyway." He wanted to get back in the habit of going when he wasn't working. It'd been a long time. A dry time.

Again Nick glanced out of the large windows. Beth and Corey had finished filling the birdfeeders and sat on a wooden swing together. Corey laughed at something Beth said. His son looked like what a seven-year-old should look like. Carefree.

Since he'd taken Corey back from his grandparents, the boy acted so careful, careful in what he did and said—if he said anything. Nick had learned to accept shrugs as their primary mode of communication. His boy had a lot to say to Miss Ryken.

Mary glanced at the clock.

Nick followed her gaze. It was closing in on four-thirty. Time to leave.

Mary smiled. "Why don't you and Corey stay for dinner?"

That surprised him, but then it didn't. If Mary Ryken cooked half as well as she baked, they were in for a real treat. He'd like to see how Corey responded to her. "Thank you, Mrs. Ryken. I appreciate your offer. We'll stay."

The woman stood. "Good, and please call me Mary."

"What can I do to help?" He also got to his feet.

"Not a thing." She waved him away and then stepped out of the sliding glass door. "Beth, why don't you show Nick around since Corey will be coming here after school. And, Corey, would you like to help me in the kitchen?"

Nick gave Mary a double take. She'd turned down his help.

As if sensing his confusion, Mary explained, "I might as well get to know the boy a little better, and you'll want to make sure everything is secure for him here. Beth will show you."

"Oh. Yeah, thanks." For a minute there, Nick thought she was throwing him and her daughter together.

Corey raced into the kitchen. "Really, I get to come here after school?"

Nick folded his arms. "That okay with you?"

His son nodded.

Nick remembered Corey's comment about Beth reminding him of his mom. Of Nick's wife. Was that why his son wanted to come here? To recapture a feeling of home and what he'd lost?

"Corey, why don't you wash your hands in the bathroom around the corner and then come back and I'll tell you what I need you to do." Mary had a nice way of issuing orders.

"Yes, ma'am." Corey had a nice way of following them, and he slipped out of sight.

Nick's sense of ease at this choice hit a speed bump when Beth walked into the kitchen. Seeing her regularly might be a problem. He couldn't muddy the waters of his life with an ill-timed relationship. Not when he needed to rebuild his relationship with Corey.

He sure could use a friend, though, and she was Corey's teacher. Keeping it friendly presented a unique challenge considering his track record. But it was only a couple of months until school was done. He'd figure out somewhere else for Corey to spend his days during the summer months because Mary worked in the mornings.

Surely he'd survive the next two months. They'd all survive.

Beth stood before him. "I'll give you the tour."

"We're staying for dinner." He watched her reaction closely.

"Mom always makes more than enough." She gave him another sunny smile.

"Do you mind?" They'd invaded her space.

"Not at all. Come on. We can chat about Corey."

Nick blanched at the serious teacher look on Beth Ryken's face. He got the feeling that she'd found something wrong with his boy and he was going to hear about it. "Lead the way."

It didn't take long to walk through the downstairs. Each room looked crowded with wall hangings and books and knickknacks. Beth's mom had collected a lot of stuff over the years, and that stuff seemed to pop up in odd spots like her flowers outside.

"There's a bathroom and two bedrooms upstairs. Just so you know, my father was in law enforcement and we have his firearms. But they're locked in a safe upstairs."

"No problem." Nick had guns at home, too, locked up where Corey couldn't get at them.

Someday he'd teach his son how to use and respect them. He'd start off with the BB gun his father had given Nick when he was Corey's age. Keeping that gun had been one of many disagreements between him and Susan. She didn't want their boy following in his father's footsteps.

Nick stepped outside with Beth. The day had grown warm enough to forego jackets. The backyard was surrounded by a tall wooden fence. Huge trees grew along the other side and their branches shaded part of the yard, lending more privacy.

One of Mary's more organized flower beds had been set up in the corner, complete with statues and greens poking up through the soil. The yard felt secluded, winsome even, as if he might find a secret passageway to some imaginary land, if a person was given to that kind of fancy. He wasn't.

He glanced at Beth. "You wanted to talk about Corey?"

She nodded and headed for the swing she'd occupied with his son earlier. "Maybe we should sit down."

He swallowed hard. "Okay…."

Whatever she had to say wasn't going to be good. It hadn't been good at Corey's previous school, either. The social worker there had said Corey displayed antisocial behavior. What was so antisocial about being quiet? Corey had been withdrawn, but Nick couldn't blame the kid. He'd lost his mom, and that school worried about how often he colored with a black crayon!

He waited for her to get comfortable before settling himself next to her, taking care to keep space between them. That pretty skirt she wore draped across her knees and swayed against her long legs, which were bare. Her feet were, too.

"What can you tell me about Corey's education?"

He gathered his wandering thoughts. "What do you want to know?"

"Corey said his grandmother was his teacher?"

Nick nodded. "For a little bit. Corey lived with his grandparents the last six months before we moved here. His grandmother pulled him out of school after Christmas break. She homeschooled him. Why?"

"Why wasn't he with you?" Beth's eyes widened as if she hadn't expected to ask that question. "I'm sorry, that's way too personal."

He felt his brow furrow. "No. It's okay. At the time, it seemed like the perfect solution. My wife's parents were glad to have him and I knew he'd be safe there. I was working a delicate undercover case that I couldn't walk away from."

"Undercover?" Beth's expression froze. She even scooted away from him a little.

There it was. That look of distaste for what he did was written all over Miss Ryken's face. Any interest she might have had in him died right then, he could tell. Probably a good thing, too.

"I worked as an undercover officer for years in Grand Rapids. I transferred into the sheriff's department here and start next week as one of their deputies."

"Oh."

Evidently, the Ryken women didn't like the idea of men in law enforcement. "I understand your father was a deputy sheriff, as well."

Beth stared at her hands. "Yes. Look, Mr. Grey, back to Corey. Can I ask why you allowed him to be pulled out of school?"

Nick leaned forward and rested his elbows on his knees. He'd been deep in finishing up his case and hadn't the time to double-check. Maybe he should have made the time. "My mother-in-law thought it might be best for Corey. I trusted her judgment and agreed."

"Did his grandmother follow a lesson plan, do you know?"

He should have known, but he didn't. Another failure. "Why? Is there a problem?"

"I'm not sure. Do you read together?"

Nick had plenty of excuses like working nights and leaving education concerns to his wife. He hadn't read to his boy since Corey started school. So many things he hadn't done for his own son. But that was changing, starting with this move north.

"No."

Beth gave him an encouraging smile. "I'll send him home with some books. Read together and see how it goes."

He narrowed his gaze. "What are you trying to say?"

"It's too soon to say anything other than I think your boy struggles with reading."

"Which means what?"

He watched her shutter her thoughts with a calm face.

"We'll cross that bridge when we know more. After I hear from Corey's previous school."

That bridge was looming awfully close considering it was April. He knew for a fact that Corey's previous school had nothing good to report. It was why Nick had agreed to his in-laws pulling the boy out.

Nick looked into Beth's eyes expecting to find more disappointment, even censure, but it wasn't there. She was a blank page with that teacher face going.

At that moment Mary Ryken poked her head out of the sliding glass door to announce that dinner was ready.

"After you, Mr. Grey." Beth stood and waited for him to do the same.

His appetite was pretty much gone, leveled flat by Beth's concerns and the half-dozen cookies he'd ingested earlier. He'd make room, though.

As they walked away from the swing, Nick couldn't get the conversation out of his head. Corey had issues with reading. His boy had enough stress in his life—he didn't need more. As his father, Nick didn't want Corey to feel like a failure or be ashamed of his lack of skill with words. His kid was smart. He'd always been good with numbers.

Before they reached the door that would take them back inside, Nick stalled Beth with the touch of his hand to her arm. "Whatever I need to do to help Corey, let me know."

"Mr. Grey—"

He cut her off. "He can't be held back."

Her eyes widened.

Nick softened his tone. "This is important."

"Of course it is. All my students are important."

"That's not what I meant."

She held up her hand. "I know, Mr. Grey. We'll do everything we can."

"Thank you." But Nick had the sinking feeling that

Corey's second-grade teacher had already written the boy off as a lost cause for this year. That didn't sit well. Nick had succeeded in getting some really bad guys off the streets, but at what cost?

Walking into the house, Nick was struck by the sound of his son chattering about baseball with Mary Ryken as they set the table.

"My mom's a die-hard Detroit Tigers fan," Beth said.

Nick nodded. Corey loved baseball. They used to watch games together on TV. One more thing they hadn't done in a long time. But all that would change, starting today with bringing his son to the Ryken house. He'd made a good move.

For Corey and maybe, with time, him, too.

Chapter Three

"Here, Corey, try this one." Beth handed him a beginning-level reader book about puppies.

Corey glanced at her and then cracked the cover. He stared at the page, muttered a couple of correctly read words and then pushed the book away. "I don't feel like reading."

She smiled at him, knowing this was the excuse he hid behind. "It'll get better with practice. I promise."

"Can I go across the street now?"

"Let's get through this book first."

The boy slumped lower in his chair.

"I know you can do it, Corey. And I'm here to help. Let's try again."

The boy let out a sigh and picked the book back up. Hearing the kid stumble over several words in a row, Beth's heart sank. Her suspicions had been correct. Corey Grey was nowhere near a second-grade reading level. "Let's sound this word out…."

It took a while to get through only a few pages. Beth was glad she'd called her mom before they'd even started and let her know that Corey was going to hang out with her after school. This was going to take patience, something she wasn't sure Corey's father had.

Nick Grey's reaction to Beth's concerns a few days ago still bothered her. He'd displayed such vehemence that his boy pass second grade. Was it a pride thing? Nick seemed to have more depth than that. She hoped he did.

Holding back a child to repeat a grade was openly debated within the LeNaro school district. Beth believed in some cases the hard choice was needed. Might even be needed here. But she wouldn't get Nick's cooperation, that was for sure. He wasn't offering up any information about Corey's old school, either. Beth called to rush those transcripts. The sooner she reviewed what was there, the sooner she'd figure out what to do. And find out why Nick had allowed his son to be pulled out.

She couldn't ignore Corey's failure to meet reading benchmarks, move him forward and hope for the best. The chances of him becoming more lost and falling further behind were too great. He excelled with math, proving the boy both was bright and could see. The need for glasses wasn't the issue here. So why did he lag so far behind in reading? What had he missed? And more important, could he catch up before the end of the school year?

By the time Beth and Corey finished the book and made their way to Beth's home across the street, Beth knew it'd take a lot of work to get Corey reading where he should. She had a theory, though. If she was correct, maybe they could go back and fix what Corey had missed.

"What took you two so long?" Beth's mom was decked out in a ruffled apron she'd purchased off a home-shopping show.

Beth smiled at Corey. "We were working."

Corey didn't look amused. Frustrated for sure.

Her mom clicked her tongue. "Corey, did you have anything to eat since lunch?"

"No."

"Well, dinner's almost ready. Go wash up and we'll eat right away. Your dad called. He'll be a little late."

Beth watched the boy do as her mother asked without hesitation, before she let loose her irritation. "This better not become a habit."

Her mom lifted her chin. "What are you talking about?"

"Corey's dad being late."

Her mother gave her a hard look. "That's between him and me. He promised to pay me extra when he's late."

Beth sighed. She couldn't really argue with that. Her father used to be late a lot, too. At least Nick had called.

"So why'd you keep Corey at school so long? The poor kid needs an afternoon snack."

Beth scrunched her nose. How much could she really share with her mom? "We were reading."

"He's behind, isn't he?"

Beth's eyes widened. "How'd you know?"

Her mom shrugged as her gaze shifted behind her before she focused back on Beth. "Set the table, would you? Corey, you can help."

The boy had returned. Reason enough for her mother's quick change of subject. But still, how'd she know? And if it was that easy for her mother to figure it out, why hadn't Nick? Or Corey's grandparents? Even worse, why hadn't someone done something to help the child?

Beth set the table, letting the dishes clunk hard as she laid them down.

Corey gave her a quick look with wide eyes. "Are you mad?"

That question stopped her cold. It wasn't exactly fear she read in his face but something close to it. Almost as if he'd braced for impact. It made her sick to ponder the implications of that single glance from a sad-eyed seven-year-old.

She wouldn't jump to conclusions. Not before reading those reports from Corey's previous school, if they ever got here.

Beth smiled, feeling like a heel. "No. I'm not mad. More irritated that I have to set the table, something I don't like to do, but I shouldn't take it out on the plates, huh?"

Corey surprised her with a big grin. The fear was gone, replaced by a sardonic expression that looked much too old for the child giving it. He looked so much like his dad. "They could break."

Beth grinned back. Had she read way too much into Corey's expression? "I suppose my mom wouldn't like it if I broke her dishes."

"No." Corey shook his head. "I don't think she would."

Beth watched him lay down forks and knives around each plate. He'd been through a lot at a young age, but were there additional concerns she should worry about?

A fierce sense of protection for Corey filled her. She'd find out, real quick. Starting with the boy's father.

Nick pulled into Mary Ryken's driveway. A few raindrops splashed against the windshield of his patrol car, promising more soon. He got out and rushed for the front porch and made it before the deluge.

Beth Ryken came out looking darker than the rain clouds overhead. "Can I talk to you a minute?"

That sounded like trouble. She looked stern. Still beautiful, though. Always beautiful. He took a deep breath. "Hey, sorry I'm late. I had to finish up the paperwork of an arrest."

"It's not that." A crease of worry marred her otherwise-perfect forehead. "Nothing serious?"

He let out a bark of laughter. "Maybe for the drunk and disorderly seventy-eight-year-old woman who refused to get out of the vehicle of the man who picked her up hitchhiking. The poor guy didn't dare touch her, so he called us. I thought the whole thing was pretty funny."

That didn't earn him any points. Beth's gaze grew cool. Icy. "Have you been using the books I sent home with Corey?"

He nodded. "Every night before bed we read one of those storybooks." Nick enjoyed revisiting that quiet time together.

"Who's doing the reading?" Her gaze narrowed.

"Both of us. Corey struggles, but I help him out." What was up with this woman? Two days ago she sent home the books. Why the grief when he followed her directions?

"They're barely first-grade level." Her voice had dropped to nearly a whisper.

The rain pounded the ground, but that was nothing compared to the bomb his son's teacher had thrown at him. "But I've seen him reading the backs of cereal boxes, and comic books."

"Probably following the pictures."

Nick stared at her with dread crawling up his spine. He didn't know what kinds of books kids read in what grades. Nick clenched his fists. Had she sent those books home to entrap him? To prove her point? That wasn't fair. Not fair to his son. To him.

At that moment Corey flew out the door. "Hi, Dad."

Nick looked at his boy. "Corey, can you wait in the car?"

His son glanced at Beth and then back at him. "Okay...."

"I'll only be a minute. Don't touch anything."

Corey's shoulders slumped and he flipped up the hood of his rain slicker and dashed for the vehicle.

Nick watched him get into the SUV cruiser and then focused on Beth. "There has to be something I can do."

"This late in the school year, I don't know. I'm sorry." Beth Ryken didn't beat around the bush, that was for sure.

"But there has to be something—"

The front screen door opened with a squeak, and Mary Ryken had a loaded plate wrapped in foil. Dinner? "We had more than enough."

Mary had made enough for both him and Corey to take home the previous night, too. "Thank you."

Nick's focus followed to where Beth pointed, toward the sheriff patrol vehicle. Corey was messing with something. "I've got to go." He stared hard at his son's teacher. "But this conversation is far from over."

He saw how Beth's eyes widened, but she didn't say another word as he ran for the car. His uniform got soaked in the process.

Nick slipped behind the wheel and set the foil-wrapped plate on the backseat. "I asked you not to touch anything."

Corey looked at him. "Are there games on this?"

Nick turned his computer monitor back around. "No. No games."

As Nick backed out of the Rykens' driveway, he glanced at the porch. Beth waved. Corey waved back. "What did you do at Mary's today?"

"I was at school with Miss Ryken."

"How come?"

Corey shrugged.

Nick drove with care, slow and sure. "Did she ask you to read?"

His boy's face fell. "Yeah."

"And you had trouble, huh? Like with the books we have."

More dejection. "Yeah."

Nick swallowed hard. "Corey, why didn't you tell me you were having a hard time reading words? I could have helped."

"You weren't there."

The barb hit hard and true, piercing his heart with bitter regret. "Grandma and Grandpa would have helped you to read better."

Corey shrugged again.

It wasn't the kid's fault. Why hadn't Susan's parents picked up on it? Nick rubbed the bridge of his nose. They were dealing, too. He couldn't blame them. Maybe if he'd made Corey read more. If he'd been around…

"Dad?"

"What?"

"I think I made Miss Ryken mad."

Nick felt himself frown. "I'm sure you didn't, son."

"But she slammed the plates on the table. But not like Mom. Miss Ryken didn't break any."

Nick couldn't breathe. He never had the right words to explain Susan's odd behavior. Couldn't excuse it, either. They'd argued so much toward the end. Way too much.

"Don't worry. Miss Ryken wasn't mad at you." She was probably madder than a hornet at him, though, for letting his boy down. And rightly so.

Nick turned left onto the road that took them north of town to where they now lived. He needed to talk to Beth Ryken.

"Hey, bud, do you have recess before your lunch break or after?"

"After," Corey said. "Why?"

"Just wondered."

Nick knew his son ate lunch around noontime. So, maybe he'd stop by tomorrow. And see if he couldn't have a chat with Miss Ryken.

Beth checked her watch and growled. She was late. Way too late for her early-morning dentist appointment. She pushed down on the gas pedal and picked up speed. And then spotted the flashing lights.

"Really?" Beth slowed and pulled over to the side of the road.

Another growl escaped while she checked her glove box for registration and proof of insurance. Beth jumped at the quick tap to her driver's-side window. And then her stomach sank.

Deputy Officer Nick Grey with a shining gold star on his chest opened the door for her. He stood there tall and solemn. His mouth twisted into a crooked grin. "In a hurry this morning, Miss Ryken?"

Her stomach, which had dropped somewhere near her sandal-clad feet, now fluttered back to life. Why'd the man have to look so good in that brown uniform?

She let out a sigh. "Late for an appointment. I guess I was going a little too fast, but there's no point now—I'll never make it in time."

"Do you know what the speed limit is on these roads?"

She squinted at him. Seriously? "My dad was a cop, remember? Fifty-five."

He cocked one eyebrow, but there was a definite twinkle in his eye. "I clocked you at sixty-eight. Not wise on back roads with deer roaming in the fields."

Irritation filled her. Irritation that she'd get a ticket, irritation that Nick Grey might be a low-down scoundrel who not only scared his little boy but didn't attend to his education. Even more irritating still was despite all that,

Nick Grey grew more attractive every time she looked. "Just give me the ticket and we'll both be on our way."

"Would you step out of the car?"

Her eyes flew wide. "What! Why? I've got my papers right here. Look me up and you'll see I don't have a history of speeding tickets. This will be my first one."

His brows drew together and he looked stern. Downright scary, too. For a skinny guy, Nick was pretty intimidating. "I'm not giving you a ticket."

"Then why...?"

"I need to talk to you. Please?"

Oh, there was no denying that pleading look he gave her. And that only fueled the anger simmering inside. She got out of her car and slammed the door harder than she'd intended. "What do you want?"

"What's with the attitude?"

Beth didn't hold back. "I saw fear in your son's eyes last night and I'd like to know why."

Again the man only cocked one eyebrow, cool as can be. "When you slammed the plates on the table?"

Beth gasped and then sputtered, "I, uh—"

"Corey told me. Look, Miss Ryken, there's something you should probably know. My wife had mood swings. During one of her more manic ones, she smashed a stack of plates because I was late for dinner. Corey's a little sensitive."

Beth's mouth dropped open, and she slapped her hand over it. She was going to be sick. Corey wasn't afraid of his father; he'd been afraid of her!

"It's okay. No harm done. But it hasn't been easy for Corey, and I didn't make it any easier by sending him to live with his grandparents. But I'd run out of options."

Beth's heart broke all over again. "I'm so sorry."

"For what? Thinking ill of me? You should. I let my boy down."

"No, for scaring your son." Beth leaned against her car and stared at the cherry orchard across the street. She'd called that one all wrong.

The sun shone on dewdrops clinging to the tree buds, turning them into sparkling crystals. Those cherry buds would soon burst open into white blossoms. Just one of many breathtaking sights in Northern Michigan. She sidled a glance at Nick. Yup, breathtaking sights everywhere.

"It's okay, really. No harm done. His grandparents sugar-coated everything, afraid to raise their voices. I don't know, maybe they thought they were protecting him."

"Is that why you moved here? To get away from them?"

He shook his head. "I need to reconnect with my boy. His mom's issues forced us into a partnership, but then I left my partner behind and abandoned him."

"Living with his grandparents for a while is hardly abandonment," Beth pointed out.

"Tell that to a seven-year-old."

Beth gave him a sharp look. "I see what you mean."

He nodded and then leaned against her car, too. Right next to her. "You see why I won't let him repeat second grade? He's had so much taken out of his hands beyond his control. This will feel like one more failure for him. Another left behind."

It would feel that way to a seven-year-old. What a tough spot. Beth dropped her head back to look up at the clouds above. Her arm brushed against Nick's, connecting with what felt like a hard beam of steel.

She scooted away and faced him. "But it's so late in the year. I don't want him to get lost in the shuffle if he's moved ahead."

"It's never too late." Nick's voice was soft.

Beth drew in a sharp breath. Awareness hummed between them as he watched her. In his eyes she saw something stark and lonely and her heart responded. But she couldn't erase his worries and fix what had gone wrong in his life. He was off-limits.

She wasn't stupid. Beth knew mutual attraction when she saw it. When she felt it. There was no way she'd let herself get romantically involved with this man. Not when Beth knew how quickly his life could be snuffed out.

"I want to ask you a favor."

Beth tipped her head. Sounded like a big favor, too. "What's that?"

"Will you tutor Corey in reading?"

Beth stood straight and stepped away from her car. Away from him. He made her dizzy.

"I'll pay you, of course. Whatever it takes." He straightened, as well.

Beth whirled around. "I can't accept your money. I won't. He's my student. It's my job to help where I can...."

"But?"

She looked Nick in the eyes. So easy to do. "Repeating second grade might be the best thing for Corey. Have you considered that? He's new—it's not like there's peer pressure to deal with. Not yet. He could even go to the other second-grade class so I'm not his teacher."

"It's not the best thing. Not for Corey. And not for me."

Beth felt her spine stiffen. "That sounds like pride talking."

Nick laughed at her then. "Is that what you think?"

She folded her arms across her chest and stared down the deputy officer in front of her, knowing that wasn't it at all.

"Look, I can work with him all summer long, every single night, but I need a game plan. Something you're trained to give. All I'm asking is to get him where I can then pick up the slack come summer. Do whatever you need to do, only don't throw your hands up and recommend he be pushed back a year because there's only two months left of this one." Nick's steely gray eyes showed resolve.

Beth frowned and rubbed her forehead. Corey was already at her house in the evening. She'd have to get it cleared through her boss, but this was a special circumstance. What she did on her own time was her business. In the few days the boy had been with her and her mom, Beth had already come to love the kid. She didn't want to let him down, either.

She glanced at Nick.

"A big difference can be made in two months." He gently thumped his ticket pad in his hand. A reminder of the speeding ticket she rightfully deserved.

She laughed. "You know, extortion is illegal."

He gave her a slow grin that made her heart race. "Blackmail was never my intent."

Beth felt herself slipping, giving in. "You'll need to finish Corey's reading assignments after he leaves my mom's. And I'm going to hound you."

"I've had worse nightmares."

She imagined that was true. There was so much strength hidden inside that wiry, well-over-six-foot steel frame of his. And a lot of feelings were locked behind those gray eyes, too.

Beth held out her hand. "I'll do what I can. Have we got a deal, Mr. Grey?"

"I think we do, Miss Ryken. And we'll work hard on our end—I promise you that." He took her hand and held on, wrapping warmth and strength and all kinds of promises in one not-so-simple handshake.

Chapter Four

Come up with a plan. Nick had said that days ago and Beth had one. It had been slow coming together between progress reports for her other students and running it by her principal, but she'd done it. She'd even made up a progress booklet for Nick.

She riffled through the papers on her desk—Corey's papers from his previous school. Corey's old school reports were as confusing as they were disheartening. The transcripts showed a downward spiral that started before Corey's mom had died and then plummeted steeply afterward.

"Poor kid." Beth felt that undeniable pull for the boy.

Corey had been jostled between special reading groups, and he'd been labeled with emotional problems that were never clearly explained. Had no one seen through to the obvious? Corey didn't have a handle on phonics. Somewhere along the line, he'd missed the mark and by the time his mother had died, his emotional stresses had kicked in and his dwindling grasp on vowel sounds and rules had slipped. It was no wonder he got lost along the way. He'd never mastered how to identify the trail markers.

Well, Beth knew a few things about marking trails.

She'd start with flash cards, games, work sheets, whatever it took to get Corey more familiar with identifying sounds. And she had a stack of books for Nick so he could continue working with Corey at home in the evenings and on his days off. If he spent half an hour every day reading with Corey, it'd make a difference.

Beth's mom even promised to help where she could. The only variable she couldn't predict was Corey's reaction. His willingness to learn was key.

She put away the sensitive papers, locked the drawer of her desk and then scooped up her stuff. Exiting her classroom, she spotted the other second-grade teacher, Julie, calling it a day, as well.

"So, Beth, are you up for sailing the Manitous again this year?" Julie's husband was a hotshot attorney with one sweet sailboat. Gerry was more than the average amateur sailor. Sailing with them had become a tradition and a fun way to celebrate the end of the school year and the start of summer.

"I sure am." Beth nodded. "Count me in, only please, no setups this year."

Julie frowned. "Oh, come on, he wasn't so bad."

Beth tipped her head. Julie and Gerry had arranged a blind date with a guy from Gerry's office. He was way too short and arrogant besides.

Julie smiled. "You bring someone, then."

Beth's mind immediately shifted to Nick, but that brown uniform he wore made her shake away any thoughts of sunset sailing with the handsome redhead. "We'll see."

When Beth made it across the street to her mom's house, she was armed with phonics lessons. Walking into the living room, she expected to find Corey in front of the TV. Instead he sat at the dining room table across from her mom. The two playing a game of Battleship.

"B-3." Corey's hair hung in his eyes.

Beth's fingers itched to brush the kid's bangs back, but she remained quiet and watched.

"Nope. Miss." Her mom wore an evil-looking grin. "My turn. F-8."

Corey's face crumpled into irritation. "Hit."

"I'm home."

Neither one acknowledged her. They were caught up in the game. And it was close. Each had only one ship left, and Beth's mom dove in for the kill on Corey's big destroyer. It made Beth smile as she slipped upstairs to change into jeans.

When she returned, Corey had put away the pieces while her mom started dinner. "Who won?"

The look of disgust on Corey's face clued her in.

"Sorry. She always beat me, too. Are you ready to play some different games?"

The boy looked cautious. "Like what?"

"Sound games." Beth spread out her flash cards.

"That's schoolwork, isn't it?"

Beth met the boy's wary eyes. "Did your dad tell you that he asked me to be your tutor?"

"Yeah."

"Did he say why?"

Corey looked down. "Because I don't read good."

Beth touched his hand and gave him a big smile. "You will, Corey. I promise, in time you will read much better."

He looked at her with a lot of doubt in his face, but she spotted hope shining in his eyes.

Thursdays after school, Beth helped staff a kids' art program. She milled between tables, helping where needed but mostly watching kids create. Corey sat at a table littered with paper, crayons and markers he hadn't touched.

Grace Cavanaugh worked beside him drawing a house on a piece of yellow construction paper. She cut out trees made of brown and green paper and then pasted them on the yellow. She glued cotton balls for clouds.

"Don't you like to color?" the little girl asked.

Corey shook his head.

"Why?"

He shrugged.

"This is our house. It's for my mom." Grace stuck the paper in Corey's face.

"My mom died." Corey flicked the edge of the paper away.

Beth sucked in a breath, but she remained quiet and watched the two kids interact.

Grace set her paper down and tipped her head. She considered what Corey had said for a few seconds and then shrugged her shoulders. "That's okay. I don't have a dad. Maybe you'll get a new mommy. Want me to help you get started? I know where everything's at."

Corey nodded.

"C'mere, then."

Beth's eyes stung when Corey followed Gracie to the paper bins. She directed him to pick a color and he did. And then he followed her back to the table while she rattled off a host of things he could draw and she promised to help. God bless little Gracie. She'd broken into Corey's shell.

"Hey, Beth, got a minute?" Diane, their school counselor, leaned against the door.

Beth scanned the room for the other teacher helping out. She spotted her assembling the supplies they'd need for tonight's lesson in painting. The kids were busy chatting and hanging up their backpacks. She could duck out for a few. "Yeah, sure."

Diane nodded toward the hall.

Beth gave the other teacher a heads-up and then followed Diane out of the art room. "What's on your mind?"

"I understand you're tutoring one of your students. The new boy, Grey, is it?"

Beth folded her arms. "Corey Grey. I cleared it through Tammy. The boy's behind in reading."

"Where are you working with him?"

"My mom watches him after school, so we work at home. Why?"

Diane looked concerned. "I had a long talk with Mr. Grey about his boy still grieving. Corey might latch on to you as a maternal replacement, so it might be wise to stay in teacher mode."

Gracie's words whispered through Beth's mind. *Maybe you'll get a new mommy.* And something deep inside twisted, wishing...

Not going there. Beth cleared her mind with a firm nod. "Gotcha."

"We should compare notes in a week or so to see how he's settling in. Check for improvement."

"Sure. That'd be great." Beth knew the routine.

Because it was a small elementary school, grade-level teachers worked together as a team sharing lesson-plan notes and progress reports. But Diane seemed more careful than usual with Corey. Was it because of Nick's position or Corey's transcripts?

Beth gestured toward the classroom. "He's working with Grace Cavanaugh right now. And Thomas Clark has taken Corey under his wing, too. They're all tablemates in the classroom."

"Good." Diane gave her a nod. "Good pairings there."

Beth wanted to roll her eyes. That was why she'd placed Corey at their table. "I thought so."

Diane nodded again. "Okay, then, I'm heading home. We'll meet soon."

"Sure thing." Beth slipped back into the art room.

"Miss Ryken, can you help us?" Gracie's hand was in the air with a tube of paint. "We can't get this open."

Beth popped the plastic top and handed it back. Both kids had donned aprons. Each one held a paintbrush.

Corey looked nervous as he stared at the blank white paper clipped to a tabletop easel.

Beth stood next to him and stared, too.

Corey looked at her, his eyes unsure.

"Let it fly, Corey."

"I don't know what to make."

Gracie was busy painting big red flowers.

Corey seemed too tentative. He did fine coloring pre-printed pictures like the tall-ship work sheets in class, but the blank page intimidated him. Was that the result of his previous school making too much of the dark pictures the boy drew?

"Sometimes playing with the colors creates something special all by itself. Give it a try."

Corey thought about that a moment and then dipped his brush into Gracie's red paint. He slathered the paper and then rinsed the brush to try another color. Blue.

"There you go." Beth patted his shoulder. "Nice."

Corey looked at her again and smiled.

"You got it, Corey. Now have fun with it." Maybe he'd paint what was inside his heart.

Beth made her rounds, helping other kids and doling out encouragement. But she made her way back to Corey, curious.

"Wow!" She stared at his painting and smiled. "That's beautiful."

Corey had made a sloppy rainbow that ran off the page,

but it arched over a corner painted black. None of the white paper showed. He'd filled it all with color. Did it mean something good? Beth couldn't help but think it did.

"You can have it."

Beth hesitated in accepting. Teacher mode, Diane had said. Her kids made pictures for her all the time. She had a slew of them in her desk. But this one was special. Like the boy in front of her. "What about your dad? He might like it, too."

Corey shrugged and looked away.

Beth regrouped. She didn't want to hurt the boy's feelings by refusing. Nick wouldn't mind, would he? "Thank you, Corey. I know right where it'll go."

His eyes brightened. "Really?"

"Really. Would you like to make another one?"

"Nope." Corey gathered up his brushes and headed for the sink. "I'm done."

Beth checked her watch. Still another forty-five minutes to go. "Corey, would you like to help me? Be my go-for?"

The boy looked thoughtful a moment. "What's a go-pher?"

Beth smiled. "Go for things the other kids might need."

He nodded. "Okay."

"All right."

By the time Beth checked her watch again, it was time to pack up. Corey had been a good helper as they cleaned up spilled paint and passed out more paper.

Every errand she sent the boy on within the room had turned into a game of timing. Could he shave his last errand time down in seconds without running? Corey had laughed and fast-walked his way through tables and chairs. When stumped, he'd ask Gracie where to find something. The kid was sharp.

Parents filtered into the art room oohing and aahing

over their kids' projects. Beth looked at Corey's. It wasn't quite dry but should be by the time they left. She'd have it framed.

Something told her this little step was huge. And her heart nearly burst with pride when she realized she'd been part of it.

Nick pulled into the Rykens' driveway. After a long workweek, he looked forward to his upcoming days off. He'd settle into the house he'd bought, mow the lawn and maybe shop for homeowner gadgets to stock the garage. Plus, he'd have time to get reacquainted with his son.

He rubbed his chin as the familiar feeling of panic shot through him quicker than a bullet. What kind of father was he to be afraid of his own son?

He slipped out of his patrol car and shrugged off his stupid fears. He was a grown man and a cop used to facing some pretty mean customers; he could do this. He'd been reading with Corey every night without making a dent of improvement that he could see. His boy couldn't read and Nick didn't know how to teach him. He sure hoped Beth had solutions stuffed up her pretty sleeves.

Charging the steps, Nick halted from stepping close enough to knock on the door. The windows were open to let in the unusually warm April evening breeze. He could hear Beth talking to Corey. He could see them at the dining room table. The soft glow of the overhead light made Beth's blond hair shine. It looked silky and real. But then, it might come from a bottle for all he knew. His wife had colored her hair, but something about Beth made him think she didn't. He watched as she raised a good-sized card. Corey made the sound of the vowel combination and Beth smiled and then moved on to the next card.

That sunny smile of hers did things to him. He'd made

the mistake of letting Susan get to him too fast, before he'd even had a chance to think. He'd never make that mistake again.

He stepped closer and knocked.

"Come in." Beth's voice.

Nick stepped inside, nodded and looked at his son. "Hey, bud."

Corey looked up. "Hey."

"Well, that's it for tonight. Good job, Corey."

"I'll get my stuff." Corey glanced at him as if trying to gauge how fast he should move.

"We've got time." Nick watched his boy relax and head for the kitchen. Nick slipped into a chair facing Beth. "So? What's the verdict?"

Beth pulled out a thin three-ring binder and slid it across the table toward him. "Here's your lesson plan."

He flipped open the cover. "My what?"

"Reading exercises to do with Corey. Have him tell you a short story, you write it down and then have him read it back. As he improves, lengthen the story. Stuff like that in addition to regular reading. I've got a checklist for you so that you can keep track of what you've done. Nursery rhymes are a great tool, and remember, repetition is a good thing."

Nick ran a hand through his hair. She'd put a lot of work into this, but then, she was used to this stuff. He wasn't. "Thanks, I think."

She smiled and his stomach flipped. "You'll be okay."

Corey returned with his backpack, and Mary followed with two foil-covered plates.

"Wow, dinner again?" Nick accepted the gifts with gratitude.

"Yes, and some cookies." Mary gave Corey's shoulder a squeeze. "Did you show your dad the gift you made?"

Corey's eyes widened. "No."

Nick tipped his head. "What gift and for who?"

"Miss Ryken." Corey stared at his feet.

Nick glanced at Beth.

She set a big piece of thick paper on the dining room table. "Corey painted this at class tonight."

Nick took in the colors. It looked like every other kid's painting he'd seen hanging in a classroom. So? "That's great, bud."

Beth glared at him.

What?

Beth knelt so she was eye level with Corey. "I'll get this framed and then when you come back we'll pick out a place to hang it. Sound good?"

His boy nodded.

Nick felt as if he'd missed something here. It was just a painting. All kids painted, right? He tried to remember pictures from Corey hanging on their apartment walls and couldn't.

Susan hadn't framed any of Corey's colorings. Neither had he. They might have stuck a couple on the fridge of their old apartment, but other than that, not a big deal was made. Another should-have-but-didn't.

Mary patted Corey's arm. "Have a good time with your dad. We'll see you in a few days."

"Okay." Corey looked wary.

Nick rubbed his jaw. He had the next three days off.

Tomorrow was Friday and then the weekend spanned before him with no real plans made. He'd have to come up with something they could do together. His fingers gripped the binder Beth had made. He'd need more than this to keep them busy. "Thanks, Mary, and thank you, Miss Ryken."

"Why don't you call her Beth, like Mary does?" Corey looked up at him.

"Because she hasn't asked me to. And you'll call her Miss Ryken, too—is that understood? She's your teacher."

"Yeah, but—"

"And Mary should be Mrs. Ryken."

Beth came away from the dining room table. She wore faded jeans and a baggy T-shirt that hid her curves. "My mom told him it was okay to call her Mary."

"I'd prefer he didn't."

"Really, Nick, it's too confusing if he calls us both by our last names. Mary is fine for me," Beth's mother piped up.

Nick nodded. Mary's argument made sense. But he didn't want his son getting too comfortable on a first-name basis with his teacher and tutor. What if he made the mistake of calling her that in school? Could lead to trouble. Corey didn't need any more trouble.

The same went with him, too.

Beth's face softened as she studied him. The hum of attraction between them wasn't a good thing, either.

Without looking away from him, she said, "Corey, you better do as your dad says."

Corey looked from Beth to him and then back at Beth.

Nick felt like a heel for insisting. "For now, it's Miss Ryken."

"Yes. For now," Beth repeated.

Nick had a plate in one hand and the binder in the other, so he nodded. "Good night and thanks. Let's go, bud."

"Good night."

Once in the patrol car with their goods in the backseat, Nick finally asked, "So how'd it go?"

Corey shrugged.

"We've got to work on this reading thing now, son. We can't let it go."

"Why?"

Nick didn't answer right away. He didn't want to threaten the boy with being held back. It was up to him as the parent to agree. Nick wouldn't, but what if Beth was right about it helping Corey instead of hindering him? Nick had already made so many mistakes.

"Dad?"

"Let's just work on it, okay?"

"Okay." Corey slumped lower.

Nick drove the rest of the way in silence. Yeah, sure, they were going to do real well the next few days.

Once they were inside their two-bedroom home, Corey went straight to his room. Nick went to his and changed out of his uniform. Nick met Corey in the kitchen. They both wore pajama bottoms and T-shirts.

"What do you say we watch a little sports and then read a book before bed." Nick nuked the plate Mary had given him. "Are you hungry?"

Corey nodded.

"Want more dinner?"

Corey shrugged and went to the cupboard. "I want cereal."

Nick watched his son grab a bowl and milk from the fridge all while he waited for the beep from the microwave. Silently they brought their dishes to the table. Nick peppered his food while Corey poured milk on his breakfast of champions.

"How was school today?" Nick couldn't stand the silence.

"Okay." Corey crunched on a mouthful of cereal.

"Do you like it here?"

Corey's eyes widened. "Yeah."

"Do you miss Grandma and Grandpa?"

Another crunch, but much slower this time. Corey looked as if he was searching for the right way to answer that question.

"It's okay if you do." Nick wouldn't blame the kid if he wanted to go back. He wasn't exactly a barrel of laughs and highly doubted he'd be up for any Father of the Year medals.

"I like it here," Corey said.

Nick nodded, satisfied with the boy's conviction. "Yeah, me, too."

The next day, Beth agreed to keep Corey in the classroom after school, where Nick would pick him up. She wondered what had happened to the boy. He tried so hard to get the vowel sounds right and to read, she thought his head might explode. Like right now. Corey stared at the page with bulging eyes.

"I'm never going to get this." The seven-year-old pushed away his practice work sheets with frustration, knocking a book to the floor with a clap.

"Sure, you will. You're doing great."

Corey shook his head and tears threatened.

Beth tipped her head. She had an itchy feeling this wasn't about reading. "What's wrong, Corey?"

The boy wiped his nose with his sleeve. "I don't want to live with Grandma and Grandpa."

Beth's stomach tightened. Surely Nick wasn't considering that. "Has your dad said that you have to?"

More sniffling. "If I don't learn to read, he's going to send me back."

That couldn't be true. Still, Beth let the breath she'd been holding out slowly. "What makes you think so?"

Corey shrugged. "I just know."

Beth didn't know Nick well enough to assure the boy that wasn't going to happen. Was Nick pushing his boy too hard? Was she? Maybe that binder she'd made had scared both of them.

Beth studied the seven-year-old. "What do you and your dad like to do together?"

Corey shrugged.

"Come on, there must be something."

"We watch baseball on TV sometimes."

Beth smiled. LeNaro High School happened to have a very good baseball team. Their opening home game was tomorrow afternoon, too. "Anything else?"

"Dad likes to mow the lawn."

Beth chuckled. "Yeah?"

"I went with him to buy a new mower. He said when I was older, he'd show me how to mow."

That didn't sound like a man ready to pack his son off to the grandparents', but then, she wasn't sure.

"Okay, back to work. Your dad's going to be here soon." Beth scooted to get comfortable on the small seat and stretched her legs out under the table. She grabbed a book of silly poems with corresponding pictures that were equally ridiculous. "I think you might like these."

She read a couple short ones, glad to hear Corey laugh as he listened and followed the pictures. Poetry was a good place for phonics, too. Hearing the beats and rhythm of the words made them less intimidating. At least she hoped so, for Corey's sake.

After only a few minutes, a soft knock at her open classroom door jerked Beth's attention away from Corey. Nick stood tall in the doorway wearing jeans and a charcoal-colored long-sleeved shirt. He looked great. Major-league great.

Couldn't she look at the guy without her pulse reacting?

The corners of his lips curved into a semblance of a smile. "Hey."

"You should do that more often," Beth said before thinking.

"What's that?"

Might as well complete the blunder she'd started. "Smile."

He tipped his head and then looked at his son. "Hey, bud, how'd you do?"

Beth glanced at Corey.

"Okay." The boy had a thoughtful expression on his face.

She should tell Nick what Corey had told her and find out if it was true, find out how hard Nick was pushing, but she couldn't do that in front of the boy. Still, it sounded as if they needed something fun to do together. Something where they could connect. "I understand you both like baseball."

Both males looked at her as if she'd stated the obvious.

Beth swallowed a laugh. "Well, I don't know what you two have planned for the weekend, but the LeNaro High School baseball team is playing at home tomorrow afternoon. Should be a good game, too, as they're playing against an equally tough team. If you're interested in going, I'll print off a schedule."

Nick smiled again and looked at Corey. "Sounds like fun. Would you like to go, bud?"

Corey shrugged. "Okay."

Beth got up and went to her desk to print off a schedule as promised.

"Miss Ryken, will you go, too?" Corey asked.

"Uhhh—" Beth stuttered, knowing she should refuse, but the words stuck in her throat.

"Corey, I'm sure Miss Ryken has other plans." But Nick

Grey had a hopeful look on his face, too. Hoping she'd refuse or agree, Beth wasn't sure.

"Please?" Corey begged.

How could she refuse those eyes?

"If you're not busy, it'd be great if you'd come with us." Nick looked sincere but guarded.

She bit her bottom lip. She needed to talk to him about his son anyway, his previous school's reports, his worries. Surely there'd be a moment to do that without making a big deal of it. And not in front of Corey.

Who was she trying to kid? Beth wanted to go, and she wanted Nick to want her to go, too. "Okay, yeah, sure."

Relief shone from Nick's eyes. "Great, do you want us to pick you up?"

Beth backpedaled a little as she handed Nick the sports schedule. "I'll meet you there. It's an easy walk from the house."

"Okay, we'll see you tomorrow, then. Corey, do you have your stuff?"

The boy shouldered his backpack. "Yup."

"See you tomorrow." Beth breathed easier.

This was a harmless afternoon baseball game. Sure, she could wait until teacher-parent conference night, but Nick needed to know what worried his son now. A child under stress couldn't focus and learn. And they desperately wanted Corey to learn.

It wasn't as if it was a date or anything. She'd stick to teacher mode and they'd meet at a school function. Beth didn't date men in law enforcement. Tomorrow she'd make that clear to Nick. He deserved to know where she stood, and Beth didn't believe in playing games.

Straightening her classroom before calling it a day, Beth

reassured herself that it'd be okay. Tomorrow would turn out fine. But she looked forward to the baseball game a little too much to really believe it.

Chapter Five

Nick made his way to the bleacher stands near the high school baseball field with Corey in tow. Players warmed up, and a few family members were already bundled on the bench seats in anticipation of the game. The day was sunny but cool. He'd be surprised if the temperatures climbed out of the fifties.

No sign of Beth yet, so Nick looked around.

The nearby concession stand opened its rolltop door with a rattle and snap, letting out the smell of freshly brewed coffee. This was small-town living at its best. The high school wasn't big by any means, but obviously the community rallied around it. An open concession stand manned by volunteers proved that.

He stared at the rolling hills dotted with orchards that lay beyond the sports fields. He thought of a show he used to watch on TV as a kid. Even then they were reruns, but Nick loved Sheriff Andy Taylor, who always had the right answer and time for his son. That was what Nick wanted.

He wanted Corey to grow up in a place where he could get involved in sports and the community. A place where they'd know people on a first-name basis. A place where they'd both belong, like Mayberry. Did he ask too much?

"There's Miss Ryken." Corey pulled on his sleeve.

Nick gave Beth a wave.

She waved back.

Beth had dressed for a chilly day in jeans and a jacket and a LeNaro Loons baseball cap. Her long hair had been pulled back into a ponytail, making her look young. He was pushing thirty-three, and if he hadn't known she taught second grade, he'd think she was college aged at best.

The closer she got, the better he could see that she didn't wear a trace of makeup. Young and unspoiled came to mind. Gawking at her, he felt stale and jaded. As if he'd been thrown in the dryer too long without a softener sheet.

Beth was fresh air and sunshine.

Did she have any idea how beautiful she was? Maybe she did and didn't care. She seemed comfortable in her skin. Being out and about without makeup was something his late wife would never have done. She had to look perfect even if they were only headed to the grocery store.

Beth smiled. "Have you been waiting long?"

Nick couldn't take his eyes off her. "We just got here."

Beth raised a woolen blanket draped over her arm. "I brought reinforcements. It can get pretty cold sitting on those metal bleachers."

He pushed aside sudden thoughts of snuggling close. "Would you like some coffee? Smells like it was just brewed."

"Sure." Beth gave him that sunny smile that hit him like a Mack truck.

Nick looked down at his son. "Corey, what about you? Do you want some hot chocolate?"

Corey wasn't listening. He waved to another little kid.

"Want to play catch?" the little boy hollered.

"Can I, Dad?"

Nick glanced at Beth. "Do you know that kid?"

Beth nodded. "That's Thomas Clark, Corey's tablemate at school. He's a good boy."

Nick nodded. "Stay where I can see you, okay, bud?"

Corey took off without another word, leaving him very aware of and alone with Miss Ryken. He gestured for Beth to take the lead to the concession stand.

The short woman behind the counter scanned him with interest before focusing on Beth. "So what brings you out to Jared's game before the finals?"

"Julie, this is Nick Grey. You remember, his son, Corey, is a new student in my class."

Julie reached out to shake his hand. "Nice to meet you, Nick. And your boy's a sweetie. Perchance do you like to sail?"

"Hmm, never done it." Nick wasn't sure what that had to do with anything.

Beth gave the woman a pointed look before turning to him. "Julie is the other second-grade teacher and Jared is her stepson. He plays third base."

"My husband and I sail. Beth goes with us at the end of the school year. It's sort of a tradition."

Nick nodded, still not sure what that had to do with him. "Great."

"We'll take two large coffees," Beth said.

"Sure thing." Julie gave him another once-over and then winked at Beth. "Inviting a guest is also somewhat of a tradition. So give it some thought."

"Ah, yeah sure." Nick paid for the coffee while Beth doctored hers with creamer and sugar.

Her cheeks were rosy pink. She was fresh faced, all right. But did her skin feel as soft as it looked?

Once seated on the folded blanket with steaming cups of coffee, Beth turned toward him. "Sorry about that."

He played dumb, which wasn't hard. "About what?"

"Julie and the sailing…" Beth waved it away.

"Was that an invitation, then?"

She looked flustered. "Yeah, but that's a long way away. Actually, I was hoping to talk to you about Corey."

Nick's stomach tightened as he took a sip of black coffee. "Everything okay?"

"I'm not sure. Corey's afraid you'll send him back to his grandparents if he doesn't read well."

Nick choked on the hot coffee. The woman didn't beat around the bush. "Where would he get that idea?"

Beth shrugged. "Corey told me in confidence, so please keep it under your hat. But I thought you should know because he's stressing about it. He's pushing himself pretty hard."

Nick nodded, but his gut felt as though it'd been shredded. He'd left Corey behind before, so it only stood to reason that his son didn't trust him not to do it again. He'd been pushing the reading exercises hard at home, too.

"You okay?" Beth's voice was soft, her cornflower-blue eyes even softer.

"I didn't tell him about being held back, so he must have concluded…" Nick ran a hand through his hair.

He spotted Corey playing catch. Someone had given him a small glove to use. His little guy had so much riding on those seven-year-old shoulders.

He shifted toward Beth. "I think Corey wanted you to come today because he's not easy around me anymore. He walks on eggshells, and maybe that's why. He thinks I'll leave him. I don't know what to do about it. He talks to you. Got any suggestions?"

Beth stirred her coffee with the little wooden stick. "Maybe what you need is something fun to do together. Find some interests in common."

Right now that interest was Beth Ryken. Corey liked her, and so did Nick. Maybe too much.

He raised his cup of coffee to her. "Like today—thanks. Maybe we can do this again."

Her eyes widened with alarm.

He'd just asked her out.

Time to be blunt, too. Before she got the idea he was trying to hit on her. "Look, Miss Ryken. I'd be a liar if I said I didn't find you attractive, but I'm in no place to get involved right now. I didn't mean for that to sound like a date."

She smiled at him without looking the least bit offended. Amazing woman. "That's good, because I don't date cops."

"Because of your father?"

Her eyes narrowed. "I saw what it did to my mom. And me when he didn't come home."

Nick nodded. Being the wife of a man in law enforcement wasn't easy. He'd seen the toll it had taken on his own mom. His parents had probably split because of it.

And then there was Susan's reaction to his job. Beth seemed made of stronger stuff. Maybe she was and that was why she wanted no part of a cop's life. Beth knew her limitations.

Susan hadn't.

At first his wife had been enamored with the idea of him being an undercover cop. But they'd eloped only weeks after meeting, and then the reality of his late-night shifts sank in and she complained. A lot. He wasn't home enough. She got pregnant right away with Corey and everything took a dive from there.

Still, the Ryken women had made it through okay. They seemed well-adjusted, except for maybe Beth's refusal to give a cop a chance. But then, maybe that was wiser still and completely understandable.

"So how'd you and your mom get through it?"

Beth shrugged. "Church and friends, mostly."

"Were you and your mom always churchgoers?"

Beth nodded. "For as long as I can remember."

"That's good. I want that for Corey. He needs to grow up in a good church and know how to live a Christian life. I've been a poor example for a man of faith. I put God on the back burner for a while."

Beth's eyes widened. "And now?"

"Now I want Him front and center."

"Easier said than done, huh?"

Nick nodded.

"Don't worry, you're a better example than you realize."

Her words soothed, and he clung to them. "I hope you're right."

"Your son's a good boy, Mr. Grey. A little withdrawn maybe, but there's a gentle politeness there, too. He tests the waters with kids in his class before putting himself out there all the way. I'd guess he gets that from you."

"Yeah, maybe." Perceptive woman. He'd learned the hard way that what glittered wasn't always gold. Especially with Susan. She'd seemed so perfect in the beginning, but then they hadn't really known each other. Once married, that became all too clear.

The ball game started, so Corey made his way back into the bleachers and sat next to Beth as if he belonged there. As if he belonged to her. But the boy smiled at him. "Thanks, Dad."

Nick leaned forward. "For what?"

Corey shrugged. "Coming here."

"You're welcome." He glanced at Beth.

She gave him a soft smile that made him rethink his comment about not getting involved. What Beth had said was dead-on. He needed to find ways to share fun experiences with his boy if he hoped to knit their torn relationship back together. Maybe even make it stronger.

Still, there was no doubt Beth's presence had helped. Corey relaxed around her, and Nick wished some of that ease would rub off toward him. Maybe it would, in time.

For now, Beth made a good buffer between them. They needed her. In fact, they both might need Beth Ryken for a whole lot more than simply a reading tutor.

As the game wore on, Corey went back to playing catch with Thomas. Beth watched the clouds roll in and smother the sun.

She shivered. "This is why I don't come to many early-season games. I end up freezing."

"Here, use the blanket." Nick scooted off their woolen cushion and helped her pull it up around her shoulders.

"Thanks. You want half?" she asked before she'd considered sitting that close to him.

He cocked one eyebrow at her as if she'd lost her mind. "No. I'm fine."

Maybe she had, considering her speech about not getting involved. She wrapped the blanket tighter, and yet part of her was disappointed that he hadn't taken her up on her offer. He'd be warm to lean against.

And Nick was a man of faith, he'd said. Maybe that was why she'd connected with him on a level other than simple attraction. They had God in common.

She'd meant what she'd said about not dating cops. Not that many had asked. A state trooper she'd met at a friend's wedding had once asked her out, but she'd declined his offer. She'd made a personal vow never to marry a police officer. But in the case of the state trooper, there'd been no spark.

She glanced at Nick. A shiver of excitement shot up her

spine that had nothing to do with the cold. Sparks didn't begin to cover their mutual attraction.

Nick had admitted to finding her attractive. Sedate-sounding words, but she'd seen the fire in his eyes when he'd said it. As a woman, she found that look super gratifying. As a woman with a brain, she knew that look was as good as a red-flag warning.

Beth had few regrets in her life and she planned to keep it that way. Losing her father early in her teens made her realize how short life could be, so she played it safe. She thought long and hard before jumping in and weighed the consequences of each decision.

Her dad would never walk her down the aisle or hold her first child. Wonderful moments she'd miss all because what should have been a routine traffic stop ended with her father dead.

She glanced at Nick again. Falling for a guy like him could be the biggest regret of her life. *If* she let it happen. She wouldn't deny the desire to help him with his son. If she could legitimately get Corey ready enough for a fighting chance in third grade, then she could step away.

"Hi, Beth." Thomas's mom climbed the bleachers to sit in front of them.

"Sandy." She forced a smile that usually came with ease.

"And this must be Corey's dad. Hi, I'm Sandy Clark." She extended her hand along with a good dose of interest. "My boy's been talking nonstop about his new friend, Corey."

"Nick Grey." He accepted her handshake.

"Welcome to the area. We're going out for pizza after the game and would love it if you joined us. Thomas would be thrilled."

Surprise registered on Nick's face before he nodded agreement. "Thanks. Corey would like that."

"Great. We'll see you at Jemola's Pizza and Wings. Beth knows where it's at." Sandy gave them both a big smile and left.

Nick turned toward her. "Please say there's a Mr. Clark."

Beth laughed at the panicked look in his eyes. "Yes. Well, no, not anymore. They split up last year and share custody of Thomas."

"You've got to go with us," Nick pleaded.

Beth tipped her head and teased, "Don't tell me a tough guy like you is afraid?"

He nodded fast. "Did you see the glint in that woman's eyes?"

Beth laughed again.

Oh, she'd seen it, all right, and her hackles had risen because of it. They shouldn't have, though. Sandy Clark was a nice woman and solid mom. "You could do worse."

Nick gave her a long look. "I could do better."

Her heart pounded harder. She opened her mouth to remind Nick about how wrong for each other they were, but nothing came out. Diane's advice to stay in teacher mode rang through Beth's brain. Why had she said that, anyway?

He gave her a boyishly crooked grin that made her stomach flip. "Hey, all I'm looking for is friendship. No worries, okay? Come with us."

"Okay." Beth wanted to believe she'd agreed to go because of her weakness for pizza, but she knew better. Her weakness was all about Nick.

Once seated inside the pizza shop around a red-and-white-checkered table, Beth perused the menu.

"Pizza or wings?" Nick peered over her shoulder. "Which do you prefer?"

She fought the urge to lean back and into him. "Both."

"Then we'll get both." Nick's voice was low and soft.

Beth was an idiot to confuse an order of pizza and wings with an endearment, but somehow Nick had made it sound that way. She quickly focused on Corey. "What do you like on your pizza?"

Corey looked thoughtful and then confused. "Huh?"

Beth smiled. "What kind of pizza do you like?"

The boy shrugged. "Pepperoni, right, Dad?"

"That's right." Nick looked pleased with his son's cheerfulness. "Good call coming here."

Thanks to Sandy. Beth bit back jealousy. "Yeah, it was."

"Hey, Beth, Mr. Grey." Her school's counselor stopped by their table.

"Hi, Diane."

"Try their specialty pizza today. It's barbecue chicken and awesome."

"Thanks." Why did Beth feel as if she'd been caught doing something wrong?

"I like pepperoni," Corey said.

"You do? Well, that's good, too." Diane smiled and then turned her attention toward Nick. "Looks like you guys are settling in."

"We are."

Corey's attention was caught by the arrival of Thomas and his mom.

"Thanks for getting a table. This place fills up pretty fast after games." Sandy slipped into a seat right next to Nick. "Hi, Diane, do you want to join us?"

Diane tapped on the tabletop. "Oh, no, my husband's waiting for me in the car. Thank you. Nice to see you."

"See you Monday." Beth was glad Sandy had shown up. She didn't need Diane thinking she and Nick were an item. Not so soon after being advised to stay in teacher mode.

Corey stared at Thomas's mom but didn't say a word.

Beth glanced at Nick to see if he'd introduce his son.

When he didn't say anything, she stepped up. "Corey, this is Mrs. Clark."

Sandy smiled. "Hello."

"Hi." Corey's voice was barely audible.

"Mom, can we have some quarters for games?" Thomas held out his hand.

Sandy dug in her purse.

Nick stood and placed his hand on Corey's shoulder. "Come on, bud, let's check out those games."

The boys followed Nick to the corner by the door where an ancient pinball machine stood proud with lights flashing. There was also one of those claw machines packed with stuffed animals that begged to be played with and lost.

Beth watched Nick instruct the boys.

He might not realize it, but Nick was pretty good with kids. He didn't try too hard to sound interested, nor did he talk down to them. Kids saw right through a patronizing tone.

"So, Beth, are you and Nick Grey seeing each other?" Sandy asked after they'd given the waitress their order while the boys continued to play.

"No." Beth shifted. Seeing the gleam in Sandy's eyes made her want to stretch the truth.

Sandy's eyes narrowed. "Oh?"

Beth came clean, partially. "My mother watches Corey after school."

"Ahh. Nick seems like a nice guy."

"He is." Beth's impression of Nick had been way different than *nice* that day he'd showed up in her classroom. He had an edge to him. A good attribute for a cop.

Beth sipped her pop.

Sandy glanced toward the pinball machine. "So what's his story? Divorced?"

"Widowed." Beth figured that was common enough

knowledge to repeat. Still, she didn't like giving Sandy any pointers. Or encouragement.

"Awww, that's too bad." Sandy's eyes had softened but they didn't look a bit sorry. More like relieved that there wasn't a Mrs. Grey lurking in the background.

"Yeah." What else could she possibly say?

"Hey, Beth!"

Beth looked up to see her friend hurrying toward her. "Eva!"

They quickly embraced, and then Eva looked around the crowded restaurant. "Wow. Not many tables open."

"Join us," Beth said, and then glanced at Sandy to see if she'd mind.

"Adam is with me, along with Ryan and Kellie. You sure there's room?"

"We'll make room." Sandy smiled and pulled a small table for two that was empty toward their larger one. She welcomed the additional people and yet Beth didn't think it was about "the more, the merrier."

Easier to corner Nick in a group. Really! What was wrong with her? If she didn't want him, she shouldn't care if someone else might.

Tamping down her venomous thoughts, Beth made the introductions as they all pitched in to help Sandy gather chairs.

"Hello." Nick had returned with the two boys. He took the increased size of their party in stride, save for the raised eyebrow he gave her.

Beth did the honors. "This is Nick Grey and his son, Corey. They recently moved to LeNaro and Corey's in my class."

Eva reached out her hand. "And this is my fiancé, Adam, my brother Ryan and his fiancée, Kellie."

After a quick round of small talk, everyone sat down.

Beth noticed that Sandy had managed to scoot next to Nick again. She shrugged it off and concentrated on Eva. "You're getting close."

Eva grinned. "Two weeks until the wedding. I can hardly wait."

"Me neither." Adam brought Eva's hand to his lips.

Eva brushed him aside. Her cheeks were pink but she beamed with joy.

"The cherry blossoms will be wide-open by then," Ryan added with a look of such sweetness toward Kellie that Beth's heart twisted.

She'd once had hopes of capturing Ryan's notice, but Kellie was perfect for him. And Beth was happy for them all. Really, she was, but when would true love happen for her?

As if her eyes had a will of their own, she glanced at Nick.

He gave her that crooked grin that wasn't much of a smile at all.

She smiled back. He looked bored out of his mind. From Sandy's chatter or the table talk about cherry farming, Beth wasn't sure. Still, meeting new people was good for him, considering his newness to town.

Eva's smile grew wider as she glanced at Nick and then back at her. "So, Beth, have you thought about who you're bringing to the wedding?"

As they left the pizza shop, rain poured from the sky with no sign of letting up. Under the red-and-white awning, Nick turned to Beth. "We'll give you a ride home."

She looked as if she might argue but nodded. Her house was only a few blocks away, but she'd be soaked through if she walked home.

He watched Beth wave goodbye to her friends as the

two couples climbed into a huge blue pickup. They were nice people. Sandy and her son raced to their car, too. Beth was right about her; he could do a lot worse, but Sandy Clark held no interest for him.

Corey didn't seem impressed, either. He'd barely spoken to the woman.

"Ready to run?" He clicked the remote to unlock his small SUV. He'd traded in his car before the move, after hearing about the winters up north. He looked forward to putting the four-wheel drive to use. Maybe he and Corey could learn to ski.

"Ready." Beth reached for Corey's hand.

His son took it as naturally as if he'd been holding hands with Beth forever. But then, she was his teacher. Little kids must be used to that sort of thing.

They made a dash for the car.

Beth pulled open the back door for Corey and waited while he climbed into his booster seat.

She slipped into the passenger side with a squeal. "Rain just dribbled down my back."

They were soaked dashing for the car. And cold.

Beth shivered and then clenched her teeth to keep them from chattering.

"Corey, hand me that blanket," Nick said.

"I'm okay." Beth rubbed her arms.

"You'll be home before the heat kicks in." Nick wrapped the blanket around her shoulders. That small movement brought them into close proximity.

Close enough to kiss.

His gaze lingered on her full lips.

"Thanks." She sounded breathless.

He leaned back fast. "You're welcome."

The air inside his car hummed with more than the drone

from the defroster on high. The scent of rain mixed with the softness of Beth's perfume had Nick's brain reeling.

Friendship. He'd said that was all he was looking for, but it sure wasn't all he wanted.

Nick glanced at Corey through the rearview mirror. The kid's eyes were wide but not wise. His boy couldn't possibly understand the currents of attraction swirling around them.

For Corey's sake, Nick wouldn't get involved with Beth. There was too much to lose if they suddenly broke up. Women could be vindictive when they wanted to be, and he wouldn't risk exposing Corey to any of that. Especially when he needed to concentrate on reading. The poor kid had had enough drama to last a lifetime.

Friendship. That was all he'd offer Beth until he knew his son had passed second grade. That was all he could handle until he knew for sure what kind of woman Beth proved to be.

Chapter Six

Sunday morning, Beth entered her small community church with her mom. Spotting Eva Marsh, Beth waved. And her friend made a beeline straight for her.

"Morning."

"So what's the deal with that redheaded guy who can't keep his eyes off you?" Eva kept her voice secret-sharing low.

Beth shook her head. "I thought you'd decided to attend your brother's church."

"We are, but we still like to visit. I grew up coming here."

Beth scanned the packed pews for her friend's outrageously handsome fiancé. He chatted comfortably with a crusty old farmer named Jim Sanborn. Although Adam was now a full-time cherry grower, he didn't fit that role today. Dressed in crisp gray slacks and a cotton sweater, Adam looked as urbane as when he'd first knocked on Eva's door over a year ago. Beth had been her roommate then, and she'd coaxed Eva to give Adam a chance. Now they ran Marsh Orchards together and would soon open a bed-and-breakfast to boot.

Eva poked her in the ribs with her elbow. "So? What gives with Nick Grey?"

"Nothing gives. His son is in my class and my mom watches Corey after school."

"And?"

"And that's it." That was all it should be.

"I don't believe you."

Beth never could pull one over on Eva. "He's a deputy sheriff."

"Oh." Eva wrinkled her nose.

She knew Beth's criteria. She also knew how much her father's death had affected her. Eva had been a strong friend through the tragedy. If not for Eva, Beth didn't know what she might have fallen into trying to cope with the loss.

"So…he's off-limits."

"Pretty much." Beth knew what it was like to wait at home and worry. She'd seen her mother do it most of her life. When Beth was old enough to understand the danger her father faced on the job, she had worried, too.

Working in a relatively safe place like Northern Michigan hadn't mattered in the end. They all had breathed easier after moving here, thinking the threat had been removed and her father was safe. But her dad hadn't been killed on the streets of suburban Detroit. He'd been shot on a lonely stretch of back road in Leelanau County and left for dead.

Eva squeezed her arm. "Well, your Mr. Grey just walked in the door and he's headed our way. Maybe he doesn't know he's on your do-not-touch list."

Nick's hair looked damp from a shower and he wore a long-sleeved navy shirt and jeans. Tall and lean, Nick wore jeans well. Even better than his sheriff's uniform.

"He knows." Beth took a deep breath.

Nick wanted to bring God onto the front burner of his life.

Even more reason to like the guy.

"Uh-huh." Eva gave her a doubtful look.

"Look, Nick doesn't want to get involved, either." With Corey's issues, moving to a new town with a new job, Nick had more things to concentrate on than her.

"And he told you that when? After you told him about your vow not to date policemen?"

Beth rubbed her forehead. Since when had Eva gotten so smart? "I don't know. Maybe."

And then Nick stood before them with Corey closing in right behind him. "Miss Ryken."

Beth smiled. "Mr. Grey." They still didn't call each other by first names. "Hi, Corey."

Eva's eyes held amusement before she extended her hand. "Nick, was it?"

He accepted it. "Yes. And you're Eva Marsh."

"Soon to be Eva Peecetorini. In fact, it…"

Beth gave her friend a pointed look. Would Eva get the hint not to invite Nick? They didn't need any matchmaking. If Beth wanted him to go, she'd ask him herself. She didn't need any help. Didn't want it, either.

"…is just a matter of waiting now." Eva smiled.

And Beth let out the breath she'd been holding.

"Congratulations." Nick nodded.

Eva barely contained the happiness that perked and gurgled within her, ready to bubble over on them. "Thanks. Nice to see you both again. Bye, Corey."

"Bye."

Beth watched Eva sidle up to her fiancé. The two were rarely far from each other for very long. The music started and folks scattered into their seats.

"After you." Nick gestured for her to lead the way.

They were going to sit together. And why shouldn't they? They were friends, right? Despite Eva's observation that Nick's gaze had lingered on her at the pizza shop, they were friends. They were adults, too. They could handle attraction for each other and not act on it.

Beth slipped into a pew next to her mom.

"Morning." Nick strategically placed Corey between them.

"Good morning, Nick. If you're not busy after church, why don't you and Corey come over for dinner?"

Beth felt the smile on her face freeze. Her mother hadn't said a thing about inviting the Greys for Sunday dinner. She'd been looking forward to an afternoon nap.

Nick glanced at her. "Thank you, but I don't think so...."

Corey turned toward his dad. "Can we, please?"

"I have more than enough, and homemade cookies are on tap for dessert. I made the dough this morning." Her mom knew how to twist the knife.

Nick hesitated.

Because of her. And that would never do, not when Corey wanted to come over. She faced Nick. "You can't turn down homemade cookies."

He gave her that crooked half smile. "What kind?"

"Peanut butter."

"My favorite."

Hers, too. Beth smiled.

He smiled back.

Were they kidding themselves to think they could maintain mere friendship? Nick needed to make summer arrangements for Corey soon. Then they'd hardly see each other. Save for maybe Sunday mornings.

Nick leaned forward. "I guess that settles it. We'll be there."

Beth ignored the flutter of excitement that zipped through her. This was going to be a long six weeks until summer break.

Throughout the worship service, Beth heard Nick's deep voice singing the songs as if he knew them. Proof that he'd been a churchgoer, as he'd said. Not that she had any reason to doubt him, but hearing him sing reassured her all the same.

When the kids were dismissed for children's church, Corey hesitated.

Beth leaned toward the boy. "You don't have to go, but you'll have more fun there than here. Do you want me to walk you down and then you can decide?"

The boy nodded and took her hand.

Beth glanced at Nick. "I'm going to go with him to check it out."

He gave his boy a reassuring nod. "It's okay, bud. See what you think." And then he looked at her and mouthed the words *thank you*.

Maybe she'd overstepped her place, but Beth got the feeling that Nick didn't expect Corey to go. And then Corey would miss out. She knew the children's program director and her aides. They'd take good care of the boy and maybe he'd make more friends.

As they descended the steps, Beth asked, "Did you go to church with your grandparents?"

"Sometimes."

"Did they have stuff for kids to do during service?"

Corey shook his head. This was clearly all new to him.

They entered the noisy lower level and Beth introduced Corey to the teenage co-teacher. "He's new to the area."

"Great." The girl gave Corey a wink. "We're going to have a snack first before we get started. Do you like animal cookies and juice?"

Corey nodded.

The girl offered her hand. "Follow me and I'll find a place for you."

Corey looked at Beth.

"I'll hang out for a little bit if you'd like to stay."

That satisfied. Corey went with the teenager and squished in between a couple other kids at the table.

After snack time and cleanup, it didn't take long for Corey to join in *their* form of singing. Beth watched for a few moments while the kids moved and wiggled to match the words of the song amid giggles and laughter.

Corey wiggled, too, and when he glanced her way, Beth gave him a wave and left for upstairs.

The minister was already into his message when she slipped in next to Nick.

He leaned close, sending a shiver through her. "He's okay?"

"Yeah, he's doing great."

Beth tried to focus on the sermon. Pretty hard to do with Nick next to her. Everything about him seemed magnified in the space of the pew. Her gaze strayed to his strong hands resting on long jean-clad thighs.

"God answers prayer," she heard the minister say. *"He doesn't always give us what we want, but He'll give us exactly what we need."*

Beth closed her eyes as those words hit her hard and took root. God knew what she wanted—a safe man to love and make a family with. But what if she needed something else?

"Try this one again." Nick had the sports page of the weekend paper open on the coffee table in the living room. He and Corey had been banished from helping in the kitchen.

Silence.

Nick glanced at Beth setting the table in the dining room. She wore a blue dress with white polka dots that skimmed the middle of her calves. Tall and trim yet with full curves, Beth looked ultrafeminine and sort of old-fashioned, as if she'd stepped right out of the Dust Bowl era. She'd kicked off her sandals when they walked in the door and puttered around in her bare feet.

He liked watching her move.

His chest tightened as it hit him that this felt like home. Listening to Beth and her mom fixing a meal together lulled him into a relaxed, sleepy sort of place. Tempted to stretch out on the couch and close his eyes, he wondered how the Rykens would react if he did just that.

Only then he'd miss watching Beth.

He looked at his son. Corey's eyes were glued to the TV screen. There was work to be done, so he tapped the newspaper. "Come on, bud. It's about the Tigers, your favorite team."

Corey shrugged. "I don't want to read it."

Nick grabbed the remote and clicked off the television. This was their ritual. Nick brought out the books, and every night Corey said he didn't feel like reading. Nick insisted. Corey slumped and tried and stumbled and grew more discouraged until Nick couldn't stand it. So he'd take over and read the rest.

That probably wasn't what Beth had in mind when she'd given him books for his son to read. He thought about what Beth had told him yesterday. Corey was stressed. Somehow he had to put his boy's fears to rest without breaking Beth's confidence.

"Corey, look at me."

His son obeyed.

"We've got all summer to work on this, but the more

progress we make now, the easier it will be. You want to be ready for third grade, right?"

Corey looked at him closely as if reading between lines, only he struggled there, too.

"Look, bud, would you rather repeat second grade?"

His son's eyes grew round with fear.

Nick hated scaring the boy but he needed to level with him.

"No…."

Nick nodded. "I don't want you to either, but we've got to work hard and show Miss Ryken you're ready to move on. Don't you think we should try?"

Corey nodded.

Nick had him. "I heard the third-grade teacher here is pretty tough."

"How do you know?" Corey responded with a look of pure skepticism.

Nick had lost him and thought quick. "Thomas's mom might have said something about it."

Corey narrowed his eyes even more and then glanced at Beth.

Nick closed the deal before his boy saw through the fib. "This is about getting you ready to learn big stuff next year. You're a smart kid and this is a hiccup we've got to cure."

"Okay." Corey sighed and pulled the paper close. "Will the Ti-eye…geerrrrs maaake the paaay-uh."

Nick cringed. "That's it. Take your time and sound it out. What do the Tigers do?"

"Play baseball. Play-offs?" Corey looked at him.

"Yeah. What do you think? Will they go this year?"

Corey grinned. "They better."

Nick ruffled his son's hair. "If they know what's good for them. Okay, let's get back to the article."

He spotted Beth standing in the dining room with a dish towel in her hands watching them. Their gazes locked and he saw the approval shining in her blue eyes. He got the feeling that he'd turned a corner with his son. Maybe with Beth, too.

"Dinner's ready," she said softly.

"Let's wash up, bud." Nick stood.

"Can we take the paper home with us?" Corey asked.

Nick could have given his son a bear hug but decided against it. Small steps required small reactions to keep them going. "Absolutely. After we make sure it's okay with Mrs. Ryken."

"We've read it. You can take the paper." Beth nodded. "Now hurry up. Mom and I are setting out the food."

Dinner smelled amazing and he wasted no time bustling Corey into the half bathroom to wash up.

Once they were seated around the table, Mary grabbed his hand. "Will you say the blessing?"

"Sure." Nick took Corey's hand and bowed his head. Beth sat across from him holding his son's other hand and her mom's. They made a tight circle around the table. "Thank You, Lord, for bringing us together. Please bless this food, and bless us as we place our trust in You. Amen."

Mary squeezed before letting go. "That was lovely."

Nick nodded. The words had sort of spilled out of him. He was grateful Beth was Corey's teacher and her mom lived right across the street from the school.

Even more grateful that they attended church and made good role models for his son. This move north was looking more and more like the right thing. And Corey might yet grow easier around him.

Nick didn't feel so lost. Not with the help he received from these two women. As he sat in the Ryken dining room spooning a healthy glop of mashed potatoes onto his plate, this felt like family. He glanced at Beth. She cut Corey's roast beef into smaller bites.

She'd make a great mom.

To Corey.

He banished the thought before it took root.

Nick needed a level of certainty in who Beth was before he could even think about pursuing her. This time, he'd know the woman inside and out before he'd allow one kiss between them. Then there was the mammoth obstacle of Beth's objection to his choice of career to consider. He couldn't promise her he'd always be safe. What had happened to Beth's father could happen to him.

But if God had truly brought them together as he'd prayed, then dating would fall into place at the right time. Or not at all.

Nick trusted his calling for law enforcement and he'd trust God to take care of preparing Beth's heart. If they were meant to be together, they would be.

Monday afternoon, Beth walked home from school with a new packet of reading material centered on sailing for Corey. The boy had worked well with Thomas on an essay assignment about tall ships. Corey had even completed a couple of answers.

The child had listened with rapt attention when Beth read a story about sailing ships and trade on Lake Michigan during the eighteen hundreds. She wondered if Julie's invite to sail the Manitou Islands wasn't something that might work as further incentive for Corey. A reward to work toward that was tangible, instead of the fear of failing. She'd have to talk to Nick about it.

"I'm home." Beth kicked off her shoes, but silence greeted her.

"Mom? Corey?" She walked into the kitchen. The house was too quiet.

Then she peered out the windows into the backyard. Both her mom and Corey were on the grass playing with a small black-and-white terrier. A small dog with a very round belly.

Beth stepped outside onto the deck. "What's this?"

Her mom grinned. "Isn't she precious?"

Had her mom brought home a pregnant dog?

The little girl came right up to her, tail wagging. Beth crouched low and scratched behind the pooch's ears. "Where did she come from?"

"She followed me home from school," Corey said.

The dog responded to Corey's voice and went straight for him, climbing onto the boy's lap to lie down as if she'd finally found safe harbor. Just like the ships they'd read about today.

Beth couldn't believe the look of adoration that little dog gave to Corey. She nuzzled under his hand, begging to be pet. "She's adorable."

And very, very pregnant. How many puppies did she carry and how much bigger could she possibly get before delivery? The dog wore no collar. Surely she belonged to someone. Or had someone dropped her off by the school because they didn't want to deal with puppies?

Beth clenched her teeth. How could anyone do something so horrible?

"She looks like a misshaped peanut," her mom said.

Beth laughed when the dog's ears perked up.

"Do you think Peanut is her name?" Corey said.

Again the dog looked up at Corey and then cuddled her head against him.

"It suits her, that's for sure." Beth had never seen a dog so enamored with a child before. As if Peanut had chosen

Corey as her own and expected him to protect her. Provide for her.

What was Nick going to say?

"We gave her some milk-soaked bread that she lapped up pretty quick." Her mom brushed off her jeans and stood. "I think she might have been wandering awhile, but she's pretty clean. No fleas that I can see."

Maybe she'd been well cared for and gotten lost. Which meant her owners might be worried sick.

Beth took a deep breath. "Corey, we should find out if her owners are looking for her."

The boy's eyes clouded over. "How? Why would they lose her if they wanted to keep her?"

Good question. "I don't know, but anything can happen with a dog."

Corey cuddled her closer.

And Beth prayed there was no one looking for little Peanut.

By the time they heard Nick pull into the driveway, they'd eaten dinner and Beth had returned from a quick trip to the store for a bag of dry dog food. Tutoring Corey on his reading had gone out the proverbial window. They'd played and fawned over Peanut the entire evening. Beth would gather books about dogs—a new subject of interest for Corey.

After a quick knock on the door, Nick stuck in his head. "Hello?"

"Come in, Nick. We're in the living room," her mother called out.

Beth met Nick in the dining room. "We've got a surprise for you."

He cocked his eyebrow.

"Dad! Dad!" Corey had jumped to his feet. "This is Peanut. Can we keep her?"

Beth watched Nick's controlled expression. "She followed Corey home."

"Is that dog fat or is there something else going on?" Nick didn't look amused.

Corey grabbed his father's hand and pulled. "She's going to have puppies. Come here and feel. They're moving around inside."

Nick glanced at her with wide eyes while following his son into the living room. He sat on the couch where Peanut lay like a miniature beached whale.

Sure enough, something inside that rounded belly moved.

"See? Did you see that?" Corey jumped up and down.

"I saw it." Nick laid his hand on the dog's stomach and his expression grew more grim. He scratched under the dog's chin before standing back up.

The dog watched him.

"I don't know, Corey. She must have owners who are looking for her."

"But there's no collar." Corey's chin lifted defiantly.

And Beth intervened. "Nick, are you hungry?"

"There's a plate for you in the kitchen." Her mother started to get up from her chair.

Beth waved her to stay put. "I'll get it for him, Mom." She gave Nick a pointed look to follow her.

He glanced back at his son, who had sat down on the couch, and Peanut climbed into his lap.

"We can't keep that dog," he said.

Beth glared at him to keep quiet until they reached the kitchen. "Come on."

"Miss Ryken…"

She held up her hand to stop him. "Before you decide, that dog loves Corey. I've never seen anything like it."

"Maybe you and your mom can keep her here until I have a chance to find out if anyone's looking for her."

Beth nodded and popped the plate of leftovers into the microwave. "We can do that. Have fun getting her away from Corey, though."

Nick sat at the table and raked his hands through his short-cropped red hair. "What are we going to do with a dog?"

"With puppies." Beth grinned.

Hard-edged Nick was one big softy. He'd caved pretty quick. He gave her an exasperated look. "With puppies."

She set the warmed plate in front of him along with a tall glass of milk. "Maybe this little dog is Godsent."

"How do you figure that?"

She sat across from him and took a deep breath. "Well, I've been praying for you and Corey to find a common interest. Something other than reading that would bring you together daily. And look what showed up."

Nick looked surprised. "You prayed for me?"

"And Corey." Beth felt her face flush.

"That's good. Keep doing that." Nick briefly bowed his head before digging into his food.

Corey wandered into the kitchen with Peanut following him. "Can we keep her, Dad?"

Nick gave his son and the dog a long look. "First we have to see if anyone claims her. If not, then yes, bud. We'll keep her."

"Yippeeeee." Corey flew at his dad and hugged him.

Nick returned it with a fierceness that made Beth's eyes sting. She got the feeling Corey and his father hadn't embraced in a while.

Beth offered up a silent prayer of thanks.

Funny, but the message from the church service the day before came back with an interesting twist. *God answers prayer.* He might not give what's wanted but always delivers what's needed.

Nick and Corey needed this little dog.

Chapter Seven

Nick peeked in on Corey. His boy slept soundly with Peanut snuggled into his armpit. In that moment the dog opened her eyes and looked at Nick as if studying him. She had a pretty black face with a white streak down her nose and small swatches of tan on her cheeks. He might be crazy, but he got the distinct feeling the dog wanted to stay with them. Maybe it was the way the dog had latched on to Corey or the relaxed look on her face as if she'd finally made it home.

"I'll do my best to keep you, girl," Nick whispered.

That seemed to satisfy the dog. She shifted and snuggled her nose right back into the crook of Corey's arm.

He stepped back and closed his son's bedroom door partway. He couldn't leave that dog behind tonight at Beth's. Corey's eyes had welled with unshed tears and he just couldn't do it. So into the car Peanut had gone with tail wagging as she settled into his son's lap for the short ride home.

Mary had told him that when he dropped Corey off at school, he could also drop Peanut off at her house before Beth left. That way the dog would only be alone during the morning hours. She'd keep her until Nick picked up Corey, watching her in case of puppy delivery.

Nick's gut tightened. What did he know about dogs having puppies?

Absolutely nothing.

He scratched a quick note on his to-do list to call a veterinarian in the morning. There was a small vet office not far from their house. Maybe they'd know something about the little dog. If not, he'd run an ad in the paper to cover all bases.

He hoped nobody claimed the pooch. Corey was smitten and Nick hated the thought of having to pry Peanut from his son's arms. He prayed he wouldn't have to.

His phone rang and he picked up before the second ring. "Nick Grey here."

"Hi, it's Beth. Sorry to call so late—"

"Miss Ryken," Nick purred. "What's up?"

She laughed. "You can call me by my first name, you know."

"I know." He might need the distance, but he liked calling her by her teacher title.

"Well, then, *Mr. Grey,* you left your sheriff's hat here."

Nick glanced at the decorative hooks by the back door where he usually hung his hat. Empty. "Thanks for calling. I would have looked all over. I'm going to try to get Peanut to the vet's tomorrow and then I'll drop her by after your mom gets home."

"How'd she do?"

"She's snuggled up with Corey and they're sleeping."

"Good."

"Which reminds me." Nick ran his hand through his hair. "I've got to cover an overnight shift this Saturday night. The guy on duty's wife had a C-section this week.

I hate to ask, but do you think your mom would watch Corey and Peanut at your place overnight?"

"Of course. It'd be fine. We'd love to have them both."

Nick breathed easy. He didn't doubt her. Beth's quick answer and upbeat tone spoke volumes. She cared for his son. A lot. "We didn't get much reading done tonight."

"We didn't either with the excitement over Peanut."

"Yeah, Peanut." Nick hoped they could keep her. "I'll try to get Corey back on track tomorrow night."

"You will."

Nick liked the confidence she had in him.

"In fact…" Beth stalled.

"What?"

"Corey has shown a marked interest in boats, and I go sailing at the end of the school year with the other second-grade teacher and her husband. Do you remember meeting Julie at the baseball game?"

He remembered. The woman had hinted at him going, too. Maybe Beth didn't want that. "You want to take Corey?"

"I thought it might be a good incentive to keep him focused on reading. Use the sailing trip as a reward for making progress. A reason not to quit trying."

"How big is this boat?"

"It's big enough for half a dozen adults and a couple kids for sure. Of course, I'd like you to come, too. So you'll feel comfortable with Corey's safety."

"Of course." Nick smiled.

She was so careful. Careful to reinforce that his invite was all about Corey. But he wondered…

"Is that a yes, then?"

He shifted his phone. "I'd say it is."

"Good. Well, I better let you go. We can talk more about the details another time."

"Yeah, sure." Nick wouldn't mind chatting a bit longer. "See you tomorrow."

"Good night, Nick." Beth's voice sounded soft, even hesitant as she called him by his first name for the first time.

He had to admit that he liked the sound of it coming from her. Even over the phone, the connection between them hummed to life. He scanned his empty kitchen and envisioned Beth setting the table for Sunday dinner here.

It was too soon, much too soon to go there.

"Good night, Beth."

By the end of the week, Beth had gone through several children's books about dogs having puppies with Corey. His reading had slowly improved after he'd finally nailed down some phonic rules. The boy's interest in the subject matter helped as well, but Beth knew they'd lose ground in keeping Corey focused when those pups were born.

Nick had reported that according to the vet, Peanut was in good health. A tangle of puppy heartbeats had showed up on the ultrasound. The vet believed she'd deliver sometime within the next two weeks. They were all on puppy watch.

A knock at the door brought Beth's nose out of the book she'd been trying to read. Peering through the window, she spotted Nick and Corey on the front porch with an overnight bag.

Tonight Nick was on patrol.

Beth hurried toward the door and opened it wide, stepping back. "Hey."

Nick carried in a duffel bag. Corey carried a bag of dog food. And Peanut trotted in behind them as if she owned the place.

Beth bent down and scratched the dog's ears. Then she

glanced at the clock. It was six in the evening. Nick's shift started at seven and ended at seven in the morning. "Did you guys have dinner?"

"We ate before we came." Nick set the duffel on the couch. "Corey's clothes and pj's."

Beth nodded.

"Dad made spaghetti." Corey sat down on the floor next to Peanut. The dog had climbed into the middle of a pink-cushioned dog bed, compliments of her mother.

Beth glanced at Nick. "Wow. I'm impressed."

"Don't be. It's not hard to open a jar and boil water." He looked around. "Where's your mom?"

"She went to the store to buy stuff for breakfast. Mom wants it ready when you come to pick Corey up."

Nick shook his head. "She doesn't have to do that."

"I know, but try to tell her that."

"I have and it doesn't work." Nick referred to all the meals she'd sent home with him.

"Now you know what I live with." Beth tried to get her mother to follow a sound budget that included a savings plan. She fought a losing battle.

"Walk me to the door?"

Beth glanced at Corey. "The Tigers are playing in Atlanta, if you want to turn on the TV. Mom had the game on before she left."

The boy nodded and grabbed the clicker. "Thanks, Miss Ryken."

"You're welcome."

Nick's gaze bore into hers. "Thank you for keeping him overnight. You've got the numbers?"

"Yes." Beth swallowed hard. Nick meant the phone numbers for Corey's grandparents. Just in case he didn't come home.

He looked so tall and foreboding in his sheriff's uniform, but Nick was lean enough to encourage someone to take a crack at him. Beth didn't like that. She didn't like the thought of him patrolling alone all night, either.

"I owe you, big-time," he whispered.

He'd paid her mom generously for her time tonight. Too much, Beth thought. She gave him a cheeky grin she didn't feel inside. "Yeah, you do."

He returned her quip with a lopsided grin. "Exact your payment, then."

Beth's stomach swirled and danced. Nick Grey could flirt when he wanted to. "Be careful tonight."

His eyes grew sober in an instant. "I'm always careful. It's my job to be ready for anything and anticipate the worst."

Beth resisted the urge to touch him. She wanted to feel the iron strength of Nick's arms wrapped around her. Maybe smooth back that red hair of his.

She wrung her hands instead. "It's the *worst* that bothers me."

Nick stepped closer and grasped her hands, stilling them. For a minute, Beth thought she might get her wish, but instead of pulling her closer, Nick nodded. "I'll see you in the morning, Beth."

"Okay." He hadn't promised, but the confidence in his voice helped. A little.

This was the reason she didn't want to fall for Nick. She hated the gnawing fear in the pit of her stomach at the thought of him roaming dark back roads in the wee hours with backup miles away.

He let go of her hands. "Good night, Corey. Listen to Mary and Miss Ryken."

"Sure." Corey nodded, but his gaze was fixed on the game.

Nick gave her a wink and then left.

Beth closed the door behind him and then leaned against it. Had her dad relaxed too much up here? Was that what had gotten him killed? Maybe he hadn't expected the worst when he approached the car he'd pulled over for speeding. Maybe her dad had been tired that night.

"Corey?" Beth's stomach turned over.

"Yeah?"

"Did your father get a nap today?"

The boy shrugged. "I don't know. Maybe."

Beth tried to shake the fear that settled around her like a misty shroud.

"Something wrong, Miss Ryken?"

Beth gave the boy a bright smile. It wasn't right to make the boy nervous with her worries. "No. Why?"

He looked her straight in the eye. "Do you like my dad?"

Beth's smile faltered and fell. What exactly was Corey asking? "Of course I like your dad. He's a nice man."

"Yeah." Corey focused back on the game. There couldn't be any hidden meaning behind his question. He was only seven years old.

Beth settled on the couch and Peanut made a wobbly jump into her lap. The dog stretched and then nuzzled her hand for pats. She stroked the dog's fur and puzzled over Corey's question. The kid wasn't looking to play matchmaker, was he?

"Corey, why did you ask me if I liked your dad?"

He shrugged. "Just wondered."

"Oh." See? Nothing.

Beth was paranoid, or maybe everyone saw through her to the truth. She liked Nick, all right. She liked him a lot. Maybe too much.

Nick stepped into Mary Ryken's warm kitchen the next morning. Sunlight streamed through the windows and the smell of sausage made his belly rumble. Corey's painting had been framed and it now hung in a place of honor on the kitchen wall. It looked good there. It looked even more cheerful as sunlight shined off the glass. A promise of better days to come?

He shook his head at such sleepy imaginings. He'd had an eventful Saturday night on patrol. He'd checked on a noisy party with a guy passed out on the ground by his car, and then he'd been called to a domestic dispute within a town smaller than LeNaro.

Domestic violence calls were the ones he hated most. They were unpredictable and scary. But not last night. The couple had made up by the time he'd arrived. They'd been verbally but not physically abusive, so all had ended well with promises of keeping it toned down in future. Nick had filled out his reports during downtime before dawn.

"Morning, Nick." Mary Ryken stood by the stove wearing a ruffled apron and flipping pancakes.

He yawned. "Sorry."

Beth peered at him with concern. "You look tired."

And you look beautiful. He didn't dare say it, but he didn't look away from her, either. Her hair was tousled from sleep and it was all Nick could do not to yank her into his arms. "I'm okay."

Silence settled in the kitchen.

Nick jerked back to the present when he realized no one was talking or paying attention to the small TV droning in the background. He glanced at his son, who wore a curious expression. Mary, too, had been watching them, a pancake poised on her plastic turner. Even the dog sat with her ears perked high as if waiting for something. Probably a scrap of food to fall.

Nick glanced back at Beth, who hunted for something in the fridge. She seemed so perfect in every way. Even cheerful in the morning. But Nick needed a bigger sign than his mushy heart beating too fast before he considered Beth Ryken right for them.

Right for him.

"Why don't you let us keep Corey for church and then Beth can run him home later. That way you can get some sleep."

"No…." Hadn't these two women done enough for him?

"It's no problem," Beth said. "I'll bring him home after lunch."

Nick looked at Corey. "That work for you, bud?"

"Yup." His son dug into a small stack of pancakes with a smile. The kid liked it here. Why shouldn't he?

Mary touched Nick's shoulder as she handed him a plate of pancakes and sausage. "Sit down and eat, and then go."

"Thanks." Nick meant it.

He couldn't begin to express his gratitude to these two women, and even the dog. Corey flourished here. And that liveliness transferred when they went home, too. Especially since the arrival of Peanut. His boy was healing.

He slipped into a chair next to Beth. She didn't have a plate of food, only an empty mug. "Aren't you eating?"

She got up fast. "More coffee first. Can I get you a cup?"

He shook his head as he jammed a forkful of fluffy pancakes into his mouth. "Milk?"

She laughed at his muffled request.

He watched Beth move around the kitchen as if trying to keep busy. When she set a glass of milk in front of him, he smiled and nodded.

She didn't sit back down. Instead she leaned against the sink and drank her coffee.

He cleaned his plate in no time, but no matter how much he ate, a stronger hunger had settled over him. It felt right. *This* felt right. He and his son and Beth in the kitchen having breakfast together. It didn't matter that they were in her mother's house. It felt as if they were a family.

"More?" Mary had another stack of pancakes ready.

"Please." He lifted his plate. Tired to the bone but not ready to leave. Not yet.

He glanced at Beth and noticed that she looked pale. Worn, even, as though she hadn't slept well. The light smudges under her eyes were barely visible, but they were there. Had Corey or the dog kept her up? He was used to getting up once a night with Peanut to let her outside, but he fell back to sleep easily enough that it didn't bother him.

"How many times did you have to get up with the dog?" he asked.

Beth shifted. "Only once."

"And Corey?"

"I didn't wake up at all," Corey said.

Nick glanced at Beth and Mary, who confirmed it with nods of agreement. "I didn't hear a thing." Mary finally sat down to eat.

"Good. I'll take off, then. I can take Peanut with me."

"I'll bring her," Beth said with a wave of dismissal. But she wouldn't look at him. "Go home and sleep."

Nick nodded. Funny, but he felt as if he was already home. He looked at the dog they'd had for nearly a week now with no claims made on her. She slept with Corey, and Nick hadn't heard a peep out of the boy ever since. His son used to stir and get up a couple of times during the night. On occasion, Corey had called out for his mom before drifting back to sleep. Those nights had torn Nick in two.

He ruffled his son's hair. "See you later, bud."

His son smiled up at him. "Bye, Dad."

His heart full, Nick glanced at Beth. "You're going to need directions to my house."

"You're right. Let me get some paper and a pen." She

hurried into the dining room like a flash of light. What was wrong with her?

He followed her.

She snatched what she needed and turned quick, almost running into his chest, and wobbled.

He steadied her by gently grabbing her shoulders. "You okay?"

"Yeah, why?" She sounded breathless. Agitated.

"I don't know. You seem…different." He slid his hands down her arms before letting them drop away from her. Before he pulled her close.

She cleared her throat. "Nope. I'm fine."

He narrowed his eyes but didn't press her. "Okay."

"Here, draw me a map." She handed him the paper and pen and backed away a few steps, absently rubbing her arms.

He looked at her closely, giving her a chance to tell him what was wrong.

"Directions?" She pointed to the paper.

He leaned over the dining room table and drew. Then he wrote down his address. She already had his cell phone number. "It's not far."

"Oh. I know where you live. I didn't recognize the street address, is all." Beth looked like her normal self again.

Nick wanted to shake his head. Women were a mystery he'd never solve. "Have you thought about how I can even up the score?"

Her pretty blue eyes clouded over with confusion.

"I owe you big-time, remember?"

She smiled. A big, bright and beautiful smile. "Oh, I'm thinking."

"Make it good."

Her eyes widened, and then she looked worried all over again. "I'll try."

Chapter Eight

Later that afternoon, Beth drove a few miles out of town with her windows down. It was hot for the first week of May and that probably boded well for a warm summer. Nick didn't live far from the northern lake of Lake Leelanau. She spotted a public-beach sign and smiled. North Lake had the best sandy beaches.

Beth loved the beach. Any beach. She had plenty to choose from, too. Living on the Leelanau Peninsula, which was surrounded by Lake Michigan and split in the middle by Lake Leelanau, Beth took advantage of the water every chance she could. Give her sun, sand and a book and she was a happy camper. She hoped Corey would enjoy those things, too, especially books.

Beth glanced at the boy buckled into a booster seat that her mom had purchased before Nick could intervene. Her mother had given Nick a lecture on the ease of keeping a seat at their house and wouldn't hear another word about it.

It wouldn't be long before Corey turned eight and wouldn't need a booster seat. It wouldn't be long before the school year ended and Corey wouldn't need her, either. The thought of not seeing the boy every day brought a sharp squeeze deep in her chest.

She'd lost her teacher mode for sure. And maybe Diane had been more concerned about her and how much it would hurt if she got too close to this little boy who'd stolen her heart from the get-go.

Too close to his father, who'd done the same thing.

"Looks like we're here," Beth said.

Peanut lay in Corey's lap, but her ears perked up when they pulled into the driveway. Did the dog know they were home? Her new home?

"This is it, right?"

"Yup." Corey got out and set Peanut on the grass. They both trotted toward the front deck.

Beth looked around. The yard was vast with mature oak trees lending shade to the south end of the house. And what a cute house! Nick had bought a ranch with a peaked roof addition on the front that gave the place a cape-cottage look. Tan with white shutters and an ornamental white picket fence in the front, it was somewhere she could easily see herself.

This was what Beth wanted, only she didn't want to share it with a man in law enforcement. She let out a sigh and walked toward the house.

Nick came out of the garage wearing khaki shorts and a faded T-shirt. His face and arms shone with sweat. The stubble along his jaw looked pretty good, too. "Hey. Wow, is it that time already?"

Beth nodded. "What are you up to?"

"Putting in a fence for the dog."

"You were supposed to sleep." The breeze played with her hair, so Beth anchored it behind her ears.

"I did. For a bit." He gestured for her to follow him. "Come on, I'll show you."

Corey and Peanut must have gone inside, because they were nowhere in sight. Beth walked behind Nick into the backyard, which seemed to go on forever. "How much land do you have?"

"Couple acres. I own to the edge of those woods."

He'd been putting in welded wire fence anchored by wooden posts. By the looks of the posts sticking out of the ground, he planned on fencing in a good-sized area, too.

"It works for now. Eventually, I'll get picket fencing for the whole backyard, but with the puppies, I'm worried they might slip right through the slats."

Beth's heart melted even more. Nick Grey was pure mush. "You're doing this for the puppies?"

"And Peanut. No one's claimed her, so she's ours. She'll need a safe place to run around outside."

"Can I help?"

Nick gave her a shocked look. "You're kidding, right?"

"I wouldn't offer if I didn't want to."

He narrowed his gaze as he took in her striped capris and white T-shirt. "You'll get dirty."

Beth laughed. Did he think she was afraid of a little dirt? "So? I wash well."

He gave her that lopsided grin that made her stomach flip. "You smell good, too."

"We'll see about that after we're done."

Nick gave her a nod. "Thanks."

"You're welcome." Beth rationalized her offer to help. The dog and the forthcoming puppies made as good an excuse as any, but she knew better.

She wanted to stick around and help Nick because it meant spending time with him. And that brought her closer and closer to breaking the vow she'd made not to date cops.

"Come on inside. I'll show you the house before we get started. Is your mom expecting you back?"

"No."

Beth's mom had practically tossed her out the door

with orders to take her time. Obviously, her mother already liked Nick and had no qualms about what he did for a living.

They stepped into the house from the back deck. A huge kitchen done in white cupboards and pale blue walls with a dining area greeted them. Beth found herself smiling again. "Nice. This is really nice."

He looked at her. "All I need to do is fill it."

Surely he meant with furniture. The place was pretty bare. No knickknacks or artwork on the walls. A table with chairs in the dining room, louvered blinds instead of curtains gracing the windows. In the living room, Nick had a recliner with a floor lamp beside it, a TV and a coffee table in front of a sofa. On that sofa a little boy lay curled up around a pregnant dog. Both were sleeping.

Nick stopped and stared a moment, his eyes softening at the sight of his son. "Why's he wiped out?"

Beth hoped Nick didn't mind. "We stayed up sort of late watching a Disney movie last night. And then Mom made a small turkey for lunch. Which reminds me, I have leftovers for you. They're in a cooler in my car."

Nick shook his head. "She doesn't have to do that."

"Trust me, you're doing her a favor. She loves to cook."

Her mom had taken the Grey boys under her wing. Cooking was something Mary Ryken enjoyed, and making sure Nick and Corey ate well gave her mom purpose. Or maybe it was feeling needed that seemed to stave off her mother's shopping sprees. Would that change come summer when Nick found other arrangements for Corey?

Beth could volunteer to watch him, but that wasn't a good idea. Spending the summer with Corey meant slipping right into a mom role. Beth wouldn't mind a bit, but how fair could it be to act like a mother to Corey if she wouldn't accept his father?

"Want to see the rest of the house?"

"Of course. Lead the way." Beth followed him.

Nice finished basement. Nice bedroom for Corey, bathroom, and then finally, they ended up in Nick's room. It was a large bedroom with a sliding glass door that opened onto the back deck. Okay. She officially loved his house. "Nice."

"I think so." He foraged through a dresser drawer and then tossed a dark blue T-shirt at her. "Here. You can wear this while we work. Do you want a pair of jeans or shorts?"

Beth clutched his T-shirt and raised her eyebrow. "Your shorts won't fit me."

He cocked his head and studied her hips. "Sure they will. Might be baggy around your waist, though."

She felt her cheeks heat. He was crazy but sweet. And his comments made her feel small and feminine. "The shirt is fine. I'll be a minute."

Beth dashed for the bathroom to change her top. A splash of cold water might be in order, too.

It didn't take long before Beth met him in the kitchen wearing his shirt. It hung on her shoulders. Her cheeks were still rosy. She was the most beautiful and caring woman he'd ever met.

"What?"

He shook his head. "Nothing. Would you like some lemonade?"

"Please." She looked away.

He poured, wondering what they were doing dancing around each other this way. He handed her a glass and noticed her feet. They were pretty, too, and in flip-flops. "Those won't do."

"Huh?"

"I'll get you a pair of work boots and socks."

A nervous-sounding giggle slipped out of her. "Okay."

Back in his bedroom, he retrieved the protective footwear. Passing the bathroom, he noticed her pristine white T-shirt folded and draped over the towel rack. The sight stopped him cold.

The fierce longing for the right woman to share in raising Corey cut him in two. But Beth didn't want to get involved with a cop, and he shouldn't get involved with anyone right now. Right?

That conviction didn't ring true anymore. Not with the attachment Corey had for Beth.

He returned to the kitchen and spotted Beth peering out of the sliding glass door. "Boots might be big, but they'll keep you safe from injury."

She turned and smiled. "Thanks."

"No, thank you for your help. It'll go much faster with two of us."

She opened her mouth and then closed it. Something was definitely on her mind.

Nick's gut tensed. He hoped it wasn't about Corey. "What?"

Beth bit her bottom lip and then cleared her throat. "I have a favor to ask you."

"Name it. I owe you big-time, remember?"

"This is big."

He stepped closer, looking forward to what she might ask of him. "It should be."

"Will you go with me to a wedding I'm in Saturday?"

He blinked. "That's it?"

"Guys hate weddings, or so I'm told."

Wearing a suit and tie, making small talk with people he didn't know and would probably never see again—yup, weddings were a drag. "You're in it?"

"A bridesmaid for my friend Eva. You met her and her fiancé at the pizza place."

Even worse. He'd end up standing around and waiting. Why was there so much waiting around with weddings? But dancing might be involved. With Beth. Nick wasn't opposed to that. He suspected holding her close would be worth it.

"Sure. I'll go."

She smiled. "Great. I thought Corey could come, too, since the whole thing is outside in a cherry orchard. My mom will be there, so she can help keep an eye on him. It'd be a great chance for you to meet some people in the community."

Nick chuckled. Dancing didn't sound promising in an afternoon garden wedding. It might be boring, too. "You don't have to sell me on it. I said I'd go."

"Right." Beth took the boots and socks from him and then sat down to put them on. Her cheeks blazed.

"What time?" This wasn't a date. Far from it. But then, if it was a garden-party thing, what did she need him for?

"The wedding's at six in the evening. You can meet me there. Maybe pick up my mom? She knows where to go."

"This is an outside wedding at night?" In May. In Northern Michigan.

Beth had laced up each boot. They were too big. Along with the baggy T-shirt, she looked as if she'd been caught playing dress-up in her father's closet. "In their cherry orchard that'll be in full bloom. It's quite a sight to see, too. Don't worry, there will be tents set up for dinner and the band. But it's not supposed to rain according to the forecast."

Even though he'd lived up north for a short time, he knew forecasts changed on a dime. There was a saying he'd heard in the department: *if you don't like the weather, just wait, it'll change.*

Anything could change in less than a week. Including his resolve to wait until he knew Beth better before asking her out. A band meant dancing, and he really liked the sound of that.

"I'll be there."

"Thank you." Beth smiled, looking relieved.

He smiled back. "Let's wrestle the fence."

"Okay." She peeked into the living room to check on Corey. "He's still asleep."

"Maybe we can get this done before he wakes up. With you helping, it shouldn't take too long since the posts are in." Nick handed Beth a pair of work gloves.

She took them without a word and followed him outside.

"I need you to pull the length of fence tight against the posts so I can hammer staples in and attach it. Sound good?"

Beth nodded. "Good."

They worked in silence at first. Together they'd unravel the length of twelve-gauge wire fencing and straighten it. Beth held it firm while he hammered it in place. She was strong and capable even clomping around in his oversize boots. They worked well as a team, nailing one post after another. She moved with him and didn't flinch when he brushed against her.

"Thanks for doing this." He slammed a staple in place.

"No problem. Glad to do it."

Nick sat back on his haunches and looked up at her. She'd pulled her hair back into a messy ponytail. "That's what amazes me."

She wrinkled her nose. "This? No biggie."

"My wife would never have done this."

"No?"

He shook his head. "No."

"What happened?"

"To her? Or to us?" Nick couldn't believe he was going there.

"Both," Beth whispered.

They unrolled the next length of fence. "She was killed in a car accident, but our marriage was a wreck long before that."

Beth's gaze flew to his. "I'm sorry."

"Yeah, me, too. I rushed into it without really knowing her." He stopped rolling fence. "Remember what I told you about Susan breaking the plates?"

Beth nodded. "Yeah."

"Looking back, I wonder if there wasn't more I could have done to help her cope. Things had really deteriorated that last year. Frustration had grown into resentment." He blew out his breath. "Maybe if I'd been around more at night, I could have seen what was happening to her. Made her get help. I don't know."

Beth laid her gloved hand on his. "Didn't her folks notice anything?"

"Her mom said it was anxiety and stress. Susan worked part-time while Corey was at school. I don't know where the stress came from, unless it all came from me."

He'd been working an undercover case he couldn't walk away from. Not then. He'd planned on going to a day shift, but the case had dragged on, and then Susan was killed.

He glanced back at Beth. "Sorry to unload."

Her eyes shone with compassion, and she gave him a bright smile. "Don't be. We're friends, right?"

"Right." She was naive to think so. He didn't know what they were.

"Hey, Dad, can Peanut come out?" Corey stood on the back deck rubbing his eyes.

"Sure, son." Nick glanced at their fence. Only two posts left to go to finish enclosing the backyard. He'd have to build a gate somewhere, but he'd figure that out later. "Keep an eye on her while we finish up."

"Okay." Corey ran in the backyard with Peanut at his heels. She moved pretty fast for a pregnant dog.

"He's settling in here, isn't he?" Beth's voice was quiet as they pulled the fence tight on the last post.

"I think so. Having the dog really helps. And you." Nick checked his watch. "You want to stick around for dinner and then do some reading together with Corey?"

"Sure." She handed him her work gloves. "I'll go wash up."

Nick watched her walk up the steps of his back deck. She slipped out of his work boots and socks and then disappeared into the house. It felt right having her here.

"Is Miss Ryken staying for dinner?" Corey was by his side.

"That okay with you?" Nick looked down at his son. Seemed silly to call her Miss Ryken now that they'd become friends. But he'd rather wait until the school year was over before he gave his son permission to call her by her first name. Maybe Miss Beth would do come summer.

Corey grinned. "Yup."

He ruffled the boy's hair, which was in need of a trim. "Come on. Let's wash up, too."

Stepping inside, Nick knew they'd become far more than friends. They'd become a family.

Beth cleared the dishes from the table to load them into the dishwasher. Nick had grilled hamburgers for dinner and Beth had made a salad. Her mother's leftovers had been tucked into his sparsely filled fridge for another day.

The guy didn't stock up much. Good thing her mom had sent leftovers.

"Last one." Nick set the greasy burger plate on the counter and then leaned close and sniffed her neck.

Beth turned. "What are you doing?"

"You still smell nice."

She wielded a butter knife. "Watch it, mister."

He cocked his eyebrow in challenge.

"Don't think I won't use it," she warned.

He laughed at her mock fierceness. "You wouldn't hurt a fly."

"My father taught me self-defense moves when I was a kid." She'd had to use it years ago to help Eva get away from her bully of a then-boyfriend.

"Care to see if they work?" Nick teased her.

She wasn't biting on his line. "I know they work."

"I used to teach a self-defense class to my fellow undercover officers. Several were women."

She touched his nose. "Is that how you got this broken? Did those women gang up on you?"

He glanced at the dining room table, but Corey had already gone into the living room.

Beth could hear the TV.

"A different gang and the odds weren't in my favor."

Beth felt her eyes widen as the reality of his work came crashing in, obliterating their easy flirtation. "That's why I don't date cops."

"Because they get their noses broken?"

She poked him in the ribs to move so she could load up the dishwasher. "No. It's how they get broken that bothers me."

He reached for a plate that she'd rinsed and settled it into the rack. "That was when I worked undercover. I had to play rough-and-tumble to prove I was a punk. No big deal."

Beth couldn't imagine what Nick might have had to do in the name of justice. She didn't want to know. She hated the thought of him getting beat up, or worse. The way he'd sloughed it off as nothing silenced her pretty good. They filled the rest of the dishwasher without another word.

When they were done, Nick turned it on. "I'm not reckless, Beth."

She glanced at him. The hum of the dishwasher spraying water nearly drowned out his softly spoken words, but she'd heard them loud and clear. He was making his case. "My father wasn't, either."

"Life has risks. Some occupations hold more than others, but you shouldn't stop living because of fear."

She narrowed her gaze.

She lived. Didn't she? *Yeah, right.* As Eva's roommate and now her mom's, what did that say about her ability to step out and take risks? She saved her pennies for what? A rainy day?

"I can choose what risks to embrace."

"But what if you miss out on something God has for you?" Nick didn't look as confident as his words sounded. Was he trying to say that they might be meant for each other?

She refused to put herself through the same pain of her father's death. This afternoon Nick had confessed to some of what he'd been through with his late wife. How much had stemmed from what he did for a living? The life of a cop's wife was filled with worry. And fear. How did a woman let go of that?

Beth didn't have to, and that was the point. She had a choice here. "Let's work on Corey's reading homework before I leave. It's getting late."

Too late to rescind her request for Nick to accompany her to Eva's wedding. She'd asked him out of pure selfishness. She didn't want to be standing on the sidelines waiting for sympathy dance requests from Eva's brothers. She didn't want to dance with men she'd tower over, either.

But the real reason she'd asked was because she didn't want to show up to such a romantic affair alone.

Nick was a lot like wedding cake. Harmless in small chunks, but too much and she'd be hurting. She made a mental promise to take him in moderation until her stopping point at the end of the school year.

"All right. We can settle around the table." Nick cleared off the salt and pepper shakers.

"I have a better idea. Let's write haiku in the living room and make a game of it."

"High-what?" Nick gave her a funny look.

Beth laughed. "Come on, and I'll show you."

They gathered around the coffee table and Beth handed out a couple of sheets of notepaper while Nick clicked off the TV.

"What are we doing?" Corey slipped down beside her.

"A game."

Corey looked at his dad. "This doesn't look like a game."

Nick chuckled. "Don't worry, bud, I don't know how to do this, either."

Beth smiled. "We're going to write a poem called a haiku."

Corey groaned.

"Haiku are fun poems and they don't have to rhyme," Beth explained. "Five syllables or beats, then seven, then back to five. Here…I'll do one so you can see what I mean."

She scribbled down a few lines and read it back using her fingers to show the number of beats in each line. "Peanut is pregnant. Her puppies will arrive soon. What will we name them?"

"Let me see that." Nick pulled the paper closer and counted, then stared at her. "How'd you do that so fast?"

Beth grinned and looked at Corey. "Practice. I love these things. Corey, do you want to give it a go?"

The boy shrugged.

"We'll help you. Let's start with a topic. How about baseball?"

Corey looked lost.

Beth gave him an encouraging nod. "How about this.... The Tigers are great."

"They like to grill big fat steaks," Nick added.

Corey giggled.

And Beth nodded. "I think you've got it. We need a last line, though, five beats."

"And throw the ball...far?" Corey counted each sound on his fingers.

Beth whooped. "Yes! That's it! Corey, you're good."

Nick gave his son a high five and then smiled at her with admiration. "Let's do more."

Beth nodded.

Nick and Corey both waited for her to give more clues, but her throat suddenly felt tight. This had really worked. Corey looked excited to continue, and Nick? She didn't want to think about how wonderful Nick looked. Or how spending a Sunday together made it feel as if they were a family.

Because thinking along those lines forced her to face the fact that she'd have to make a choice and soon. Follow her head or follow her heart.

No matter which one she followed, someone was bound to get hurt. Eventually.

Chapter Nine

"Beth, Mr. Grey, thanks for meeting with me." Diane sat back down at her desk.

"Of course." Beth was used to this sort of thing.

She and Diane had met with the parents of at-risk kids before. Sometimes the parents were willing, sometimes they weren't. But this was weird because she knew Nick pretty well.

And cared for him, too.

"No problem." Nick wore his deputy sheriff's uniform. At least he'd left his hat in the car so he didn't look quite so formidable. "What's this about? Beth said we'd discuss how Corey has been settling in, but there's more, isn't there?"

Diane nodded. "A little. Yes. Corey's previous school had some troubling notations—"

Nick snorted contempt. "They labeled him without understanding what he'd been through."

Beth held her tongue. And her hands neatly in her lap. She'd nearly reached out to Nick at the strain in his voice. But that wouldn't be good, not in front of Diane. The counselor had seen them out together, and Nick had called her by her first name.

Diane didn't falter. "He's showing improvement. He's socializing, making friends, and his reading is progressing."

"Then you won't recommend he be held back, right?" Nick had moved forward in his seat.

Diane looked at her for help.

"We don't make those recommendations until closer to the end of the year," Beth said.

Nick's eyes narrowed. "How close?"

"The last couple of weeks."

"Miss Ryken knows I won't agree to hold my son back."

Diane nodded. "Yes, she told me that. Look, Mr. Grey, if Beth believes it's best for Corey, and he scores well for repeating second grade, you'll need to sign a waiver that you're refusing retention. Those forms follow Corey until he graduates."

Nick nodded. "Understood. But he's doing better."

"I'd say." Diane leaned back in her chair. "Thanks to both of you working together instead of in opposition."

Nick looked surprised.

Beth was, too. Where was Diane going with this?

"The first time I met with Corey, he said that he wanted a family. A new family that would never leave."

Beth's belly tumbled. Diane hadn't told her that. That whole teacher-mode warning made sense now.

Nick puffed out his cheeks, then released his breath in a whoosh. "He feels abandoned after I had him live with his grandparents."

Diane looked even more serious. "Not now, he doesn't. Whatever it is that you two are doing outside of schoolwork and tutoring, keep it up. Corey is settling in nicely because he has both his teacher's and his father's support. Inside the classroom and out of it. But if you're dating, that will play right into Corey's new-family fantasy."

Beth glanced at Nick. "We're not dating."

He looked determined. "Not yet."

Diane looked between the two of them. "Whatever you decide to do, keep in mind that the outcome of your relationship will have an impact on Corey. Now, let's go over Corey's progress in detail."

Beth cringed. She knew what Diane said without really saying it. Getting romantically involved with Nick had to be a one-way street. Go all the way or don't go at all. Marriage or maintain friendship. From Corey's perspective, a breakup would be a form of abandonment. Another loss and possible setback. But if they were to remain friends until Corey was truly settled, would that make a positive difference?

Diane went over the transcripts from Corey's old school and compared those sparse notes to where he was now. Beth kept progress logs on all her students. She had to. Part of her job was comparing those with the other second-grade class. She and Julie worked as a team to ensure everyone met their benchmarks. Nick listened, but his expression grew darker the more they went over Corey's transcripts from his old school. "I never realized it had been that bad."

Diane shrugged. "The information is incomplete. And contradictory."

Beth remembered reading one teacher's notes that Corey had cried a lot. He'd isolate himself from the other students and cry. And like most kids that age who had no idea how to help, they left him alone. And Nick had been gone, too.

Beth's heart bled for the little guy who'd felt all alone. Corey wanted a family. But he had one. He had grandparents and a good father. What else was he after?

A mom.

Of course he was. Poor kid. But Beth wasn't sure she

could fill that role. Not if it meant becoming the wife of a cop.

After their meeting, Beth turned to Nick in the hallway of the administration office. "Are you ready to pick up Corey at my mom's or do you have to return to work?"

"I'm done for the day. I'll walk you over."

Beth agreed.

Slipping outside into late-May sunshine, Nick stalled her with a touch. "You're not going to suggest holding Corey back, after all those good things your school counselor had to say?"

Beth had to make him understand so many things. "It's not solely a matter of opinion. We look for certain criteria and aptitude when completing the required paperwork that recommends retention. Scoring helps narrow that decision."

He shook his head. "Corey's a smart kid. He's going to catch up."

Beth hoped so. "And we've got to remain a team in agreement on our friendship. No dating, Nick."

He nodded but didn't look convinced.

"Are you going to talk to my class for Jobs Day?" Corey bounced on the bed. "Thomas's dad is a chef and he's going to be there."

"Uh-huh." Nick attempted to tie his tie for the third time. "We'll see, bud."

"Miss Ryken said it was okay, didn't she?" Corey threw himself in the middle of the bed once again.

"Yes, she did." Nick had been formally invited to speak for Occupation Day in Beth's class.

He wasn't thrilled about it, but he'd do it because Corey wanted him to. He'd do anything to help Beth and that school counselor pull for Corey to pass second grade. Staying involved helped with that. His son's old school had passed unfair judgment on Corey because Susan's parents had gone to all the parent-teacher meetings at school. That hadn't done his boy any favors.

So he'd talk to Beth's class to prove he was involved. He cared. But kids loved all the gore of excitement-filled stories. Those kind of tales would only reinforce Beth's fears and maybe scare his son. He'd keep it tame. Thankfully, that wasn't hard to do since moving here.

He looked through the mirror at his son. "And stop jumping on my bed. You'll wrinkle your suit."

Corey pulled at his tie as he slipped to the floor. "Why do I have to wear this, anyway?"

Nick smiled. "Because it's a wedding."

"So?"

"So we're supposed to look nice at weddings."

"Stupid wedding. Do I have to go?"

Nick chuckled. Corey had wanted to go before he knew about wearing a suit. Maybe Nick should have arranged for Corey to go to Thomas's house instead. Too late now. "Yes, you do. We're picking up Mrs. Ryken on the way."

Corey smiled. "Does Mary have to wear a suit?"

"No, bud. She's probably going to wear a dress." Nick still didn't like it that Beth's mom had given his boy permission to call her by her first name. But Mary liked it that way. Who was he to refuse the woman's wish?

Nick stepped back, finally satisfied that his tie was straight. He hadn't worn a suit in ages. Susan's funeral might have been the last time. A day he'd rather not remember. Corey had been devastated. Lost.

He glanced at the boy. His son had come back to life. He read, too. Brokenly still, but better than before. The haiku poetry game Beth had taught them Sunday night had been a huge hit with Corey. Every night this week, they spent time making up different haiku and laughing at their results.

Nick had framed the first poem Corey wrote on paper with Beth's help. It had cracked them all up and Nick cherished the memory of seeing his boy laugh so hard. It'd been a long time, and Nick didn't want to forget that moment. A milestone.

He glanced at the framed piece of paper displayed on his bedroom wall.

I like scary bugs
Icky, yucky, crawly, splat
Hairy legs and eyes

Nick smiled. He owed Beth a whole lot more than attending a wedding with her. He owed her his patience. *Friendship,* she'd said. That was getting increasingly difficult to maintain.

"Ready, Dad?"

He looked down at his son with his freshly cut red hair. Nick had gotten a trim, too. A Saturday morning spent at the barbershop in town as father and son. Then they went out for breakfast. Corey had read the menu and chose pancakes. They'd come a long way.

"I'm ready."

After letting Peanut inside from a potty run, they left through the garage and climbed into his SUV. It didn't take long to reach town. When they'd pulled into Mary Ryken's driveway, Nick got out and headed for the house.

Mary met him on the porch. An attractive woman in her fifties, she wore a yellow dress that fluttered when she walked. "How nice you look, Nick."

"Thanks. You, too." Nick held open the passenger-side door for Beth's mom.

He was perplexed that Mary hadn't remarried. Had she even dated in the twelve years since her husband's death? If she had, would Beth still have held on to the fear from her dad's death? Maybe Beth would have accepted him if she'd finished growing up with a stepfather who'd taken away the sting of her loss.

At Corey's tender age, he needed another mom, wanted another mom, but she had to be the right woman. A woman like Beth. According to the school counselor, they shouldn't jump into anything until they were sure. Nick agreed.

"Oh, Corey, you look very handsome."

Nick gave his son a pointed look through the rearview mirror.

Corey straightened up from slouching in his booster seat. "Thanks, Mary."

"You're welcome." Mary fussed with her dress before buckling up. "You're going to drive out of town and then head north on Eagle Highway. Marsh Orchards is only a few miles out."

Nick nodded. He had an idea where they were going. In the month he'd been patrolling the county, he'd come to know the area pretty well. Leelanau County was filled with cherry orchards and vineyards. A safe area, too, all things considered.

Would he ever convince Beth of that?

By the time they pulled into the long driveway that led to Marsh Orchards, Nick was taken by the beauty of the place. A cherry-red farmhouse sat on a hilly mound with good views. Following the signs, Nick parked, got out and stared at the vista before him. Beth had been right. The orchard was something to see. The cherry trees were heavy with white blossoms, and petals fluttered to the ground like falling snow. Fat and soft.

"Come on. We'll sit on the bride's side." Mary bustled forward.

Nick followed with his hand tight around Corey's. He didn't need the boy running off somewhere. Especially after they spotted a couple of kids close to Corey's age darting around the cherry trees. The sun hung in the western sky, but it was a good three hours from setting and still shone with warmth. Another benefit to moving so far north, the days were even longer, especially as summer approached. And this was one beautiful spring day.

They sat down in white folding chairs as a woman with a harp began playing typical wedding music. It was light and airy sounding, and Nick felt as if he'd walked into one of Corey's books. If a giant white rabbit showed up, he'd worry.

Chuckling at his thoughts, he spotted the tent Beth had mentioned. It was a huge white wedding variety with roll-down walls positioned on high ground beyond a pole barn. Inside he glimpsed tall propane heaters to ward off the night chill. Should be an interesting evening.

A hush settled among the guests and the music changed tempo. Nick felt a tug on his sleeve and looked down. "Yeah, bud?"

"What happens now?"

Nick smiled. "The bride will come out and meet her groom."

"Who are they?" Corey pointed at the men who had taken their places in front near a flowered arch. Two of them Nick remembered from the pizza shop. Adam and Ryan. The third man standing was older and bald. And the minister looked like a lighter version of Ryan. Brother, maybe?

"That's the groom and his friends. The groom is the one getting married today."

Corey nodded.

The music changed again and everyone stood.

Corey, on tiptoe, craned his neck to peer around the adults who watched the bride come down the steps of the house. "There's Miss Ryken."

"Doesn't she look beautiful?" Mary cooed.

"Yeah." Nick wasn't sure if she meant the bride or her daughter. Didn't matter. Beth looked amazing.

Beth and another bridesmaid lifted the back of the bride's dress, keeping it from snagging on the gravel of the driveway. Once they reached grass, the women fluffed the bride's dress and then slipped into single file in front of her. A dark-haired woman and then Beth.

The pink dress Beth wore accentuated every fine curve and long length of her. Her hair had been bundled on top of her head, giving her even more height. Walking between the two petite women, Beth stood regal. Gorgeous.

Once the women were standing in place, Beth looked his way.

Nick smiled.

She smiled back.

Nick drank in the sight of her. From a distance it was easy to do without being caught. But then Beth glanced his way a couple times and each time, he smiled instead of looking away. She nearly forgot to take the bride's bouquet so the couple could exchange rings.

Enough staring. Beth had a job to do.

Thankfully, the ceremony was brief. Corey's fidgets weren't too bad. The kid asked only twice what they were doing and why. Finally, the bride and groom kissed to seal the deal as a married couple.

Nick felt another tug on his sleeve. "Yeah, bud?"

"Will you marry Miss Ryken?"

It was a rare occurrence for Nick to be struck speechless. He might not use a whole lot of words, but he'd always found a few when he needed them.

Not now, though. "Uh…"

"She could be my new mom," Corey added as if trying to convince him to agree.

Nick didn't need to be convinced. He glanced at Mary, who hid a smirk behind a tissue. He'd get no help there.

He faced his son, who waited for an answer. "I don't know, bud. We'll talk about that later."

"Okay." Corey shrugged, not realizing the bomb he'd just thrown had confirmed everything the school counselor had said.

Nick felt the shrapnel like pinpricks all over his skin as that question reverberated through his brain. Hadn't he thought along those same lines? But he couldn't rush. For Corey's sake, he had to be sure. And he had to be sure she'd say yes.

After the ceremony and another round of pictures, Beth slipped into a seat at the table for four with her mom, Corey and Nick. Shame on him for staring during the service. Shame on her for staring back.

"Hey."

Nick looked surprised. "No wedding-party table?"

"Nope. The bride and groom have their own, so the rest of us can mingle." She chose a couple hors d'oeuvres offered by a waiter.

"Nice."

Beth gulped her water. Something about the way Nick looked at her made her feel warm all over. Nervous, even.

"You look pretty," Corey said around a mouthful of dried cherries and chocolate. Small dishes of the stuff graced every table.

"Thank you, Corey." She didn't dare look at Nick. Beth

had read the appreciation in his gaze several times. She didn't need his words, didn't want them, either. And certainly not in front of her mother.

After a brief silence while Nick and Corey pounded down the snacks and cherry mix, Beth breathed a little easier. Nick didn't say anything about the way she looked.

"Lovely wedding." Her mother fluffed the brand-new dress she wore.

"It is."

Her mother had ordered the yellow confection from an online store before Beth could intervene. One more frilly dress headed for the back of her mother's closet after tonight, never to be worn again. Beth supposed only one extravagant purchase wasn't too bad considering her mom had a habit of ordering a few to try on and choose from. Her mom was trying to curb her spending habits and making some progress.

"So what's next?" Nick asked.

"Dinner and then the band will set up and emcee the rest of the usual wedding stuff." Beth had been given the reception plan by Eva months ago. They'd cut the cake and throw the bouquet and garter all in between an evening of dancing.

"Good. The sound of that harp is getting old."

"I agree." Beth laughed.

Being sandwiched between two tiny women in pictures had been bad enough, but tromping around in a short pink sheath of silk with harp music playing in the background made her feel like a giant. An underdressed one, at that.

Dinner was barely served when the tinkling of glasses started. The bride and groom had only just sat down.

"What's that for?" Corey's eyes went wide.

The crowd cheered as Adam and Eva shared a quick kiss. Beth glanced at Nick, and he nodded for her to go ahead and explain. "At weddings people tap their glasses so the bride and groom will kiss."

Corey made a face. "Why?"

Beth gestured that it was Nick's turn this time.

"I don't know, bud. Maybe because kissing is fun."

"Ewww."

They all laughed, but Beth caught Nick looking at her again.

"Trust me. You'll think so one day."

Corey stuck out his tongue and clutched at his throat, playing dead. "No way."

Relieved by the arrival of food, Beth heard her stomach growl. She was hungry, all right, having skipped lunch, but anticipation for the evening ahead gnawed at her. She almost couldn't eat. Almost.

Glancing sideways at Nick, so handsome in his navy suit, Beth could hardly wait to feel his arms around her. Not exactly smart thinking for a woman who didn't want to date a cop, but tonight she intended to put all that aside and enjoy the dance floor.

A Scripture from First Corinthians flashed through her mind, reminding her that all things were lawful but not all things were profitable. Or wise. Could she dance close to Nick and still stay friends? There was more to lose than friendship if she didn't keep her mind clear and heart safe tonight.

Glasses were again tapped and Corey made a face.

Beth felt her cheeks heat even though they laughed and cheered with the rest of the guests. She considered Nick's words to his son, admitting to the fun of kissing. Foolish girl, but Beth wanted to experience some of that fun with a certain redheaded man.

By the time dinner was over, Corey had slid down in his seat, looking bored and tired.

Beth's mom leaned toward Nick. "Would it be all right if Corey and I left? I can use Beth's car."

Nice, Mom. Real nice and obvious.

But part of her wanted to pat her mother on the back for a job well done. "Don't you want to stay for cake?"

"No." Her mom gripped her midsection. "I'm way too full. Well, Nick, what do you say?"

Nick cleared his throat. "Yeah, that's fine. Here, take my car. It has his booster seat. I'll bring Beth home and pick up Corey."

She laid her napkin on the table and stood. "No need. I put one in Beth's car, you know, just in case." Her mom gave them a wide smile.

Beth wanted to roll her eyes.

"Might be late. Would you like me to pick up the dog?"

Nick nodded and handed over his house key. "Thank you, Mary. That'd be great. Call me if needed. You have my cell."

"Will do." She smiled. "You two have fun. Come on, Corey, let's go and get Peanut."

"Can she come to your house?"

"Sure, she can." Her mom took Corey's hand and looked back. "You two stay as late as you like."

Beth watched them leave, acutely aware of Nick sitting next to her. In the midst of a tent full of people, she felt as if they were utterly alone. "So."

He didn't bother to move over to another seat. He gave her that lopsided grin instead. "So."

She rolled her eyes.

He leaned close. "Relax. I owe you, remember?"

She hadn't forgotten. Worse, how could she exact payment without landing herself in dangerous waters?

The band had set up during dinner and the lead member announced that the bride and groom would open the floor with a first dance. Beth smiled as she watched Adam and Eva swirl in each other's arms. She'd been there when the two met, and they'd overcome so much since then.

Namely Eva's trust issues and fear.

"You look happy." Nick's voice sounded soft.

"I am. For them. Eva's a good friend."

"As you are." Nick stood and offered her his arm. "Come on."

He led her to the parquet bit of wood that served as a dance floor. A dance floor that had filled up fast. Eva's brothers were out there with their ladies, as were Eva's parents and others. Rose Marsh gave her a wave and a curious look toward Nick.

Beth waved back.

She'd introduce Nick later. For now, she wanted to pretend they had no worries. No issues. She wanted to enjoy the night on the arm of one handsome man.

The song was slow and old, but Beth recognized the tune. The lead singer purred lyrics from a Frank Sinatra hit as Nick pulled her close.

Something about flying to the moon and dancing in the stars had Beth's head spinning. She slipped her hand into Nick's, but when he tightened his hold around her waist, her breath caught.

"Relax—you're stiff as a board."

"Sorry." She settled her other hand on his shoulder, felt the solid man beneath the suit coat and concentrated on moving with Nick. "I don't dance much. Only at weddings."

He winked. "Then we've got some ground to cover."

They were at eye level, and Beth wore heels. She smiled.

Suddenly, Nick spun and then twirled her away from him only to pull her back in.

She gripped his shoulder to keep from stumbling. "Warn me next time you do that."

"Follow my lead and you'll know."

Beth furrowed her brow as it dawned on her. "Hey, wait a minute, you're good at this."

He smiled and his gray eyes crinkled at the corners. Her stomach flipped. "Where'd you learn to dance?"

"Had to for my first undercover stint."

"Why? I don't get it."

Nick tipped his head. "Drug sales in the back of a ballroom-dancing studio."

"Oh."

A harmless answer said lightly, but it made her shiver all the same. He'd seen and done things she didn't ever want to know about. She was fooling herself if she thought they could escape what he did for a living. Not tonight. Not ever.

Nick kept Beth busy on the dance floor. The music was mixed between current and long-ago hits. They laughed with friends of hers during some of the hokier songs and finally took a break for the cutting of the cake and coffee.

Nick wolfed down his slice of marbled wedding confection in seconds flat while Beth picked at hers. Some of her hair had fallen out of its trap and hung down her soft neck past her bare shoulders. He wanted to release the rest of it.

"What?" she asked.

"Aren't you going to eat that?"

She pushed her plate toward him. "You can have it."

Nick loosened his tie. Beth fanned her face, so he pushed a glass of water toward her. "You can have my water."

"Thanks." She took a long drink. "Do you want to, um, get some fresh air?"

"Absolutely." He stood after she did, trying not to look eager to get her out of the vinyl walls of the tent.

Outside he breathed deep the chilly but sweet air from the trees in bloom surrounding them.

Beth wobbled and grabbed his arm. She slipped off her heels. "I won't get far with these things sinking in the grass."

How far did she plan on walking? "Where are we going?"

"There's a picnic table around here somewhere. I stayed with Eva for a while and I practically lived here during high school, I came over often enough. Follow me."

He did. Silently.

They reached a wooden picnic table and Beth sat on the top, her bare feet resting on the bench seat below. She rubbed her arms.

He slipped out of his jacket and handed it to her.

"Thanks." She shrugged into it.

The air was cold, but it felt good after the heated tent. Their breaths made little white puffs in front of them. He pointed to the table. "You're going to snag that dress."

"That's okay. I'll never wear it again."

"Too bad." Nick stepped closer. "You look amazing."

"Thanks." Beth snuggled deeper into his jacket, burying her hands in the pockets. "What's this?"

She'd found his string-tie restraints and pulled them out of the left side pocket.

He shrugged. "Easier to carry off duty than regular handcuffs."

"And you thought you'd apprehend someone here, at an outdoor wedding?"

He gave her a wicked grin. "Never know."

Beth's eyes widened, and then she gave him a thorough once-over. "You're carrying, aren't you?"

"I always do." Nick patted his lower back where he wore a pancake holder for his SIG Sauer. A smaller gun than his Glock, it fit well under the tuck of his shirt, where he could reach it quick, if needed.

Beth closed her eyes. "At a wedding."

"At night, in a remote place I'm not familiar with and with people I don't know. Yeah, Beth, at a wedding."

She pulled his jacket closer around her shoulders. "Did I ever tell you how my father died?"

"No." Nick looked up at the night sky filled with shimmering stars and a crescent moon.

Here it comes.

"You might have read the official report, but what really happened is that a guy he'd stopped for speeding was high on something. Instead of obeying my dad's request for his registration, the guy grabbed my father's gun and shot him." Beth talked in her usual calm teacher voice, but her eyes looked glassy.

Nick didn't know her father had been killed with his own firearm. There hadn't been a trial since the perp accepted a plea bargain and was sentenced clean as a whistle. The details of the weapon used to commit the crime had been left out. Maybe for the sake of the family or in honor of Ryken's sterling tenure, Nick didn't know.

So how did Beth know? "Who told you?"

"I overheard a couple of deputies talking at Dad's funeral. The ones who'd found him—" her voice broke "—on a dark stretch of road."

"I'm sorry, Beth." He took her cold hands in his own and chafed them softly. "Sorry for you and your dad."

"I never told my mom. She would have freaked. She'd been beside herself with worry that night when my dad didn't come home. He'd been late before, but for some reason my mom was frantic. She had called the station and

I remember her screaming over the phone asking when he'd last checked in, bawling that something wasn't right. It was late when the sheriff came to our house. My father had been found dead beside his cruiser. He died alone."

"Beth—"

She sniffed and pulled her hands from his. "Don't you see why I won't go through that again?"

He brushed away a single tear with his thumb. He couldn't make her any promises, and that was what made it so tough. "I'm not your dad."

She glared at him. "You could be."

"We have something here." He pulled his jacket closed in front of her and gently tugged on the lapels, drawing her against him. "I know you feel it, too."

She surprised him by giving him a wan smile. "Why do you think I'm telling you this?"

He caressed her face. "To scare me off."

She shook her head. "No. To scare me off. To remind me why…"

"You don't date cops," he finished for her.

"Right."

"So don't call it dating." Nick searched her pretty blue eyes rimmed with dark eye shadow.

"That's not going to work."

His lips were mere seconds from hers. "We can make it work."

"We can't." But Beth's eyes drifted closed.

He touched his lips to hers and wrapped his arms around Beth's waist. *Easy, take it easy.*

Nick didn't deepen the kiss. He heard the band leader announce the bouquet toss, and the guy expressly asked for the two bridesmaids. Beth and Anne.

He couldn't keep Beth out here. "We've got to go."

Beth's eyes flew open and in them Nick saw horrified

regret. Whether she regretted the interruption or kissing him, he didn't know. All he knew was that they had to get back inside that tent.

"Come on." He gave her his hand.

Beth didn't take it. She slipped on her high heels and made a sink-in-the-grass dash back where they'd come from. He followed close behind her and then took his jacket from her when they slipped through an opening in the tent.

Beth made her way onto the dance floor but hung back toward the side.

Nick noticed that Eva had been searching the group for her. The bride smiled when she spotted Beth amid the cluster of single ladies. Turning her back on them, Eva tossed the bridal bouquet behind her head. The thing had some height to it as it sailed past women literally throwing themselves forward to catch it.

But it landed.

Right in Beth's arms.

She bobbled it but managed to keep the bundle of flowers from hitting the ground. Beth looked surprised. She looked embarrassed. And then she looked at him.

Nick smiled at her. If ever he'd been given a sign about Beth being the one for him—and Corey—that was it.

Chapter Ten

"Go to dinner with me Friday night." Nick held open the passenger door for her.

"Thank you, but no." Beth plucked at a broken stem of a pink rosebud from the bridal bouquet and held it to her nose as she slid into the seat.

He started the engine and then looked at her. "Come on, Beth. Don't you think we're inevitable?"

She sighed. "Because I caught the bride's flowers and you caught the garter? Really, Nick, that's nothing but superstition."

"Maybe. Or maybe it confirms what we feel."

Beth didn't want to examine what she felt for Nick. "Look, I'm sorry if I led you on by inviting you to this wedding."

Nick smiled. "You didn't lead me on. We've been dancing around this attraction since the day we met."

He was right about that. "Doesn't mean we have to act on it."

"Too late. It's deeper now. I trust you. Especially with Corey."

Corey.... Beth closed her eyes. She'd fallen for the boy since his first day in her class.

"He needs you, Beth." Nick knew how to fight dirty without so much as raising his voice.

"That's not fair."

"Neither is your fear."

Maybe not, but it was real. The risks Nick took every day were real, too. "Have you ever considered leaving law enforcement?"

She glimpsed a flash of anger in his eyes.

"Would you leave teaching?" His voice was soft and dangerously low.

She understood where he came from. Nick's job was his calling, as teaching was hers. "No. I suppose not."

They were almost to her mom's house. The silence that settled between them in the car was louder than any radio cranked up on high volume. The space echoed with tension. And regret. At least on her part. She wanted to go out with him but knew better. What might have happened had they not been interrupted from that kiss?

Probably a good thing she didn't know.

Beth glanced at Nick driving. His lips were a grim line and his hands gripped the steering wheel. He'd rolled up his shirtsleeves and she marveled at the steel of those lean arms. Even the hairs on his forearms were reddish-gold. She closed her eyes, remembering the feel of them wrapped around her on the dance floor.

When he kissed her…

They pulled into her mother's driveway.

"I'm sorry," Beth muttered.

Nick slammed the car in Park and turned toward her. "Yeah, me, too."

"I'll get Corey so you don't have to come in." Beth opened the door, but Nick stalled her with the touch of his hand to her shoulder. Her shoulder was encased in his jacket again.

His touch was gentle. Coaxing. "I'm not giving up."

Beth's belly flipped.

And then he gave her that lopsided grin of his. "Just so you know."

"Thanks." At least they were still friends. "I'll get your son."

The porch light came on, and Beth's mom opened the door. A sleepy-looking Corey stumbled out onto the porch. Peanut flew past him toward the car, her tail wagging furiously, but she couldn't make the jump into the backseat.

Beth bent down and picked up the little dog. Peanut cuddled right into her neck. The dog couldn't weigh more than fifteen pounds, but her belly felt bigger and more hard. "She's got to be getting close."

"Yeah. I'm afraid so."

"Hopefully, Corey will get to see the puppies born." Beth knew what an educational experience that would prove to be. She'd watched their family Lab deliver pups long ago, and she hoped Peanut waited until the end of the school day. Summer break was only two weeks away, but she didn't think the dog had that long.

Corey climbed into his booster seat in the back, buckled in and then sprawled.

Beth settled the dog next to the drowsy boy. Her heart ached with the knowledge of what she gave up because she was too afraid to say yes to Nick.

"Good night, Beth."

"Your jacket."

"I'll get it later." He winked.

Beth shut the passenger door and watched as Nick backed out of her mother's driveway. Seconds turned into minutes, but she didn't move.

"Beth, honey. Are you coming in? It's cold out there."

It was. Beth pulled Nick's coat closer and inhaled his

clean-scented aftershave, but she was already too chilled to feel any warmth from it. "Yeah. I'm coming."

She walked into her mother's house and tossed Eva's bridal bouquet on the dining room table.

"Everything all right?" Her mom's eyes shone with concern.

"Yes." Things were as they should be.

So why did she feel so horrible?

"Good night, Mom, and thanks for watching Corey." Beth kissed her mother's forehead and made her way upstairs.

Slamming her hands in the coat pockets, she felt that string restraint and frowned. It was better to feel the hurt now rather than later, after she gave everything she had to Nick only to lose him.

Wednesday morning, Beth checked her watch. Today was Occupation Day, but her first of three speakers was late. She'd asked Julie's husband, Gerry, to talk about sailing since her class had been studying historic ships of the Great Lakes.

Not to mention the biggest third-grade field trip in the fall was sailing on a tall ship out of Traverse City. Gerry must have been held up at his firm. Hopefully, the other two speakers showed.

One of them was Nick.

A knock at the door brought Thomas's father, Todd Clark, a chef by trade, peeking in the door. "Am I too early?"

Beth smiled. "Not at all. Our first speaker didn't show. Come in."

Todd brought props: his chef's hat, an apron and what looked like the ingredients to make bread. "I'm going to need a table."

Beth stepped closer. "Can you make whatever it is you're making in twenty minutes? I have another speaker scheduled."

"It'll be tight, but yes. This is a hands-on chemistry lesson about how gluten is formed."

"Your hands on or theirs?" Beth giggled.

Todd donned his apron and hat with a smile. "Both. I brought everything I need with me, and I see you have a sink with hot and cold water. Perfect."

Beth nodded. The kids were going to love it, but not because of anything to do with chemistry. Her kids would simply want to stick their fingers in the dough.

She introduced Chef Todd and then stepped to the side to let him take over.

Leaning against the wall, she watched as Todd opened a sack of flour. He measured and then with a sinister face, Todd tossed the flour into a bowl, causing dust to fly.

Her students laughed.

Beth shook her head. Thomas's dad was quite the showman.

The kids laughed harder when Todd made more faces as he ran the water until it reached the right temperature. "Who'd like to touch this water and see how warm it feels?"

Kids swarmed.

Halfway through Chef Todd's mixing of the dough, she smelled the yeasty concoction clear across the room.

"Ewww, it smells." Gracie Cavanaugh plugged her nose.

Beth smiled. Her mom must not make homemade bread.

"That's the yeast doing its thing," Todd explained.

After some kneading, Todd separated out bits of sticky dough. "Feel it. Now add more flour—that's it. See? That's elasticity forming. The smelly yeast eating up the flour will make the dough rise."

"Ooooooooh."

Beth didn't hear the door open, but she felt Nick's presence as he quietly stepped into her classroom.

"Looks like I've got a tough act to follow," he whispered.

"You've got your work cut out." She glanced at him.

Nick stood next to her, looking rigid as a soldier in his brown sheriff's uniform complete with hat.

Formidable and distant.

For a man who'd said he wasn't giving up on her, he certainly hadn't tried very hard. After the wedding, she didn't see him or Corey at church the next morning, or the rest of the day. The past two nights when Nick picked up Corey and Peanut after his shift, he hadn't stayed long.

"That's an understatement, Miss Ryken." His eyes were full of mischief and he winked at her.

Was Nick lying low on purpose? Absence makes the heart grow fonder and all that sort of thing? Clenching her jaw, Beth had to admit it had worked. She'd missed him.

Her attention was snagged by her students' clapping.

Chef Todd's demonstration was over. "Thank you, kids. Drop your dough balls into this bag. Yup, that's it."

He cleaned up his props and threw away the dough in seconds. Only the flour-covered table remained. And the yeasty smell of dough and chalky flour.

"Thank you, Mr. Clark. Don't worry about the table. I'll take care of it." She shook the man's hand and then brushed away the dusty flour left behind.

"Okay, kids, everyone wash up and then take your seats. Our next speaker is Deputy Officer Grey."

Beth heard the oohs and aahs and spotted a couple of kids poking Corey in the side. They knew Nick was his dad, but that didn't diminish the awe shining on the boy's face. Corey was proud of his father.

And Nick looked equally proud of his son, if the softening of his features was any indication. Nick gave Corey a quick nod as he walked to the front of the room.

Once her students were seated, Beth pushed the table into the corner and then turned the time over to Nick. He started with the usual police officer speech encouraging kids to steer clear of strangers and never accept candy or a ride from anyone without their parents' approval.

He looked tall and fierce but friendly. How could he not when construction-paper sailboats hung from the ceiling over his head? His hat touched a couple as he slowly paced in front of the chalkboard, giving a brief description of his daily duties.

Looking around the room, he asked, "Any questions?"

Several hands flew in the air, so Beth picked one. "Grace."

"Do you pull over a lot of speeders?" the little girl asked.

Nick had pulled her over. She'd never forget that morning.

He glanced her way with a half smile. "Some days, yes."

The kids laughed.

Beth felt her cheeks heat. Obviously, Nick hadn't forgotten, either.

"What's the fastest speeder you ever caught?" another called out.

Nick rubbed his chin. "A man driving one hundred and twenty."

"Wow…" the students seemed to chant.

"Did he go to jail?" Grace asked.

Nick smiled. "Yes, he did."

"Did you ever shoot anyone?"

Beth cringed. A typical question, but she dreaded the answer. She glanced at Nick and waited.

Would he answer?

He looked stern. Nick's demeanor changed to very serious. "It's not like you see on TV. A police officer never brags about shooting, nor does he pull his firearm unless there's no other option. Unless he intends to use it."

The room fell silent and the kids stared at Nick with wide eyes.

"Did you ever get shot?"

"Ahh…" Nick hesitated.

Beth looked at Corey, whose face had gone pale. No way could she let Nick answer that here. Not with her heart pounding hard in her ears.

"Okay, Officer Grey, I believe our time is up. Thank you for coming." She rushed to the front of the room.

His eyes narrowed, but he nodded. "Thank you."

The kids clapped.

Beth took Nick's arm and ushered him toward the door.

"Are you trying to get rid of me?"

"For now, yes." Beth would explain later. Maybe.

Gerry stuck his head inside the room right when Beth opened the door for Nick. "Sorry I'm late."

"Oh, no, it's okay. This is Nick Grey. Nick, Gerry."

Gerry extended a hand. "You're the one sailing with us in a couple weeks. With your boy, right?"

"Yes." Nick ended the handshake.

Gerry glanced at Beth and then back at Nick with a curious smirk. "Excellent. Excellent. You'll love it. We're gone all day to the Manitou Islands. They're a beautiful place."

Nick gave her a questioning look. They hadn't gone over the details.

She'd tell him all that later, as well. She practically pushed Nick out the door. "Yeah, great. Come on, Gerry, the kids are waiting."

"Maybe Nick here wants to stay and see the slide show? See what he's in for."

Beth stopped pushing and heat flooded her face. What was wrong with her? "Do you want to stay?"

He stared at her a long time before he answered. "I'm on duty. Maybe another time."

Beth swallowed hard. "Another time."

He tipped his hat and left.

"You okay?" Gerry asked.

"Yeah. Why?"

Because she'd rudely shoved Nick out the door? Because she was afraid of his answers to the kids' questions? Because she was falling for the guy?

Gerry shrugged. "No reason. You seem…agitated."

Beth shook her head and tried to look innocent. "No."

"You've got yourself a tall one there." Gerry patted her shoulder before making his way to the front of the class to load his DVD into the TV's player.

Beth wanted to deny it, but Nick was hers for the asking.

She glanced at Corey. The boy's color had returned and he laughed at something Thomas said. No harm done. But her stomach still roiled. Had Nick answered yes to the last question, that he'd been shot, did he know what that knowledge would do to his boy? To her?

This weekend was Memorial Day weekend—a time when folks got rowdy with the unofficial start of summer. Parties and fireworks and calls made to 911. Nick was on duty this weekend. He'd be out there on patrol. Right in the thick of it.

Nick hesitated on the porch of Mary Ryken's house. The front door was open, but a screen door stood in his way. He could hear his son's voice as he read a story about himself. Corey still hesitated and stuttered, but he could read.

Nick's heart nearly burst when he overheard Corey read the last few lines.

"I want to be a cop when I grow up, just like my dad."

"That's good, Corey. Very good." Beth's voice sounded soft. "You've earned your sailing trip, that's for sure. But you'll have to keep at it over the summer. Promise?"

Corey nodded. "I promise."

Good thing he had the following weekend off. He'd never been much of a boater and wouldn't want his son sailing the big lake without him. He rapped his knuckles on the wood of the screen door before stepping inside the warm house. "Hello?"

"Dad!" Corey tore down the hall out of the kitchen toward him.

"Hey, bud."

"Wait till you see the sailboat we're going on. It's so big and really cool!"

Nick glanced at Beth. "You could have let me stay."

Beth's pretty mouth opened but nothing came out for a second or two. "I did, but you said you were on duty."

"After you shoved me out the door." Nick gave her a playful wink. He looked around for the dog. "Where's Peanut?"

"In here on the couch in the living room sleeping." Mary looked up from knitting or whatever it was she was doing with yarn. "I think she's close to puppy time, poor thing."

"I've got the next two days off, so hopefully, they'll come then." He looked at his son. "Ready, Corey?"

"Aren't you going to eat dinner?" Corey looked confused as he glanced back and forth between them.

Did his boy notice the awkwardness between them? Probably.

Since the wedding, Nick hadn't been around much. Sunday, Susan's parents had called. They'd driven up to visit

Corey and "inspect" their new house. They'd been pleased with what they'd seen, but Nick thought they might have been a little hurt from Corey's constant chatter about Miss Ryken.

Nick had explained only that she was Corey's teacher and tutor, but they saw through that. They knew Beth was someone special and not only to his boy.

The past couple of nights when he'd picked up Corey, Nick hadn't stayed. Mary had given him foil-covered plates as she used to. All because Nick could barely stand being in the same room with Beth and not pulling her close.

He was falling pretty hard.

"I don't know, bud." He looked at Beth. Did she want him to stay?

She'd been in a hurry for him to leave her class this morning. She'd been rattled pretty good by her students' questions, too. He could tell. What would she do if she saw the old bullet wound on his shoulder or the knife stab in his lower back?

"Mom made spaghetti," she said. "And it's best served straight from the pot."

He thought spaghetti tasted better reheated, but then, his had always come from a store-bought jar. "I'll stay."

"Corey, how about a game of Battleship?" Mary peered over her glasses at him. "You two go ahead. We've eaten."

His son jumped at the chance to play his favorite game, and Nick knew a setup when he saw it. He didn't mind. He gave Mary a grateful nod and followed Beth into the kitchen.

Silently, he washed his hands at the sink while Beth served up plates and set them on the table.

"What do you want to drink? Milk, water or pop?"

He sat down and sprinkled cheese atop his pasta and

sauce, which smelled better than anything he'd ever made. "Water's fine."

Beth brought two iced glasses of water and sat down.

He took her hand and bowed his head. "Thank You, Lord, for this food, and show us that there's nothing to fear in You. Amen."

Beth slipped her hand from his. "Nice."

He didn't miss her sarcasm. "You fear what I do, but I'm in God's hands every day. You are, too. And Corey. Your mom."

"What about my dad?"

"He was, too." Nick took a bite of spaghetti and closed his eyes. "This is good."

Beth nodded. "My mom's got skills."

He chuckled. Beth did, too. She'd taught his son to read, to laugh again and show his love. For that Nick would always be grateful.

He sighed. "I don't have the answer why your dad was killed. I don't know why Susan had the troubles she did or why it all ended wrapped around a tree one night. All I know is that we're not meant to live in fear."

Beth nodded and they ate in silence.

"You've been shot before, haven't you?" Beth whispered.

He nodded around another mouthful. "Yeah."

Beth closed her eyes tight.

He kept his voice low so Corey wouldn't hear. "It was a random bullet during a domestic dispute. I got in the way."

"And that's supposed to make it okay?" Beth's eyes went wide. "Does Corey know?"

Nick shook his head. "When he's older, I'll tell him like my dad told me."

Beth looked at him. "Is your dad alive?"

"No—"

She pushed her plate aside and gripped her forehead. "And now you've got another Grey who wants to join the force."

"My father died from cancer."

"Oh."

He reclaimed her hand. "Beth, life's fleeting. We're not supposed to get too comfy down here, right? We've got to make our days count for as many as God gives us. Count yours with me." He caressed the back of her hand with his thumb. "And Corey."

She didn't look convinced, but Nick had made a dent in her resolve. There was no need to rush things. He'd pleaded his case. He'd give Beth some space for it to sink in.

He wiped his mouth with a napkin. "Now, tell me about this sailing trip."

"Well, it's fun, and the boat is really nice with a cabin and galley. Gerry's a good sailor. He's been sailing all his life."

"We'll be gone all day?"

Beth nodded. "You'll need swimwear, sunscreen and something warm to slip on in case it gets cool."

Nick nodded. "Where are we going again?"

"South Manitou Island. You'll love it."

He'd love spending the day with Beth on a beach. But sailing? He'd never been a big fan. Seemed like too much work.

"After school's out?" He'd know by then if Corey legitimately passed second-grade reading. He didn't want to force advancement to the third, but he would if he had to. Corey needed to move forward, not step back.

"The weekend right before."

"Something to look forward to, then."

Chapter Eleven

Beth couldn't sit still while Corey read. She paced her classroom, listening and not listening. Her mind wandered to thoughts of Nick.

They were all in God's hands.

She knew that on an intellectual level, but deep down did she really? Did she trust God with what she couldn't control—her future? She sighed.

"Something wrong, Miss Ryken? Did I miss a word?" the boy asked.

She looked into gray eyes that were so like his father's. "Oh, no. You're doing very well. I think we can call it a day."

Her cell phone rang and she grabbed it on the third ring. It was Nick. "Hello?"

"Hey, can you bring Corey home? Peanut's water broke, so I don't want to leave her alone." Nick sounded nervous.

Beth smiled. "We're on our way. Need anything?"

"Just you, here. I don't know what I'm doing."

Beth let loose a soft laugh even as his words gave her butterflies. "Don't worry, Peanut knows what to do. See you in a few."

At the mention of the dog's name, Corey stopped shoving books into his backpack. "What's wrong with Peanut?"

"It's puppy time. Let's go."

Corey grinned and scrambled for the door.

Beth hurried right behind him.

She tapped her mom's name in her phone and then cradled it against her ear. "Hey. Peanut's water broke, so I'm taking Corey home. I don't know how long I'll be."

Her mom laughed. "Take your time, honey. This is so exciting. Let me know what she has, okay?"

"Will do." Beth disconnected. Stuffing the phone back in her purse, she opened the car door for Corey.

He threw his backpack inside before climbing into his backseat booster chair.

"Buckled?" Beth checked before slipping in behind the wheel.

"Yup."

She pulled out of the parking lot and headed for Nick's. It didn't take long. Once there, Beth and Corey raced through the side door that led from the laundry room to the kitchen.

"Nick?" Beth called out to let him know they were there.

He sat at the kitchen table with messy hair. His feet were bare beneath loose cotton pants and a T-shirt. He looked up, relieved. "She keeps pacing."

Beth watched Peanut. Sure enough, the little dog panted and paced. She scratched at the bedding on the floor in the kitchen and lay down only to get back up again.

Corey sat on the linoleum floor and the dog crawled into his lap and settled down. But only for a few moments. She got back up and paced some more.

Beth looked at the huge pile of bedding. Afternoon sunshine streamed in through the sliding glass door onto the blankets. Peanut loved to lie in the sun, but maybe not today. Not now. "We should set her bed in a quieter place. What about your room?"

Nick scrunched his face. "I've got carpet."

"Do you have a kiddie pool?"

Corey bounced up. "It's in the garage."

"We'll make up a bed for her in the pool in your room and close the blinds. I think she needs quiet."

They got busy getting the pool down from the garage rafters, cleaned it thoroughly and then set everything up in Nick's room.

Beth drew the blinds while Nick carried Peanut in followed by Corey.

Beth checked her watch. It was getting close to dinnertime. "Maybe if we leave her alone for a bit, things will start moving."

"And we'll have puppies?" Corey asked.

Nick tousled his boy's hair. "That's the plan."

"Got plans for dinner? I can make something quick," Beth offered. Corey had to be hungry.

"How's frozen pizza sound?"

Beth glanced at Corey, who was inching down the hallway to peek into Nick's room. "Sounds perfect. I'll make a salad, too, if you have the stuff."

"I do." Nick spotted Corey, too. "Come on, bud. Give Peanut some space."

Half an hour later, Beth finished slicing veggies for a salad while the pizza baked in the oven. Corey was in Nick's room checking on Peanut, but there was still no hint of puppies. Nick was scanning the internet for information on dog deliveries when the oven timer sounded.

Beth turned off the oven and set the bowl of salad on the table. "Find anything?"

Nick's face looked grim. "Lots of stuff."

Beth walked over to stand behind him. "Like what?"

"Puppies are supposed to be born within minutes of a dog's water breaking."

Beth leaned over Nick's shoulder to read the website page, and dread filled her. "How long has it been?"

"Too long." Nick pointed to the screen. "Says here that after two hours call the vet."

Beth chewed her bottom lip. It had been at least that long since Nick had called her at school. "Corey should eat something. I'll have him wash up while you call your vet."

Nick nodded.

Beth headed down the hall and peered through the door to Nick's room. Corey lay on the floor and stroked the little dog's head. Peanut appeared calm. No more panting or pacing. No sign of puppies coming, either.

She could hear Nick's muffled voice as he talked on the phone. "Corey, it's time for dinner. You need to wash up."

"Okay." The boy dashed for the bathroom.

Beth knelt beside the kiddie pool in the corner of Nick's darkened room. A heavy-laden Peanut looked so small amid a swirl of blankets in that big blue plastic circle.

"How is she?" Nick knelt next to her and scratched beneath the dog's chin.

"Calm as can be. What did the vet say?"

Nick's eyes looked worried. "He'll meet us at his office in half an hour."

"Did he say anything else?"

"Only that time's not on our side."

Beth closed her eyes. That didn't sound good. Not good at all.

Nick glanced at Corey through the rearview mirror. His boy sat in the backseat with Beth. Peanut lay on a couple towels in Beth's lap and nudged under her hand for more pats. The dog acted as if nothing was wrong. He knew better. He'd read the online articles.

"Is Peanut going to die?" Corey's eyes were grave.

Nick wanted to lie, say everything would be fine and erase that crease of worry in his son's forehead. "I don't know, son. Let's pray that she doesn't."

Corey nodded. "We prayed for Mom."

"I know." Nick's stomach turned.

He glanced at Beth through the mirror. Her eyes watered as she looked back.

Nick and his son had prayed in the emergency waiting room the day of Susan's accident. Along with her parents, they'd all prayed. Susan had still died. How did he explain why to a seven-year-old?

"Take my hand, Corey." Beth's voice sounded thin. "Dear Lord, please touch our little Peanut and her pups. Bring her through this. Amen."

"Amen," Corey echoed.

Nick kept praying, though, begging God not to take his boy's dog. Wasn't losing his mother enough?

He glanced again at Beth. She felt like an anchor here. Calm in the face of the storm ahead. Her eyes were closed and she held Corey's hand. Both petted the dog, but Beth continued to pray. Silently. He could see her lips move.

They pulled into the veterinarian's office and Nick shut off the engine. Corey was already out of his booster chair and tearing around the other side of the car reaching for Peanut.

"I've got her, bud." Nick lifted the little dog from Beth and held her close. Peanut nuzzled under his chin and Nick patted the dog's back.

His eyes burned. It had to be okay.

Beth got out and Corey reached for her hand. She took it and the two walked into the vet's ahead of him.

Please, God. Let Peanut live.

"It's going to be okay, Corey." Beth wrapped her arms around a very worried little boy.

He melted into her embrace.

They sat on the same vinyl-covered bench in the lobby where they'd been given the bad news. Corey had heard it right along with her and Nick, and the boy's eyes had gone wide as marbles. A no-nonsense kind of man in his sixties, the country vet didn't mince words. Peanut's contractions had stopped, and while she was not distressed, her puppies' heartbeats were tragically low. Much lower than what he liked for a C-section. Lower than those of puppies expected to live.

After hearing their options, Nick wanted to try the shots that should induce labor. So they waited. And waited.

The office loomed silent. Even the dogs in the back that had been barking quieted down. An exotic bird in a cage behind the desk nodded off, too. No more swaying from foot to foot. Could animals tell when one of their own was in trouble? The silence lingered, interrupted only by the tick-tick of the giant clock over the doorway.

Beth let her head fall back against the wall. Corey had curled up on the bench and his head rested in her lap. She ran her fingers through the kid's hair. So much for staying in teacher mode. Beth had moved right into comforter.

Like a mom.

"I'll be right back." Nick stood and exited the office.

"Where's he going?" Corey asked.

"I don't know." Beth watched Nick on his phone as he paced outside in front of the plate-glass window. Who was he calling?

After a few minutes, Nick stepped back inside. He crouched down in front of Corey. "I called the pastor, bud. We've got the church praying for Peanut."

Corey lifted his head and gave his dad a brave smile.

And Beth's heart broke.

A gut-wrenching sound suddenly came from the back, making the hairs on her arms rise.

The dogs started barking again and the bird fluttered against its cage and squawked.

Beth looked at Nick. "Was that Peanut?"

"It must be."

Corey sat up with wide eyes and a white face.

She didn't remember her Lab screaming when she delivered her puppies. What if these puppies were too big to come out?

Beth pulled Corey close. Whether to soothe the boy's fear or her own, she wasn't sure. "It's okay, Corey. Keep praying. God's with us. He's always with us."

"How do you know?" His seven-year-old voice was raw.

She brushed back his bangs. "Because the Bible tells us so. And so does your dad."

"She's right, bud." Nick wrapped his arms around them both and hung on.

This was what families did. They clung to each other in times of trouble. Beth closed her eyes and kept praying.

Fifteen minutes later, the vet came out with a big smile on his face. "Mr. Grey, we've got our first puppy and it's alive. Shocked my socks off. Born back feet first. I had to help pull the pup out. Little thing was clogging up the whole process. Come on back. I think you're in for a treat."

Corey jumped up.

He and Nick followed the vet. But then Nick turned. "Are you coming?"

Beth shook her head. Peanut was their dog. This was

a moment Nick should have with his son. She needed the distance. "You two go ahead."

Nick stared a moment longer.

Corey peeked around the corner and pulled on Nick's hand. "Come on, Dad."

Beth smiled. "Go ahead. I have an e-reader in my purse and I need to call my mom. I'll be fine."

Nick disappeared with his boy and all was quiet again, save for the murmurs of him and Corey and the vet in the next room and the occasional yip from the dogs boarded in back. No more screaming from Peanut.

Beth slumped in her seat, her stomach a mess of knots that wouldn't loosen. "Thank You, Lord."

Another half hour passed and the vet came out to get her. "They'd like you to come back. Peanut's doing great."

Beth took a deep breath and let it out with a whoosh. Grabbing her purse, she followed the vet into the dimly lit examining room. Peanut lay on several towels on the floor with three squirming little puppies around her. A heat lamp had been turned on overhead, warming the entire area.

Nick sat on the floor a short distance away and Corey lay on his belly next to him.

When she entered, Nick looked up at her with shining eyes. "We're waiting for one more."

Beth glanced at the vet, feeling sorry for pulling the old man away from his evening. The animal doctor didn't seem to mind. He gave her a cheerful nod and left the room whistling. No doubt to attend to his office business or the dogs in back while they watched the wonder of puppy birth.

Nick held out his hand. "Come here."

She set her purse on the floor. Without taking his hand, Beth sat on the floor beside Corey.

Corey sat up. "Isn't this cool? Four puppies."

Where had that little dog stowed four pups all these weeks? "Wow."

Nick grinned. "Yeah, right. Wow."

Beth smiled.

Peanut didn't notice them much. She was busy sniffing and licking her three puppies, nuzzling them as they wiggled and latched on to nurse.

Beth glanced at Nick over Corey's head. God had given them a huge blessing. No, five blessings if they included the arrival of Peanut. That little dog had helped bond father and son. Watching Corey lean against his father's arm, Beth's eyes stung. They'd healed. They were going to be okay.

Peanut got up, turned a couple of times and then moved away from her pups. The puppies wobbled and rolled around and the last little blessing made its appearance. Another puppy slipped out in a matter of seconds, black-and-white nose first. And Peanut got to work cleaning up the last baby.

Nick chuckled. "That's it, then. They're all accounted for."

"Amen." It was all Beth could manage around the lump of emotion in her throat. God had saved Corey's dog and she was grateful.

He hadn't saved Nick's wife, though. What had Nick gone through with his son as they'd waited in a different kind of hospital not so long ago? They'd made it through. Battle scarred for sure, but they'd made it.

Could she?

By the time they pulled out of the vet's and headed for home, Peanut had been x-rayed to make sure nothing had been left behind. The puppies were checked over and sexed. Peanut had three girls and one boy—all were given a clean bill of health.

Nick would receive his bill in the mail, but the guy

didn't even blink at the cost. It was much less than it could have been. Much better outcome, too.

Corey sat in the back with a box holding Peanut and her puppies next to him. "What are we going to name them?"

"Whatever you want." Nick smiled at his son through the rearview mirror.

"I don't know any girl names."

"We could name them different kinds of nuts like their mom."

Corey laughed. "What other kinds of nuts?"

"Almond or Hazelnut or Cashew or even Filbert."

Corey laughed harder. "Or Walnut."

Nick laughed. "Sure, why not?"

Beth stared out the window into the darkness that settled over cherry orchards that had lost their white blooms. Nick grabbed her hand with a squeeze. She looked at him.

"What do you think?"

Beth tried to sound cheerful. "What about Brittle, Butter, Cookie and Cake?"

Nick gave her an odd look. "I think we'll come up with something." He threaded his fingers through hers. "Thank you."

She squeezed back before pulling away. He needed both hands on the wheel for the upcoming curve in the road. "You're welcome."

"I mean it, Beth. You've done a lot for us. This weekend I'm taking Corey to stay with his grandparents while I'm on duty. Would you go with me? You know, so you can meet them."

"Let me think about it." Beth had to admit she was curious about them, but meeting them was a big step. Maybe in the wrong direction.

She peeked in the backseat. Corey's head bobbed against his chest as sleep took him. "He's done in."

"Corey was a trouper through all this because you were his anchor tonight. He needed you. I needed you, too."

"Thanks." What else could she say? The whole way home, Beth couldn't stop envisioning a different kind of scene—one with Nick in the hospital instead. How would Corey deal with that after losing his mom?

They pulled into Nick's garage. Beth sat in her seat a moment while Nick unbuckled and then lifted Corey out of his seat. She got out and grabbed the box of dog and puppies while Nick carried his son.

They entered through the laundry room without a word. He walked down the hall to settle Corey into bed, and Beth transferred Peanut and her pups into the blanketed kiddie pool.

The dog licked her hand and then turned her back, shielding her puppies from view.

"Okay, Mama, I'll give you some space." Beth understood those feelings. "You're a good girl, Peanut. A good mama, too."

Beth left the door open and headed for the kitchen. She'd managed to put the salad and pizza in the fridge before they'd left, but the sink was a mess with all her veggie clippings. She scooped up the waste into a plastic grocery bag and threw it in the garbage.

She washed her hands and then rinsed a clean cloth to wipe down the counter. Corey's face kept coming back to her. A scared, wide-eyed little boy who'd waited so bravely for news of his dog. Was he brave because he'd been through this before with his mom?

Why did some live and others die?

Beth's vision blurred. She leaned against the counter and closed her eyes against the burning tears, but they leaked out anyway.

"Hey, hey…." Nick was behind her.

She hadn't heard him come into the kitchen.

He rubbed her shoulders with strong hands that moved softly. "Beth, honey, what's going on?"

Beth shook her head, her throat so tight she coughed.

He turned her around and pulled her into his arms.

She welcomed his embrace. Took the warmth he gave, but that was all she'd take. Who was she trying to fool? She fought a losing battle if she thought she could keep herself from falling for him.

"It's okay. Everything's okay now."

But it wasn't.

He pulled back and looked into her face and rubbed away tears on her cheeks with his thumbs. "Why are you crying?"

She shook her head and sniffed.

Would he be angry if she told him? He'd made it clear he wouldn't leave law enforcement. Whining about it now was no better than nagging. Beth didn't want to do either.

She hunted behind her for the roll of paper towels they'd used for napkins at dinner. She grabbed one and wiped her face, blew her nose.

Nick chuckled, but he hadn't let go of her. His arms hung loosely around her waist. He gave her a gentle shake. "Tell me."

"I, ah, I don't know what I would have done if we'd lost Peanut." Beth couldn't come clean.

She couldn't share the visions she'd had of a worried Corey in a hospital waiting room. Didn't Nick realize the impact on his son if he were injured—or worse—from his job? Sure, he'd moved to where he thought it was safe, but Beth's father had thought the same thing. She and her mom had, too.

He narrowed his gaze. "We didn't."

She looked away.

Nick cupped her cheeks and searched her eyes. "What's going on in that beautiful head of yours?"

"I don't deal with loss very well," she managed.

"We didn't lose the dog, or her pups."

"But we could have." Her voice broke.

He ran a hand through her hair. "You're stronger than you realize, Beth."

She felt ready to crack into pieces. "I don't know about that...."

"I do."

"What if—"

He traced her bottom lip with his fingertip. "Stop thinking about all the what-ifs. You won't lose me."

She clung to that promise.

Nick tipped up her chin and kissed her. Really kissed her.

And she kissed him back.

The tidal wave of feelings hit hard, weakening her resolve to pull back when he deepened their kiss.

She loved Nick.

She loved Corey, too, and more than anything she wanted to protect that boy from any more losses. But how, when she couldn't even protect herself?

Chapter Twelve

"You got home late last night." Beth's mom scrambled eggs with a whisk and then poured the mixture into a hot skillet. "Want some breakfast?"

"Sure." Beth sat down, rubbing her eyes.

"Everything okay?"

Beth nodded a little too quickly.

Her mom turned off the burner, brought two cups of coffee to the table and sat down across from her. She couldn't fool her mom, who narrowed her gaze with concern. "Tell me, honey. What's wrong?"

Nick had called her honey. And later, when she'd left his house, he'd told her that she'd brought sweetness to his and his son's life.

Beth closed her eyes a couple of seconds before zeroing in on her mother. "If you had the chance to go back, knowing what would happen to Dad, would you have married him anyway?"

Her mother smiled. "You're in love with Nick."

Beth took a sip from her steaming mug. "It takes more than love to make it work. You've said so yourself."

"True." She patted her hand. "Hmm, what's this all about, Beth?"

Beth continued to sip the gourmet coffee from the coffee club her mother had signed up for. She received regular shipments every month. Too expensive by far, but Beth had to admit it sure tasted good.

They'd never talked about how her father's death had impacted her mom. It had always been the elephant in the room. Sure, Beth got on her mom about her spending habits and frivolous purchases, but she'd never examined too closely the core reason for them. Beth had been afraid to ask her mom to seek help. She'd been afraid to point out the obvious, as well. Her mom used shopping to fill the void left in the wake of her husband's death.

Her mother's eyes filled with tears. "The pain of losing a spouse well before their time is something I wouldn't wish on anyone."

It hurt to hear her mother's voice so thick with emotion. "It's okay, Mom. You don't have to talk about it."

Her mother grabbed her hand and gently squeezed. "You need to hear it, Beth. I know you miss your dad. I do, too. And it still stings, even after all this time. I think about him every day."

Her mom took a sip of her own coffee. "Sometimes I find myself looking forward to telling your father something when he gets home. Like when Peanut followed Corey. Your father would have loved that little dog."

Beth's eyes blurred.

"But I'll see him again. You will, too, Beth. Death is never final."

She nodded and a tear leaked out.

Her mom patted her hand. "To answer your question, yes, I would gladly marry your father a hundred times over, even though I've never felt equipped to handle his death. I'd do it all over again."

Beth wondered if maybe her mother was far better

equipped than she'd ever thought. It was Beth who was the coward here.

"If you want to build a future with Nick and Corey, you need to prepare for the worst but hope for the best. And God is our hope."

Her mom's words echoed something Nick had said before. That was the way he prepared for his workday. He prepared for the worst. He truly believed he was in God's hands.

We're all in God's hands.

Even so, Nick carried a gun off duty. Proof of his readiness to act in any given situation. Being a cop was part of who he was, not simply what he did for a living. She'd have to accept that. Embrace it, even.

"Has Nick told you how he feels?"

Beth shrugged. Her heart whirled at the memory of his kisses and the way he'd made her feel. Protected and cherished.

Loved.

Her mom chuckled softly. "Well, it's obvious he's crazy about you. Corey is, too."

Beth ran her fingertip around the rim of her mug. "Tonight Nick's taking Corey to his grandparents' for the long weekend since he'll be working extended shifts. He wants me to go with him."

"Will you?"

"I would like to meet them." Beth didn't add that she wanted to see for herself if they were worthy of caring for Corey in case something happened to Nick.

In case Beth couldn't follow through on her feelings.

Her mother looked at her long and hard. "Beth, this isn't something you can figure out with your head. You have to pray for God's leading and then follow your heart. That's where He'll speak to you. Inside your heart, you'll know, but you have to trust that small voice. Listen for it and you'll hear."

"I'll try." That was all she could commit to.

For now.

That afternoon, Nick stepped into Mary Ryken's dining room. The familiar scent of cinnamon and melted butter hung in the air as always. "Ready, bud?"

His son shifted his backpack on his narrow shoulders. "What about Peanut and the puppies?"

"They'll be fine at home. I'll check on them during my rounds." He glanced at Mary, who held a plastic container of cookies to take with them on the two-hour trip south to Susan's parents'.

"Beth will be right down," Mary said. "And Corey had a PB&J and milk and cookies after school."

"Thanks."

His son ate better afternoon snacks than Nick typically ingested for lunch. Today was no exception. The hot dog he'd wolfed down lay like a lead pipe in his gut.

He waited for Beth. Was she going with them? She'd never said for sure the night before. But then, he'd never given her the chance to answer before kissing her good-night.

Nick rubbed the back of his neck.

He wanted Susan's parents to know that he'd not only moved on, but he was settling down for real. They'd seen his house, and he wanted them to meet the woman who would be a good mom to his boy, their grandson.

If Beth agreed to take up the role.

As usual, Nick put the cart before the horse, thinking about a lifetime ahead when they hadn't gone out yet. He may have kissed Beth only last night, but he already had them married. Would she have him?

"Hi."

He looked up to see her coming down the stairs dressed in long denim shorts and a pretty yellow top. A light blue sweater hung over her arm. Her purse dangled from the other.

And his heart took a nosedive.

Beth had better have him, because he wanted her. No matter how long it took, Nick made a silent vow he'd convince her to give them a chance. Somehow.

"Hi." His fingers itched to touch her.

"Thanks for inviting me along." Beth was at the bottom step.

"Thanks for going." Nick couldn't help it. He tucked a strand of her blond hair behind her ear and let his fingers swipe her jaw.

Beth's cheeks went pink and she looked away. And turned toward Corey. "Are you looking forward to visiting your grandparents?"

"I guess." His boy shrugged.

Nick tried to shake off the awkwardness that had bloomed overnight between them. "Well, let's go, then."

Mary gave him a knowing smile and that gave him hope. As the wife of a cop killed on duty, Mary must have good advice for her daughter. The right advice. But then, Mary hadn't been excited about him being a deputy, either. He didn't need any more strikes against him.

"Not sure when I'll have her back." Nick made it sound like a date. Maybe it would be. If they stopped somewhere for dinner on the way home.

"No worries." Mary's smile was broader yet.

He hoped so.

Beth gave her mom a sharp look.

Mary trusted him, but he wasn't sure about Beth. Her fear kept her rolled up tight as a ball of string, and Nick couldn't find the end in order to unravel it. Beth needed a little unraveling.

By the time they made it to his former in-laws' house, they'd discussed at length possible names for the puppies. Corey wanted to name them after colors—Blue, Pink, Periwinkle and Red. Nick still pulled for nut names, and Beth thought the puppies should be called Disney character names. Having nothing agreed, they played a rousing game of word rhymes that had eaten up the travel time.

Beth never stopped being a teacher. But then, he never stopped being a cop.

"This is lovely," Beth whispered as they pulled into the driveway.

"Yeah." Nick stared at the small farmhouse situated on a large lot in a small village north of Grand Rapids. He'd never given it much notice before. Every other time he'd come here, he'd been in some sort of turmoil—job or Susan related. Now he noticed the flowers that grew in clumps along the walkway. Mary would like them.

"There's a bunch of cider mills and apple orchards around here." He and Susan had gotten in an argument at one. Ruined the day, too.

"Similar to home." Beth smiled, but she looked tense.

"Yeah, sort of." Nick stalled her with a touch of his hand to her elbow. "Relax—they won't bite."

Susan's parents were standing at the front door. "Corey!"

"Hi, Grandma." His boy ran into his grandmother's arms.

"You sure about that?" Beth whispered.

"I got your back." Nick walked forward and extended his hand to his former father-in-law. "Greg, this is Beth Ryken. Corey's teacher and tutor."

"Nice to meet you." His father-in-law shook Beth's hand and shared a look with his wife. "Ellen, this is Beth."

"Hello."

Beth offered her hand to Ellen, who accepted it politely, but the two women sized each other up. Beth towered over his short and stout mother-in-law, but the women didn't seem to notice differences in stature. Like a couple of cats squaring off, the two stared hard at each other.

Ellen broke eye contact first. "Come in, please."

Corey had already raced into the house straight for the exotic saltwater aquarium.

As they followed his former in-laws inside, Nick hoped this didn't turn out to be a bad idea, forcing Susan's parents to meet the new woman in his life. Forcing anything never worked. He should know that by now.

Once inside, Ellen turned to Beth. "Would you like the tour? Corey's got his own room here—for when he visits."

"I'd like that." Beth followed his mother-in-law up the stairs, but she glanced at him.

Nick gave her a nod of encouragement as he watched them go up the rest of the way. Following Greg into the kitchen, he asked, "Are they going to be okay up there?"

Greg chuckled. "Ellen looked forward to meeting Corey's tutor. She won't knock her out. Yet. Are you serious about this woman?"

His father-in-law didn't mince words. Neither did Nick. "I am."

"Hmm. And Corey likes her?"

Nick narrowed his gaze. "He does."

"Kind of soon, don't you think?"

"It's been over a year now." Nick had mourned enough.

Greg shook his head. "Not what I meant. You've known this woman how long?"

"Two months."

Greg nodded but kept quiet.

Twice as long as he'd known Susan before they ran off and eloped. But he got the point. Loud and clear.

Corey joined them in the kitchen. "Hey, Dad, can I watch TV?"

Nick looked at his son. "Ask your grandfather."

"For a few minutes. I need your help in the garden before dinner." Greg looked at Nick. "Are you staying?"

Nick shook his head. "I was hoping to take Beth to dinner on our way back."

He looked forward to alone time with her. Find out where he stood, where they were headed.

Susan's parents were by no means old, only in their early sixties, but they were wise. Maybe Greg was right and it was too soon. Maybe Nick needed to relax and let the relationship develop on its own.

His former in-laws had Susan and then her brother later in life. Ellen had retired early in order to care for Corey after Susan's death. She was a finicky woman, and that intrusion into their ordered and unhurried life had no doubt taken some getting used to. But Nick never doubted how much Susan's parents loved Corey.

Greg opened the fridge. "How 'bout some iced tea while we wait for the women?"

"Sure." Nick scratched his temple and looked up at the ceiling, hearing the creaks in the floor of the women walking around up there. How long was this tour going to take?

Beth followed Ellen into each room while she explained that they'd moved here after Susan married Nick and their son had joined the military. A quiet place to retire, Ellen had said. Beth was glad that Nick's late wife hadn't grown up here. Fewer painful memories for everyone. But Susan's memory lingered like cloying perfume. Pictures were everywhere.

"This is Corey's room."

Beth stepped into the boyishly decorated bedroom with its race-car bed and NASCAR curtains. Corey wasn't into NASCAR. He liked baseball and sailboats and puppies. "Did Nick tell you their dog had puppies?"

Ellen smiled with surprise. "He didn't. How many?"

"Three girls and one boy. They haven't named them yet. Can't agree on what to call them."

Ellen chuckled. "Corey loves animals, but I won't deal with the mess. That's why we have fish. They're Greg's hobby."

Expensive hobby. Ellen's home might be spotless, but Beth would rather have dog hair and PB&J fingerprints on the fridge. As an elementary teacher, Beth was used to her noisy, messy world. Bright and vibrant.

Her gaze caught on a picture resting atop a dresser. Like a marionette on a string, Beth stepped closer as if pulled. The family portrait was recent. Corey looked only a little younger, but Nick's hair was long and wavy.

He'd worked undercover then and he looked like a dude with a 'tude in that picture. Nick's arm was draped around a very thin blonde wearing a lot of makeup and poufed-up hair. Fussy. Susan looked high maintenance.

"That's my daughter, Susan. You sort of resemble her."

Beth backed up. That was a weird thing to say. She glanced at Ellen, looking for clues that weren't there. "You think so?"

Ellen cocked her head. "No, maybe not."

Beth studied the portrait harder, but only for seconds. They had the same coloring perhaps, but Beth wasn't anywhere near as coiffed. Her features were not as perfectly chiseled, either.

She glanced at Ellen. "I'm sorry for your loss."

"Thank you. It hasn't been easy. Especially letting Corey go."

Beth swallowed hard. What did she mean? "I'm sure. He's a wonderful boy."

"Nick told us how well you've tutored him. Greg and I appreciate all that you've done. Corey showed us his storybooks when we visited and mentioned a sailing trip?"

Beth nodded. "Friends of mine sail, and Corey earned the chance to go. Nick agreed that it'd be good for him to work toward a reward instead of against the threat of repeating second grade."

"Will he?"

Beth cocked her head. "What?"

"Pass second grade."

Beth had to remember to stay in teacher mode, but it was tough. She was the grandmother, and Beth wasn't sure how much Nick had shared with the woman.

But under this grandmother's scrutiny, Beth believed blunt honesty was best. "He's borderline considering his reading level. Nick wouldn't agree to hold him back."

Ellen's direct gaze pierced her. "What do you think?"

"I think Corey's not done. He needs to work hard this summer to prepare for third grade and the testing he'll face. What made you pull him out of school?"

Ellen's expression clouded over. "I wasn't very good at homeschooling, but I couldn't leave him in that school where he'd been so lost and alone. He cried every day."

Beth's heart twisted, remembering what Diane had said. Poor kid. He missed his mother and wanted a new one. He wanted a whole family. He'd been so withdrawn when he first came, but with Thomas and Gracie and her mother he'd blossomed. Why hadn't they looked for a different school? One that could better meet Corey's needs? But then, they were grieving, too. Maybe having Corey home was a way to hold on to their daughter's memory a little longer.

"He needed us," Ellen added. "He still needs us."

Beth nodded, feeling a little lost herself. "Of course. You were there for him when he needed you most."

Ellen gave her a curt nod.

Stupid thing to say to a grandparent. Of course they'd been there. They'd always be there, too. Especially if Nick wasn't. Ellen made that perfectly clear.

Beth glanced back at the picture. She thought about Susan breaking those plates and Corey's reaction when Beth had roughly set her mom's table. They did look a little bit alike in a relative sort of way. Weird. Was that why Corey had been at ease with her that first day in school?

Ellen's smile was tight. "I loved my daughter, but I'd be lying if I didn't admit that she put Nick through a lot. Put us all through a lot."

"I'm so sorry."

"I wouldn't have blamed Nick had he left Susan, but he didn't. Not with Corey so young." Ellen gave her a pointed look. "Nick came from a broken home."

Beth hadn't known that. There was a lot about Nick she didn't know, but she knew what kind of man he was. A man with a mother-in-law who defended him. "He's a good father."

Ellen nodded. "Corey needs him now more than ever. My grandson needs stability in his life."

Beth agreed.

Ellen wasn't only stating the obvious here. She sent a message. One Beth didn't have much trouble deciphering. Ellen might not welcome another woman stepping in to raise her grandson, but she wouldn't stand for her grandson or Nick being jerked around. Or hurt.

"We're here if anything happens to threaten that stability."

"Of course." Beth swallowed.

Would Susan's parents fight for Corey if something ever happened to Nick? They were the boy's flesh and blood. They seemed like good people, solid and respectable. But anything was possible when it came to a question of custody.

Beth followed Ellen back downstairs, where Nick waited for her on the deck with an empty glass in his hand. Exiting through the sliding glass door, she spotted Corey helping his grandfather in the garden. They stuck fat wooden markers into the soil, labeling the seeds and seedlings planted in neat rows.

Would Corey be lonely growing up here? He'd made friends at school and had a dog with puppies. Would Ellen take Peanut along with the boy?

The knot in Beth's stomach pulled tighter.

"We better get going." Nick called out to Corey. "We're leaving, bud."

The boy waved, unfazed. "See you later."

Nick smiled.

"Corey, you should give your father a hug." Ellen stood next to Nick.

"It's okay."

Beth bit her lip. She agreed with Ellen but didn't say a word. It wasn't her place.

Corey trotted up onto the deck and Nick gave his son a bear hug, squeezing tight until Corey squirmed and squealed with laughter. "Bye, Dad."

"See you in a couple days."

Corey nodded and then launched himself at her. "Bye, Miss Ryken."

Beth hesitated before returning the little boy's embrace.

She hugged him tight and fought the urge to kiss his forehead. "Bye, Corey. Have fun, okay?"

"Yup." He broke away and ran to join his grandfather back in the garden.

She glanced at Ellen. The woman's gaze was cool, but Beth reached out her hand. "Nice to meet you."

Ellen took it for a brief shake, her smile polite. "You, too."

She felt Nick's hand at the small of her back.

"Let's go. Thanks, Ellen. I'll call you when I leave to pick up Corey."

"Perfect, we'll meet you halfway."

"Sounds good."

Beth didn't think Ellen was a meet-halfway kind of woman. She got her way or worked hard until she did. Maybe Susan had rebelled against that. Had she married Nick to spite her staid parents?

Beth couldn't wait to get out of there.

Nick glanced at Beth in the passenger seat. She sat quietly straight with her hands in her lap. A quiet Beth was a troubled one.

"Okay, spill it."

She looked at him with wide eyes. "Spill what?"

"What's on your mind. You haven't said a word since we left."

"Do I remind you of your first wife?"

Where had that question come from?

"No, not really. There's a slight similarity with your blond hair and blue eyes, but that's where it ends. You're nothing like Susan. For one, you're quiet when you're upset."

She nodded. That was true. Beth liked even-keeled.

"I saw a picture of her, and Ellen thinks I resemble her."

Nick blew out his breath. Nice. What woman wanted to be told something like that? "Ellen's a little hard around the edges but soft once you get to know her."

Beth didn't look as if she believed him. "Do they still work?"

"They're both lawyers. Greg practices part-time, and Ellen retired after Susan died."

"I see." Beth closed her eyes and leaned her head back.

"Give them time. Right now they're afraid of you."

"Afraid of *me?*" She bolted upright and stared at him. "Why?"

Nick chuckled. "Because they don't know you yet."

He couldn't point out the obvious. His in-laws knew Corey was nuts about her. And now they knew he was, too. Beth wasn't a threat to their place in Corey's life but a welcome addition. Susan's parents would see that, too. Eventually.

"Where do you want to go for dinner?"

"Doesn't matter. You choose."

Great. This wasn't turning into the date he'd hoped for. Not with Beth practically hugging the passenger-side door as if she wanted to jump out. Obviously, a romantic dinner wasn't going to happen.

"We'll be okay, Beth. We're going to make this work."

She gave him a teasing smile, but it didn't cover the worry in her eyes. "I don't know. You come with a lot of baggage."

He chuckled again. "We both do, honey. We both do."

"Beth," a deep voice intruded.

She opened her eyes and stared into gray eyes that were awfully close to her own. "Yeah?"

"We're home."

She sat up and yawned. She'd fallen asleep after dinner, a very quiet dinner, while Nick drove home. "Sorry."

"Don't be. You're pretty when you sleep."

Beth laughed. "Yeah, right. Did I snore?"

"No."

"Good."

Silence settled heavy in the car.

Would Nick kiss her good-night? Should she let him?

After meeting Corey's grandparents, there were other things to consider before moving forward. Her mom had said to follow her heart, but how could she when it was silent? Too many other variables to consider with a relationship with Nick. Namely what might happen to Corey if Nick died. If she was only a stepmom, would that mean anything in a court of law?

"Thanks for going with me tonight."

"You're welcome. I'm glad I went." Her eyes had been opened wider.

Nick leaned toward her. "I guess we should say goodnight, then."

Beth didn't want to get out of the car. She didn't want Nick to leave, either. "Can you do me a favor?"

"Sure."

"Will you call me when you're done with your shift tomorrow?"

Nick smiled. "At seven on a Sunday morning?"

Beth nodded.

"You got it." He softly ran his finger down her cheek. "Maybe we can do dinner next week. Someplace nice."

"Not good. That's the last full week of school and a final push for Corey." She didn't ask for a rain check.

He narrowed his gaze. "You're not still considering holding him back?"

"No. Honestly, that wouldn't be good for him now. Not

when there's been so much improvement. But he's still not near a third-grade reading level."

Nick looked at her with hope in his eyes. "You could work with him over the summer."

Beth hesitated. "We'll see."

Nick sighed. "We'll talk more next week, then. While we're sailing."

"Yes."

"Beth…" Nick stopped and then leaned back in his seat. "Good night."

She tamped down her disappointment. He wasn't going to kiss her. A good thing, too, considering Beth's state of mind. The only whispers she heard from her heart told her to get out now before she got in too deep and drowned.

"Good night, Nick."

Chapter Thirteen

Beth held Corey's hand as they walked down the dock toward Gerry's boat. Nick held his son's other hand. She loved the strength that had developed between father and son. They were fine. They'd be fine, too. She'd done her job helping Corey read. And that was a good thing, even if it hurt to think about them without her.

Today she'd pretend they were any ordinary couple. She wouldn't ruin the day thinking about the what-ifs and what-she-should-dos. She'd simply enjoy her last outing with the Grey men and call it good.

"Wow. Is that it?" Corey pulled against Nick's other hand.

But Nick didn't let go. "Stay with me, bud."

Gerry's beautiful white sailboat rocked gently against a wave left behind by a motorboat. Beth nodded. "That's it."

Nick gave her a sharp look. "The *Showoff*? Does this guy have something to prove?"

Beth shook her head. "No, no. He's fine, really. Julie has always called Gerry a show-off, so when they got the boat, it was a natural choice for a name."

Nick looked skeptical.

Beth scanned the marina that was already bustling with

activity. Boaters headed for town and breakfast and others prepped their sailboats and motorboats for a day on Lake Michigan. And what a day it promised to be. Not a cloud in the sky and temperatures climbing but with a steady breeze.

Perfect for sailing. Perfect for hitting the beach on South Manitou Island. And perfect for falling in love…. Wait, she'd already done that against her better judgment.

She glanced at Nick. Of all the guys she'd ever wanted, why'd she have to fall for this one? Nick had the potential to break her heart forever. And if anything happened to Nick, she might lose Corey, too.

That was a double whammy she didn't want to risk taking. Better to get out now. But after today. She wanted to enjoy today. She wasn't supposed to think about those nasty what-ifs.

"Morning!" Julie popped up out of the sailboat's cabin. "Have you guys had breakfast? We've got leftover fruit salad and sweet rolls."

"Thanks, but we ate at my mom's." Beth let go of Corey's hand and stepped down into the boat. She faced Nick when he didn't follow, shielding her eyes from the sun.

Standing on the dock holding on to a seven-year-old who strained to climb aboard, Nick hesitated.

"You coming aboard?"

"I'm not much of a boating guy, but I thought… I don't know what I thought."

Julie grinned. "You expected a big motorboat, didn't you?"

Nick nodded and finally let go of Corey, who jumped in with a whoop of delight.

"Can I go up there?" Corey pointed toward the front.

"No!" Nick's voice was sharp. Then he glanced at Julie and explained, "I don't want him falling over."

Julie opened one of the bench-seat compartments and pulled out a child-sized life vest. "One rule on our boat is that kids have to wear a life vest on deck. We've got enough for the adults, too. You boys okay with that?"

Corey nodded.

Nick looked as if he relaxed, a little. He helped his son into the life vest. Not one of those cheesy orange puffy ones but a Coast Guard–approved personal flotation device. Gerry had bragged about them last year after he'd upgraded his gear.

"A cool one," as Corey put it, making her heart pinch.

Beth ruffled the boy's hair.

"Coffee, anyone?" Julie offered. "We're waiting on Gerry's brother and his wife, and then we'll head out. They have a little girl around Corey's age. I imagine the kids will want to play in the berth."

"Berth?" Nick cocked his head.

"It's way up front in the cabin with a flat bed. The kids can play games and look out the windows. It's a good place for them while we're moving out. They can't fall out anywhere down there."

Nick nodded. "Then sure, I'll take a cup of coffee."

Beth declined. Once Julie slipped back into the cabin, she turned to Nick. "You sure you're okay with this?"

Nick gave her a tight smile. "Corey has been talking about nothing else all week. I can't chicken out now. You've done this before, right?"

Beth nodded. "Several times. Gerry's a good sailor. He grew up in Leland and has sailed Lake Michigan his whole life. He knows what he's doing."

Nick's gaze traveled the nearly thirty-foot sailboat while he ran his hand along the railing surrounding the back of the boat.

He finally blew out a breath. "Okay, then. Good. I'm good."

Beth chuckled and slipped into the cabin. She set the duffel bag she'd brought on a cushioned bench seat in the cabin's galley. She'd packed sweatshirts and windbreakers for the three of them, as well as beach towels and sunscreen. Nick had left his gun at home. Dressed for the beach, he couldn't exactly *conceal* it very well. Both Nick and Corey wore their swim shorts with T-shirts. Beth had her bathing suit on under her shorts and T-shirt.

Julie had informed her yesterday that the shoreline water temps were above normal for this time of year, so they might actually get in the water instead of wading around the beach.

Beth rolled her shoulders. She really needed this. A relaxing day spent in the sun with sand and surf.

It wasn't long before the other couple arrived. Their daughter, Millie, was a year older than Corey and in third grade.

"Millie, tell Corey about the tall-ship field trip." Beth wanted to stir Corey's interest and give him something to look forward to at school next year. Something more than how well he could read.

The little girl's eyes lit up. "Oh my gosh, it was so fun. We didn't go nearly as fast as Uncle Gerry, but we all got a turn to steer. It's a super-big boat with, like, these tall sails that make a lot of noise."

Corey listened with rapt attention.

True to Julie's words, the kids gladly followed her into the cabin toward the front. They seemed happy to stay put and play games until Uncle Gerry got the boat out into open water.

"Open water, huh? Like how open?" Nick sat beside

her on the molded cushioned benches that made a horse-shoe around the cabin entrance, surrounding the wheel.

Beth patted Nick's knee. "Don't worry. We're only fifteen miles or so from South Manitou Island and it's a straight shot. This is going to be fun."

He draped his arm around the ledge behind her. His fingers teased her neck along the collar of her T-shirt, sending shivers through her. "If you say so."

"I do." Beth forced a smile and then got up for a bottle of water.

She'd never have expected Nick to be nervous about sailing. He seemed so ready to face whatever came his way, but this was different. Maybe because he had to trust someone else's expertise for their safety. And maybe now he'd know a little about how she felt.

They made it. Nick climbed out of the inflatable dinghy with a small motor onto warm sand. They'd anchored in the crescent-shaped harbor of South Manitou Island, and a prettier place he'd never been. He felt like a pirate coming ashore to paradise, where a pristine sandy beach awaited them. He'd never seen water so blue.

He offered Beth his hand. "Watch your step."

She took it but gave him a "yeah, right" expression as she hopped out and skipped up the beach to lay out a blanket. Beth looked right at home, too, already kissed by the sun. Tall and blonde and tanned, she lured Nick's gaze often.

But she seemed distant today. Almost too cheerful, as if trying to keep something that bothered her at bay.

"C'mere, Corey. More sunscreen." Beth sprayed down his boy, whose red hair flamed and freckles multiplied in the sunshine.

Nick's did, too, so he'd keep his shirt on for a while yet. No need showing off his scars, either.

"So what'd you think?" Gerry slapped him on the back after setting down the cooler while his wife stuck a huge beach umbrella in the sand and opened it.

"Great trip. Thanks for inviting us."

Nick had to admit after they'd pulled out of the harbor and set sail across the Manitou Passage, he'd started to enjoy it. The light wind and soft waves and warm sunshine coaxed his muscles to relax.

Nick had even allowed Corey to follow Gerry around the railings that encompassed the deck to the front of the boat. The bow, as it was called. Corey had loved watching their vessel cut through the wide-open water.

His boy had been beside himself with excitement when they spotted a long freighter to the north. If Corey's interest in boating stuck, Nick might have to find a little boat for them to use on the lake across the street. He had a smidgen of Lake Leelanau lake rights.

Gerry gave him a wink. "Good, now what about Beth?"

"She's amazing." Nick had no trouble admitting that, too.

Beth turned and smiled, but it was a sad sort of smile. He smiled back.

Gerry laughed and slapped his back again. "We'll watch your boy if you two want to take a walk."

Nick glanced at his son. Corey and Millie had plunked down near the shoreline with sand buckets and shovels in hand.

Gerry pointed toward the lighthouse tower peeping up over the tree line. "That way is a shipwreck you can see from shore. It's a pretty good hike along the shoreline, but Beth knows the trail through the woods."

"Corey's going to want to see that."

"We'll meet you over there in a bit. Go on. It's quite a sight."

"Thanks."

Gerry nodded. "No problem."

Nick walked over to Beth sitting on the beach blanket. Sunlight shimmered in her hair. He sighed and offered his hand. "Let's take a walk."

Beth's eyes widened. "What about Corey?"

"They'll watch him and then meet us by the shipwreck. Gerry said you knew the way."

Beth took his hand and stood. "I do."

Nick needed to talk with Beth alone. "Corey, we're going for a walk. Mind Julie and Gerry, okay, bud?"

"Okay." His son continued piling sand.

He glanced at Beth. "He's good." Nick wasn't so sure about himself, though. Walking along the gorgeous stretch of shoreline in silence, he ran the question through his mind. Over and over, he came up with the same plan, and the same reasoning. But he couldn't nail down the answer.

"You're awfully quiet." Beth gave his hand a squeeze.

"Yeah." He glanced at her and his stomach dropped. He hadn't been this nervous in a long time. He stopped walking and reached for Beth's other hand. "I can say the same about you, too. What's going on, Beth?"

Her eyes widened but she didn't pull away. She didn't say anything either, but shrugged.

"Talk to me."

Her blue eyes clouded over. Guarded. "About Corey?"

"And us."

"I don't think we should do this now." She tried to pull her hands away, but he held firm.

"Why?"

She looked around. "It's too beautiful a day—"

That came like a kick in the gut. He'd hoped for so much

more. "Would you consider watching Corey through the summer?"

Her eyebrows went up. "As his tutor?"

"No. Although, I sure could use your help with his reading."

Beth tipped her head. "You mean like in the mornings until my mother gets home?"

He pulled her closer and wrapped his arms loosely around her waist. "I mean to complete our family. For real. For good."

"Nick…" she warned.

He knew what he wanted. It hadn't taken long to know Beth was the woman he wanted to share his life with. Tired of dancing around the obvious, he dove straight in. "Marry me."

Her eyes went wide and softened and then watered.

"I can't." Her voice was whisper-low and full of regret.

"Why?"

She pushed out of his arms. "You know why."

"Because you won't date a cop? Come on, Beth. Don't you think we're past that?"

"It's bad enough worrying about you now. But if we— No. I can't go through that for the rest of my life. I won't."

"We're already a stable family for Corey. Doesn't that count for anything?" He threw his arms wide. "Look at this sailing trip. You recognize Corey's interests and feed them. You inspire him to succeed."

"So, you—"

He cut her off. "So, he needs both of us. He needs you as much as he needs me."

She closed her eyes and a single tear tripped over her lashes to run down her cheek.

He didn't want to make her cry and felt like a heel for

doing so. Gently, he wiped the tear away as he tucked her hair behind her ear.

"He wants you for a mom," he said softly.

"That's not fair." Her voice was barely above a whisper.

"Love's not fair, but isn't it worth exploring?"

Her eyes flew open.

"I love you, Beth."

"Stop! Just stop." She backed away as if scared to listen. "I'm not marrying you, Nick. There's too much for me to lose."

Nick understood her fears, but he didn't want their lives ruled by it. Or their relationship stunted as friendship or ended because of it. How could he make her see that they had the right stuff to make it?

"But isn't there far more to gain, even if our life together is shortened?"

Beth searched his solemn gray eyes. So dear, this man, but he didn't get it. Her mother said she never once regretted marrying Beth's father, but had her mom really moved on? She still grieved. Still tried to fill the void left from her father's death.

She sighed. "Can we discuss this later?"

"If you'll reconsider."

· "No. I'm pretty solid on this." Beth didn't flinch or look away, emboldened now that she'd finally made a choice. Was it the right choice?

Nick nodded, defeated. "Then let's see this shipwreck. The rest of the group expects to meet us there."

"Okay." Beth felt sick for doing this to him.

She walked alongside Nick as they rounded the corner toward the lighthouse. They shuffled through the water's edge and up on shore. Not all the sand was as smooth as in the protected harbor. They both wore their beach sandals, so it didn't matter.

Without a word, they crunched through zebra mussel shells bleached white by the sun. The beauty was lost to her. She'd made the right decision. Her mind ran through all the reasons why they'd struggle. She mentally listed the risks. Deep down she knew they all made sense. Logical reasons to refuse him, but it still hurt.

"This place is incredible," Nick said softly.

Beth jumped at the chance to act normal. Even if it was only small talk about the area, it was something. Something to stop the noisy thoughts inside her head.

"Wait till you see the shipwreck. It's sort of eerie but really neat and stands right out of the water. This whole area is a diving preserve because of all the sunken ships. Gerry and Julie have dived here before."

"Really? I didn't know. Lake Superior, sure, everyone's heard that song."

Beth chuckled despite the heaviness in her heart. Who hadn't heard about the wreck of the *Edmund Fitzgerald?* "There's quite a seafaring history on Lake Michigan as well as Superior. Amazing how these lakes can turn deadly."

Nick's brow furrowed and his skin paled. "Ah, I didn't need to hear that."

Beth stopped walking and faced him. The noise was back in her brain. "That's how I feel, Nick. Every time you go to work."

He kicked a piece of driftwood. "I know it's not easy. My parents may have split up because my mom couldn't handle the demands of my dad's job. But you're strong, Beth. More so than you realize."

She hadn't planned on doing this today. She'd wanted to discuss it later, but the words seemed to bubble up and flow out of her before she could stop them. "I don't know if I can handle it. If I can handle *us*. You can't promise to come home unharmed."

Nick looked at her. His eyes looked red-rimmed and lost. His nose was sunburned and his hair shone like burnished copper in the sun. He tipped his head back to look at the sky and then zeroed in on her. "Can anyone make that promise? Beth, we're in God's hands. Not our own."

Looking into Nick's somber eyes, she couldn't say another word. What argument did she have for that one? Other than her lack of trust in God to see her through the heartache of losing Nick. And that's what it all boiled down to. A matter of trust in the unseen and unknowable future. A strong person might be able to do that. But she wasn't strong. Not at all.

"What about Corey?" Nick asked.

Beth nodded. She fought against the pounding headache that echoed deep in her heart.

Corey needed stability and like it or not she was part of that stability for now. "I'll help through the summer as his tutor, but that's all I can be. It might be best for you to find another care provider."

Nick gave her that lopsided smile that wasn't much of a smile at all. "Corey's going to his grandparents' for a couple weeks. They'll keep up with Corey's reading and I'll look for someone else then."

Beth fought for control and managed a clipped nod. Her mother knew from the get-go that Nick would find someone else through the summer months, but this still felt like a betrayal. An end.

She couldn't hear any whispers from her heart now. Nothing came to her but a dull ache. She sighed. "Come on, let's see that wreck."

Nick looked at her with gloomy eyes, as though he'd lost his best friend. And maybe she had, too.

"I don't like the look of those clouds." Julie packed up what was left of dinner.

Nick overheard that muttered comment over the sound of the beach umbrella flapping furiously in the wind. Wind that had really picked up. He scanned the horizon, where those dark clouds Julie had mentioned hovered far away.

He'd hinted at leaving early a couple of times. It was pretty tough hanging out with Beth. Pretty tough to act normal when his heart had taken a beating. There was no getting her back from this one. No pushing for something more between them. Beth didn't want to be the wife of a cop. End of story.

"Wind's coming out of the west, southwest. I think we can outrun it." Gerry gave his wife a wide grin.

It was a braggart kind of grin that didn't give Nick much comfort. Great, this guy wanted to play cowboy.

They'd lingered too long over dinner, but Gerry wanted to wait and sail back by sunset. He said there was nothing like it. Well, Nick could have done without the added treat if it meant getting home safe and sound.

After an afternoon spent hiking and lounging on the beach, everyone was beat. But Gerry suddenly kicked into high gear. He and Julie moved quickly, getting their beach gear loaded onto the dinghy while the rest of them trudged along.

Nick remembered that kind of adrenaline rush. The anticipation of a challenge ahead. He could feel it bouncing off Gerry like a rubber ball. Only Nick wasn't feeling up to a challenge today. And he had a bad feeling this day was about to get worse. Fast.

"Come on, everybody. Let's go." Gerry waved his arm, gesturing to load up.

Nick looked at his beautiful but cowardly Beth. She wanted to run away from what they had, thinking it'd be easier. For who? Her? But the reality of how right she was hit hard. As the daughter of an officer, Beth had seen what it was like to be married to a cop. Her eyes were wide-open. Maybe he was the naive one thinking that love and faith were enough to keep them together. All he knew was that he loved her. Blindly, deeply and forever.

And that's why he'd let her go.

Beth didn't seem the least bit concerned about the clouds as she helped the kids climb into the smaller boat they used to shuttle back to the *Showoff.*

He thought about that wreck of the *Morazan* freighter they'd seen offshore sticking straight up out of the water. Gerry had explained that she'd run aground in the fall of 1960. There were a whole lot of shipwrecks littering this Manitou Passage. Big ships.

Bigger than the *Showoff.*

Nick rubbed the back of his neck where the hairs felt prickly. He grabbed the life vest on the bench seat of the dinghy. "Corey. Put this on."

His son's eyes went wide at his sharp tone.

"Please," Nick said softly.

He glanced at Beth.

She'd quieted, too, at his barked order.

Millie's parents gusseted her up in a life vest, too. And the girl's father kept staring toward the west and those clouds that were building.

The ride from shore was quick, but a distant rumble of thunder quieted the chatter as they climbed aboard the sailboat.

Nick looked around the cockpit and then asked Beth, "Where's the adult vests?"

She patted the cushioned benches. "Under here."

"Let's get them on."

"Dude." Gerry slapped him on the back after securing the dinghy to the back of the boat. "We're fine. We'll stay ahead of it. Might even miss it entirely, according to radar."

Nick reached under the bench anyway. "I'm used to wearing a different kind of life vest at work, so I'd feel better with one on."

"Suit yourself." Gerry ducked into the cabin.

"Beth?" He handed her one.

She narrowed her gaze and then slipped it over her T-shirt and secured it. She gave him a quick nod. Better to be safe.

The air hadn't cooled in spite of the stiffer wind. Warm southwest wind, Gerry had said. Nick didn't care where it came from. All he knew was that the chop on the water had increased by the time they had pulled out from the protection of the island's harbor into the open waters of the Manitou Passage.

Nick tried to remain calm, but forty-five minutes later the sun had been swallowed whole by those clouds. The ones Julie didn't like.

Nick didn't like them, either.

Those clouds had made a dark bluish-gray wall. The wall was gaining on them. Moving fast. He spotted a fork of lightning, but he kept his mouth shut. He didn't know how to sail; what orders could he possibly give?

Wouldn't have mattered if he'd spoken aloud—the wind would have stolen his words and thrown them away. He could barely hear himself think over the constant slapping of the wind against the sails and waves sloshing against the boat. Not to mention Gerry and his brother spouting out terms Nick had never heard.

They sort of tilted in the water. Nick held on tight and wedged himself in the corner where the cabin met the cockpit. When he spotted Gerry and his brother pulling on life vests, his stomach turned. They were in for a rough time ahead.

"Anything I can do?"

Gerry shook his head. "Go below for now with the women and children. It's going to get a little dicey and wet up here."

Nick swallowed a bruising retort.

"Wet and wild." Gerry's brother, on the right side deck, had a big grin on his face.

The two men enjoyed this a little too much. Nick understood the feelings from working undercover. Man against man, Nick knew his chances. Man against nature was something else entirely and completely unpredictable. He clenched his teeth as he slipped into the cabin. There were bigger reasons for this boat's name and he'd not spout them here and now. But he prayed those reasons wouldn't get them all into trouble.

In the cabin, Beth and Millie's mom sat tucked in by the little galley table. Julie had stashed things in cupboards and compartments that locked with a click before they left South Manitou. But she kept finding things that might dislodge and fly across the cabin, like the card game the kids played earlier.

Right now those two kids stared wild-eyed out the little cabin windows while they huddled on that flat surface in the front.

Julie and Millie's mom wore their life vests, too.

"This is so cool." Corey watched the waves that were too close to the left side window for Nick's comfort.

He didn't care for the spray of water that occasionally came into the cabin, either. "Yeah, cool."

Nick looked at Beth. She'd slipped on her windbreaker over her vest but still looked pretty calm. Maybe there was nothing to worry about. He was a novice at this kind of thing.

But when he sat down next to her and took her hand in his, she held on tighter than a death grip.

They were moving so fast. And the sound of distant thunder grew louder.

Closer.

Beth rethreaded her fingers through Nick's, glad for his steely calm. If she held on tight enough, maybe some of that strength would seep into her, too. The rocking motion wasn't treating her well. All of them looked as if dinner wasn't getting along well with the waves. Except for Corey. The rough seas didn't seem to bother the kid at all.

They kept the cabin door open for air. Spray from the waves spattered through. Occasionally water whooshed right over the side into the cockpit, soaking Gerry at the wheel. The cold water spit against her bare legs and she wished she'd thought to bring pants.

The wind had considerably increased. She thought she heard twenty-five knots, maybe even thirty, bandied about by the guys above. The boat heeled far to the side when hit by a sudden gust and Gerry yelled directions to his brother.

Millie squealed and her mom reached for her.

Beth had slipped from her seat, but Nick caught her and pulled her against him. He looked a little green, too.

"You kids okay?" he called out.

Corey's eyes were huge as he lay on the bed in the V-shaped front of the boat. "What was that?"

"Hang on, bud." Nick's arms stayed locked around her.

Julie shrugged. "A hard gust of wind. We might have to go topside or we'll all be sick down here."

Beth glanced at the kids and shuddered. She felt safer in the cabin, where the water couldn't pull them off the boat.

"Why can't we use the engine to motor us home?" Nick asked.

"The engine is for calm days and maneuvering around a harbor or close to shore. Totally ineffective in wind like this. It's okay—the storm will pass."

Beth took a deep breath. Hunker down and wait it out. They were safe in the cabin and dry. Julie and her husband had sailed in storms before. They'd ride this one out.

She closed her eyes and let her head fall onto Nick's shoulder. Helpless. She prayed they'd make it to shore soon, before she got sick. It'd been a long time since they'd left South Manitou. They had to be halfway across to Leland's harbor by now.

The wind only increased, taunting them, laughing at the men's attempts to harness it with sailcloth. Why had they done this, anyway? The sound of the wind was nothing compared to the roar of the rain. At first big drops hit the cabin roof with a *tap, tap, tap.* Then a deluge shrieked over the lake.

The boat heeled again, tipping farther this time. The kids screamed and even Julie looked concerned when a wave of water sloshed over the side of the stern into the cockpit.

"I'm going to get sick, Mama." Millie started to cry.

Nick got up but had to hold on to the table to keep from falling back down. "I can't stay in here."

Beth watched him make his wobbly way out of the cabin, but he leaned in the corner of the cockpit, hanging on to the railing. The rain, the waves and the lake were one color. Gray. She could barely see where the edge of the white boat stopped and the lake started, it rained so hard.

No way was she going out there.

"Yeah, we should all go up top." Julie tried to get up but slipped backward when the boat pitched again.

"No," Beth whispered. She wouldn't leave the cabin. "Corey, come sit by me, bud."

The boy scooted close and Beth held him tight.

"What's that?" Nick shouted.

"That's the crib!" Gerry yelled above the roaring rain. "It was portside a moment ago. Come about!"

"I can't see a thing," his brother screamed back. "Gerry!"

"Come about now!"

More howling wind and roaring rain.

The boat heeled hard. Beth came off her seat and fell on the floor, taking Corey with her.

"Get to the high side!" Julie pulled herself along the table.

Beth tried to get up but spotted the windows along the low side of the boat. They were covered by water. Her stomach dropped and then it felt as if they'd been lifted and tossed. She felt a shuddering crunch that made her teeth chatter.

"What was that?" Millie's mom whispered.

Turning her head, Beth saw that the young woman was on the floor, too. Millie had thrown up.

Beth's stomach lurched, but the bile inching up her throat froze. She trembled, closed her eyes and prayed her belly would settle when she realized what they'd hit.

How could Gerry not have seen the North Manitou Shoal Lighthouse smack in the middle of the passage? They'd passed it on the way, but its red light had been doused then, not needed. But what about a few moments ago?

An alarm rang.

"What's that?"

"Bilge alarm." Julie's eyes were huge, her face white.

"Julie, get everyone up here. We hit the corner of the shoal light. I don't know how bad it is."

Millie cried harder.

"How do we check it out?" Nick's deep voice echoed.

She opened her eyes in time to see Julie feeling along the cabin floor.

"What?" Beth cried.

Julie wobbled to the cockpit. "Gerry! We're taking on water into the cabin!"

"Grab the helm!" Gerry slipped around the corner to the cabin desk devoted to charts and the radio. "Everyone out now! Nick, tether them in the stern for now. Julie will help you."

Beth watched as Nick sprung into action, helping Millie and her mom first out into the cockpit. Rain pelted them, pasting their hair against their heads as it soaked them through.

She glanced at the floor. Her feet were tucked up underneath her, and she was dry. Corey, too, because he sat in her lap. Where was the water coming in? Why did they have to go up top?

She couldn't move. Gripping Corey close, she tried to breathe evenly and think. Think!

"Mayday, Mayday, this is the *Showoff,* over." Gerry's voice sounded strained now.

She watched him as if she'd fallen into a bad dream.

The radio crackled to life and someone answered.

"We hit the crib and we're taking on water. Six adults and two children on board."

Beth listened as Gerry gave them their location, as well as their water situation. Something about pumps not keeping up but they had time.

They were taking on water! How much time did they have before they sank?

They were going to sink!

Beth couldn't hear the rest of what was said, because Gerry's voice had grown fuzzy.

They were going to sink.

"Nick!" she choked out.

"Come on, Beth. You and Corey. Now!" Nick shouted again. "Beth!"

She looked at him. He was tethered on to the railing and held out another tether. How would they unclip in time before they sank?

The wind still whipped. The boat sort of wallowed in the water but it wasn't going down. Gerry had adjusted the sails that now flapped in the wind. She glanced at the floor. Still pretty dry except for the darkening of the carpet toward the front end of the boat. Maybe they'd be okay. At least they weren't flying sideways anymore.

Corey clung to her.

She took a deep breath and stood.

Lord, please help us.

Gerry grabbed her arm. "Come on, Beth. It's okay. Help's on the way. The Coast Guard's already in the area somewhere. We're not the only one in trouble today. Once the storm passes, we'll abandon onto the dinghy. We'll be okay."

She looked at him and then at Nick.

"Come on, honey." Nick's smile was sweet.

She stepped out of the cabin, still clutching Corey, who walked beside her. Rain assaulted their faces. "Take care of him first."

Beth held on to Corey while Nick tethered in his son.

Another gust hit and the boat tilted.

Beth slipped and fell against the bench seat. Clawing

against the cushioned seats, she couldn't grip the slippery vinyl. She slammed against the railing, flipped and went over.

"Beth!" Nick screamed.

She fought the waves, choked on them as they splashed over her face. The water was cold, but not as cold as the rain slicing her face.

She heard yelling and screaming. "Man overboard!"

Beth caught a glimpse of the sailboat. It rocked back and forth in the water. With all her might, she kicked and moved forward to the boat. The dinghy bounced on the waves behind it.

If she could reach the dinghy, she could pull herself in. She kicked with all her might and tried to swim forward but was tugged farther away by the waves.

Away from the sailboat.

Nick threw the life ring her way. "Grab it."

She tried. Felt the rope slip through her fingers and come up short as she was pulled away.

"Beth. Hang on."

"I'm trying."

Again with the life ring. But it didn't reach her this time. Beth swam forward. The water dragged her back.

This time Nick threw something else her way. It hit the water and floated, tossed by the waves.

"Grab the seat cushion." Nick's voice barely skipped across the water's surface.

She swam toward the cushion, still out of reach. Sputtering after another wave swamped her. She tried again and managed to grip the canvas loop. Pulling herself onto the small square cushion, Beth rested, exhausted.

She watched as Gerry and his brother struggled to raise the sails, only to drop them back down. Everyone hunkered in the cockpit, hanging on. Gerry fought the waves but pulled the dinghy close to the stern. The *Showoff* didn't look as if it was sinking, but it rode lower in the water. Or was that the waves?

She saw someone pointing her way. Nick.

"I'm coming!" he screamed.

"No!" Beth reached out her hand. He couldn't leave Corey alone.

The boat waffled. Maybe they couldn't maneuver. She saw Julie let go of the rope to the dinghy. They couldn't come get her in that!

No. The dinghy wasn't going anywhere. And the waves pulled her farther away. She was on her own. Alone.

Chapter Fourteen

"Dad, no!" Corey clung to him.

Nick cupped his son's cheek. "I'll be back. It's okay, Corey. They've got you. You're safe until help gets here."

Nick scanned the horizon. No Coast Guard in sight. But then, Search and Rescue could come by boat out of Frankfort or by air in Traverse City. Didn't matter. Help was on the way.

His boy wouldn't let go.

"I'll get Beth and come back. I promise." Nick added that last bit praying God would make it so.

Beth was a strong woman and a swimmer to boot. He'd seen the lithe muscles in her arms and legs. If anyone could tread water for days, it'd be her. Only they didn't have days; they had hours. How many, he wasn't sure. Exposure to the warming but still-cold water temperatures worried him.

"Noooo." His boy sobbed.

Nick's gut twisted.

He was leaving his son behind again, but he couldn't leave Beth out there all alone. The seas were still too rough to take the dinghy and risk the kids' safety.

No, he had to go. Beth would have a better chance staying warm with both of them huddled close.

The storm was already blowing itself out, leaving so much damage in its wake. The *Showoff* was broken, but it wouldn't completely sink, according to Gerry. Too much flotation, he'd said. Whatever that meant. In Nick's mind, any boat could sink, including this one.

He glanced at the two men hanging on to the railing at the back, exhausted from their fight against the wind. The front end of the *Showoff* dipped below the water but then bobbed back up.

Smaller swells churned the dinghy against the sailboat, but their tie held firm. Julie had instructions to unclip the dinghy loose if the sailboat sank any farther.

Julie gripped Corey close. They both huddled with Millie and her mom. All of them shivering. But safe. His boy was safe.

Beth wasn't.

Nick could barely see Beth bobbing farther away from them, struggling to swim. "Corey, I have to go after Beth. We can't leave her out there all alone, can we?"

"No." His son hiccuped on a sob.

Nick pulled away, but Corey screamed. "Dad!"

"It'll be okay." He looked at Julie, who pulled his boy back away from the edge of the dinghy. "Don't let go of him."

"I won't."

"I'll be back, bud. I promise. I love you, son. I love you very much."

His son cried harder.

Nick looped a life ring over his shoulder and slipped into the water. His breath caught. It wasn't polar-bear-dipping cold, but certainly not shoreline warm like the harbor at South Manitou.

With the Coast Guard on its way and Gerry's boat

equipped with a satellite tracking system, they'd be found. Hopefully soon.

But he had to get to Beth.

Nick swam hard and choppy. The waves pushed him forward. Toward Beth instead of away from her. God was with him. He knew that, but his legs tingled in the cold water. His fingers did, too. How long before they got into real trouble out here?

"Help me, Lord."

She was so tired.

And cold.

Pushing herself up on the seat cushion Nick had thrown her, Beth tried to paddle, but her arms felt as if they'd fallen off. She couldn't feel her fingers anymore. She couldn't feel anything…but regret.

Regret stung sharper than the cold water twisting the skin on her toes and numbing her fingertips. Why had she gone sailing, why had she brought Nick and Corey along, and even more troubling, why was she so afraid to make them a real family with a marriage license?

She'd always lived a safe life. Through high school, college and even now Beth weighed the risks of every decision she made, choosing the easy way. The safe way. She'd always prided herself on being practical. But she was practically scared of her own shadow, if the truth be told.

She spotted the boat as it bobbed up on a swell. Then it disappeared. So far away.

Glancing to the west, where the leftover clouds had turned dark peach from the late-day sun pushing its way down behind them, Beth wondered if this might be her last sunset.

She closed her eyes. "Lord, I'm so sorry…."

What was she sorry for?

"Everything. Not trusting You. Not telling Nick and Corey how much I love them."

Nick...

Beth started to cry.

Nick had said they were all in God's hands. But Beth didn't want to believe it, not really. She'd been too wrapped up in keeping her heart safe from hurt.

God hadn't given her what she wanted; He'd given her what she needed. Who Beth needed in order to rely more on Him. Nick and Corey were gifts she'd refused.

How selfish could she be? Hurt was part of life, right? God never promised a carefree life without suffering. Yet she'd been striving for exactly that. Why rob them all of the blessing of being together because she was afraid of pain?

The fear of loss.

Beth never regretted a moment spent with her dad, even though his time with her had been cut short. Her father had taught her the importance of passion and love. But she'd traded those in for fear. She didn't want to face the possibility of Nick's death, and yet here she was facing her own.

She was going to die in this cold water.

And she'd never told Nick that she loved him.

A sob welled up and spilled over. Water splashed against her face as a wave lapped over her shoulders. She coughed and slipped back into the water. The seat cushion popped forward. Out of reach.

She didn't care.

Death is never final.

Was that her mom speaking?

Life is eternal.

Love never fades....

Beth let her head fall forward. Her face dipped into the water, startling her. Her hair had soaked up the cold water like a sponge and lay like stringy icicles against her neck. Her nose seared icy cold. With eyes closed, she smiled. At least, she thought she smiled; she couldn't feel her cheeks anymore.

God was with her. She felt Him drawing near. Lifting her up out of the water and breathing warmth on her face.

"I'm ready, Lord."

"Beth?"

Nick?

"Beth, honey. Come on, baby, talk to me." He swatted her face.

"Owww."

He laughed and then kissed her.

Heat.

Beth grabbed his hair and pulled.

"Owww."

"You're real." Beth's teeth chattered.

He chuckled. "Of course I'm real."

"Corey?"

"He's safe with the others. Help's on its way."

"Thank You, Lord." Her head flopped against Nick's shoulder encased in the life vest. He wore one at work, too. He was a careful man. Why hadn't she realized that before?

She kicked her legs, tried to stave off that tingling sensation.

"Come on, Beth. Fold your arms close to your body and keep still." He wrapped his arms and legs around her, pulling her close.

"Hmm, this is nice." She felt his body's heat seep into hers as they huddled together. Bobbing like human buoys.

He kissed her again.

Too brief.

She searched his storm-gray eyes, feeling stronger now. Now that he was with her. She slipped down and water splashed over her face again. She coughed and closed her eyes.

Nick lifted her higher, onto the life ring, and then held on to them both. "Stay with me. Don't sleep. We're going to be fine. And you're not leaving me. I'll get a desk job or something, anything to keep you with me. Is that understood?"

"No." She shook her head.

"What do you mean, no? No? I said you're not leaving me."

She smiled at how fierce he sounded.

Beth couldn't let him give up his passion because of her fear. She was done trading on fears and worries. "I love you, Nick. I love that you're a good father, a wonderful man and a careful cop."

He hugged her closer, if that was possible considering their life vests made a barrier between them. "Then marry me. You, me and Corey. Make us a family and we'll figure out the rest."

"Don't forget Peanut."

He rubbed his nose against hers. His was cold, too. "And the puppies, too. I love you, Beth."

"I'm glad." Her eyes itched and her lids lagged too heavy to keep open.

Her mom was right. God had whispered through her heart when she'd finally stopped and listened. Once the noise of her thoughts clamoring inside her practical, reasoning mind quieted. Out here in the water, she couldn't do anything but listen to the whispers in her heart. Did she really need to flip overboard for that? Why couldn't she have lain down on a bed of soft grass to hear…?

"Beth." Nick shook her.

She startled awake.

Nick held her close. "Kiss me."

She tried. She was so tired she could barely rally the strength to kiss him, but she managed. This was where she wanted to be and where she belonged.

Beth didn't know how long they huddled together in the middle of the Manitou Passage. When the sun finally dropped beneath the line of the lake's water, a Coast Guard rescue boat drew near.

Noisy, too.

Men shouted orders and their boat engine purred as it idled.

She shook her head. "Small boat."

Beth couldn't see the faces of the men leaning down to get them up and out of the water because of the glare of lights that shone from behind them.

Nick laughed. "It'll do."

As they were pulled into the boat, Corey lunged for his father.

"Dad!"

Nick pulled him close and squeezed him tight.

Beth glanced at everyone huddled in blankets, but she couldn't raise a hand to wave. She was ushered into the cramped cabin before she could say another word. But then her teeth chattered something fierce and her eyelids grew heavy again. Someone helped her out of her windbreaker, life vest and clothes. Right down to her bathing suit.

And then a warm blanket was wrapped around her with packs of something warm placed directly on her skin. Her vitals were taken, including her temperature.

The heat washed over her like a warm wave followed by sharp needle pricks of tingling. Her feet went into warm slippers, and a warm hat with long woolly flaps was wound around her neck and head. Someone gave her a cup of hot chocolate, but her hand shook.

"Drink slowly." Someone held it for her.

Beth took a couple sips and then leaned back against the wall. Her head felt heavy.

"Is she okay?" Nick stripped off his wet T-shirt on his own.

Beth spotted a small, round puckered scar on Nick's shoulder with a bigger one on his back before the same kind of blanket went around him, too. A bullet wound. She'd touch that scar and make sure it didn't taunt her.

"Groggy, but good vitals. You're both hypothermic." The Coast Guard guy pointed at her. "She's borderline moderate, but I think she's warming well. Keep her still and we'll check her vitals again soon."

Nick nodded and sat down next to her. He scooped up Corey, also bundled in a blanket, onto his lap. Both were given hot chocolate.

"You okay?"

"Not the way I envisioned our sailing trip." Beth gave him a watery smile. "I'm so sorry."

He caressed her cheek before helping her take another sip of hot chocolate. "I'm not."

Corey looked up at his father. "I'm never going on a boat again."

Beth reached out her hand and patted the boy's knee. "Sometimes bad things happen, like today, but we can't let it make us afraid of living." She thought about Nick's scars. He might receive more over the course of his career, and she'd have to deal with that. Trust God to help her through the fear. "Or enjoying the beauty around us and trying again."

Corey's eyes went wide and he looked up at Nick.

"She's right, son. But we'll take it easy for a while. Maybe stick to Lake Leelanau."

Corey looked as if he thought hard about that one.

Beth smiled at the boy. "There's a great beach by your house."

"Soon to be our house." Nick took hold of her hand and kissed it.

Beth smiled. "Yes, soon to be our house. Nick, I don't want you to change what you do. Not for me."

"Beth—"

She cut him off with her fingers against his lips. They'd handle this together with openness and honesty. She was a cop's daughter who could teach Corey a thing or two about being the child of a deputy officer. She'd trust God to help her be a good cop's wife. One who'd give her fear and worry to God. He could handle it. She couldn't on her own.

"Bad things happen, but we're not going to live in fear. God is with us and we're in His hands. Right, Corey?" Nick echoed her words, but his gaze remained locked on hers.

Corey poked his dad in the ribs. "Is Miss Ryken going to be my new mom?"

"Is that okay with you?"

Corey nodded, but he wore a serious look on his face.

"What is it, bud?" Nick asked.

Beth held her breath.

"I'm glad because we're already a family."

"Yeah, bud. We are." Nick gave her that lopsided grin that wasn't much of a grin.

It made her heart ooze. Completely thawed out and pliable.

"Dad?"

"Yes, son?"

"Do I have to still call her Miss Ryken?"

Beth laughed.

Nick did, too. "I think it'll be okay if you call her Beth."

"I love you. I love you both." She leaned forward and

hugged these two men brought into her life so that she might truly live.

They were a family. And they would remain a family no matter what.

Nick wrapped his arms around her. They had Corey trapped between them, but he snuggled in close.

This was real warmth. Real peace. And Beth was never so grateful for God's whispers into her heart in the dark waters of Lake Michigan. He had been with her then and she needn't fear the future, because He'd always be with her. With all of them.

Epilogue

The first Saturday in August shone like a gemstone. A perfect summer day that remained warm and calm into early evening. It was the perfect day for Beth and Nick to exchange their wedding vows aboard a passenger ferry boat while cruising the Manitou Passage shoreline.

Beth had come up with this plan for a couple of reasons. She wanted to face the waters where they could have lost each other with a new memory of celebration. She also wanted to show Corey that they didn't need to live in fear of what had happened. God had been with them, and Beth wanted to honor that by marrying Nick where he'd proposed and she'd accepted.

Beth smiled as Corey led her down the aisle of the lower deck. The boy looked handsome in his khaki pants and crisp linen shirt that matched his father's. No suits and no ties. That had been the only request from her Grey men.

The lower deck's windows were open to let in the warm evening air too still for even a breeze. But that was okay with Beth. She'd take balmy to breezy on this special day.

The sides of the benches had been decorated with white bows and sprays of evergreens and wildflowers that she and her mother and Corey's grandmother had gathered earlier in the day in an open field near Nick's house.

Beth carried a small bouquet of the same.

"This is weird," Corey whispered. "Getting married on a boat."

"It's worth it, though, don't you think? Kinda fun, even?"

Corey shrugged. "I guess." Beth smiled down on the boy who'd stolen her heart the day he'd shown up in her class.

"Hey, Beth?" He looked up with a frown. "Do you think the puppies will be okay?"

"We'll take good care of them while you're with your grandparents." She squeezed Corey's hand and then smiled at Nick, who looked curious about their chitchat. She'd fill him in later.

Her mom had promised to stay with the dogs while they drove a couple hours north to spend a few days in a little cottage on Lake Michigan. The plan was for her mom to take two of the puppies by summer's end. And they'd keep Peanut and her other two. Much to Nick's chagrin, Beth didn't have the heart to send those puppies too far. And Corey had agreed.

They finally reached Nick standing tall and handsome with their minister and the boat's captain. Beth leaned down and kissed Corey's forehead when he handed her over to Nick.

"Thanks, Corey."

He gave her a serious nod and then sat down next to his grandparents.

"You look beautiful." Nick lifted her hand and kissed it.

"Thanks. You, too." Beth wore a simple white dress with her hair pinned up with more wildflowers. Even her strappy sandals were comfortable.

They had a long evening ahead of them. After the wedding followed by light hors d'oeuvres on the boat, dinner and dancing awaited at a restaurant overlooking the beach. Beth and Nick's guest list had been small. Family and a few friends.

The minister started the ceremony, and Beth stared into Nick's eyes and held tight his hands.

"To have and to hold in sickness and in health…"

Nick had held her in the water. He'd kept her warm and safe from slipping into a more serious situation. He helped her realize who to trust with her life and his. "I do."

Nick smiled at her.

"Nicholas, do you take Elizabeth to be your lawfully wedded wife…" the minister continued.

Beth experienced a renewed sense of pride in Nick's position. He enforced the law. Something not everyone could do. She'd support him in his calling. All things were possible in God, who'd strengthen her.

"I do."

"Then go ahead and kiss your bride."

Nick pulled her close. "I love you."

"I love you," Beth whispered before kissing Nick.

"Mr. and Mrs. Grey, folks," the minister announced.

Their guests cheered.

Beth spotted her mom, who dabbed her eyes with a tissue. And then she was practically tackled by Corey as he hugged them both.

She laughed and squeezed the boy closer. "I love you, Corey."

"Me, too." He buried his head into her waist.

He was her little boy now. For always.

* * * * *

Dear Reader,

Thank you so much for picking up a copy of my book. I hope you enjoyed reading Beth Ryken's journey to a happily-ever-after of her own. Beth was one of those secondary characters who demanded a book. At first I thought she and Eva's brother might get together, but no. They would never have worked!

And then I realized something about Beth. She needed to be needed but also played it much too safe because of the death of her police officer father when she was fourteen. Enter Nick Grey, a simple man called to be a cop. Both have emotional baggage, but when they finally place their trust in God and give Him their fears, their happily-ever-after is truly possible.

I love to hear from readers. Please visit my website at jennamindel.com or drop me a note c/o Love Inspired Books, 233 Broadway, Suite 1001, New York, NY 10279.

Many blessings to you,

Jenna

Questions for Discussion

1. When the book opens, Beth is worried about her mom's spending habits. Should she be? How could Beth have approached the issue more effectively?

2. Nick's relationship with his seven-year-old son is strained. What could Nick have done better to reach his boy?

3. Many youngsters struggle in first and second grade. Do you believe in having a child repeat those grades if they are behind grade-level standards? Why or why not?

4. Beth's and Nick's attraction to each other is immediate but they let their fears get in the way of deepening the relationship. Why were they afraid? How did they finally overcome those fears? And in what ways did their faith help?

5. Nick believes his previous mother-in-law feels threatened by his relationship with Beth. Should he have shared those thoughts with Beth? What steps can they take to keep Corey's maternal grandparents feeling connected?

6. Nick tries to overcome Beth's concerns regarding the possible dangers of his job by telling her that they are ultimately in God's hands. Do you believe that? If so, how can that put worry to rest in your life?

7. When their dog Peanut is in trouble with her labor, Nick calls his minister for prayer. How concerned

do you believe God is about our pets? Have you ever prayed for yours? If so, what were the circumstances and how did God answer those prayers?

8. By the end of the book, Beth faces her biggest fear. Are there any fears you'd rather not deal with? And if so, how can you give them to God?

9. The Scripture verse of Isaiah 43:1–2 really spoke to me for this book. No matter how deep our troubles, God is with us and we won't "drown." What does this verse mean to you?

10. Heroes and heroines in romance novels often fall in love quickly. Do you think couples should date for a certain amount of time before marrying? If so, how much time is enough time? Why?

11. Beth agrees to tutor Corey and she uses a lot of games to teach. How essential is having fun to learning?

12. Do you remember your favorite book as a child? What was it?

HIS MONTANA BRIDE
Big Sky Centennial • by Brenda Minton

Cord Shaw's had enough of romance. So when he and pretty Katie Archer are suddenly in charge of a fifty-couple wedding in honor of the town's centennial celebration, he's surprised when he's one of the grooms saying I do.

ALASKAN SWEETHEARTS
North to Dry Creek • by Janet Tronstad

Alaskan single mom Scarlett is determined to claim the land Hunter Jacobson's grandfather promised her. Though their families have been feuding for years, and her head's saying Hunter's all wrong for her, her heart is telling her something different....

NORTH COUNTRY DAD
Northern Lights • by Lois Richer

Handsome widower Grant Adams is in over his head raising twins. Dahlia Wheatley's offer to help find a new mom for the girls makes him realize it's *her* he wants for his family's future.

THE FOREST RANGER'S CHRISTMAS
by Leigh Bale

Hoping to save her grandfather—and herself—from a lonely holiday season, Josie Rushton heads home for Christmas. Soon she's the one being rescued by widowed forest ranger Clint Hampton and his adorable matchmaking daughter.

THE GUY NEXT DOOR
by Missy Tippens

Returning to town to sell his family home, lawyer Luke Jordan notices his old best friend Darcy O'Malley has become a beautiful woman. Could it be that love has been right next door all along?

A HOME FOR HER FAMILY
by Virginia Carmichael

He's a successful businessman. She's a hardworking mechanic. Though they come from different worlds, when Jack Thorne helps Sabrina Martinez gain custody of her nieces, they discover love knows no boundaries.

———

REQUEST YOUR FREE BOOKS!

2 FREE INSPIRATIONAL NOVELS
PLUS 2
FREE
MYSTERY GIFTS

Love Inspired

YES! Please send me 2 FREE Love Inspired® novels and my 2 FREE mystery gifts (gifts are worth about $10). After receiving them, if I don't wish to receive any more books, I can return the shipping statement marked "cancel." If I don't cancel, I will receive 6 brand-new novels every month and be billed just $4.74 per book in the U.S. or $5.24 per book in Canada. That's a saving of at least 21% off the cover price. It's quite a bargain! Shipping and handling is just 50¢ per book in the U.S. and 75¢ per book in Canada.* I understand that accepting the 2 free books and gifts places me under no obligation to buy anything. I can always return a shipment and cancel at any time. Even if I never buy another book, the two free books and gifts are mine to keep forever.

105/305 IDN F47Y

Name   (PLEASE PRINT)

Address   Apt. #

City   State/Prov.   Zip/Postal Code

Signature (if under 18, a parent or guardian must sign)

Mail to the Harlequin® Reader Service:
IN U.S.A.: P.O. Box 1867, Buffalo, NY 14240-1867
IN CANADA: P.O. Box 609, Fort Erie, Ontario L2A 5X3

**Are you a subscriber to Love Inspired books
and want to receive the larger-print edition?
Call 1-800-873-8635 or visit www.ReaderService.com.**

* Terms and prices subject to change without notice. Prices do not include applicable taxes. Sales tax applicable in N.Y. Canadian residents will be charged applicable taxes. Offer not valid in Quebec. This offer is limited to one order per household. Not valid for current subscribers to Love Inspired books. All orders subject to credit approval. Credit or debit balances in a customer's account(s) may be offset by any other outstanding balance owed by or to the customer. Please allow 4 to 6 weeks for delivery. Offer available while quantities last.

Your Privacy—The Harlequin® Reader Service is committed to protecting your privacy. Our Privacy Policy is available online at www.ReaderService.com or upon request from the Harlequin Reader Service.

We make a portion of our mailing list available to reputable third parties that offer products we believe may interest you. If you prefer that we not exchange your name with third parties, or if you wish to clarify or modify your communication preferences, please visit us at www.ReaderService.com/consumerchoice or write to us at Harlequin Reader Service Preference Service, P.O. Box 9062, Buffalo, NY 14269. Include your complete name and address.

LI13R

SPECIAL EXCERPT FROM

Love Inspired

*Get ready for a Big Sky wedding…or fifty! Here's a
sneak peek at
HIS MONTANA BRIDE by Brenda Minton,
part of the **BIG SKY CENTENNIAL** miniseries:*

"**B**ad news," Cord said. "That was the wedding coordinator. She's quitting."

"Ouch. So now what?"

"I'm not sure."

"With no coordinator to help, will you call off the wedding?" Katie asked.

"No." There was too much at stake. The town needed this wedding and the money it would bring in. They had a bridge in need of repairs and a museum they couldn't finish without more funds. "I'll just figure out how to pull off a wedding for fifty couples, maybe get some media attention for Jasper Gulch and hopefully not mess up anyone's life."

"I think you'll do just fine. Remember, it's all about the dress."

"How long are you going to be in town, Katie?" He placed a hand on her back and guided her up the sidewalk.

"I'm not sure. I'm supposed to be helping my sister, but she seems to have escaped and left me here." She sighed and glanced at him.

"Do you think that as long as you're here…"

They were standing in front of the massive wooden doors that led to the church. She had a slightly red nose from the cool morning air and her lips were tinted with pink gloss. As long as she was there, she could be a friend. That wasn't

LIEXP0914

what he'd planned to say, but the thought framed itself as a question in his mind.

She was studying his face, waiting for him to finish.

"Maybe you could help me with this wedding?"

"I thought maybe you wanted me to run interference and keep the single women at bay. 'Hands off Cord Shaw,' that kind of thing." As she said it, somehow her palm came to rest on his shoulder as if they'd been friends forever.

It was the strangest and maybe one of the best feelings. It tangled him up and made him lose track of the reality that he was standing in front of the church. The door could open at any moment. And for the first time in years, a woman had made him feel at ease.

Can rancher Cord Shaw and Katie Archer pull off Jasper Gulch's latest centennial event without getting their hearts involved? Find out in HIS MONTANA BRIDE by Brenda Minton, available October 2014 from Love Inspired.

THEY SAID IT BEST . . .

ON ADVERTISING . . .

"Half the money I spend on advertising is wasted, and the trouble is I don't know which half."

JOHN WANAMAKER

ON MARKETING . . .

"These are difficult days for automobile manufacturers; they're thinking up ways to make their products safer and new names to make them sound more dangerous."

THOMAS la MANCE

ON ACCOUNTING . . .

"Auditors are the people who go in after the war is lost and bayonet the wounded."

P. RUBIN

ON PROFIT . . .

"Volume times zero isn't too healthy."

LEE IACOCCA

ON ENTREPRENEURS . . .

"Launching your own business is like writing your own personal declaration of independence from the corporate beehive. . . . Becoming an entrepreneur is the modern-day equivalent of pioneering on the old frontier."

PAULA NELSON

FROM THE TOP TO THE BOTTOM LINE, IT'S ALL IN . . .
THE GREAT BUSINESS QUOTATIONS

THE GREAT

BUSINESS

QUOTATIONS

Compiled by

ROLF B. WHITE

A Dell Book

Published by
Dell Publishing Co., Inc.
1 Dag Hammarskjold Plaza
New York, New York 10017

Dell ® TM 681510, Dell Publishing Co., Inc.

ISBN: 0-440-13098-0

Reprinted by arrangement with Lyle Stuart Inc.

Printed in the United States of America

September 1987

10 9 8 7 6 5 4 3 2 1

PREFACE

This book is a miscellany of quotations and quips, sayings and satire, wisecracks and witticisms, proverbs and precepts, dictums and doggerel, epigrams and aphorisms, truisms and adages, axioms and maxims, poems and rhymes, limericks and graffiti as an anthology.

That's what it is, but forget it!

Treat it as an interesting Business Digest and you have a unique collection of the best that has been said or written on this subject from all over the world since records began. This will benefit all those connected with business and is a useful source of information to repeat in letters, speeches and everyday conversation. With this book you can impress others with your wit and wisdom in this world so dominated by profit motivation.

More than that, it is a fund of hints and useful tips, memory joggers and general guidance to help you through the myriad complications of business. If it fails sometimes to show you how to deal with various situations, at least you can learn from the many examples of how not to do it.

This is a book for inspiration and amusement at odd moments. Keep it where you do most of your creative thinking: this might be at work, by your bedside or in the smallest room of the house, but perhaps we ought not to recommend in your car, where so many people get their brilliant ideas.

One fact that is absolutely certain is that the principles of trading have not changed since commerce began with bartering between primitive human beings. It may still be somewhat barbaric at times but it remains simply a matter of dealing; dealing with money and people. As there are plenty of books on various commercial techniques, an attempt has been made to cover the emotional and more personal aspects of business and how it affects the individual.

The offerings of the many management gurus with their new systems and buzzword phraseology tend to confuse proceedings even more. Few of these wonderful theories have been included, because we doubt the ability of these fashionable trends to survive and become standard equipment. Their shortlived popularity is the result of the continuous search for short answers to problems and the need to keep up to date and improve at all costs.

Every time you turn to *The Great Business Quotations,* we hope that you will find something humorous and that you learn or will be reminded of an idea for your own benefit. If this does not happen, we must assume that you are either perfect or a perfect fool. As you are reading this book, neither is likely!

Should you be wondering why this need not be regarded as just a reference book, if you turn to the chapters entitled Books on page 302 and Perseverance on page 350, you may be persuaded to read further.

Like most things in life, some parts of this book are better than others. Old-fashioned quotations are here because often the cleverest ideas were originally recorded back in the old days, and these more literary inclusions tend to be near the end of each chapter. If you find the going a trifle heavy, you can skip these sections, but, although the language may be somewhat pedantic, their meaning still holds good today.

The difference between this work and most other business books is that the editor does not agree with everything in it. In fact, there is violent disagreement with the sentiments expressed in many of the items. It is up to the readers to interpret their own view, remembering always that an opposite opinion can provoke the correct response.

One of the advantages that go with the compilation of a collection like this is that the blame for what is said rests squarely with the author of each entry and not with the editor. This applies in particular to the anti-feminism and the male/female ratio of the subject matter. Any objections can be countered with indisputable fact that the vast majority of recorded sayings were expressed by men and that, until recently, "man" was a popular collective word for the human race as a whole. That's our excuse and we're sticking to it!

It has taken many years to accumulate these prime remarks about Business and, before I decided to produce this collection in book form, the source of quotations was not always recorded. The result is that a very small number can only be acknowledged as anonymous. My apologies to those who may be offended by non-recognition and to anyone whom I was unable to contact for permission to use their material. Omissions will be rectified in subsequent editions.

I accept that it would be wrong to consider the nonsense rhymes at the start of each chapter as some of the world's greatest comments. These have been included to add some originality and perhaps some humor to a subject that can be taken too seriously. If you think you could have done better, it is only fair to point out that you probably didn't!

If you appreciate making use of this book half as much as I have enjoyed the compilation, you will realize that I have had twice the fun.

R. B. W.

CONTENTS

THE GREAT
BUSINESS
QUOTATIONS

1 · BACKGROUND

Work

The ones who wash
The most
Are those who work
The least

Work is much more fun than fun. NOEL COWARD

If you don't want to work, you have to work to earn enough money so that you won't have to work.
OGDEN NASH

We forget what gives money its value—that someone exchanged work for it. NEAL O'HARA

Unless you are willing to drench yourself in your work beyond the capacity of the average man, you are just not cut out for positions at the top. J. C. PENNEY

No one ever got very far by working a 40-hour week. Most of the notable people I know are trying to manage a 40-hour day. CHANNING POLLOCK

If hard work is the key to success, most people would rather pick the lock. CLAUDE McDONALD

Better to wear out than rust out.
BISHOP RICHARD CUMBERLAND

Work is love made visible. KAHLIL GIBRAN

Hard work is often an accumulation of the easy things you didn't do when you should have. ANON

The harder you work, the luckier you get.
GARY PLAYER

Work is the greatest thing in the world, so we should always save some of it for tomorrow.
DON HEROLD

Luck is what you have left over after you give 100%.
LANGSTON COLEMAN

I believe the twenty-four hour day has come to stay.
MAX BEERBOHM

I haven't got time to be tired.
EMPEROR WILHELM I

As a rule, from what I've observed, the American captain of industry doesn't do anything out of business hours. When he has put the cat out and locked up the office for the night, he just relapses into a state of coma from which he emerges only to start being a captain of industry again. PELHAM GRENVILLE WODEHOUSE

Hard work describes the amount more often than the difficulty. ANON

When a man tells you that he got rich through hard work, ask him whose?
DONALD ROBERT PERRY MARQUIS

I do most of my work sitting down; that's where I shine. ROBERT BENCHLEY

Work is the curse of the drinking class.
OSCAR WILDE

Work expands to fill the time available for its completion. C. NORTHCOTE PARKINSON

He who considers his work beneath him will be above doing it well. ALEXANDER CHASE

My father taught me to work, but not to love it. I never did like to work, and I don't deny it. I'd rather read, tell stories, crack jokes, talk, laugh—anything but work. ABRAHAM LINCOLN

All work and no play makes Jack a dull boy—and Jill a wealthy widow. EVAN ESAR

Anyone can do any amount of work provided it isn't the work he is supposed to be doing at the moment.
ROBERT BENCHLEY

Robinson Crusoe started the 40-hour week. He had all the work done by Friday. LEOPOLD FECHTNER

If it were not for the demands made upon me by my business, I would provide living proof that a man can live quite happily for decades without ever doing any work.　　　　　　　　　　　J. PAUL GETTY

I'm against retiring. The thing that keeps a man alive is having something to do. Sitting in a rocker never appealed to me. Golf or fishing isn't as much fun as working.　　　　COLONEL HARLAN SANDERS

When a man has had to work so hard to get money, why should he impose on himself the further hardship of trying to save it.　　　　　　　DON HEROLD

Times have changed. Forty years ago people worked 12 hours a day, and it was called economic slavery. Now they work 14 hours a day and it's called moonlighting.　　　　　　　ROBERT ORBEN

What most persons consider as virtue after the age of 40 is simply a loss of energy.
　　　　　　　　　　　FRANCOIS VOLTAIRE

Work is accomplished by those employees who have not yet reached their level of incompetence.
　　LAURENCE J. PETER and RAYMOND HULL

The rise in the total of those employed is governed by Parkinson's Law, and would be much the same whether the volume of work were to increase, diminish or even disappear.
　　　　　　　C. NORTHCOTE PARKINSON

If you work like a horse all you want to do afterwards is hit the hay.　　　　　　　　　ANON

"Don't you ever feel like work?" a lazy boy was asked, and he answered, "Yes, sir, but I do without."
                              SALVADOR de MADARIAGA

Do not tell me how hard you work, Tell me how much you get done.   JAMES J. LING

The best investment a young man starting out in business could possibly make is to give all his time, all his energies to work, just plain, hard work.
                              CHARLES M. SCHWAB

We often wondered when Henry Ford slept because he was putting in long hours working and when he went home at nights he was always experimenting or reading.   CHARLES T. BUSH

The continuing increases in purchasing power and leisure time that have made many Americans the envy of working people everywhere have not come from working ever harder—but from working ever smarter.
                              WILLIAM C. FREUND

Most people like hard work. Particularly when they are paying for it.   FRANKLIN P. JONES

Work is of two kinds: first, altering the position of matter at or near the earth's surface relatively to other matter; second, telling other people to do so. The first kind is unpleasant and ill-paid; the second is pleasant and highly-paid.   BERTRAND RUSSELL

Work is not the curse, but drudgery is.
                              HENRY WARD BEECHER

More men are killed by overwork than the importance of this world justifies.   RUDYARD KIPLING

I believe in work, hard work and long hours of work. Men do not break down from overwork, but from worry and dissipation.   CHARLES E. HUGHES

Labor is the capital of our working men.
GROVER CLEVELAND

If you have great talents, industry will prove them: if moderate abilities, industry will supply their deficiencies. Nothing is denied to well-directed labor; nothing is ever to be attained without it.
SIR JOSHUA REYNOLDS

The very last thing the ordinary industrial worker wants is to have to think about his work.
GEORGE BERNARD SHAW

Industry need not wish, and he that lives upon hopes will die fasting. There are no gains without pains. He that hath a trade hath an estate, and he that hath a calling hath an office of profit and honor; but then the trade must be worked at, and the calling followed, or neither the estate nor the office will enable us to pay our taxes. If we are industrious, we shall never starve; for, at the workingman's house hunger looks in, but dares not enter. Nor will the bailiff or the constable enter, for industry pays debts, while idleness and neglect increase them.   BENJAMIN FRANKLIN

Corporations

As a sort of explanation
From the days of Botticelli,
Today's word "corporation"
Was used to mean "pot belly."

Corporation. An ingenious device for obtaining individual profit without individual responsibility.
AMBROSE BIERCE

Without great, powerful organizations, Americans cannot hope to compete successfully with the world.
HENRY FRICK

Corporations have neither bodies to be kicked nor souls to be damned. **ANDREW JACKSON**

A corporation cannot blush. **HOWELL WALSH**

Humans must breathe, but corporations must make money. **ALICE EMBREE**

Breakages, Limited, the biggest industrial corporation in the country. **GEORGE BERNARD SHAW**

God is always on the side of the big battalions.
MARSHAL TURENNE

It is truly enough said that a corporation has no conscience; but a corporation of conscientious men is a corporation without a conscience.
HENRY DAVID THOREAU

Every great institution is the lengthened shadow of a single man.   THOMAS EDISON

There was a time when corporations played a minor part in our business affairs, but now they play the chief part, and most men are the servants of corporations.
THOMAS WOODROW WILSON

I resent large corporations. They flatter personalities.
BOB NEWHART

The modern corporation is a political institution; its purpose is the creation of legitimate power in the industrial sphere.   PETER F. DRUCKER

Concentration of economic power in all-embracing corporations represents a kind of private government which is a power unto itself—a regimentation of other people's money and other people's lives.
FRANKLIN DELANO ROOSEVELT

A criminal is a person with predatory instincts who has not sufficient capital to form a corporation.
HOWARD SCOTT

The myth that holds that the great corporation is a puppet of the market, the powerless servant of the consumer, is in fact, one of the services by which its power is perpetuated.
JOHN KENNETH GALBRAITH

A holding company is the people you give your money to while you're being searched.   WILL ROGERS

Today the large organization is lord and master, and most of its employees have been desensitized much as were the medieval peasants who never knew they were serfs.
RALPH NADER

Corporations, which should be the carefully restrained creatures of the law and the servants of the people, are fast becoming the people's masters.
GROVER CLEVELAND

It is idle to suppose that corporations will not be brought more and more under public control.
ALFRED NORTH WHITEHEAD

Corporations cannot commit treason, nor be outlawed, nor excommunicate, for they have no souls.
SIR EDWARD COKE

The ancient Hebrews had a goat on which all the sins were placed, so the holding company idea isn't new.
ANON

We all make the mistake of thinking about institutions, such as business, and government, as ends in themselves.
ADLAI STEVENSON

Big business is basic to the very life of this country; and yet many—perhaps most—Americans have a deep-seated fear and an emotional repugnance to it. Here is a monumental contradiction.
DAVID LILIENTHAL

The growth of a large business is merely a survival of the fittest.
JOHN D. ROCKEFELLER

Concentration of wealth and power has been built upon other people's money, other people's business, other people's labor. Under this concentration, independent business was allowed to exist only on sufferance. It has been a menace to . . . American democracy. FRANKLIN DELANO ROOSEVELT

Free enterprise ended in the United States a good many years ago. Dig oil, dig steel, dig agriculture, avoid the open marketplace. Big corporations fix prices among themselves and drive out the small entrepreneur. In their conglomerate forms, the huge corporations have begun to challenge the legitimacy of the State. GORE VIDAL

Corporate bodies are more corrupt and profligate than individuals, because they have more power to do mischief, and we are less amenable to disgrace and punishment. WILLIAM HAZLITT

The large corporations, though still primarily a private economic entity, has such vast social impact (where it locates, whom it hires, what technology it pursues) that it has become a public trust with a communal constituency. STEPHEN B. SHEPPARD

We demand that big business give people a square deal; in return we must insist that when anyone engaged in big business honestly endeavors to do right, he shall himself be given a square deal.
THEODORE ROOSEVELT

Every monopoly and all exclusive privileges are granted at the expense of the public, which ought to receive a fair equivalent. ANDREW JACKSON

Corporations, especially the large and complex ones with which we have to live, now appear to possess some of the qualities of nation states including, perhaps, an alarming capacity to insulate their members from the moral consequences of their actions.

PAUL EDDY, ELAINE POTTER and BRUCE PAGE

A corporation is an artificial being, invisible, intangible, and existing only in the contemplation of the law. Being the mere creature of the law, it possesses only those properties which the charter of its creation confers on it, either expressly or as incidental to its very existence. There are such as are supposed best calculated to effect the object for which it was created. Among the most important are immortality, and, if the expression be allowed, individuality; properties by which a perpetual succession of many persons are considered the same and may act as a single individual.

JOHN MARSHALL

In all likelihood we must brace ourselves for the consequences of . . . "wars of redistribution" or of "pre-emptive seizure," the rise of social tensions in the industrialized nations over the division of an ever more slow-growing or even diminishing product, and the prospect of a far more coercive exercise of national power as the means by which we will attempt to bring these disruptive processes under control.

ROBERT HEILBRONER

Entrepreneurs

One of the sums
Known by scholars;
That the sense comes
Before the dollars.

The American system of rugged individualism.
                    HERBERT CLARK HOOPER

The greatest works are done by the ones. The hundreds do not often do much—the companies never; it is the units—the single individuals, that are the power and the might. Individual effort is, after all, the grand thing.   CHARLES HADDON SPURGEON

Small is beautiful.
                    PROFESSOR E. F. SCHUMACHER

The man who opened the first restaurant must have been a person of extraordinary genius.
                    ANTHELM BRILLAT-SAVARIN

The fact that 25% of businesses fail in the first year and less than 20% are still in business 10 years later is because of lack of proper planning.
                    JESSE WERNER

I'm a self-made man, but I think if I had it to do over again, I'd call in someone else.   ROLAND YOUNG

Never have partners.
HOWARD HUGHES'S FATHER

When you paddle your own canoe, you can do the steering.
ANON

Chop your own wood and it will warm you twice.
PROVERB

I'm not saying I carry a lot of insurance, but when I go so does the company!
ANON

He was a self-made man who owed his lack of success to nobody.
JOSEPH HELLER

A man isn't a man until he has to meet a payroll.
IVAN SHAFFER

He found it inconvenient to be poor.
WILLIAM COWPER

The trouble with some self-made men is that they insist on giving everybody else the recipe.
MAURICE SEITTER

If you can build a business up big enough, it's respectable.
WILL ROGERS

Most self-made men are smart enough to employ college professors to train their sons.
ANON

Launching your own business is like writing your own personal declaration of independence from the corporate beehive, where you sell bits of your life in forty-hour (or longer) chunks in return for your paycheck.

Going into business for yourself, becoming an entrepreneur is the modern-day equivalent of pioneering on the old frontier.　　　PAULA NELSON

No bird soars too high, if he soars with his own wings.
　　　　　WILLIAM BLAKE

After the first years of pioneering, the employer wants security just as much as the employee.
　　　　　HERMAN W. STEINKRAUS

No one can go on being a rebel too long without turning into an autocrat.　　　LAURENCE DURRELL

Opportunity is luck's entrepreneur.　　　　ANON

The way to love anything is to realize that it might be lost.　　　GILBERT KEITH CHESTERTON

A man is likely to mind his own business when it is worth minding.　　　　ERIC HOFFER

If you observe people long enough, you'll realize that the self-made ones have an abundance of working parts.　　　　BOB TALBERT

If I would be a young man again and had to decide how to make my living, I would not try to become a scientist or a scholar or teacher. I would rather choose to be a plumber or a peddler, in the hope to find that modest degree of independence still available under present circumstances.　　　ALBERT EINSTEIN

Of course everybody likes and respects self-made men. It is a great deal better to be made in that way than not to be made at all.

OLIVER WENDELL HOLMES

I've always acted alone. Americans admire that enormously. Americans admire the cowboy leading the caravan, alone astride his horse, the cowboy entering a village or city alone on his horse.

HENRY KISSINGER

A man becomes a conservative at that moment in his life when he suddenly realizes he has something to conserve.

ERIC JULBER

People who work for themselves often discover what poor employers they are.

ANON

It is a paradox of the acquisitive society in which we now live, that although private morals are regulated by law, the entrepreneur is allowed considerable freedom to use and abuse the public in order to make money.

GORE VIDAL

The first of earthly blessings, independence.

EDWARD GIBBON

Self-made men are most always apt to be a little too proud of the job.

JOSH BILLINGS

The very people who have done the breaking through are themselves often the first to try to put a scab on their achievement.

IGOR STRAVINSKY

Self-made men are very apt to usurp the prerogative of the Almighty and overwork themselves.
EDGAR WILSON NYE

Keep thy shop, and thy shop will keep thee.
ENGLISH PROVERB

First secure an independent income, then practice virtue.
GREEK PROVERB

The highest manifestation of life consists in this: that a being governs its own actions. A thing which is always subject to the direction of another is somewhat of a dead thing.
ST. THOMAS AQUINAS

Commerce

When someone gets
Something for nothing,
Someone else gets
Nothing for something.

Commerce is the art of exploiting the need or desire someone has for something.
EDMOND and JULES de GONCOURT

Every dollar spent for missions has added hundreds to the commerce of the world.
N. G. CLARK

Someone has suggested that America's greatest gifts to civilization are three: cornflakes, Kleenex and credit.

LOUIS T. BENEZET

The purpose of industry is the conquest of nature in the service of man.   R. H. TAWNEY

When a merchant speaks of sheep he means the hide.

SWISS PROVERB

America is a company town, and the company is General Motors.   ANON

The American industrial machine is a unit, just like an automobile. It is made of big parts and little parts, each of which does its own particular job and all of which are intricately fitted together. You may think that it would be fun to sort them all out into neat piles according to size to please the statisticians. You could even pass a law declaring that all the parts must be the same size; and the theorists, no doubt, would be delighted. But when you get through, your automobile won't run—and neither will American industry.

BENJAMIN FAIRLESS

The musician, the painter, the pet, are, in a larger sense, no greater artists than the man of commerce.

W. S. MAVERICK

The McDonald's fast food chain uses up more beef per year than any one of most of the countries in Africa.

L. M. BOYD

No nation was ever ruined by trade.
                    BENJAMIN FRANKLIN

In matters of commerce the fault of the Dutch
Is offering too little and asking too much.
The French are with equal advantage content,
So we clap on Dutch bottoms just twenty percent.
                    GEORGE CANNING

The commerce of the world is conducted by the strong, and usually it operates against the weak.
                    HENRY WARD BEECHER

You recognize but one rule of commerce; that is to allow free passage and freedom of action to all buyers and sellers whoever they may be.
                    FRANCOIS QUESNAY

With the supermarket as our temple and the singing commercial as our litany, are we likely to fire the world with an irresistable vision of America's exalted purpose and inspiring way of life?
                    ADLAI STEVENSON

Whoever controls the volume of money in any country is absolute master of all industry and commerce.
                    ABRAHAM LINCOLN

Commerce links all mankind in one common brotherhood of mutual dependence and interests.
                    JAMES A. GARFIELD

The commercial man almost has to be a romanticist because he so often deals with unrealities.
                    GILBERT KEITH CHESTERTON

Merchants have no country. The mere spot they stand on does not constitute so strong an attachment as that from which they draw their gains.
THOMAS JEFFERSON

No matter who reigns, the merchant reigns.
HENRY WARD BEECHER

Industry is the root of all ugliness. OSCAR WILDE

In transactions of trade it is not to be supposed that, as in gaming, what one party gains the other must necessarily lose. The gain to each may be equal. If A. has more corn than he can consume, but wants cattle; and B. has more cattle, but wants corn; exchange is gain to each; thereby the common stock of comforts in life is increased. BENJAMIN FRANKLIN

The social and economic welfare of the country is inseparably connected with the welfare of its industries.
OTTO KAHN

Piracy, n: commerce without its folly-swaddles—just as God made it. AMBROSE BIERCE

A merchant's happiness hangs upon chance, winds and waves. EDMUND FULLER

What recommends commerce to me is its enterprise and bravery. It does not clasp its hands and pray to Jupiter. HENRY DAVID THOREAU

We rail at trade, but the historian of the world will see that it was the principle of liberty; that it settled

33

America, and destroyed feudalism, and made peace and keeps peace, that it will abolish slavery.
RALPH WALDO EMERSON

Commerce, however we may please ourselves with the contrary opinion, is one of the daughters of fortune, inconstant and deceitful as her mother.
SAMUEL JOHNSON

Commerce is, in its very essence, satanic. Commerce is return of the loan, a loan in which there is the understanding; give me more than I give you.
CHARLES BAUDELAIRE

The selfish spirit of commerce knows no country, and feels no passion or principles but that of gain.
THOMAS JEFFERSON

America is not a mere body of traders; it is a body of free men. Our greatness built upon our freedom—is moral, not material. We have a great ardor for gain; but we have a deep passion for the rights of man.
THOMAS WOODROW WILSON

Perfect freedom is as necessary to the health and vigor of commerce, as it is to the health and vigor of citizenship.
PATRICK HENRY

Commerce is the great civilizer. We exchange ideas when we exchange fabrics.
ROBERT GREEN INGERSOLL

Commerce defies every wind, outrides every tempest and invades every zone.
GEORGE BANCROFT

The crossroads of trade are the meeting place of ideas, the attrition ground of rival custom and beliefs; diversities beget conflict, comparison, thought; superstitions cancel one another, and reason begins.

WILL DURANT

The prosperity of a people is proportionate to the number of hands and minds usefully employed. To the community, sedition is a fever, corruption is a gangrene, and idleness is an atrophy. Whatever body or society wastes more than it acquires must gradually decay; and every being that continues to be fed, and ceases to labor, takes away something from the public stock.

SAMUEL JOHNSON

Commerce is of trivial import; love, faith, truth of character, the aspiration of man, these are sacred.

RALPH WALDO EMERSON

Reputation

Reputation's an impression
Other's get with lines uncrossed;
It's a personal possession
Rarely noticed till it's lost.

After I am dead I would rather have men ask why Cato has no monument than why he had one.

CATO the ELDER

Your reputation is what others are not thinking about you.　　　　　　　　　　　　　TOM MASSON

Few people think more than two or three times a year; I have made an international reputation for myself by thinking once or twice a week.
　　　　　　　　　　　GEORGE BERNARD SHAW

Reputation is a bubble which bursts when a man tries to blow it up for himself.　　EMMA CARLETON

There are few persons of greater worth than their reputation; but how many are there whose worth is far short of their reputation!
　　　　　　　　　　　LESZINSKI STANISLAUS

It is easier to add to a great reputation than to get it.
　　　　　　　　　　　　PUBLIUS SYRUS

Fame is chiefly a matter of dying at the right moment.
　　　　　　　　　　　　　　　ANON

A sign of celebrity is often that his name is worth more than his services.　　DANIEL J. BOORSTIN

How many people live on the reputation of the reputation they might have made?
　　　　　　　　　　OLIVER WENDELL HOLMES

Who has once the fame to be an early riser may sleep till noon.　　　　　　　　　JAMES HOWELL

Now when I bore people at a party, they think it's their fault.　　　　　　　　HENRY KISSINGER

The only time you realize you have a reputation is when you're not living up to it.   JOSE ITURBI

It is better to be famous than notorious, but better to be notorious than obscure.

JAMES K. FEIBLEMAN

A large reputation often depends on a small geographical sphere of influence.   BERTRAM TROY

A celebrity is one who is known to many persons he is glad he doesn't know. HENRY LOUIS MENCKEN

Whatever reputation I have is due to the fact that I never open my mouth unless I have something to say.

GEORGE BERNARD SHAW

It is one of the pleasant ironies of history, and cause of hope for all of us, that it is possible for a man to achieve great reputation and even enduring fame by doing something just a little worse than anyone else.

EDWARD McCOURT

If fame is to come only after death, I am in no hurry for it.   MARTIAL

It is difficult to make a reputation, but it is even more difficult to mar a reputation once properly made—so faithful is the public.   ARNOLD BENNETT

Fame: the advantage of being known to those who do not know us.   NICHOLAS CHAMFORT

A bull does not enjoy fame in two herds.

RHODESIAN PROVERB

Respectability: The offspring of a liaison between a bald head and a bank accountant.

AMBROSE BIERCE

Character is what God and the angels know of us; reputation is what men and women think of us.

HORACE MANN

Money is like the reputation for ability—more easily made than kept. **SAMUEL BUTLER**

After a fellow gets famous, it doesn't take long for someone to bob up that used to sit by him at school.

FRANK McKINNEY HUBBARD

I am better than my reputation.

FREIDRICH von SCHILLER

Good and bad men are each less so than they seem.

SAMUEL TAYLOR COLERIDGE

To be somebody you must last. **RUTH GORDON**

When one has never heard a man's name in the course of one's life, it speaks volumes for him; he must be quite respectable. **OSCAR WILDE**

Some men's reputation seems like seed-wheat, which thrives best when brought from a distance.

ARCHBISHOP RICHARD WHATELEY

The most serviceable of all assets is reputation . . . it works for you automatically . . . 24 hours a day. Unlike money, reputation cannot be bequeathed. It is always personal. It must be acquired. Brains alone, however brilliant, cannot win it.   OTTO KAHN

Respectability is the dickey on the bosom of civilization.   ELBERT HUBBARD

These are people who think that everything one does with a serious face is sensible.
GEORG CHRISTOPH LICHTENBERG

One may be better than his reputation, but never better than his principles.
NICHOLAS VALENTIN de LATENA

A reputation for good judgment, for fair dealing, for truth, and for rectitude, is itself a fortune.
HENRY WARD BEECHER

No man, however great, is known to everybody and no man, however solitary, is known to nobody.
THOMAS MOORE

Fame lies in being able to do what I like . . . The Academie Française and the renown of being a great writer—this great crown, so to speak, permits me to wear, in season or out of season and wherever I choose, my old gray felt hat. If I wanted, I could go to the opera in slippers.   ANATOLE FRANCE

Talk to every woman as if you loved her, and to every man as if he bored you, and at the end of your first season you will have the reputation of possessing the most perfect social tact.   OSCAR WILDE

Conspicuous consumption of valuable goods is a means of reputability to the gentleman of leisure.
THORSTEIN VEBLEN

There are people who are followed all through their lives by a beggar to whom they have given nothing.
KARL KRAUS

Have regard for your name, since it will remain for you longer than a great store of gold. *Ecclesiasticus*

Reputation has one advantage: it allows us to have confidence in ourselves and to declare our thoughts frankly.   ALFRED de VIGNY

There are two modes of establishing our reputation: to be praised by honest men, and to be abused by rogues. —It is best, however, to secure the former, because, it will invariably be accompanied by the latter.
CHARLES CALEB COLTON

Fame is a vapor; popularity an accident; the only earthly certainty is oblivion.   MARK TWAIN

Ethics

When you're considering any sort of tempta-
*   tion,*
You should think hard about your reputation.
Then make up your mind with no hesitation
To turn it down firmly without reservation.
If another good chance is your expectation,
You can try it again at the next presentation.

The quality of moral behavior varies in inverse ratio to the number of human beings involved.

> ALDOUS LEONARD HUXLEY

There is no admission charge to the straight and narrow path.

> ANON

It is not best that we use our morals week days; it gets them out of repair for Sundays.   MARK TWAIN

The truth is, hardly any of us have ethical energy enough for more than one really inflexible point of honor.   GEORGE BERNARD SHAW

Good resolutions are simply checks that men draw on a bank where they have no account.

> OSCAR WILDE

Thou canst not serve cod and salmon.

> ADA LEVERSON

Without doubt half the ethical rules they din into our ears are designed to keep us at work.
LLEWELLYN POWYS

Men of business must not break their word twice.
THOMAS FULLER

Always do right. This will surprise some people and astonish the rest.　　MARK TWAIN

It makes a great difference whether a person is unwilling to sin, or does not know how.
LUCIUS ANNAEUS SENECA

Gamesmanship or The Art of Winning Games Without Actually Cheating.　　STEPHEN POTTER

The best way to keep your word is not to give it.
NAPOLEON BONAPARTE

Most people are good only so long as they believe others to be so.　　FRIEDRICH HEBBEL

The first step in the evolution of ethics is a sense of solidarity with other human beings.
ALBERT SCHWEITZER

The only way to get rid of a temptation is to yield to it. Resist it, and your soul grows sick with longing for the things it has forbidden to itself.　　OSCAR WILDE

Faith makes many of the mountains which it has to remove.　　DEAN WILLIAM RALPH INGE

The strength of a man's virtue should not be measured by his special exertions, but by his habitual acts.

BLAISE PASCAL

Be good and you will be lonesome. MARK TWAIN

Would that the simple maxim, that honesty is the best policy, might be laid to heart; that a sense of the true aim of life might elevate the tone of politics and trade till public and private honor become identical.

MARGARET FULLER

Never esteem anything as of advantage to thee that shall make thee break thy word or lose thy self-respect. MARCUS AURELIUS

If your morals make you dreary, depend on it they are wrong. ROBERT LOUIS STEVENSON

Where wealth and freedom reign, contentment fails,
And honour sinks where commerce long prevails.

OLIVER GOLDSMITH

Technology

The principle charm
Of a new technology
Is to cure the harm
Of the old technology.

Technology or perish. JOHN R. PIERCE

In guessing the direction of technology it is wise to ask who is in the best position to profit most.

BEN H. BAGDIKIAN

If automation keeps up, man will atrophy all his limbs but the push-button finger.

FRANK LLOYD WRIGHT

There are three ways of courting ruin—women, gambling and calling in technicians.

GEORGE POMPIDOU

The genius of modern technology lies in making things to last fifty years and making them obsolete in three.

ANON

Just the other day I listened to a young fellow sing a very passionate song about how technology is killing us and all that. But before he started, he bent down and plugged his electric guitar into the wall socket.

PAUL GOODMAN

If people really liked to work, we'd still be plowing the ground with sticks and transporting goods on our backs. WILLIAM FEATHER

Before technology, things didn't work but people did. Nowadays, neither! ANON

The robot is going to lose. Not by much. But when the final score is tallied, flesh and blood is going to beat the damn monster. ADAM SMITH

If the human race wants to go to hell in a basket, technology can help it get there by jet. It won't change the desire or the direction, but it can greatly speed the passage. CHARLES M. ALLEN

Technology—the knack of so arranging the world that we don't have to experience it. MAX FRISCH

The science of today is the technology of tomorrow. EDWARD TELLER

Technology made large populations possible; large populations now make technology indispensable. JOSEPH WOOD KRUTCH

Our great-grandfathers were certainly not horrified by automation. After all, they did provide the ribbed washboard, the crossbuck saw, the spinning wheel, and other labor-saving devices in order to enable great-grandma to do the work of three hired girls. ANON

The danger of the past was that men became slaves. The danger of the future is that men may become robots. ERICH FROMM

In the space age, man will be able to go around the world in two hours—one hour for flying and the other to get to the airport. NEIL McELROY

Technological progress has merely provided us with more efficient means for going backwards. ALDOUS LEONARD HUXLEY

Technocracy is just communism with spats. JOHN C. STEVENS

These men of the technostructure are the new and universal priesthood. Their religion is business success; their test of virtue is growth and profit. Their bible is the computer printout; their communion bench is the committee room. The sales force carries their message to the world, and a message is what it is often called.   JOHN KENNETH GALBRAITH

Any sufficiently advanced technology is indistinguishable from magic.   ARTHUR C. CLARKE

Electronic calculators can solve problems which the man who made them cannot solve; but no government-subsidized commission of engineers and physicists could create a worm.

JOSEPH WOOD KRUTCH

A world technology means either a world government or world suicide.   MAX LERNER

It is a distinction between science and technology that technology must always be useful, whereas science need not be.   SIR PATRICK LINSTEAD

Established technology tends to persist in the fact of new technology.   GERRIT A. BLAAUW

The characteristic of the exploding technological society is that changes sooner or later must take place in a fraction of the time necessary even to assess the situation.   JOHN WILKINSON

Progress is dangerous because it is based on perfect technology.   JEAN RENOIR

One consequence of postwar technology has been the acceleration of change in our society, so that we seem to produce a new generation about every five years.

ROSS MACDONALD

Where there is the necessary technical skill to move mountains, there is no need for the faith that moves mountains.

ERIC HOFFER

We cannot get grace from gadgets. In the bakelite house of the future, the dishes may not break, but the heart can. Even a man with ten shower baths may find life flat, stale and unprofitable.

JOHN BOYNTON PRIESTLEY

People are so overwhelmed with the prestige of their instruments that they consider their personal judgment of hardly any account.

PERCY WYNDHAM LEWIS

The high stage of world industrial development in capitalistic production finds expression in the extraordinary technical development and destructiveness of the instruments of war.

ROSA LUXEMBURG

However far modern science and technics have fallen short of their inherent possibilities, they have taught mankind at least one lesson: nothing is impossible.

LEWIS MUMFORD

Only science can hope to keep technology in some sort of moral order.

EDGAR FRIEDENBERG

For tribal man space was the uncontrollable mystery. For technological man it is time that occupies the same role.   MARSHALL MCLUHAN

Technology means the systematic application of scientific or other organized knowledge to practical tasks.   JOHN KENNETH GALBRAITH

It is crucial vision alone which can mitigate the unimpeded operation of the automatic.   MARSHALL MCLUHAN

It was naïve of the 19th century optimists to expect paradise from technology—and it is equally naïve of the 20th century pessimists to make technology the scapegoat for such old shortcomings as man's blindness, cruelty, immaturity, greed and sinful pride.   PETER F. DRUCKER

We live as we live because of the decisions, however explicit or however undefined, that were taken yesterday about which technological developments to encourage to satisfy man's enduring urge for an ever better life.   LORD ZUCKERMAN

2 · BUSINESS

Good Business

There is no minimum
  At the start
And there's no maximum
  At the end.

Boldness in business is the first, second, and third thing.　EDMUND FULLER

A man can never leave his business. He ought to think of it by day and dream of it by night.
　　　　　　　　HENRY FORD

To be successful in business, be daring, be first, be different.　WILLIAM MARCHANT

One of the rarest phenomena is a really pessimistic businessman.　MIRIAM BEARD

The two leading recipes for success are building a better mousetrap and finding a bigger loophole.
　　　　　　　　EDGAR A. SHOAFF

Put all good eggs in one basket and then watch that basket.   ANDREW CARNEGIE

Live within your income. Always have something saved at the end of the year. Let your imports be more than your exports, and you'll never go far wrong.
          SAMUEL JOHNSON

What's good for the country is good for General Motors and vice versa.   CHARLES ERWIN WILSON

The art of winning in business is in working hard—not taking things too seriously.   ELBERT HUBBARD

Solvency is entirely a matter of temperament and not of income.   LOGAN PEARSALL SMITH

Business is never so healthy as when, like a chicken, it must do a certain amount of scratching for what it gets.   HENRY FORD

Business is more exciting than any game.
          LORD BEAVERBROOK

Why is it that businessmen manage their affairs so much more successfully than politicians? Because businessmen have only businessmen to compete with.
          ANON

If America is to be civilized, it must be done (at least for the present) by the business class.
          ALFRED NORTH WHITEHEAD

The submachine gun is the greatest aid to bigger and better business the criminal has discovered in this generation. *Collier's Magazine*

Never refuse a good offer. PROVERB

What we want is a story that starts with an earthquake and works its way up to a climax.
SAMUEL GOLDWYN

Hitch your wagon to a star; keep your nose to the grindstone; put your shoulder to the wheel; keep an ear to the ground; and watch the handwriting on the wall. HERBERT V. PROCHNOW

The man who attends strictly to his own business usually has plenty of business to attend to. ANON

What's lost upon the roundabouts we pulls up on the swings! PATRICK REGINALD CHALMERS

In many businesses, today will end at five o'clock. Those bent on success, however, make today last from yesterday right through to tomorrow.
LAWRENCE H. MARTIN

Whenever you see a successful business, someone once made a courageous decision. PETER F. DRUCKER

Had an Optimist, Co-operative, Exchange, Lions, Kiwanis or a Rotary Club flourished in the days of the Exodus with . . . Moses as president, the children of Israel would have reached the promised land in forty days instead of forty years.
STEWART C. McFARLAND

Punctuality is one of the cardinal business virtues: always insist on it in your subordinates.
DONALD ROBERT PERRY MARQUIS

Let a man start out in life to build something better and sell it cheaper than it has been built or sold before; let him have that determination and the money will roll in. **HENRY FORD**

Business must be profitable if it is to continue to succeed, but the glory of business is to make it so successful that it may do things that are great chiefly because they ought to be done. **CHARLES M. SCHWAB**

You've removed most of the road-blocks to success when you've learnt the difference between motion and direction. **BILL COPELAND**

Business only contributes fully to society if it is efficient, successful, profitable and socially responsible.
LORD SIEFF

A great society is a society in which men can serve the needs of others whom they do not know.
F. A. HAYEK

Not because of any extraordinary talents did he succeed, but because he had a capacity on a level for business and not above it. **TACITUS**

If you wish to succeed in life, make perseverance your bosom friend, experience your wise counselor, caution your elder brother, and hope your guardian genius.
JOSEPH ADDISON

There is a sense in which the business men of America represent America, because America has devoted herself time out of mind to the arts and achievements of peace, and business is the organization of the energies of peace. THOMAS WOODROW WILSON

To business that we love, we rise betimes, and go to it with delight. WILLIAM SHAKESPEARE

Talk of nothing but business and despatch the business quickly. ALDUS MANUTIUS

Real success in business is to be found in achievements comparable rather with those of the artist or the scientist, or the inventor or the statesman. And the joys sought in the profession of business must be like their joys and not the mere vulgar satisfaction which is experienced in the acquisition of money, in the exercise of power, or in the frivolous pleasure of mere winning. LOUIS BRANDEIS

Bad Business

Without a doubt
It's bad business
To talk about
Your bad business.

Business without profit is not business any more than a pickle is candy. CHARLES F. ABBOTT

It is not the crook in modern business that we fear, but the honest man who does not know what he is doing.
OWEN D. YOUNG

Expenditure rises to meet income.
C. NORTHCOTE PARKINSON

Things that are bad for business are bad for the people who work for business.   THOMAS E. DEWEY

Monopoly is business at the end of its journey.
HENRY DEMAREST LLOYD

Businessmen get together and complain about bad business over the most expensive dinners.   ANON

Most of the trouble with most people in America who become successful is that they can really and truly get by on bullshit alone. They can survive on it.
SAMMY DAVIS, JR.

If I went managing a store today and one of my clerks told a lie to sell merchandise, I would fire him—or her —on the spot. Not only would it be wrong. It would be poor business.   J. C. PENNEY

Nothing is harder on your laurels than resting on them.   ANON

Nice guys finish last.   LEO DUROCHER

The business of everybody is the business of nobody.
THOMAS MACAULAY

A business that makes nothing but money is a poor kind of business.　　　　　　　　HENRY FORD

Too often the American dream is interrupted by the Japanese alarm clock.　　　　　　　　ANON

The "tired business man" is one whose business is usually not a successful one.
　　　　　　　SENATOR JOSEPH R. GRUNDY

The history of every dead and dying "growth" industry shows a self-declining cycle of bountiful expansion and undetected decay.　　THEODORE LEVITT

The great menace to the life of an industry is industrial self-complacency.　　DAVID SARNOFF

The cosmetics industry is the nastiest business in the world.　　　　　　　ELIZABETH ARDEN

If everybody minded their own business, the world would go round a deal faster than it does.
　　　　　　　　　　LEWIS CARROLL

Half the failures in life arise from pulling in one's horse as he is leaping.
　　　　　　　JULIUS CHARLES HARE and
　　　　　　　AUGUSTUS WILLIAM HARE

You never expected justice from a company, did you? They have neither a soul to lose, nor a body to kick.
　　　　　　　　　　SYDNEY SMITH

In this business, you can't win 'em all.
　　　　　　　　　　JOHNNY ROSELLI

Why always "Not yet?" Do flowers in spring say "Not yet?"   NORMAN DOUGLAS

At some time in the life cycle of virtually every organization, its ability to succeed in spite of itself runs out.   RICHARD H. BRIEN

Forgive us for frantic buying and selling, for advertising the unnecessary and coveting the extravagant, and calling it good business when it is not good for you.   UNITED PRESBYTERIAN CHURCH

A market is a place set apart for men to deceive and get the better of one another.   ANACHARVIS

He that thinks his business below him will always be above his business.   EDMUND FULLER

If small business goes, big business does not have any future except to become the economic arm of a totalitarian state.   P.D. REED

If a business be unprofitable on account of bad management, want of enterprise or out-worn methods, that is not a just reason for reducing the wages of its workers.   POPE PIUS XI

Those who have little but business to attend to, are great talkers. The less men think, the more they talk.   CHARLES de SECONDAT MONTESQUIEU

One must now apologize for any success in business as if it were a violation of the moral law so that today it is worse to prosper than to be a criminal. ISOCRATES

Men of great parts are often unfortunate in the management of public business, because they are apt to go out of the common road by the quickness of their imagination.   JONATHAN SWIFT

There is reason to think the most celebrated philosophers would have been bunglers at business, but the reason is because they despised it.
                    MARQUESS of HALIFAX

When a mass movement begins to attract people who are interested in their individual careers, it is a sign that it has passed its vigorous stage, that it is no longer engaged in molding a new world but in possessing and preserving the present. It ceases then to be a movement and becomes an enterprise.   ERIC HOFFER

Many persons have an idea that one cannot be in business and lead an upright life, whereas the truth is that no one succeeds in business to any great extent, who misleads or misrepresents.   JOHN WANAMAKER

I think that there is nothing, not even crime, more opposed to poetry, to philosophy, ay, to life itself than this incessant business.
                    HENRY DAVID THOREAU

What Is Business?

However they scoff it,
Business is profit;
However they doubt it,
We can't do without it.

Business is other people's money.
DELPHINE de GIRARDIN

Business has only two basic functions—marketing and innovation.
PETER F. DRUCKER

Gross National Product is our Holy Grail.
STEWART UDALL

The nature of business is swindling.
AUGUST BEBEL

The aim of legitimate business is service, for profit, at a risk.
BENJAMIN C. LEEMING

Prosperity is what business creates for politicians to take the credit.
ANON

Nothing links man to man like the frequent passage from hand to hand of cash.
WALTER SICKERT

Running a business these days is like Dudley Moore dancing with Raquel Welch. The overhead is fantastic!
ANON

Business is like oil. It won't mix with anything but business.   J. GRAHAM

The outlook for the businessman is usually brighter than the outlook of the businessman.   ANON

The craft of the merchant is to bring a thing from where it abounds to where it is costly.
RALPH WALDO EMERSON

A railroad is 95 percent men and 5 percent iron.
A. H. SMITH

Business is a combination of war and sport.
ANDRE MAUROIS

There are few ways in which a man can be more innocently employed than in getting money.
SAMUEL JOHNSON

A friendship founded on business is better than a business founded on friendship.
JOHN D. ROCKEFELLER

Formerly when great fortunes were only made in war, war was a business; but now when great fortunes are only made by business, business is war.
CHRISTIAN NESTELL BOVEE

The business of America is business.
CALVIN COOLIDGE

The secret of business is to know something that nobody else knows.   ARISTOTLE ONASSIS

Commercialism is doing well that which should not be done at all. GORE VIDAL

The playthings of our elders are called business. ROBERT WOODRUFF

It's such a cuckoo business. And it's a business you go into because you're egocentric. It's a very embarrassing profession. KATHARINE HEPBURN

The companies that employ four people or less in the U.S. outnumber the companies that employ 100 people or more by 23 to one. L. M. BOYD

The propensity to truck, barter and exchange one thing for another . . . is common to all men, and to be found in no other race of animals. ADAM SMITH

That's the definition of business; something goes through, something else doesn't. Make use of one, forget the other. HENRY BECQUE

In thousands of years there has been no advance in public morals, in philosophy, in religion or in politics, but the advance in business has been the greatest miracle the world has ever known. EDGAR WATSON HOWE

The maxim of the British people is "Business as usual." SIR WINSTON CHURCHILL

There is nothing so useful to man in general, nor so beneficial to particular societies and individuals, as trade. This is that alma mater, at whose plentiful breast all mankind are nourished.

HENRY FIELDING

Money-getters are the benefactors of our race. To them we are indebted for our institutions of learning, and of art, our academies, colleges and churches.

PHINEAS TAYLOR BARNUM

The fact that a business is large, efficient and profitable does not mean it takes advantage of the public.

CHARLES CLORE

Our very business in life is not to get ahead of others, but to get ahead of ourselves.

THOMAS L. MONSON

America can no more survive and grow without big business than it can survive and grow without small business. Every fact of our economic and industrial life proves that the two are interdependent. You cannot strengthen one by weakening the other; and you cannot add to the stature of a dwarf by cutting the leg off a giant.

BENJAMIN FRANKLIN

Business is religion, and religion is business. The man who does not make a business of his religion has a religious life of no force, and the man who does not make a religion of his business has a business of no character.

MALTBIE BABCOCK

After all, what the worker does is buy back from those who finance him, the goods that he himself produces. Pay him a wage that enables him to buy, and you fill your market with ready consumers.

JAMES J. DAVIS

Business is a public trust and must adhere to national standards in the conduct of its affairs.

HARRY S. TRUMAN

Business, more than any other occupation, is a continual dealing with the future: it is a continual calculation, an instinctive exercise in foresight.

HENRY R. LUCE

Business underlies everything in our national life, including our spiritual life. Witness the fact that in the Lord's Prayer, the first petition is for daily bread. No one can worship God or love his neighbor on an empty stomach.   THOMAS WOODROW WILSON

Business may not be the noblest pursuit, but it is true that men are bringing to it some of the qualities which actuate the explorer, scientist, artist; the zest, the open-mindedness, even the disinterestedness, with which the scientific investigator explores some field of pure research.   EARNEST ELMO CALKINS

Business should be like religion and science; it should know neither love nor hate.   SAMUEL BUTLER

The notion that a business is clothed with a public interest and has been devoted to the public use is little more than a fiction intended to beautify what is disagreeable to the sufferers.

OLIVER WENDELL HOLMES

Business is so much lower a thing than learning that a man used to the last cannot easily bring his stomach down to the first.   LORD HALIFAX

Business is really more agreeable than pleasure; it interests the whole mind, the aggregate nature of man more continuously, and more deeply. But it does not look as if it did.   WALTER BAGEHOT

Most of the trades, professions, and ways of living among mankind, take their original either from the love of pleasure, or the fear of want. The former, when it becomes too violent, degenerates into luxury, and the latter into avarice.   JOSEPH ADDISON

People in Business

Making fun of all your bosses
Makes business more complex;
It will add some to your losses,
Like ridiculing sex.

People of the same trade seldom meet together but the conversation ends in a conspiracy against the public or in some diversion to raise prices.   ADAM SMITH

Men always try to keep women out of business so they won't find out how much fun it really is.
                              VIVIEN KELLEMS

A businessman is one who talks golf all morning at the office and business all afternoon on the links. ANON

My father always told me that businessmen were sons of bitches.　　　　　　　　　JOHN F. KENNEDY

People are the principle asset of any company, whether it makes things to sell, sells things made by other people, or supplies intangible services.
　　　　　　　　　J. C. PENNEY

A businessman is a hybrid of a dancer and a calculator.　　　　　　　　　PAUL VALERY

Any survey of what businessmen are reading runs smack into the open secret that most businessmen aren't.　　　　　　　　　MARILYN BENDER

A businessman is aggressive; a businesswoman is pushy. He's good on details; she's fussy. He loses his temper because he's so involved in his job; she's bitchy. He follows through; she doesn't know when to give up. His judgments are her prejudices. He is a man of the world; she's been around. He climbed the ladder of success; she slept her way to the top. He's a stern taskmaster; she's hard to work for.　*Today's Woman*

There are three categories of people in industry—the few who make things happen, the many who watch things happen, and the overwhelming majority who have no idea what happened.　　O. A. BATTISTA

It very seldom happens to a man that his business is his pleasure.　　　　　　　　　SAMUEL JOHNSON

Half the time men think they are talking business, they are wasting time.　　　　　EDGAR WATSON HOWE

The first Rotarian was the first man to call John the Baptist, Jack.   HENRY LOUIS MENCKEN

Women in business are a problem: if you treat them like men they start complaining; if you treat them like women, your wife may find out.   EVAN ESAR

Running a business is no trouble at all as long as it is not yours.   ANON

It is not by any means certain that a man's business is the most important thing he has to do.
ROBERT LOUIS STEVENSON

The more women become rational companions, partners in business and in thought, as well as in affection and amusement, the more highly will men appreciate home.   LYDIA CHILD

My own business always bores me to death; I prefer other people's.   OSCAR WILDE

A man is known by the company he merges.
LEONARD LOUIS LEVENSON

It is very easy to manage your neighbor's business, but our own sometimes bothers us.   JOSH BILLINGS

This is a puzzling world, and Old Harry's got a finger in it.   GEORGE ELIOT

Trade could not be managed by those who manage it if it had much difficulty.   SAMUEL JOHNSON

Regarded as a means, the businessman is tolerable; regarded as an end he is not so satisfactory.

JOHN MAYNARD KEYNES

The business man is the only man who is for ever apologizing for his occupation.

HENRY LOUIS MENCKEN

So long as a man attends to his business the public does not count his drinks. When he fails they notice if he takes even a glass of root beer.

LORNA MAY HARRIS

A small business man is any businessman who cannot afford to have a full-time representative in Washington D.C.

ANON

Business was his pleasure: pleasure was his business:

MARIA EDGEWORTH

My people belong to the old-fashioned English middle class in which a businessman was still permitted to mind his own business.

GILBERT KEITH CHESTERTON

The challenge to think systematically about large, ambiguous questions is inherently daunting and is one that many businessmen—activists by nature—may be reluctant to take up. But if businessmen are to manage events rather than be managed by them, there is no alternative.

W. S. RUKEYSER

A man often thinks he has given up business, when he has only exchanged it for another.

MICHEL de MONTAIGNE

A merchant may, perhaps, be a man of an enlarged mind, but there is nothing in trade connected with an enlarged mind. **SAMUEL JOHNSON**

Men that have much business must have much pardon. **EDMUND FULLER**

That man is but of the lower part of the world who is not brought up to business and affairs.
OWEN FELTHAM

Swept along in the concepts of their business oriented culture, many people berate themselves if they are not as consistent and productive as machines.
GAY GAER LUCE

Most are engaged in business the greater part of their lives, because the soul abhors a vacuum, and they have not discovered any continuous employment for man's nobler faculties. **HENRY DAVID THOREAU**

Freebooter. A conqueror in a small way of business whose annexations lack the sanctifying merit of magnitude. **AMBROSE BIERCE**

The plain fact is that businessmen do not possess the super qualities which, either in laudation or in condemnation, are frequently attributed to them. They have neither the craftiness and greed with which they are charged nor the profundity and farsightedness with which they are credited. **OTTO H. KAHN**

Businessmen tend to grow old early. They are committed to security and stability. They won't rock the boat and won't gamble, denying the future for a near-

sighted present. They forget what made them successful in the first place.   PETER C. GOLDMARK

A man of business may talk of philosophy; a man who
has none may practise it.   ALEXANDER POPE

There are three classes of men—lovers of wisdom, lovers of honor, lovers of gain.   PLATO

The man who makes an appearance in the business
world, the man who creates personal interest, is the
man who gets ahead. Be liked and you will never
want.   ARTHUR MILLER

We are gradually reaching a time, if we have not already reached that period, when the business of the
country is controlled by men who can be named on
the fingers of one hand, because these men control the
money of the nation, and that control is growing at a
rapid rate. There is only a comparatively small part of
it left for them to get, and when they control the
money, they control the banks, they control the manu-
facturing institutions, they control the aviation companies, they control the insurance companies, they
control the publishing companies, and we have had
some remarkable instances of the control of the publishing companies presented before a subcommittee of
the Committee on the Judiciary.
     SENATOR GEORGE W. NORRIS

It is up to businessmen to sell our economic system to
the public. They must do as good a job on that as they
do on their own products. Unless the advantages of
our system over others are brought home to everyone,

there is no reason to believe that the trend toward more and more government will be checked.

JOSEPH P. KENNEDY

Business Opinions

When all agree
In harmony,
It's not too long
Before they're wrong.

The successful businessman sometimes makes his money by ability and experience, but he generally makes it by mistake.

GILBERT KEITH CHESTERTON

Business will be better or worse.

CALVIN COOLIDGE

There is now scarcely any outlet for energy in this country except business.   JOHN STUART MILL

Everybody has two businesses—his own and show business.   EDDIE CANTOR

Big business makes its money out of by-products.

ELBERT HUBBARD

Some day the ethics of business will be universally recognized, and in that day Business will be seen to be the oldest and most useful of all the professions.
HENRY FORD

American business needs a lifting purpose greater than the struggle of materialism.   HERBERT HOOVER

Breakfast first, business next.
WILLIAM MAKEPEACE THACKERAY

There is much more hope for humanity from manufacturers who enjoy their work than from those who continue in irksome business with the object of founding hospitals.   ALFRED NORTH WHITEHEAD

He would not blow his nose without moralizing on conditions in the handkerchief business.
CYRIL CONNOLLY

There is no kind of idleness by which we are so easily seduced as that which dignifies itself by the appearance of business.   SAMUEL JOHNSON

Thank heaven for the military industrial complex. Its ultimate aim is peace in our time.
BARRY GOLDWATER

It is easy to escape from business, if you will only despise the rewards of business.
LUCIUS ANNAEUS SENECA

The greatest part of the business of the world is the effect of not thinking.   LORD HALIFAX

Big business is not dangerous because it is big, but because in bigness is an unwholesome inflation created by privileges and exemptions which it ought not to enjoy.   **THOMAS WOODROW WILSON**

Don't let business interfere with your civic enterprise.   **RICHARD KING MELLON**

I hold it to be our duty to see that the wage-worker, the small producer, the ordinary consumer, shall get their fair share of the benefit of business prosperity. But it either is or ought to be evident to everyone that business has to prosper before anybody can get any benefit from it.   **THEODORE ROOSEVELT**

The lawyer and the doctor and other professional men have often a touch of civilization. The banker and the merchant seldom.   **JIM TULLY**

If the Golden Rule is to be preached at all in these modern days, when so much of our life is devoted to business, it must be preached specially in its application to the conduct of business.   **FERDINAND S. SCHENCK**

Business is more agreeable than pleasure; it interests the whole mind, the aggregate nature of man more continuously and more deeply. But it does not look as if it did.   **WALTER BAGEHOT**

When we depend less on industrially produced consumer goods, we can live in quiet places. Our bodies will become vigorous; we discover the serenity of living with the rhythms of the earth. We cease oppressing one another.   **ALICIA BAY LAUREL**

One of the surest ways of killing a tree is to lay bare its roots. It is the same with institutions. We must not be too ready to disinter the origins of those we wish to preserve. All beginnings are small.

JOSEPH JOUBERT

Everything which is properly business we must keep carefully separate from life. Business requires earnestness and method: life must have a free handling.

JOHANN WOLFGANG von GOETHE

Business is so much a lower thing than learning that a man used to the last cannot easily bring his stomach down to the first.   **LORD HALIFAX**

He that hath little business shall become wise.

Ecclesiasticus

Business Advice

If you want to save your business skin,
It's not as you might have guessed;
'Cos it never goes to those who win
The popularity contest.

Do other men, for they would do you, that's the true business precept.   **CHARLES DICKENS**

Those who invented the law of supply and demand have no right to complain when the law works against their interest.   ANWAR SADAT

A man who is always ready to believe what is told him will never do well, especially a businessman.
                                                    PETRONIUS

Don't forget until too late that the business of life is not business but living.   B. C. FORBES

Everybody's business is nobody's business.
                                                    PROVERB

You've got to go into a dying business otherwise you only get six per cent of the profits. This way, if the gamble comes off, you get it all.   SY WEINTRAUB

People who don't mind their own business either have no mind or no business.   LEOPOLD FECHTNER

People who knock their employer are under-estimating his value to them.   ANON

Call on a business man at business times only, and on business, transact your business and go about your business, in order to give him time to finish his business.   DUKE of WELLINGTON

What most people don't seem to realize is that there is just as much money to be made out of the wreckage of civilization as from the upbuilding of one.
                                                    MARGARET MITCHELL

Business, you know, may bring money, but friendship hardly ever does. JANE AUSTEN

Nearly every man in the city wants a farm until he gets it. JACOB M. BRAUDE

There's one sure way to make a businessman worry. Tell him not to. LEOPOLD FECHTNER

War is good business. Invest your sons. JAMES A. MICHENER

The merchant has no country. THOMAS JEFFERSON

Man's boldness and woman's caution make an excellent business arrangement. ELBERT HUBBARD

Few people do business well who do nothing else. LORD CHESTERFIELD

Leaving business at the office sounds like a good rule, but it is one that can easily be carried too far because, to my mind, a man who intends to make a success should be collecting ideas and tips, and mapping out programs during every waking hour. Dismissing business after office hours has a nice sound, but I have found that often the business does not come back after the recess! JOHN H. PATTERSON

Try to find something that works and stay with it. ROBB SAGENDORPH

Businessmen are notable for a peculiarly stalwart character which enables them to enjoy without loss of self-reliance, the benefits of tariffs, franchises and even outright Government subsidies.

HEBERT J. MULLER

A man is to go about his business as if he had not a friend in the world to help him in it.

LORD HALIFAX

All business proceeds on beliefs, or judgments or probabilities, and not on certainties.

CHARLES W. ELIOT

Business needs more of the professional spirit. The professional spirit seeks professional integrity, from pride, not from compulsion. The professional spirit detects its own violations and penalizes them.

HENRY FORD

If you destroy a free market you create a black market. If you have ten thousand regulations you destroy all respect for the law.

SIR WINSTON CHURCHILL

The world can forgive practically anything except people who mind their own business.

MARGARET MITCHELL

The first mistake in public business is going into it.

BENJAMIN FRANKLIN

Anybody goes into business, they ought to start their own union.

JOEY GALLO

Unmitigated seriousness is always out of place in human affairs. Let not the unwary reader think me flippant for saying so; it was Plato in his solemn old age, who said it.   GEORGE SANTAYANA

Everything which is properly business we must keep carefully separate from life. Business requires earnestness and method; life must have a freer handling.
          JOHANN WOLFGANG von GOETHE

Go to your business, I say, pleasure, whilst I go to my pleasure, business.   WILLIAM WYCHERLEY

In civil business; what first? Boldness; what second, and third? Boldness. And yet boldness is a child of ignorance and baseness.   FRANCIS BACON

3 · FINANCE

Profit

Look at profit's true role
As one of your bosses;
It sure meets the payroll
much better than bosses.

The only real gauge of success we have is profit—
honest profit.   **REX BEACH**

The next guy who talks to me about tonnage is going
to get his salary in tons, and we'll see how he converts
that into dollars.   **JOHN C. LOBB**

Profits are part of the mechanism by which society
decides what it wants to see produced.
                                        HENRY C. WALLICH

Volume times zero isn't too healthy.
                                        LEE IACOCCA

It is not from the benevolence of the butcher, the brewer, or the baker that we expect our dinner, but from their regard to their own interest.

ADAM SMITH

The only way to keep score in business is to add up how much money you make.

HARRY B. HELMSLEY

Little by little, the pimps have taken over the world. They don't do anything, they don't make anything—they just stand there and take their cut.

JEAN GIRAUDOUX

If profits are evil, losses must be ten times worse.

BERTRAM TROY

The smell of profit is clean and sweet, whatever the source. **DECIMUS JUNIUS JUVENAL**

No man can be said to be making too much profit if many others are trying to beat him at his own game, and none can succeed. The larger his profit, the greater will be the number of those who will try and the greater the chance that they will succeed.

CLARENCE B. RANDALL

More men come to doom through dirty profits than are kept by them. **SOPHOCLES**

There are no gains without pains.

ADLAI STEVENSON

If one has not made a reasonable profit, one has made a mistake. **LI XIANNIAN**

It is well known what a middle-man is: he is the man who bamboozles one party and plunders the other.
BENJAMIN DISRAELI

The trouble with the profit system has always been that it was highly unprofitable to most people.
ELWYN BROOKS WHITE

The worst crime against working people is a company which fails to operate at a profit.
SAMUEL GOMPERS

Zoologist Desmond Morris once did an experiment that exposed an ape to the "profit motive." First of all he got it to draw and paint, and found that it was doing lovely things. Then he started rewarding the ape with peanuts for its work.
"Soon it was doing any old scrawl to get the peanuts," Morris said wryly. "I had introduced commercialism into the ape's world, and ruined him as an artist!"
THOMAS WISEMAN

The percentage of student activists who regard business as overly concerned with profits as against social responsibility has increased sharply in just one year.
JOHN D. ROCKEFELLER

Profitability is the sovereign criterion of the enterprise.
PETER F. DRUCKER

Profits are not bedfellows of honor.
TAYLOR CALDWELL

We all have our eyes on the amount of our profits— but one good way to increase them is to watch the percentage of profit. The relation of profits to the selling price—and to your investment—is the real index of business success.   LESTER WITTE

There are occasions when it is undoubtedly better to incur loss than to make gain.
                           TITUS MACCIUS PLAUTUS

Even genius is tied to profit.   PINDAR

If you don't profit from your investment mistakes, someone else will.   YALE HIRSCH

Prefer a loss to a dishonest gain: the one brings pain at the moment, the other for all time.   CHILON

Losing potential profits hurts the ego; losing money really hurts.   GERALD APPEL

I believe in profit sharing—I believe it will ultimately settle the labor problem.   CHARLES M. SCHWAB

Civilization and profits go hand in hand.
                           CALVIN COOLIDGE

Most of the occasional nonsense written in this country to decry the profit motive is either ignorance or hypocrisy; it either is failure to understand the importance of self-interest in increasing the total wealth of all of the people, or just plain shutting of the eyes to the truth. For myself, I have never known a man who did not at times seek to advance his own self-interest.
                           CLARENCE B. RANDALL

A business with an income at its heels
Furnishes always oil for its wheels.

WILLIAM COWPER

Accounting

> *When accounting,*
> *Don't be rash;*
> *There's no such thing*
> *As "petty cash."*

Net—the biggest word in the language of business.

HERBERT CASSON

When you make the mistake of adding the date to the right side of the accounting statement, you must add it to the left side too.   **ACCOUNTANT'S MAXIM**

Few have heard of Fra Luca Parioli, the inventor of double-entry bookkeeping; but he has probably had much more influence on human life than has Dante or Michelangelo.   **HERBERT J. MULLER**

Our Accounting Department is the office that has the little red box on the wall saying "In case of emergency break glass." And inside are two tickets to Brazil.

ROBERT ORBEN

A budget is telling your money where to go instead of wondering where it went. C. E. HOOVER

Auditors Are the People Who Go in After the War Is Lost and Bayonet the Wounded. P. RUBIN

"Absorption of Overhead" is one of the most obscene terms I have ever heard. PETER F. DRUCKER

An accountant is a man hired to explain that you didn't make the money you thought you had.

ANON

If my business was legitimate, I would deduct a substantial percentage for depreciation of my body.

XAVIERA HOLLANDER

Budgeting is a system of additions and subtractions more honored in breach than in observance.

EUGENE E. BRUSSELL

I don't know how much money I've got. I did ask the accountant how much it came to. I wrote it down on a bit of paper but I've lost the bit of paper.

JOHN LENNON

Did you ever hear of a kid playing accountant—even if he wanted to be one? JACKIE MASON

Is Chapter Eleven the result of following the Ten Commandments? ANON

A budget tells us what we can't afford, but it doesn't keep us from buying it. WILLIAM FEATHER

Bankruptcy is a legal proceeding in which you put your money in your pants pocket and give your coat to your creditors.   JOEY ADAMS

A budget is a method of worrying before you spend instead of afterwards.   ANON

The law of diminishing returns holds good in almost every part of our human universe.
                    ALDOUS LEONARD HUXLEY

Accounts receivable are bill-gotten gains.
                    ROBERT ORBEN

There can be mathematicians of the first order who cannot count.   BARON NOVALIS

Remember that even though work stops, nevertheless the expenses continue to mount up.
                    MARCUS CATO

Budget: A mathematical confirmation of your suspicions.   JOHN A. LINCOLN

A financial analyst thinks he sees the forest clearing but keeps bumping into trees.   EVAN ESAR

Evolution has her own accounting system and that's the only one that matters.
                    R. BUCKMINSTER FULLER

A receiver is appointed by the court to take what's left.   ROBERT FROST

Over the long haul of life on this planet, it is the ecologists, and not the bookkeepers of business, who are the ultimate accountants.   STEWART L. UDALL

It's simply a matter of creative accounting.
                                                    MEL BROOKS

Those who work out our federal budget
Have a policy—really a honey
We shall live on our national income,
Even if we must borrow the money!
                                              LEVERETT LYON

A budget is the way to go broke methodically.
                                                            ANON

The loss which is unknown is no loss at all.
                                          PUBLILIUS SYRUS

Economics

Give the minimum,
Gain the maximum.

I learned more about economics from one South Dakota dust storm than I did in all my years in college.
                                          HUBERT HUMPHREY

The trouble with today's economy is that when a man is rich, it's all on paper. When he's broke, it's cash.
SAM MARCONI

One of the greatest pieces of economic wisdom is to know what you do not know.
JOHN KENNETH GALBRAITH

A completely planned economy ensures that when no bacon is delivered, no eggs are delivered at the same time.
LEO FRAIN

It's called political economy because it has nothing to do with either politics or economy.
STEPHEN LEACOCK

Political economy: two words that should be divorced —on Grounds of Incompatability.
The Wall Street Journal

Our nation's economy seems to be based on the belief that we shouldn't practice it.
HAROLD COFFIN

In economics, the majority is always wrong.
ANON

One of the difficulties of economics is that it is too easy to explain after a particular event has happened, why it should have happened; and too easy to explain before it happens, why it should not happen.
M. G. KENDALL

A study of economics usually reveals that the best time to buy anything is last year.
MARTY ALLEN

To have national prosperity we need to spend, but to have individual prosperity we must save.   ANON

The economy may suffer if auto sales drop—but that's the American way; we have to buy more cars than we need or we'll never be able to afford them.
                              JACK WILSON

If ignorance paid dividends, most Americans could make a fortune out of what they don't know about economics.   LUTHER HODGES

Everything now seems to be under federal control except the national debt and the budget.
                              BOB GODDARD

There are three things not worth running for—a bus, a woman or a new economic panacea: if you wait a bit another will come along.
                    DERICK HEATHCOAT AMORY

The American economy is the eighth wonder of the world, and the ninth is the economic ignorance of the American people.   BURTON CRANE

There's one way to solve all the biggest problems of life: make complacency taxable.   ANON

Economics is all about the two biggest problems of life: how to make money and how to get along without it.   BERTRAM TROY

We have become to some extent, I think, economic hypochondriacs. You get a wiggle in a statistic . . . and everyone runs to get the thermometer.
                          PAUL W. McCRACKEN

What is wholly mysterious in economics is not likely to be important. JOHN KENNETH GALBRAITH

Economics is like being lost in the woods. How can you tell where you are going when you don't even know where you are? ANON

What economic history needs at present is not more documents but a pair of stout boots.
R. H. TAWNEY

Economics is a subject that does not greatly respect one's wishes. NIKITA KHRUSHCHEV

One of the soundest rules I try to remember when making forecasts in the field of economics is that whatever is to happen is happening already.
SYLVIA PORTER

Nine out of ten economic laws are economic laws only till they are found out. ROBERT LYND

Modern political theory seems to hold that the way to keep the economy in the pink is to run the government in the red. NATHAN NIELSEN

A systematic application and critical evaluation of the basic analytic concepts of economic theory, with an emphasis on money and why it's good. Fixed coefficient production functions, costs and supply curves, and nonconvexity comprise the first semester, with the second semester concentrating on spending, making change, and keeping a neat wallet. The Federal Reserve System is analyzed, and advanced students are coached in the proper method of filling out a deposit slip. Other topics include inflation and depression—how to dress for each—loans, interest, welching.

WOODY ALLEN

The idea of imposing restrictions on a free economy to assure freedom of competition is like breaking a man's leg to make him run faster.

N. R. SAYRE

An economic system prouder of the distribution of its products than of the products themselves.

MURRAY KEMPTON

Economics is about the cost of our appetites.

GEORGE F. WILL

A nation is not in danger of financial disaster merely because it owes itself money.

ANDREW WILLIAM MELLON

Like theology, and unlike mathematics, economics deals with matters which men consider very close to their lives.

JOHN KENNETH GALBRAITH

The only type of economic structure in which government is free and in which the human spirit is free is one in which commerce is free.

THOMAS ARNOLD

There are in the field of economic events no constant relations, and consequently no measurement is possible.

LUDWIG ELDER von MISES

The most important law in the whole of political economy is the law of "variety" in human wants; each

separate want is soon satisfied, and yet there is no end
to wants.   W. S. JEVONS

We may go down in history as an elegant technological
society which underwent biological disintegration
through lack of economic understanding.
                                           DAVID M. GATES

The dynamo of our economic system is self-interest
which may range from mere petty greed to admirable
types of self-expression.   FELIX FRANKFURTER

Risk

When you insure
All you are getting
Is a mature
Method of betting.

There's no such thing as "zero risk."
                                         WILLIAM DRIVER

Whatever you have, you must either use or lose.
                                            HENRY FORD

In the bad old days . . . there were three easy ways
of losing money, racing being the quickest, women the
pleasantest, and farming the most certain.
                              LORD AMHURST of HACKNEY

During the first period of a man's life the greatest danger is: not to take the risk.

> SOREN KIERKEGAARD

The worst financial risks are those that think the world owes them a living.

> ANON

Take calculated risks. That is quite different from being rash.

> GEN. GEORGE SMITH PATTON

A pinch of probability is worth a pound of perhaps.

> JAMES THURBER

Insurance is death on the installment plan.

> PHILIP SLATER

To win you have to risk loss.

> JEAN-CLAUDE KILLY

A man sits as many risks as he runs.

> HENRY DAVID THOREAU

The oil business, you know, is liable to sudden and violent fluctuations.

> JOHN D. ROCKEFELLER

Be wary of the man who urges an action in which he himself incurs no risk.

> JOAQUIN SETANTI

Whoever plays deep must necessarily lose his money or his character.

> EARL OF CHESTERFIELD

He who does not open his eyes must open his purse.

> GERMAN PROVERB

Insurance is a guarantee that, no matter how many necessities a person has to forgo all through life, death was something to which he could look forward.

FRED ALLEN

Progress means taking risks, for you can't steal home and keep your foot on third base.

HERBERT V PROCHNOW

Being grown up means we can have our own way—at our expense. HAL ROGERS

There is only one thing about which I am certain, and that is that there is very little about which one can be certain. WILLIAM SOMERSET MAUGHAM

To be alive at all involves some risk.

HAROLD MACMILLAN

If at first you do succeed, don't take any more chances. FRANK McKINNEY HUBBARD

In putting off what one has to do, one runs the risk of never being able to do it.

CHARLES BEAUDELAIRE

Not every bullet kills. ALPHONSE DAUDET

There are risks and costs to a programme of action. But they are far less than the long range risks and costs of comfortable inaction. JOHN F. KENNEDY

Risk is essential. There is no growth or inspiration in staying within what is safe and comfortable. Once you find out what you do best, why not try something else?
ALEX NOBLE

Hope is a risk that must be run.
GEORGE BERNARD SHAW

Danger can never be overcome without taking risks.
LATIN PROVERB

We can be absolutely certain only about things we do not understand.
ERIC HOFFER

Rashness succeeds often, still more often fails.
NAPOLEON BONAPARTE

First weigh the considerations, then take the risks.
HELMUTH von MOLTKE

The profits of good luck are perishable; if you build on fortune, you build on sand; the more advancement you achieve, the more dangers you run.
MARQUIS de RACAN

Every man has the right to risk his own life in order to save it.
JEAN-JACQUES ROUSSEAU

If you dip your arm into the pickle pot, let it be up to the elbow.
MALAY PROVERB

If you leap into a well, providence is not bound to fetch you out.
THOMAS FULLER

To win without risk is to triumph without glory.
PIERRE CORNEILLE

Risk! Risk anything! Care no more for the opinions of others, for those voices. Do the hardest thing on earth for you. Act for yourself.
KATHERINE MANSFIELD

To get profit without risk, experience without danger, and reward without work, is as impossible as it is to live without being born.
A. P. GOUTHEY

Gambling

When you gamble once again,
It's hard to justify;
You recall both where and when
But can't remember why.

The strength of Monaco is the weakness of the world.
H. A. GIBBONS

The gambling known as business looks with austere disfavour upon the business known as gambling.
AMBROSE BIERCE

Poker exemplifies the worst aspects of capitalism that have made our country so great.
WALTER MATTHAU

Gambling with cards or dice, or stocks, is all one thing; it is getting money without giving an equivalent for it.   HENRY WARD BEECHER

Remember this house doesn't beat a player. It merely gives him the chance to beat himself.
                    NICK 'THE GREEK' DANDALOS

God does not play dice.   ALBERT EINSTEIN

Back of the bar,
in a solo game,
sat Dangerous Dan McGrew,
and watching his luck,
was his light o'love,
the lady that's known as Lou.
                    ROBERT W. SERVICE

If you bet on a horse, that's gambling. If you bet you can make three spades, that's entertainment. If you bet cotton will go up three points, that's business. See the difference?   BLACKIE SHERRODE

Insurance: An ingenious modern game of chance in which the player is permitted to enjoy the comfortable conviction that he is beating the man who keeps the table.   AMBROSE BIERCE

I backed the right horse, and then the wrong horse went and won.   HENRY HERMAN

The odds on hitting the slot machine jackpot are about one in 2,000.   ANON

True luck consists not in holding the best of the cards at the table: luckiest he who knows just when to rise and go home.   JOHN HAY

There is enough energy wasted in poker to make a hundred thousand successful every year.
ARTHUR BRISBANE

Gambling promises the poor what property performs for the rich—something for nothing.
GEORGE BERNARD SHAW

The apparent desire to accept the certainty of losing money in the long run in return for the remote possibility of winning it in the short.   BERNARD LEVIN

Man is the only animal that plays poker.
DON HEROLD

It doesn't say much for society, if gambling is the main method of raising money for good causes.
BERTRAM TROY

There is but one good throw upon the dice, which is to throw them away.   PAUL CHATFIELD

If you must play, decide upon three things at the start: the rules of the game, the stakes, and the quitting time.
CHINESE PROVERB

No dog can go as fast as the money you bet on him.
BUD FLANAGAN

Horse racing is a particular interest in that the spectators, who lose money, set many fashions; while the bookmakers, who make money, set none.

QUENTIN BELL

He who can predict winning numbers has no need to let off fire-crackers.   ERNEST BRAMAH

A poker face is the face that launches a thousand chips.   ANON

The better the gambler, the worse the man.

PUBLIUS SYRUS

I'd sooner live among people who don't cheat at cards than among people who are earnest about not cheating at cards.   CLIVE STAPLES LEWIS

It's in gambling that we see the most amazing strokes of luck.   JEAN BAPTISTE MOLIERE

Life consists not in holding good cards but in playing those you do hold well.   JOSH BILLINGS

Gambling: The sure way of getting nothing for something.   WILSON MIZNER

Gambling is a revolt against boredom.

STUART CHASE

The good luck that comes to us in our relations with the industrial world is always the good luck of the gambler—not the glory of the warrior or the reward of the cultivator.

ELEMIRE ZOLLA

Gambling: a disease of barbarians superficially civilized.   DEAN WILLIAM RALPH INGE

Millions of words are written annually purporting to tell how to beat the races, whereas the best possible advice on the subject is found in the three monosyllables, 'Do not try.'   DAN PARKER

Play not for gain, but sport: who plays for more than he can lose with pleasure stakes his heart.
      GEORGE HERBERT

A gambler is nothing but a man who makes his living out of hope.   WILLIAM BOLITHO

Man is a gaming animal. He must be always trying to get the better in something or other.
      CHARLES LAMB

Every one knows that horse-racing is carried on mainly for the delight and profit of fools, ruffians, and thieves.   GEORGE GISSING

Nine gamblers could not feed a single rooster.
      YUGOSLAV PROVERB

One throw of the dice will never abolish chance.
      STEPHANE MALLARME

Remember that time is an avid gambler who has no need to cheat to win every time. That's the law!
      CHARLES BAUDELAIRE

I must complain the cards are ill-shuffled till I have a good hand.   JONATHAN SWIFT

If you won't gamble enough to hurt you, it won't do you any good to win.   BILL LEAR

Gaming is the son of avarice, and the father of despair.
                                        FRENCH PROVERB

Gambling is the child of avarice, but the parent of prodigality.   CHARLES CALEB COLTON

Gambling is the child of avarice, the brother of iniquity, and the father of mischief.
                                        GEORGE WASHINGTON

Gambling is a kind of tacit confession that those engaged therein do, in general, exceed the bounds of their respective fortunes; and therefore they cast lots to determine on whom the ruin shall at present fall, that the rest may be saved a little longer.
                                        SIR WILLIAM BLACKSTONE

The urge to gamble is so universal and its practice so pleasurable that I assume it must be civil.
                                        HEYWOOD HALE BROUN

I think the primary motive in back of most gambling is the excitement of it. While gamblers naturally want to win, the majority of them derive pleasure even if they lose. The desire to win, rather than the excitement involved, seems to me to be the compelling force behind speculation.   JOSEPH P. KENNEDY

4 · MONEY

Definitions of Money

I've always wondered why it's so,
That money never lingers.
Now I know why it's called "dough,"
It sticks to other's fingers.

Money is what you'd get on beautifully without if only other people weren't so crazy about it.
MARGARET CASE HARRIMAN

Money is the god of our time, and Rothschild is his prophet.
HEINRICH HEINE

Money doesn't always bring happiness. People with ten million dollars are no happier than people with nine million dollars.
HOBART BROWN

Money is round. It rolls away.
SHOLEM ALEICHEM

Money is more troublesome to watch than forget.
MICHEL de MONTAIGNE

If you can actually count your money, then you are not really a rich man.
PAUL GETTY

Money is the fruit of evil and often is the root of it.
HENRY FIELDING

Money is the poor people's credit card.
MARSHALL McLUHAN

What's money? It's the only thing that's handier than a credit card.
ANON

Money is a stupid measure of achievement, but unfortunately it is the only universal measure we have.
CHARLES STEINMETZ

Money is paper blood.
BOB HOPE

Money is an article which may be used as a universal passport to everywhere except Heaven, and as a universal provider of everything but happiness.
Wall Street Journal

Money is the only substance which can keep a cold world from nicknaming a citizen "Hey, you!"
WILSON MIZNER

Money is so unlike every other article that I believe a man has neither a legal or a moral right to take all that he can get.
PETER COOPER

Money has no ears, but it hears.
JAPANESE PROVERB

Money is always there but the pockets change; it is not in the same pockets after a change, and that is all there is to say about money. **GERTRUDE STEIN**

Money has little value to its possessor unless it also has value to others. **LELAND STANFORD**

Money is a singular thing. It ranks with love as man's greatest source of joy. And with his death as his greatest source of anxiety.
JOHN KENNETH GALBRAITH

Money, which represents the prose of life and which is hardly spoken of in parlors without an apology, is, in its effects and laws, as beautiful as roses.
RALPH WALDO EMERSON

Money is the wise man's religion. **EURIPIDES**

Maybe money is unreal for most of us, easier to give away than things we want. **LILLIAN HELLMAN**

Character is money; and according as the man earns or spends the money, money in turn becomes character. **EDWARD BULWER-LYTTON**

Money is the power of impotence. **LEON SAMSON**

Power of Money

Some say this and some say that
But when all is said and done,
Money makes the plutocrat
And keeps him number one.

The only people who claim that money is not important are people who have enough money so that they are relieved of the ugly burden of thinking about it.
                                    JOYCE CAROL OATES

Money, it turned out, was exactly like sex, you thought of nothing else if you didn't have it and thought of other things if you did.
                                    JAMES A. BALDWIN

The chief value of money lies in the fact that one lives in a world in which it is overestimated.
                                    HENRY LOUIS MENCKEN

Money isn't everything but it's a long way ahead of what comes next.   **SIR EDWARD STOCKDALE**

Money talks. The more money, the louder it talks.
                                    ARNOLD ROTHSTEIN

When a man needs money, he needs money, and not a headache tablet or a prayer. **WILLIAM FEATHER**

If a man runs after money, he's money-mad; if he keeps it he's a capitalist; if he spends it, he's a playboy;

if he doesn't get it, he's a ne'er do-well; if he doesn't try to get it, he lacks ambition; if he gets it without working for it, he's a parasite and if he accumulates it after a lifetime of hard work, people call him a fool who never got anything out of life.   VIC OLIVER

Money is not an aphrodisiac; the desire it may kindle in the female eye is more for the cash than the carrier.
MARYA MANNES

When I was young I used to think that money was the most important thing in life; now that I am old, I know it is.   OSCAR WILDE

A billion here, a billion there—pretty soon you're talking about real money.
SENATOR EVERETT DIRKSEN

There is no fortress so strong that money cannot take it.   CICERO

No one would remember the Good Samaritan if he only had good intentions. He had money as well.
MARGARET THATCHER

It isn't enough for you to love money—it's also necessary that money should love you.
BARON ROTHSCHILD

Money differs from an automobile, a mistress or cancer in being equally important to those who have it and those who don't.
JOHN KENNETH GALBRAITH

We ought to change the legend on our money from "In God We Trust" to "Money We Trust." Because, as a nation we've got far more faith in money these days than we do in God.   ARTHUR HOPPE

Life is short and so is money. BERTOLT BRECHT

Two men were walking along a crowded sidewalk in a down-town business area. Suddenly one exclaimed, 'Listen to the lovely sound of that cricket.' But the other could not hear. He asked his companion how he could detect the sound of a cricket amid the din of people and traffic. The first man, who was a zoologist, had trained himself to listen to the voice of nature. But he didn't explain. He simply took a coin out of his pocket and dropped it to the sidewalk, whereupon a dozen people began to look about them. "We hear," he said, "what we listen for."   KERMIT L. LONG

In national affairs a million is a drop in the budget.
                              BURTON RASCOE

If American men are obsessed with money, American women are obsessed with weight. The men talk of gain, the women talk of loss, and I do not know which talk is the more boring.   MARYA MANNES

Where money talks, there are few interruptions.
                              HERBERT V. PROCHNOW

Remember that time is money.
                              BENJAMIN FRANKLIN

Time is money—says the vulgarest saw known to any age or people. Turn it round about and you get a precious truth—money is time.   GEORGE GISSING

I like Paris. They don't talk so much of money, but more of sex.　　　　　　**VERA STRAVINSKY**

In an age when we would rather have money than health, and would rather have another man's money than our own, he lived and died unsordid.

MARK TWAIN

When I had money everyone called me brother.

POLISH PROVERB

It happens a little unluckily that the persons who have the most infinite contempt of money are the same that have the strongest appetite for the pleasures it procures.　　　**WILLIAM SHENSTONE**

Money never goes to jail.　　　**ARAB PROVERB**

It is extraordinary to what an expense of time and money people will go to get something for nothing.

ROBERT LYND

I didn't inherit any money.　　　**MOE DALITZ**

Money does not pay for anything, never has, never will. It is an economic axiom as old as the hills that goods and services can be paid for only with goods and services.　　　**ALBERT JAY NOCK**

The man who damns money has obtained it dishonorably; the man who respects it has earned it.

AYN RAND

A man's treatment of money is the most decisive test of his character—how he makes it and how he spends it.　　　　　　　　　　　　　JAMES MOFFATT

I've realized, after fourteen months in this country, the value of money, whether it is clean or dirty.
　　　　　　　　　　　　　NGUYEN CAO KY

Money swore an oath that nobody who did not love it should ever have it.　　　　　IRISH PROVERB

It is a kind of spiritual snobbery that makes people think they can be happy without money.
　　　　　　　　　　　　　ALBERT CAMUS

In our culture we makes heroes of the men who sit on top of a heap of money, and we pay attention not only to what they say in their field of competence, but to their wisdom on every other question in the world.
　　　　　　　　　　　　　MAX LERNER

Trade is the mother of money.　　　　　　ANON

Jesus went into the temple and overthrew the tables of the money changers.　　　　　　*St. Mark*

What I as a human being cannot do, in other words, what all my individual faculties cannot do, I can do by means of MONEY. Hence money makes every one of these faculties into something which it is not in itself, i.e., turns it into its opposite.　　　KARL MARX

We Americans worship the mighty dollar! Well, it is a worthier god than Hereditary Privilege.
　　　　　　　　　　　　　MARK TWAIN

Money does all things; for it gives and it takes away, it makes honest men and knaves, fools and philosophers; and so on to the end of the chapter.
SIR ROGER L'ESTRANGE

The value of a dollar is social, as it is created by society.   RALPH WALDO EMERSON

Money is human happiness in the abstract; he, then, who is no longer capable of enjoying human happiness in the concrete devotes himself utterly to money.
ARTHUR SCHOPENHAUER

It is true that money attracts; but much money repels.
CYNTHIA OZICK

Life and money—you can't separate them. Not on this planet. Not in the kind of life you have to live.
THOMAS H. RADDALL

All thinges obeyen to moneye.
GEOFFREY CHAUCER

Lack of Funds

*If money does not do
As much for us as it did,
Perhaps we do not do
As much for it as we did.*

Nothing is sadder than having worldly standards without worldly means.   VAN WYCK BROOKS

I can remember when you used to kiss your money good-bye. Now you don't even get a chance to blow in its ear. **ROBERT ORBEN**

Lack of money is the root of all evil.
GEORGE BERNARD SHAW

To have money is to be virtuous, honest, beautiful and witty. And to be without it is to be ugly and boring and stupid and useless. **JEAN GIRADOUX**

I owe much; I have nothing; the rest I leave to the poor. **FRANCOIS RABELAIS**

When you're down and out something always turns up —and it's usually the noses of your friends.
ORSON WELLES

When a man says money can do everything, that settles it; he hasn't any. **EDGAR WATSON HOWE**

A deficit is what you have when you haven't got as much as you had when you had nothing.
GERALD F. LIEBERMAN

I have the feeling that in a balanced life one should die penniless. The trick is dismantling.
ART GARFUNKEL

There were times my pants were so thin that I could sit on a dime and tell if it were heads or tails.
SPENCER TRACY

He who has no bread has no authority.
TURKISH PROVERB

We haven't the money, so we've got to think.
LORD RUTHERFORD

I've got all the money I'll ever need if I die by 4 o'clock.
HENNY YOUNGMAN

I would not say millionaires were mean. They simply have a healthy respect for money. I've noticed that people who don't respect money don't have any.
PAUL GETTY

I got what no millionaire's got, I got no money.
GERALD F. LIEBERMAN

Subject to a kind of disease, which at that time they called lack of money.
FRANCOIS RABELAIS

I must say I hate money but it's the lack of it I hate most.
KATHERINE MANSFIELD

Necessity knows no Sunday.
AGNES REPPLIER

The distance from nothing to a little is ten thousand times more than from it to the highest degree in this life.
JOHN DONNE

No one can worship God or love his neighbor on an empty stomach.
WOODROW WILSON

I know a fellow who's as broke as the Ten Commandments.
JOHN P. MARQUAND

If you have no money, be polite.
DANISH PROVERB

An optimist is always broke.
> FRANK McKINNEY HUBBARD

Many of the optimists in the world don't own a hundred dollars, and because of their optimism never will.
> EDGAR WATSON HOWE

Beggars can never be bankrupts.
> AMERICAN PROVERB

Life is short and so is money.   BERTOLT BRECHT

A miser is ever in want.   GREEK PROVERB

They who have little are thought to have no right to anything.   JOHN LANCASTER SPALDING

It is a kind of spiritual snobbery that makes people think that they can be happy without money.
> ALBERT CAMUS

A beggar's purse is bottomless.   PROVERB

That I should make him that steals my coat a present of my cloak—what would become of business?
> KATHERINE LEE BATES

He is not poor that hath not much, but he that craves much.   PROVERB

No man needs money so much as he who despises it.
> JEAN PAUL RICHTER

He that wants money, means, and content, is without three good friends.   WILLIAM SHAKESPEARE

Wealth

Money saved is money earned;
There's nothing less perverser.
It is true when it is learned
But seldom vice versa.

Wealth is the product of man's capacity to think.
AYN RAND

Riches are the savings of many in the hands of one.
EUGENE DEBS

If all the rich people in the world divided up their money amongst themselves, there wouldn't be enough to go round. CHRISTINA STEED

Just pretending to be rich keeps some people poor.
ANON

True, you can't take it with you, but then that's not the place where it comes in so handy.
BRENDAN FRANCIS

The average man is rich enough when he has a little more than he has got and not till then.
DEAN WILLIAM RALPH INGE

If you aren't rich, you should always look useful.
LOUIS-FERDINAND CELINE

Wealth—Any income that is at least one hundred dollars more a year than the income of one's wife's sister's husband.   HENRY LOUIS MENCKEN

God help the rich, the poor can look after themselves.
                    ENGLISH PROVERB

If you want to know what the Lord God thinks of money, you have only to look at those to whom he gives it.   MAURICE BARING

Better be born lucky than rich.   PROVERB

There are reckoned to be three times as many women than men who are worth more than $1 million.
                          ANON

I've been rich, and I've been poor; rich is better.
                    SOPHIE TUCKER

People who have what they want are fond of telling people who haven't got what they want that they don't really want it.   OGDEN NASH

A man who has a million dollars is as well off as if he were rich.   JOHN JACOB ASTOR

It is no longer a distinction to be rich . . . People do not care for money as they once did . . . What we accumulate by way of useless surplus does us no honor.   HENRY FORD

I have no complex about wealth. I have worked hard for my money producing things which people need. I believe that the able industrial leader who creates wealth and employment is more worthy of historical notice than politicians or soldiers. J. PAUL GETTY

Until the age of twelve I sincerely believed that everybody had a house on Fifth Avenue, a villa in Newport and a steam-driven, ocean-going yacht.
CORNELIUS VANDERBILT, JR.

Well, yes. You could say we have independent means.
JOHN D. ROCKEFELLER

You are affluent when you buy what you want, do what you wish, and don't give a thought to what it costs.   J. P. MORGAN

Rich men without convictions are more dangerous in modern society than poor women without chastity.
GEORGE BERNARD SHAW

Riches exclude only one inconvenience, and that is poverty.   SAMUEL JOHNSON

Be rich to yourself and poor to your friends.
JUVENAL

If your riches are yours, why don't you take them with you to t'other world?   BENJAMIN FRANKLIN

The time will never come when everybody is richer than everybody else.   C. E. AYRES

There'll be no pockets in your shroud.
JAMES J. HILL

Wealth consists not in having great possessions, but in having few wants.   EPICURUS

I don't think one can spend oneself rich.
                              RHODA THOMAS TRIPP

I am absolutely convinced that no wealth in the world can help humanity forward, even in the hands of the most devoted worker in this cause.
                              ALBERT EINSTEIN

The rich would have to eat money, but luckily the poor provide food.   RUSSIAN PROVERB

How easy it is for a man to die rich if he will but be contented to live miserable.   HENRY FIELDING

Some folks seem to get the idea that they're worth a lot of money just because they have it.
                              SETH PARKER

The foolish sayings of a rich man pass for wise ones.
                              SPANISH PROVERB

Every man is rich or poor according to the degree in which he can afford to enjoy the necessaries, conveniences, and amusements of human life.
                              ADAM SMITH

He is a great simpleton who imagines that the chief power of wealth is to supply wants. In ninety-nine cases out of a hundred it creates more wants than it supplies.   ANON

The pride of dying rich raises the loudest laugh in hell.
JOHN FOSTER

The concentration of wealth is made inevitable by the natural inequality of men.   WILL DURANT

A full cup must be carried steadily.
ENGLISH PROVERB

Whoever is rich is my brother.
RUSSIAN PROVERB

There are men who gain from their wealth only the fear of losing it.   ANTOINE RIVAROLI

Few of us can stand prosperity. Another man's, I mean.   MARK TWAIN

Prosperity is only an instrument to be used, not a deity to be worshiped.   CALVIN COOLIDGE

Riches serve a man, but command a fool.
ENGLISH PROVERB

No man can tell whether he is rich or poor by turning to his ledger—It is the heart that makes a man rich—He is rich, according to what he is, not according to what he has.   HENRY WARD BEECHER

Wealth is the sinews of affairs.   BION

The ass loaded with gold still eats thistles.
GERMAN PROVERB

This, then, is held to be the duty of the man of wealth: First, to set an example of modest, unostentatious living, shunning display or extravagance; to provide moderately for the legitimate wants of those dependent upon him; and after doing so consider all surplus revenues which come to him simply as trust funds, which he is called upon to administer, and strictly bound as a matter of duty to administer in the manner which, to his judgment, is best calculated to produce the most beneficial results for the community—the man of wealth thus becoming the mere agent and trustee for the his poorer brethren, bringing to their service his superior wisdom, experience, and ability to administer, doing for them better than they would or could for themselves. ANDREW CARNEGIE

Believe not much them that seem to despise riches, for they despise them that despair of them.
FRANCIS BACON

Wealth, after all, is a relative thing, since he that has little, and wants less, is richer than he that has much, and wants more. CHARLES CALEB COLTON

So long as a man enjoys prosperity, he cares whether or not he is beloved. MARCUS LUCAN

Benefits of Wealth

By those who ain't got it
Wealth is often abused.
But given a lot it
Is so rarely refused.

Wealth is not without its advantages and the case to the contrary, although it has often been made, has never proved widely persuasive.
                    JOHN KENNETH GALBRAITH

Money doesn't buy friends but it allows a better class of enemies.   LORD MANCROFT

A rich man is one who isn't afraid to ask the salesman to show him something cheaper.
                    Ladies Home Journal

The majority would prefer to be miserably rich than happily poor.   ANON

With money in your pocket, you are wise, and you are handsome, and you sing well too.
                    JEWISH PROVERB

I'm so happy to be rich, I'm willing to take all the consequences.   HOWARD ABRAMSON

Gucci, Gucci, Goo.   **GRAFFITI**

A man who has money may be anxious, depressed, frustrated and unhappy, but one thing he's not—and that's broke.   **BRENDAN FRANCIS**

The life of the rich is one long Sunday.
                    GEORG BOCHNER

I'd like to be rich enough so that I could throw soap away after the letters are worn off.
                    ANDY ROONEY

All heiresses are beautiful.   **JOHN DRYDEN**

The great luxury of riches is that they enable you to escape so much good advice. The rich are always advising the poor, but the poor seldom venture to return the compliment.   **SIR ARTHUR PHELPS**

It must be great to be rich and let the other fellow keep up appearances.
                    FRANK McKINNEY HUBBARD

He has so much money that he could afford to look poor.   **EDGAR WALLACE**

He that is rich will not be called a fool.
                    SPANISH PROVERB

In wealth many friends, in poverty not even relations.
                    ANON

The rich man is everywhere expected and at home.
                    SA'DI

Not even a collapsing world looks dark to a man who is about to make his fortune.
ELWYN BROOKS WHITE

I have tried to teach people that there are three kicks in every dollar: one, when you make it—and how I love to make a dollar; two, when you have it—and I have the Yankee lust for saving. The third kick is when you give it away—and it is the biggest kick of all.
WILLIAM ALLEN WHITE

It is better to live rich than to die rich.
SAMUEL JOHNSON

I'd like to live like a poor man with lots of money.
PABLO PICASSO

Wealth is not his that has it, but his that enjoys it.
BENJAMIN FRANKLIN

Riches attract the attention, consideration and congratulations of mankind.
JOHN ADAMS

Riches are not an end of life, but an instrument of life.
HENRY WARD BEECHER

If a man who is born to a fortune cannot make himself easier and freer than those who are not, he gains nothing.
JAMES BOSWELL

A man's true wealth is the good he does in this world.
MOHAMMED

In big houses in which things are done properly, there is always the religious element. The diurnal cycle is observed with more feeling when there are servants to do the work.　　　　ELIZABETH BOWEN

The greatest and most amiable privilege which the rich enjoy over the poor is that they exercise the least —the privilege of making them happy.
　　　　CHARLES CALEB COLTON

Only the brave deserve the fair, but only the rich, fat, cowardly merchants can afford same.
　　　　CHINESE PROVERB

Don't try to die rich but live rich.
　　　　THOMAS BIRD MOSHER

I wish to become rich so that I can instruct the people and glorify honest poverty a little, like those kind-hearted, fat, benevolent people do.　　MARK TWAIN

Wealth does not corrupt nor does it ennoble. But wealth does govern the minds of privileged children, gives them a particular kind of identity they never lose, whether they grow up to be stockbrokers or communards, and whether they lead healthy or unstable lives.　　　　ROBERT COLES

The privilege of the great is to see catastrophes from a terrace.　　　　JEAN GIRADOUX

It is extraordinary how many emotional storms one may weather in safety if one is ballasted with ever so little gold.　　　　WILLIAM McFEE

The world is his who has money to go over it.
　　　　RALPH WALDO EMERSON

To be poor without murmuring is difficult. To be rich without being proud is easy.   CONFUCIUS

The best way to realize the pleasure of feeling rich is to live in a smaller house than your means would entitle you to have.   EDWARD CLARKE

Being very rich, as far as I am concerned, is having a margin. The margin is being able to give.
          MAY SARTON

The gratification of wealth is not found in mere possession or in lavish expenditure, but in its wise application.   MIGUEL de CERVANTES

A man is rich in proportion to the number of things he can afford to let alone.
          HENRY DAVID THOREAU

Nowadays, we think of a philanthropist as someone who donates big sums of money, yet the word is derived from two Greek words, philos (loving) and anthropos (man); loving man. All of us are capable of being philanthropists. We can give of ourselves.
          EDWARD LINDSEY

Gold will buy the highest honours and gold will purchase love.   OVID

Disadvantages of Wealth

> *However much the whole world bitches*
> *All about money's attendant hitches,*
> *Called to account*
> *Most would discount*
> *The problems that accompany riches.*

No Rockefeller in the record is ever known to have had a good time. **LUCIUS BEEBE**

It is tragic that Howard Hughes had to die to prove that he was alive. **WALTER KANE**

When the rich wage war, it's the poor who die.
JEAN-PAUL SARTRE

It's possible to own too much. A man with one watch knows what time it is; a man with two watches is never quite sure. **LEE SEGALL**

Another bad thing about "prosperity" is that you can't jingle any money without being under suspicion.
FRANK McKINNEY HUBBARD

The prosperous man is never sure that he is loved for himself. **MARCUS LUCAN**

If you pick up a starving dog and make him prosperous, he will not bite you. This is the principal difference between a dog and a man. **MARK TWAIN**

You can't take it with you.
MOSS HART and GEORGE KAUFMAN

Rich men feel misfortunes that fly over poor men's heads.
ANON

One of the penalties of wealth is that the older you grow, the more people there are in the world who would rather have you dead than alive.
C. H. B. KITCHIN

Since I am known as a "rich" person, I feel I have to tip at least $5 each time I check my coat. On top of that, I would have to wear a very expensive coat, and it would have to be insured. Added up, without a topcoat I save over $20,000 a year.
ARISTOTLE ONASSIS

The more money an American accumulates, the less interesting he becomes.
GORE VIDAL

Sometimes the pilgrimage from rags to riches is a journey from rage to wretchedness.
R. W. HUBER

Poor men seek meat for their stomach, rich men stomach for their meat.
ENGLISH PROVERB

The rich never feel so good as when they are speaking of their possessions as responsibilities.
ROBERT LYND

Money alone can't bring you happiness, but money alone has not brought me unhappiness. I won't say my previous husbands thought only of my money, but it had a certain fascination for them.
BARBARA HUTTON

For many men, the acquisition of wealth does not end their troubles, it only changes them.
LUCIUS ANNAEUS SENECA

The rich are the real outcasts of society, and special missions should be organized for them.
NORMAN MACLEOD

He who multiplies riches multiplies cares.
BENJAMIN FRANKLIN

Keep company with the very rich and you'll end up picking up the check. STANLEY WALKER

To suppose, as we all suppose, that we could be rich and not behave as the rich behave, is like supposing that we could drink all day and stay sober.
LOGAN PEARSALL SMITH

We see how much a man has, and therefore we envy him; did we see how little he enjoys, we should rather pity him. JEREMIAH SEED

An accession of wealth is a dangerous predicament for a man. At first he is stunned if the accession be sudden, and is very humble and very grateful. Then he begins to speak a little louder, people think him more sensible and soon he thinks himself so.
RICHARD CECIL

Worldly riches are like nuts; many clothes are torn in getting them, many a tooth broke in cracking them, but never a belly filled with eating them.
RALPH VENNING

Watch lest prosperity destroy generosity.
                    HENRY WARD BEECHER

Let us not envy some men their accumulated riches; their burden would be too heavy for us; we could not sacrifice, as they do, health, quiet, honor and conscience, to obtain them: it is to pay so dear for them that the bargain is a loss.   JEAN de La BRUYÈRE

To teach rich men to enjoy life would mean to ask them to give money away, which is difficult, to say the least.   LI LIWENG

Better go to heaven in rags than to hell in embroidery.
                    PROVERB

The rich man and his daughter are soon parted.
                    FRANK McKINNEY HUBBARD

A fortune is usually the greatest of misfortunes to children. It takes the muscles out of the limbs, the brain out of the head, and virtue out of the heart.
                    HENRY WARD BEECHER

If you are poor, though you dwell in the busy market place, no one will inquire about you: if you are rich, though you dwell in the heart of the mountains, you will have distant relatives.   CHINESE PROVERB

I have a rich neighbor that is always so busy that he has no leisure to laugh; the whole business of his life is to get money, more money, that he may still get more. He considers not that it is not in the power of riches to make a man happy; for it was wisely said that 'there be as many miseries beyond riches as on this side of them.'   IZAAK WALTON

When you ascend the hill of prosperity, may you not meet a friend.   MARK TWAIN

For one rich man that is content there are a hundred that are not.   ANON

It is poor encouragement to toil through life to amass a fortune to ruin your children. In nine cases out of ten, a large fortune is the greatest curse which could be bequeathed to the young and inexperienced.
JEAN de la BRUYERE

Riches do not delight us so much with their possession as torment us with their loss. SAMUEL GREGORY

To acquire wealth is difficult, to preserve it more difficult, but to spend it wisely most difficult of all.
EDWARD PARSONS DAY

The man who dies leaving behind him millions of available wealth, which was his to administer during his life, will pass away "unwept, unhonored and unsung" no matter to what uses he leaves the dross which he cannot take with him. Of such as these the public verdict will then be: "The man who dies thus rich dies disgraced."

Such, in my opinion, is the true Gospel concerning Wealth, obedience to which is destined some day to solve the problem of the Rich and the Poor, and to bring "Peace on earth, among men Good Will."
ANDREW CARNEGIE

Riches enlarge, rather than satisfy appetite.
                              THOMAS FULLER

Many of our rich men have not been content with
equal protection and equal benefits but have besought
us to make them richer by act of Congress. By attempting to gratify their desires we have in the results
of our legislation arrayed section against section, interest against interest, and man against man in a fearful
commotion which threatens to shake the foundations
of our Union.   ANDREW JACKSON

If you look up a dictionary of quotations you will find
few reasons for a sensible man to desire to become
wealthy.   ROBERT LYND

Very few men acquire Wealth in such a manner as to
receive pleasure from it. As long as there is the enthu-
siasm of the chase they enjoy it. But when they begin
to look around and think of settling down, they find
that that part by which joy enters in, is dead to them.
They have spent their lives in heaping up colossal piles
of treasure, which stand at the end, like pyramids in
the desert, holding only the dust of things.
                    HENRY WARD BEECHER

There is a burden of care in getting riches; fear in
keeping them; temptation in using them; guilt in abus-
ing them; sorrow in losing them; and a burden of account at last to be given concerning them.
                         MATTHEW HENRY

Riches are apt to betray a man into arrogance.
                           JOSEPH ADDISON

There is nothing keeps longer than a middling fortune, and nothing melts away sooner than a great one. Poverty treads on the heels of great and unexpected riches.
FREDERICK SAUNDERS

The acquisition of wealth is the work of great labor; its possession a source of continual fear; its loss, of excessive grief.
LATIN SAYING

Nothing is so hard for those who abound in riches as to conceive how others can be in want.
JONATHAN SWIFT

The richer and bigger you are, the more considerate you have to be of other people's feelings if you are to succeed in taking the curse off being rich.
J. OGDEN SEYMOUR

There never was a banquet so sumptuous but someone dined poorly at it.
FRENCH PROVERB

What has destroyed every previous civilization has been the tendency to the unequal distribution of wealth and power. This same tendency, operating with increasing force, is observable in our civilization today, showing itself in every progressive community, and with greater intensity the more progressive the community.
HENRY GEORGE

Golden shackles are far worse than iron ones.
MOHANDAS GHANDHI

Abundance is a blessing to the wise;
The use of riches in discretion lies;

Learn this, ye men of wealth—a heavy purse
In a fool's pocket is a heavy curse.
                    RICHARD CUMBERLAND

They who lie soft and warm in a rich estate seldom
come to heat themselves at the altar.
                    ROBERT SOUTH

It is the curse of prosperity that it takes work away
from us, and shuts the door to hope and health of
spirit.   WILLIAM DEAN HOWELLS

Wealth is nothing in itself; it is not useful but when it
departs from us; its value is found only in that which it
can purchase. As to corporal enjoyment, money can
neither open new avenues of pleasure, nor block up the
passages of anguish. Disease and infirmity still continue to torture and enfeeble, perhaps exasperated by
luxury, or promoted by softness. With respect to the
mind, it has rarely been observed that wealth contributes much to quicken the discernment or elevate the
imagination, but may, by hiring flattery, or laying dili-
gence asleep, confirm error and harden stupidity.
                    SAMUEL JOHNSON

The problem of our age is the proper administration of
wealth so that the ties of brotherhood may still bind
together the rich and the poor in harmonious
relationships.   ANDREW CARNEGIE

What good does this huge weight of gold and silver if
fear forces you to bury it secretly in the ground?
                    HORACE

5 · SELLING

Selling

Whoever buys
Should have two eyes,
But one's enough
To sell the stuff.

To open a shop is easy, to keep it open is an art.
CONFUCIUS

Buy cheap, sell dear. **THOMAS LODGE**

The dearer a thing is, the cheaper as a general rule we
sell it. **SAMUEL BUTLER**

I detest life-insurance agents; they always argue that
some day I shall die, which is not so.
STEPHEN BUTLER-LEACOCK

Visit, that ye be not visited. **DON HEROLD**

Q. What's two and two?
A. Buying or selling?   LORD GRADE

When buyers don't fall for prices, prices must fall for buyers.   ANON

I remember well the time when a cabbage could sell itself just by being a cabbage. Nowadays it's no good being a cabbage—unless you have an agent and pay him a commission. Nothing is free any more to sell itself or give itself away.   JEAN GIRAUDOUX

When I sell liquor, it's called bootlegging; when my patrons serve it on silver trays on Lake Shore Drive, it's called hospitality.   AL CAPONE

When you buy something wholesale and sell it retail, is it double-dealing?   ANON

No one has insurance like the man who sells insurance.   LEOPOLD FECHTNER

Look out for the fellow who lets you do all the talking.
            FRANK McKINNEY HUBBARD

The Romantic Hero was no longer the knight, the wandering poet, the cowpuncher, the aviator, nor the brave young district attorney but the great sales manager who had an Analysis of Merchandising on his glass-topped desk, whose title of nobility was 'go getter.'   SINCLAIR LEWIS

For the most accurate results of sales forecasting, forget your present volumes; start with the future trends of the economy, then mix in projections of market demands and customer needs, and then finally evaluate your own firm's prospects for expansion and growth.

JESSE WERNER

I do not know any reading more easy, more fascinating, more delightful than a catalogue.

ANATOLE FRANCE

I have great faith in the people; as for their wisdom—well, Coca-Cola still outsells champagne.

ADLAI STEVENSON

The psychological batteries that propel a man onward day after day need constant recharging. Communication—with the boss and with home-office personnel—helps to do this. It gives a man confidence to know that he has an organization behind him, one he can draw on for backup and support.

WALTER E. BRUNAUER

A well-informed employee is the best sales person a company can have. E. J. THOMAS

When a man is trying to sell you something, don't imagine that he is that polite all the time.

EDGAR WATSON HOWE

We are inclined to believe those whom we do not know because they have never deceived us.

SAMUEL JOHNSON

It's a hectic crazy life. You're not like a shoe salesman, who can get rid of his wares. You're stuck with a product—yourself. NANCY SINATRA

If I see something I like, I buy it, then I try to sell it.
LORD GRADE

Without some dissimulation no business can be carried on at all.   LORD CHESTERFIELD

Pleasing ware is half sold.   GEORGE HERBERT

In nature nothing can be given, all things are sold.
RALPH WALDO EMERSON

I was successful because you believed in me.
ULYSSES S. GRANT

He that will do right in gross must needs do wrong by retail.   MICHEL de MONTAIGNE

Buying and selling is good and necessary; it is very necessary, and may, possibly, be very good; but it cannot be the noblest work of man; and let us hope that in our time it may not be esteemed the noblest work of an Englishman.   ANTHONY TROLLOPE

Promotion

You sell below cost
Just to save the day,
But I seem to be lost,
When they buy that way.

One-third of the people in the United States promote, while the other two-thirds provide. WILL ROGERS

In the factory we make cosmetics. In the store we sell hope. CHARLES REVSON

The sign brings customers. JEAN de la FONTAINE

Too many crooks spoil the percentage.
H. CHANDLER

The manufacturer who waits in the woods for the world to beat a path to his door, is a great optimist. But the manufacturer who shows his "mousetrap" to the world keeps the smoke coming out of his chimney.
O. B. WINTERS

Promoters are just guys with two pieces of bread looking for a piece of cheese. EVEL KNIEVEL

Everything comes to him who hustles while he waits.
THOMAS A. EDISON

What we think we know is that young sells better than old, pretty sells better than ugly, sports figures don't do very well, TV sells better than music, music does better than movies, and anything does better than politics. RICHARD STOLLEY

The perfect impasse is Avon calling and Revlon answering! ROBERT ORBEN

It comes in three sizes. Large, Giant and Super. I gave you the smaller size—Large. ANON

Don't ever slam a door: you might want to go back.
DON HEROLD

To be persuasive, we must be believable.
To be believable, we must be credible.
To be credible, we must be truthful.
EDWARD R. MURROW

We are all pretty much alike when we get out of town.
FRANK McKINNEY HUBBARD

Every crowd has a silver lining.
PHINEAS TAYLOR BARNUM

A promoter will provide the ocean if you will provide the ships.
ANON

He would sell even his share of the sun.
ITALIAN PROVERB

If you hype something and it succeeds you're a genius, it wasn't a hype. If you hype it and it fails then it's just a hype.
NEIL BOGART

Promoter: A man that wants to sell you something you don't want that he ain't got.
GERALD F. LIEBERMAN

The showmanship idea of yesterday was to give the public what it wanted. This is a fallacy. You don't know what they want and they don't know what they want.
S. L. ROTHAFEL

A hustler is a man who will talk you into giving him a free ride and make it seem as if he is doing you a great favour.
BILL VEECK

Everyone lives by selling something.
ROBERT LOUIS STEVENSON

He who sells what isn't his'n
Must buy it back or go to prison.   DANIEL DREW

The only promotion rules I can think of are that a
sense of shame is to be avoided at all costs and there is
never any reason for a hustler to be less cunning than
more virtuous men. Oh yes—whenever you think
you've got something really great, add ten percent
more.   BILL VEECK

The go-between wears a thousand sandals.
JAPANESE PROVERB

Your most important sale in life is to sell yourself to
yourself.   MAXWELL MALTZ

The wise guy is the sucker after all.
DIAMOND JIM BRADY

Beat your gong and sell your candies.
CHINESE PROVERB

Oratory is the power to talk people out of their sober
and natural opinions.   PAUL CHATFIELD

Auctioneer: The man who proclaims with a hammer
that he has picked a pocket with his tongue.
AMBROSE BIERCE

Cast thy bread upon the waters: for thou shalt find it
after many days.   *Ecclesiastes*

If the hill will not come to Mahomet, Mahomet will go to the hill. FRANCIS BACON

Man's feelings are always purest and most glowing in the hour of meeting and of farewell.
JEAN PAUL RICHTER

Fuel is not sold in a forest, nor fish on a lake.
CHINESE PROVERB

If you want to persuade people, show the immediate relevance and value of what you're saying in terms of meeting their needs and desires. HERB COHEN

Salesmanship

We tell
It well,
To sell
It well.

A salesman is one who sells goods that won't come back to customers who will. ANON

Salesmanship consists of transferring a conviction by a seller to a buyer. ARNOLD H. GLASGOW

In baiting a mouse-trap with cheese, always leave room for the mouse. SAKI

Better wear out shoes than sheets.   PROVERB

A salesman is the high priest of profits.   ANON

A salesman is an optimist who finds the world full of promising potential.   JERRY DASHKIN

Always go for the top man. WENDELL PHILLIPS

There is no such thing as "soft sell" and "hard sell." There is only "smart sell" and "stupid sell."
CHARLES BROWER

Sales resistance is the triumph of mind over patter.
EDMUND FULLER

Inequality of knowledge is the key to the sale.
DEIL O. GUSTAFSON

He who has a thing to sell
   And goes and whispers in a well,
Is not so apt to get the dollars
   As he who climbs a tree and hollers.   ANON

You must put the worm on the hook before the fish will bite.   REVEREND JIM JONES

When you are skinning your customers, you should leave some skin on to grow so that you can skin them again.   NIKITA KHRUSHCHEV

The soft spoken salesman strikes the hardest bargain.
ANON

Don't try to explain it; just sell it.   TOM PARKER

The best salesman we ever heard of was the one who sold two milking machines to a farmer who had only one cow. Then this salesman helped finance the deal by taking the cow as down payment on the two milking machines.   HERBERT V. PROCHNOW

To sell something, tell a woman it's a bargain; tell a man it's deductible.   EARL WILSON

Today's sales should be better than yesterday's—and worse than tomorrow's.   ANON

When my client gives me an absolute no, I blow a whistle and announce, "The second half is just beginning."   LARRY LEVITT

If you can't convince 'em, confuse 'em.
                        HARRY S. TRUMAN

He told me never to sell the bear's skin before one has killed the beast.   JEAN de la FONTAINE

He that speaks ill of the mare will buy her.
                        BENJAMIN FRANKLIN

There's no way to recondition a welcome when it's worn out.   FRANK McKINNEY HUBBARD

A man without a smiling face must not open a shop.
                        CHINESE PROVERB

A salesman is someone who it is always a pleasure to bid goodbye to.   ANON

Never lie when the truth is more profitable.
STANISLAW J. LEC

The cheaper the crook, the gaudier the patter.
DASHIELL HAMMETT

A salesman is got to dream, boy. It comes with the territory.
ARTHUR MILLER

No one has endurance
Like the man who sells insurance.
INSURANCE BROKERS' AXIOM

He travels the fastest who travels alone.
RUDYARD KIPLING

One must always have one's boots on and be ready to go.
MICHEL de MONTAIGNE

Good salesmanship will find a cure for the common cold shoulder.
ANON

We may not know when we're well off, but investment salesmen get on to it somehow.
FRANK McKINNEY HUBBARD

Man does not only sell commodities, he sells himself and feels himself to be a commodity.
ERICH FROMM

One of the best ways to persuade others is with your ears—by listening to them.
DEAN RUSK

Try novelties for salesmen's bait.
For novelty wins everyone.
JOHANN WOLFGANG von GOETHE

Be first at the feast, and last at the fight.
INDIAN PROVERB

Friendliness stops as soon as the sale is made.
JONATHAN LARKIN

Ours is the country where, in order to sell your product, you don't so much point out its merits as you first work like hell to sell yourself.
LOUIS KRONENBERGER

He that travels much knows much.
THOMAS FULLER

There is hardly any man so strict as not to vary a little from truth when he is to make an excuse.
LORD HALIFAX

Keep your broken arm inside your sleeve.
CHINESE PROVERB

Few human beings are proof against the implied flattery of rapt attention.
JACK WOODFORD

Negotiation

If you won't negotiate
With those intent on stealing,
You must either deviate
Or might as well stop dealing.

Agreement is brought about by changing people's minds—other people's.　　　　S. I. HAYAKAWA

If you think you have someone eating out of your hand, it's a good idea to count your fingers.
　　　　　　　　　　　　　　MARTIN BUXBAUM

There's no such thing as a free lunch.
　　　　　　　　　　　　　　MILTON FRIEDMAN

You can learn more about America watching one half-hour of 'Let's Make a Deal' than by watching Walter Cronkite for an entire month.　　　MONTY HALL

Whenever two people meet there are really six people present. There is each man as he sees himself, each man as the other person sees him, and each man as he really is.　　　　　　　　　WILLIAM JAMES

One catches more flies with a spoonful of honey than with twenty casks of vinegar.
　　　　　　　　　　　　HENRY IV King of France

Everybody's negotiable.   MUHAMMAD ALI

When a person tells you, "I'll think it over and let you know"—you know.   OLIN MILLER

Don't let your mouth write no cheque your tail can't cash.   BO BIDDLEY

. . . Successful collaborative negotiation lies in finding out what the other side really wants and showing them a way to get it, while you get what you want.
          HERB COHEN

Never tell them what you wouldn't do.
          ADAM CLAYTON POWELL

It is hard to believe that a man is telling the truth when you know that you would lie if you were in his place.   HENRY LOUIS MENCKEN

If you are scared to go to the brink, you are lost.
          JOHN FOSTER DULLES

The fellow that agrees with everything you say is either a fool or he is getting ready to skin you.
          FRANK McKINNEY HUBBARD

Once the toothpaste is out of the tube, it's hard to get it back in!   H. R. HALDEMAN

It is taken for granted that by lunchtime the average man has been so beaten down by life that he will believe anything.   CHRISTOPHER MORLEY

Chaplin is no business man—all he knows is that he can't take any less.   SAMUEL GOLDWYN

With someone who holds nothing but trumps, it is impossible to play.   FRIEDRICH HEBBEL

We cannot negotiate with those who say, "What's mine is mine, what's yours is negotiable."
JOHN F. KENNEDY

Whenever you accept our views we shall be in full agreement with you.   MOSHE DAYAN

I am firm. You are obstinate. He is a pigheaded fool.
KATHARINE WHITEHORN

Negotiation in the classic diplomatic sense assumes parties more anxious to agree than to disagree.
DEAN ACHESON

Everything in this country, whether it be commercial or literary, begins with lunch and ends with dinner.
A. BARTON HEPBURN

We promise according to our hopes, and perform according to our fears.
FRANCOIS DUC de la ROCHEFOUCAULD

Flattery is the infantry of negotiation.
LORD CHANDOS

Let us never negotiate out of fear, but let us never fear to negotiate.   JOHN F. KENNEDY

Some persons make promises for the pleasure of breaking them. **WILLIAM HAZLITT**

Promises and pie-crust are made to be broken. **JONATHAN SWIFT**

When a man repeats a promise again and again, he means to fail you. **EDMUND FULLER**

Always define your terms. **ERIC PARTRIDGE**

"No" and "yes" are words quickly said, but they need a great amount of thought before you utter them. **BALTASAR GRACIAN**

Better break your word than do worse in keeping it. **THOMAS FULLER**

A dinner lubricates business. **WILLIAM SCOTT**

Vows begin when hope dies. **LEONARDO da VINCI**

Between cultivated minds the first interview is the best. **RALPH WALDO EMERSON**

Let every eye negotiate for itself, and trust no agent. **WILLIAM SHAKESPEARE**

If a man deceives me once, shame on him; if he deceives me twice, shame on me. **PROVERB**

For of all the hard things to bear and grin,
The hardest is being taken in. **PHOEBE CARY**

The greater the contrast, the greater is the potential. Great energy only comes from a correspondingly great tension between opposites.   CARL JUSTAV JUNG

Hail fellow, well met,
All dirty and wet;
Find out, if you can,
Who's master, who's man.   JONATHAN SWIFT

There be that can pack the cards, and yet cannot play well.   FRANCIS BACON

The most advantageous negotiations are those one conducts with human vanity, for one often obtains very substantial things from it while giving very little of substance in return. One never does so well when dealing with ambition or avarice.
                    ALEXIS de TOCQUEVILLE

Only that mind draws me which I cannot read.
                    RALPH WALDO EMERSON

Boldness is an ill-keeper of promise.
                              FRANCIS BACON

I like not fair terms and a villain's mind.
                    WILLIAM SHAKESPEARE

Customers

Make sure you'll be,
With any luck,
The only (s)he
To pass the buck.

No one ever went broke underestimating the taste of the American public. HENRY LOUIS MENCKEN

The consumer is not a moron—she is your wife.
DAVID OGILVY

Warning—Customers Are Perishable. STORE SIGN

The best mental effort in the game of business is concentrated on the major problem of securing the customer's dollar before the other fellow gets it.
STUART CHASE

Keep in mind the fact that Ralph Nader could be the first customer for your new product. ANON

Women aren't embarrassed when they buy men's pajamas, but a man buying a nightgown acts as though he were dealing with a dope peddler.
JIMMY CANNON

Nothing is more satisfying than when timing and delivery occur in perfect sequence. ANON

The old days of caveat emptor—let the buyer beware
—are gone. ALVAN MACAULEY

Tipping started when gratuities were dropped in a box
marked T.I.P.S.—to insure prompt service.
BERTRAM TROY

Don't a fellow feel good after he gets out of a store
where he nearly bought something?
FRANK McKINNEY HUBBARD

On the subject of confused people, I liked the store
detective who said he'd seen a lot of people so confused that they'd stolen things, but never one so confused that they'd paid twice.
BARONESS PHILLIPS

No customer can be worse than no customer.
LEOPOLD FECHTNER

A lady is known by the product she endorses.
OGDEN NASH

The public doesn't know what it wants. We offer beautiful things that we like. Anyone who disagrees with
our taste is free to go elsewhere. TIFFANY and CO.

The customer who's always right probably waits on
himself. LAURENCE J. PETER

The buyer needs a hundred eyes, the seller not one.
GEORGE HERBERT

If you don't see what you want, Japan hasn't copied it
yet. STORE SIGN

People will buy anything that's one to a customer.
                                    SINCLAIR LEWIS

A consumer is a shopper who is sore about something.
                                    HAROLD COFFIN

Today the future occupation of all moppets is to be
skilled consumers.   DAVID REISMAN

A floor-walker, tired of his job, gave it up and joined
the police force. Several months later a friend asked
him how he liked being a policeman. "Well," he replied, "the pay and the hours are good, but what I like
best of all is that the customer is always wrong."
                                    SALES SCRAP BOOK

Shopping can be fun. It can be an emotional outlet.
Women go shopping to buy friendship or flattery from
the assistant. For some women, shopping is a sex com-
pensation. So the shop must seduce the customer.
                                    LADY DARTMOUTH

The American consumer is not notable for his imagination and does not know what he "wants."
                                    ANDREW HACKER

Advertising created in the consumer an insatiable desire for goods, and the installment plan gave him the
immediate means to satisfy his desires.
                                    HENRY MORTON ROBINSON

The customer is an object to be manipulated, not a
concrete person whose aims the businessman is interested to satisfy.   ERIC FROMM

If you want good service, serve yourself.
SPANISH PROVERB

The public buys its opinions as it buys its meat, or takes in its milk, on the principle that it is cheaper to do this than to keep a cow. So it is, but the milk is more likely to be watered.   SAMUEL BUTLER

Nothing is as irritating as the fellow that chats pleasantly while he's overcharging you.
FRANK McKINNEY HUBBARD

You pays your money and takes your choice. *Punch*

The only part of the hog that the packers waste is the squeal, and the consumers furnish that.   ANON

If you sell diamonds, you cannot expect to have many customers. But a diamond is a diamond even if there are no customers.   SWAMI PRABHUPADA

A little bit of quality
  Will always make 'em smile;
A little bit of courtesy
  Will bring 'em in a mile;
A little bit of friendliness
  Will tickle 'em 'tis plain—
And a little bit of service
  Will bring 'em back again.   ANON

When you buy, use your eyes and your mind, not your ears.   CZECHOSLOVAKIAN PROVERB

Of what value would mass production be without mass consumption? How could we stimulate mass consumption without mass merchandising? And how could we have mass merchandising without mass advertising? PAUL GARRETT

Every human being has a vote every time he makes a purchase. No one is disenfranchised on account of age, sex, race, religion, education, length of residence, or failure to register. Every day is election day . . . Moreover, minorities count.
  W. T. FOSTER and W. CATCHINGS

If the customers don't want to come, you can't keep them from it. WOLFE KAUFMAN

Human service is the highest form of self-interest for the person who serves. ELBERT HUBBARD

"Scorn not the common man," says the age of abundance. "He may have no soul; his personality may be exactly the same as his neighbors; and he may not produce anything worth having. But, thank God, he consumes." JOSEPH WOOD KRUTCH

The consumer today is the victim of the manufacturer who launches on him a regiment of products for which he must make room in his soul.

  MARY McCARTHY

In the jungle of the marketplace, the intelligent buyer must be alert to every commercial sound, to every snapping of a selling twig, to every rustle that may signal the uprising arm holding the knife pointed toward the jugular vein. DEXTER MASTERS

Consumer wants can have bizarre, frivolous, or even immoral origins, and an admirable case can still be made for a society that seeks to satisfy them. But the case cannot stand if it is the process of satisfying wants that creates the wants.

JOHN KENNETH GALBRAITH

He who findest fault meaneth to buy.

THOMAS FULLER

It is naught, it is naught saith the buyer. But when he is gone his way, then he boasteth. *Proverbs*

6 · MARKETING

Marketing

The essential allegory
Of marketing strategy
Is apropos
The Socio-
Economic Category.

They say if you build a better mousetrap than your neighbor, people are going to come running. They are like hell. It's the marketing that makes the difference.
ED JOHNSON

In a consumer society, the best product you can manufacture is one that must be replaced immediately. Like munitions . . . You make a bomb and sell it to the government. They . . . blow it up . . . They have to come right back to you and buy another one.
GENE LEES

It is amazing how complete is the delusion that beauty is goodness.
LEO TOLSTOY

You don't buy coal, you buy heat;
You don't buy circus tickets, you buy thrills;
You don't buy a paper, you buy news;
You don't buy spectacles, you buy vision.
You don't buy printing, you buy selling.   ANON

If Botticelli were alive today he'd be working for *Vogue*.   PETER USTINOV

For every credibility gap there is a gullibility gap.
                    RICHARD CLOPTON

It is only the modern that ever becomes old-fashioned.
                    OSCAR WILDE

Since both Switzerland's national products, snow and chocolate, melt, the cuckoo clock was invented solely in order to give tourists something solid to remember it by.   ALAN COREN

A hamburger by any other name costs twice as much.
                    EVAN ESAR

For the historian, as distinct from the critic of art, the chocolate-box is one of the most significant products of our age, precisely because of its role as a catalyst.
                    ERNST GOMBRICH

These are difficult days for automobile manufacturers; they're thinking up ways to make their products safer and new names to make them sound more dangerous.
                    THOMAS la MANCE

The market is the place set apart where men may deceive each other.   ANACHARSIS

We ain't got hold of culture yet, but when we do get her, we'll make her hum. ANON

The search for the best possible product at the most possible mark-up with the shortest possible duration for the earliest possible replacement. JOHN CIARDI

What the public like best is fruit that is overripe.
JEAN COCTEAU

Next to the American corpse, the American bride is the hottest thing in today's merchandising market.
KITTY HANSON

I am the world's worst salesman: therefore I must make it easy for people to buy.
F. W. WOOLWORTH

We follow the law of demand and supply. ANON

Benjamin Franklin may have discovered electricity but it was the man who invented the meter who made the money. EARL WILSON

The armpit had its moment of glory, and the toes, with their athlete's foot . . . We went through wrinkles, we went through diets . . . We conquered hemorrhoids. So the businessmen sat back and said, "What's left?" And some smart guy said, "The vagina" . . . Today the vagina, tomorrow the world.
JERRY DELLA FEMINA

What's in a name? A 35 percent markup.
VINCE THURSTON

The market potential in China
is one billion toothbrushes and two billion armpits.
ANON

I once made a design for Zenith, and they turned it
down because it was a design that would not go out of
fashion. They asked, "What will we do next year?"
ISAMU NOGUCHI

Had a look at the alligators. Just floating handbags,
really.
TREVOR GRIFFITHS

Begin with another's to end with your own.
BALTASAR GRACIAN

I persuade, you educate, they manipulate.
DR. ALLEN CRAWFORD

The water closet like the harp is essentially—a solo
instrument.
GRAFFITI

Imitation is criticism.
WILLIAM BLAKE

The world is quite right. It does not have to be
consistent.
CHARLOTTE PERKINS GILMAN

The Bathtub: When producers want to know what the
public wants, they graph it as curves. When they want
to tell the public what to get, they say it curves.
MARSHALL McLUHAN

If the package doesn't say "New" these days, it better
say "Seven Cents Off."
SPENCER KLAW

We live in a world of things, and our only connection with them is that we know how to manipulate or to consume them.   ERICH FROMM

It is true that America produces and consumes more cars, soap and bathtubs than any other nation, but we live among these objects, rather than by them.
                               MARY McCARTHY

God will not have any human being know what will sell, nor even when anyone is going to die, nor even whether or not it is going to rain.
                               SAMUEL BUTLER

A living is made, by selling something that everybody needs at least once a year. Yes, sir! And a million is made by producing something that everybody needs every day. You artists produce something that nobody needs at any time.   THORNTON WILDER

Those marketing guys would love the Jolly Green Giant to get brown around the edges so they could launch a new brand.   ANON

The cure for "Materialism" is to have enough for everybody and to spare. When people are sure of having what they need they cease to think about it.
                               HENRY FORD

New links must be forged as old ones rust.
                               JANE HOWARD

We can vary things so as to make them bigger or smaller, heavier or lighter, thicker or thinner. In its new form the article may serve its purpose more efficiently or more cheaply, or it may adapt itself to an altogether different purpose.

ROYAL BANK of CANADA

Pleasing ware is half sold.   PROVERB

"What's new?" is an interesting and broadening eternal question, but one which, if pursued exclusively, results only in an endless parade of trivia and fashion, the silt of tomorrow. I would like, instead, to be concerned with the question "What is best?" a question which cuts deeply rather than broadly, a question whose answers tend to move the silt downstream.

ROBERT M. PIRSIG

Statistics

Logistics are never static;
Statistics are never logic.

A group of numbers looking for an argument.

ANON

In the field of marketing and advertising, statistics are like bikinis; they reveal a good deal that is both interesting and instructive, but they usually conceal what is really vital.

HARRY HENRY

How far would Moses have gone if he had taken a poll in Egypt?   HARRY S. TRUMAN

Facts speak louder than statistics.
                          MR. JUSTICE STREATFIELD

It is now proved beyond doubt that smoking is one of the leading causes of statistics.
                          FLETCHER KNEBEL

I guessed it would happen sooner or later—the latest figures show 100 percent undecided or don't know.
                          ANON

Do not put faith in what statistics say until you have carefully considered what they do not say.
                          WILLIAM W. WATT

A statistician is one who collects data and draws confusions.   HYMAN MAXWELL BERSTON

He uses statistics as a drunken man uses lamp-posts— for support rather than for illumination.
                          ANDREW LANG

One of the questions was, "Do you think contraceptives are 100 percent reliable?" Unfortunately, the word "contraceptive" was not always understood so when the answer was "I don't know," it was not clear if the answer referred to the reliability of contraceptives or merely that the question was not understood.
                          M. SCHOFIELD

I could prove God statistically.
                          GEORGE GALLUP, JR.

There are two kinds of statistics, the kind you look up and the kind you make up.   REX STOUT

There are three kinds of lies; lies, damned lies, and statistics.   MARK TWAIN

Statistics are for losers.   SCOTTY BOWMAN

The object of statistics is to discover methods of condensing information concerning large groups of allied facts into brief and compendious expressions suitable for discussion.   FRANCIS GALTON

Statistician—A man who can go directly from an unwarranted assumption to a preconceived conclusion.
        C. KENT WRIGHT

Statistics are no substitute for judgment.
        HENRY CLAY

Statisticians have figured the time lost in every other business but never the time wasted figuring statistics.
        ANON

A single death is a tragedy, a million deaths is a statistic.   JOSEPH STALIN

Statistics indicate that, as a result of overwork, modern executives are dropping like flies on the nation's golf courses.   IRA WALLACH

Statistics are like alienists—they will testify for either side.   FIORELLO La GUARDIA

Statistics is the art of lying by means of figures.
DR. WILHELM STEKHEL

Our present addiction to pollsters and forecasters is a symptom of our chronic uncertainty about the future. Even when the forecasts prove wrong, we will go on asking for them. We watch our experts read the entrails of statistical tables and graphs the way the ancients watched their soothsayers read the entrails of a chicken. ERIC HOFFER

Prolonged statistics are a lethal dose, which if it does not kill will certainly dispel your audience.
ILKA CHASE

Definitions of Advertising

> *The ad*
> *Can make*
> *The Bad*
> *Seem better.*

Advertising is what you do when you can't go to see somebody, that's all it is. FAIRFAX CONE

When business is good it pays to advertise;
When business is bad you've got to advertise. ANON

Ads are the cave art of the twentieth century.
MARSHALL McLUHAN

Advertising is the principal reason why the businessman has come to inherit the earth.
JAMES R. ADAMS

Advertising may be described as the science of arresting the human intelligence long enough to get money from it.
STEPHEN LEACOCK

Something which makes one think he's longed all his life for a thing he's never even heard of before.
ANON

Advertising is the lubricant for the free-enterprise system.
LEO ARTHUR KELMENSON

Promise, large promise, is the soul of an advertisement.
SAMUEL JOHNSON

Advertising is the place where the selfish interests of the manufacturer coincide with the interests of society.
DAVID OGILVY

The true role of advertising is exactly that of the first salesman hired by the first manufacturer—to get business away from his competitors.
ROSSER REEVES

An advertising agency—85 per cent confusion and 15 per cent commission.
FRED ALLEN

Advertising is the art of making whole lies out of half truths.
EDGAR A. SHOAFF

The message of the media is the commercial.
                              ALICE EMBREE

Advertising can't sell any product; it can only help to
sell a product the people want to buy.
                              JEREMY TUNSTALL

Advertising is the mouthpiece of business.
                              JAMES R. ADAMS

Advertising is the rattling of a stick inside a swill
bucket.   **GEORGE ORWELL**

Advertisements contain the only truths to be relied on
in a newspaper.   **THOMAS JEFFERSON**

Advertising is a valuable economic factor because it is
the cheapest way of selling goods, especially if the
goods are worthless.   **SINCLAIR LEWIS**

Advertising is the modern substitute for argument.
                              GEORGE SANTAYANA

Advertising is the principle of mass production applied to selling.   **DR. J. T. DORRANCE**

Advertising isn't a science. It's persuasion. And persuasion is an art.   **BILL BERNBACH**

Ads push the principle of noise all the way to the
plateau of percussion . . . They are quite in accord
with the procedures of brainwashing.
                              MARSHALL McLUHAN

Advertising is the life of trade.
CALVIN COOLIDGE

The advertisement is one of the most interesting and difficult of modern literary forms.
ALDOUS HUXLEY

If advertising encourages people to live beyond their means, so does marriage. BRUCE BARTON

Advertising is the whip which hustles humanity up the road to the Better Mousetrap. It is the vision which reproaches man for the paucity of his desires.
E. S. TURNER

Advertising is the essence of public contact.
CYRUS H. K. CURTIS

Advertising is legalized lying.
HERBERT GEORGE WELLS

Advertisements are now so numerous that they are very negligently perused, and it is therefore become necessary to gain attention by magnificence of promises, and by eloquences sometimes sublime and sometimes pathetic. SAMUEL JOHNSON

Advertising promotes that divine discontent which makes people strive to improve their economic status.
RALPH STARR BUTLER

Advertising ministers to the spiritual side of trade.
CALVIN COOLIDGE

Advertising is the key to world prosperity; without it today modern business would be paralyzed.

JULIUS KLEIN

Advertising nourishes the consuming power of men . . . It spurs individual exertion and greater production.

SIR WINSTON CHURCHILL

As a whole, advertising is committed to the ways of business, and as the ways of business are seldom straight and narrow, advertising perforce must follow a dubious path.

J. THORNE SMITH

Advertising

Adverts use the female form,
Isn't it a caper?
Why does everyone conform,
Right down to toilet paper?

Doing business without advertising is like winking at a girl in the dark. You know what you're doing but no one else does.

STEWART H. BRITT

Nothing's so apt to undermine your confidence in a product as knowing that the commercial selling it has been approved by the company that makes it.

FRANKLIN P. JONES

Half the money I spend on advertising is wasted, and the trouble is I don't know which half.
JOHN WANAMAKER

It may be the way the cookie crumbles on Madison Avenue, but in Hong Kong it's the way the egg rolls!
ROBERT ORBEN

In the ad biz, sincerity is a commodity bought and paid for like everything else.
MALCOLM MUGGERIDGE

I think that I shall never see
a billboard lovely as a tree.
Indeed unless the billboards fall
I'll never see a tree at all.   OGDEN NASH

On CBS Radio the news of Ed Murrow's death, reportedly from lung cancer, was followed by a cigarette commercial.   ALEXANDER KENDRICK

I have been against commercial broadcasting ever since I heard a Toscanini radio concert in New York interrupted by the sponsor's slogan—"It may be December outside, ladies; but it is always August under your armpits."   JOHN SNAGGE

Advertising costs in the U.S. amount to approximately $100 per person per year.   ANON

Few people at the beginning of the nineteenth century needed an adman to tell them what they wanted.
JOHN KENNETH GALBRAITH

In a society where people get more or less what they want sexually, it is much more difficult to motivate them in an industrialised context, to make them buy refrigerators and cars. WILLIAM S. BURROUGHS

The best ad is a good product. ALAN H. MEYER

A good ad should be like a good sermon; it must not only comfort the afflicted, it also must afflict the comfortable. BERNICE FITZ-GIBBON

Content is more important than form. What you say in advertising is more important than how you say it. DAVID OGILVY

The guy you've really got to reach with your advertising is the copywriter for your chief rival's advertising agency. If you can terrorize him, you've got it licked. HOWARD L. GOSSAGE

The number of agency people required to shoot a commercial on location is in direct proportion to the mean temperatures of the location. SHELBY PAGE

Many a small thing has been made large by the right kind of advertising. MARK TWAIN

I must say we really enjoy all the commercials in our household but I always get a tense feeling in case anyone picks the wrong pile of washing in that detergent advertisement. *TV Times*

In advertising there is a saying that if you can keep your head while all those around you are losing theirs —then you just don't understand the problem. HUGH M. BEVILLE, JR.

If you call a spade a spade you won't last long in the advertising business.   ANON

The modern little Red Riding Hood, reared on singing commercials, has no objection to being eaten by the wolf.   MARSHALL McLUHAN

They took a poll on Madison Avenue and here is what people in the advertising industry are worried about most:
Inflation, unemployment, crime, and armpits . . .
Not necessarily in that order.   ROBERT ORBEN

It is our job to make women unhappy with what they have.   B. EARL PUCKETT

The business that believes that advertising is not necessary may find that customers take the same attitude about the business.   ANON

You can fool all the people all of the time if the advertising is right and the budget is big enough.
                    JOSEPH E. LEVINE

Those who prefer their English sloppy have only themselves to thank if the advertising writer uses his mastery of vocabulary and syntax to mislead their minds.   DOROTHY L. SAYERS

The philosophy behind much advertising is based on the old observation that every man is really two men —the man he is and the man he wants to be.
                    WILLIAM FEATHER

From any cross-section of ads, the general advertiser's attitude would seem to be: If you are a lousy, smelly, idle, status-seeking neurotic moron, give me your money.   KENNETH BROMFIELD

Those who most enjoy ads, already own the products.
                    EDMUND CARPENTER

The advertising man is a liaison between the products of business and the mind of the nation. He must know both before he can serve either.   GLENN FRANK

A slogan is a form of words for which memorability has been bought.   RICHARD USBORNE

Advertising has annihilated the power of the most powerful adjectives.   PAUL VALERY

I do not read advertisements—I would spend all my time wanting things.
                    ARCHBISHOP of CANTERBURY

The vice-president of an advertising agency is a bit of executive fungus that forms on a desk that has been exposed to conference.   FRED ALLEN

It used to be that a fellow went on the police force after everything else failed, but today he goes in the advertising game.   ELBERT HUBBARD

Never write an advertisement which you wouldn't want your family to read. You wouldn't tell lies to your own wife. Don't tell them to mine. Do as you would be done by. If you tell lies about a product, you will be found out—either by the Government, which will prosecute you, or by the consumer, who will punish you by not buying your product a second time. Good products can be sold by honest advertising. If you don't think the product is good, you have no business to be advertising it.   DAVID M. OGILVY

Living in an age of advertisement, we are perpetually disillusioned.   JOHN BOYNTON PRIESTLEY

If I were starting life over again, I am inclined to think that I would go into the advertising business in preference to almost any other. The general raising of the standards of modern civilization among all groups of people during the past half-century would have been impossible without that spreading of the knowledge of higher standards by means of advertising.
     FRANKLIN D. ROOSEVELT

Have you ever considered what anxious thought, what consummate knowledge of human nature, what dearly-bought experience go into the making of an advertisement?   WILLIAM J. LOCKE

It is far easier to write ten passably effective sonnets, good enough to take in the not too inquiring critic, than one effective advertisement that will take in the few thousand of the uncritical buying public.
     LEONARD ALDOUS HUXLEY

You can tell the ideal of a nation by its advertisements.
     NORMAN DOUGLAS

Production goes up and up because high pressure advertising and salesmanship constantly create new

needs that must be satisfied; this is Admass—a consumer's race with donkeys chasing an electric carrot.
JOHN BOYNTON PRIESTLEY

The trouble with us in America isn't that the poetry of life has turned to prose, but that it has turned to advertising copy.　LOUIS KRONENBERGER

Who are the advertising men kidding? Between the tired, sad, gentle faces of the subway riders and the grinning Holy Families of the Admass, there exists no possibility of even a wishful identification.
MARY McCARTHY

The deeper problems connected with advertising come less from the unscrupulousness of our "deceivers" than from our pleasure in being deceived, less from the desire to seduce than from the desire to be seduced.
DANIEL J. BOORSTIN

We live surrounded by a systematic appeal to a dream world which all mature scientific people readily would reject. We quite literally advertise our commitment to immaturity, mendacity and profound gullibility. It is the hallmark of the culture.
JOHN KENNETH GALBRAITH

With regard to anything that is likely to obsess a society, it is important not to give it too much advertisement.　PERCY WYNDHAM LEWIS

The advertiser is the overrewarded court jester and court pander at the democratic court.
JOSEPH WOOD KRUTCH

The more facts you tell, the more you sell. An advertisement's chance for success invariably increases as the number of pertinent merchandise facts included in the advertisement increases.

DR. CHARLES EDWARDS

Quality

It's not cheaper things
That we want to possess
But expensive things
That cost a lot less.

There is hardly anything in the world that some men cannot make a little worse and sell a little cheaper.

JOHN RUSKIN

Anybody can cut prices, but it takes brains to make a better article.

PHILIP D. ARMOUR

Progress is a continuing effort to make the things we eat, drink and wear as good as they used to be.

BILL VAUGHAN

When Queen Victoria once complained to Gladstone, her Prime Minister, that there were not many good preachers, he is said to have replied, "Madam, there are not many good anything."

KATIE LOUCHHELM

A wide screen just makes a bad film twice as bad.
SAMUEL GOLDWYN

If every new product is stamped "improved," what were we buying before? ANON

Less is more. ROBERT BROWNING

More will mean worse. KINGSLEY AMIS

I feel when people say "bigger and better" they should say "bigger and badder."
MARIE ELIZABETH KANE

If a man write a better book, preach a better sermon, or make a better mousetrap than his neighbor, though he build his house in the woods, the world will make a beaten path to his door.
RALPH WALDO EMERSON

He who builds a better mousetrap these days runs into material shortages, patent-infringement suits, work stoppages, collusive bidding, discount discrimination —and taxes. H. E. MARTZ

Never judge a cover by its book.
FRAN LEBOWITZ

Better is the enemy of good.
FRANCOIS VOLTAIRE

If it's good, they'll stop making it.
HERBERT BLOCK

Let advertisers spend the same amount of money improving their product that they do on advertising and they wouldn't have to advertise it.   WILL ROGERS

There's so much plastic in this culture that vinyl leopard skin is becoming an endangered synthetic.
LILY TOMLIN

If it works, it's out of date.   STAFFORD BEER

Here in Texas maybe we got into the habit of confusing bigness with greater.   EDNA FERBER

Who can tell what goes into a car today? The consumer won't know and the dealers get angry if you ask them.   RALPH NADER

Quality, not quantity, is my measure.
DOUGLAS JERROLD

The history of almost every civilization furnishes examples of geographical expansion coinciding with deterioration in quality.   ARNOLD J. TOYNBEE

In the past human life was lived in a bullock cart; in the future it will be lived in an aeroplane, and the change of speed amounts to a difference in quality.
ALFRED NORTH WHITEHEAD

You should not say it is not good. You should say you do not like it, and then, you know, you're perfectly safe.   JAMES McNEILL WHISTLER

How to improve goods and services? Learn to complain, politely and firmly, when you receive what you

believe to be inferior goods or services. Don't register your complaint with the salesperson or the waiter, but with the boss or the owner. He'll listen.
STANLEY MARCUS

Polished brass will pass upon more people than rough gold. **LORD CHESTERFIELD**

Good is not good, where better is expected.
THOMAS FULLER

Measure a thousand times and cut once.
TURKISH PROVERB

If fools went not to market, bad wares would not be sold. **PROVERB**

In doing of either, let wit bear a stroke,
For buying or selling of pig in a poke.
THOMAS TUSSER

You should buy the best you can afford, not the poorest or what you can't. From the best quality you will get the most satisfaction, the longest wear and the enjoyment of knowing it is the best without having to apologize for it. **STANLEY MARCUS**

If a thing is old, it is a sign that it was fit to live. The guarantee of continuity is quality.
EDDIE RICKENBACKER

Good merchandise, even hidden, soon finds buyers.
TITUS MACCIUS PLAUTUS

Those who enter to buy, support me. Those who come to flatter, please me. Those who complain, teach me how I may please others so that more will come. Only those hurt me who are displeased but do not complain. They refuse me permission to correct my errors and thus improve my service.   MARSHALL FIELD

When a man sells eleven ounces for twelve, he makes a compact with the devil, and sells himself for the value of an ounce.   HENRY WARD BEECHER

In the physical world, one cannot increase the size or quantity of anything without changing its quality. Similar figures exist only in pure geometry.
                                        PAUL VALERY

Absence of Quality is the essence of squareness.
                                        ROBERT PIRSIG

Bring your work back to the workshop twenty times. Polish it continuously, and polish it again.
                                        NICOLAS BOILEAU

The qualities we have do not make us so ridiculous as those which we affect.
        FRANCOIS DUC de la ROCHEFOUCAULD

Nothing is lasting that is feigned.
                                        ENGLISH PROVERB

How many pretenses men that sell goods weave! What poor articles, with what a good face, do they palm off on their customers!   HENRY WARD BEECHER

Quality—in its classic Greek sense—how to live with grace and intelligence, with bravery and mercy.
                                        THEODORE H. WHITE

Research

Re-search is a very good word
And the meaning is certainly plain;
When results are still quite absurd,
It literally means "search again."

Research is cheap if you want to stay in business, expensive if you don't. ANON

Research is to see what everybody has seen, and to think what nobody else has thought.
ALBERT SZENT-GYORGYI

Research is the process of going up alleys to see if they're blind. MARSTON BATES

You can analyse a glass of water and you're left with a lot of chemical components but nothing you can drink. J. B. S. HALDANE

Enough research will tend to support your theory.
ARTHUR BLOCH

No amount of experimentation can ever prove me right; a single experiment can prove me wrong.
ALBERT EINSTEIN

The outcome of any serious research can only be to make two questions grow where only one grew before.
THORSTEN VEBLEN

Basic research is when I'm doing what I don't know I'm doing.   WERNHER von BRAUN

I am going in search of a great perhaps.
    FRANCOIS RABELAIS

You can't make a baby in a month by getting nine women pregnant.   ANON

Research is an organized method for keeping you reasonably dissatisfied with what you have.
    CHARLES F. KETTERING

Nature is usually wrong.
    JAMES ABBOTT McNEIL WHISTLER

The firmest line that can be drawn upon the smoothest paper is still jagged edges if seen through a microscope. This does not matter until important deductions are made on the supposition that there are no jagged edges.   SAMUEL BUTLER

Research is something that tells you that a jackass has two ears.   ALBERT D. LASKER

The way to do research is to attack the facts at the point of greatest astonishment.   CELIA GREEN

No experiment is ever a complete failure. It can always be used as a bad example.   P. DICKSON

He had been eight years upon a project for extracting sunbeams out of cucumbers, which were to be put into phials hermetically sealed, and let out to warm the air in raw inclement summers.   JONATHAN SWIFT

I love fools' experiments. I am always making them.
CHARLES DARWIN

What is research but a blind date with knowledge?
WILL HENRY

If an experiment works, something has gone wrong.
ARTHUR BLOCH

Successful research impedes further successful researches.
KEITH J. PENDRED

What is wanted is not the will to believe but the wish to find out, which is the exact opposite.
BERTRAND RUSSELL

If politics is the art of the possible, research is surely the art of the soluble.
SIR PETER MEDAWAR

A research laboratory is not simply a building that contains apparatus for conducting experiments. I contend that it is a state of mind . . . The research man ought to be thought of as the fellow you keep up in the crows'-nest to see beyond your horizon, to tell you where there is another prize ship to be taken or a man-o'-war to be avoided.
CHARLES F. KETTERING

If you copy from one author, it's plagiarism. If you copy from two, it's research.
WILSON MIZNER

The ass went seeking for horns and lost his ears.
ARABIAN PROVERB

It may be a weed instead of a fish that, after all my labour, I may at last pull up.

MICHAEL FARADAY

True research requires an objective, even if the results turn out to be different from expectation.   ANON

Research means going into the unknown with the hope of finding something new to bring home. If you know what you're going to do, or even to find there, then it is not research at all, then it is only a kind of "honourable occupation."

ALBERT SZENT-GYORGYI

The feeling of, "aha, that's it," which accompanies the clothing of a situation with meaning, is emotionally very satisfying, and is the major charm of scientific research, or artistic creation, and of the solution of crossword puzzles. It is why the intellectual life is fun.

HUDSON HOAGLAND

Prosperity and obsolescence are absolutely tied together, and obsolescence makes prosperity. A research organization is the originator of obsolescence.

CHARLES F. KETTERING

7 · PLANNING

Planning

Use all the methods analytical,
Bring every detail into play;
Planning just to please the critical
Can cause the team to lose their way.

Adventure is the result of poor planning.
COLONEL BLATCHFORD SNELL

Long-range planning does not deal with future decisions, but with the future of present decisions.
PETER F. DRUCKER

Any business must always plan ahead, either to capitalize on success or to reverse the trend if not successful. **ANON**

The more concrete and complete the plans, the more likely it is to earn the respect of outsiders and their support in necessary financial matters.
JESSE WERNER

The more human beings proceed by plan, the more efficiently they may be hit by accident.
FRIEDRICH DURRENMATT

Things almost always turn out otherwise than one anticipates.
MAURICE HULST

An Act of God was defined as something which no reasonable man could have expected.
SIR ALAN PATRICK HERBERT

Advice would be more acceptable if it didn't always conflict with our plans.
ANON

Hindsight is good, foresight is better; but second sight is best of all.
EVAN ESAR

Hindsight is always twenty-twenty.
BILLY WILDER

Business more than any other occupation is a continual dealing with the future; it is a continual calculation, an instinctive exercise in foresight.
HENRY R. LUCE

Planning is the process by which profitable growth is sought and attained in a changing and uncertain world.
ANON

Too many businessmen never stop to ponder what they are doing; they reject the need for self-discipline: they are satisfied to be clever, when they need to be wise.
LOUIS FINKELSTEIN

I sometimes think that strategy is nothing but tactics talked through a brass hat.   R. V. JONES

Proposed sales figures or net profits that are ahead of this year's figures are merely pious hopes. Planned goals and objectives can only be built up by a careful series of chartered steps based on concrete judgments of what the market holds for you. JESSE WERNER

You can never plan the future by the past.
    EDMUND BURKE

Never take anything for granted.
    BENJAMIN DISRAELI

Make no little plans. They have no magic to stir men's blood. Make big plans: aim high in hope and work.
    D. H. BURNHAM

The same system that produced a bewildering succession of new model, style-obsolescent autos and refrigerators can also produce an endless out-pouring of new-model, style-obsolescent science.
    HARVEY WHEELER

What is clear beyond question is that the immediate foreground is obscure.   *Daily Telegraph*

A perambulator hasn't much choice of tactics against a furniture van.   GEORGE BERNARD SHAW

It is a bad plan that admits of no modification.
    PUBLILIUS SYRUS

Long range planning should consider buying other companies, merging or joint venture possibilities to obtain new sources or markets.   JESSE WERNER

I shall always consider the best guesser the best prophet.   MARCUS TULLIUS CICERO

The wisest prophets make sure of the event first.
HORACE WALPOLE

Particulars are not to be examined till the whole has been surveyed.   EMANUEL CELLER

Our main business is not to see what lies dimly at a distance, but to do what lies clearly at hand.
THOMAS CARLYLE

When we are planning for posterity, we ought to remember that virtue is not hereditary.
THOMAS PAINE

In action, be primitive, in foresight, a strategist.
RENE CHAR

Hope nothing from luck, and the probability is that you will be so prepared, forewarned, and forearmed, that all shallow observers will call you lucky.
EDWARD GEORGE BULWER-LYTTON

He who every morning plans the transaction of the day and follows out that plan, carries a thread that will guide him through the maze of the most busy life. But where no plan is laid, where the disposal of time is surrendered merely to the chance of incidence, chaos will soon reign.   VICTOR HUGO

One cannot plan too carefully, but it is well to do this disinterestedly, as if you were planning for someone else, not committing yourself to execution nor drawing in advance upon that fund of emotion which you will need when you come to act. There are no such wastes as those of the anticipative imagination.

CHARLES HORTON COOLEY

The pursuit of novelty is one of the least original and most meretricious of aesthetic strategies.

STANLEY KUNITZ

The empires of the future are empires of the mind.

CHARLES CHURCHILL

Detail

*It's the little things that vex us
And put us on the rack;
We can sit anywhere in Texas
But not upon a tack.*

Doing little things well is the way towards doing big things better.　　　　　　　　　　　　　　　　ANON

We think in generalities, but we live in detail.

ALFRED NORTH WHITEHEAD

Life is hard.
By the yard.
But by the inch.
Life's a cinch!   JEAN L. GORDON

Show me a man who cannot bother to do little things
and I'll show you a man who cannot be trusted to do
big things.   LAURENCE D. BELL

It has long been an axiom of mine that the little things
are infinitely the most important.
                    SIR ARTHUR CONAN DOYLE

Looking at small advantages prevents great affairs
from being accomplished.   CONFUCIUS

In great matters men show themselves as they wish to
be seen; in small matters as they are.
                    GAMALIEL BRADFORD

A tendency to handle petty details can be a subcon-
scious hiding from inadequacy.   ANON

For want of a nail the shoe was lost;
For want of a shoe the horse was lost;
For want of a horse the rider was lost;
For want of a rider the battle was lost;
All for want of care about a horseshoe nail.
                    BENJAMIN FRANKLIN

Details often kill initiative, but there have been few
successful men who weren't good at details. Don't ignore details. Lick them.   WILLIAM B. GIVEN

The Americans believe they answered all first questions in 1776: since then they've just been hammering out the practical details.   RAY SMITH

Less is more.
God is in the details.   MIES van der ROHE

He that can see a louse as far away as China is unconscious of an elephant on his nose.
                    MALAY PROVERB

Having precise ideas often leads to a man doing nothing.   PAUL VALERY

People talk fundamentals and superlatives and then make some changes of detail.
               OLIVER WENDELL HOLMES

Look after the molehills and the mountains will look after themselves.   RAYMOND HULL

What deserves your attention most is the last thing to get it.   EPICTETUS

Men trip not on mountains, they stumble on stones.
                HINDUSTANI PROVERB

Watch out for the little things in life; a fish bone is much more dangerous than a soup bone.
                    O.A. BATTISTA

Small minds are much distressed by little things. Great minds see them all but are not upset by them.
          FRANCOIS DUC de la ROCHEFOUCAULD

The displacement of a little sand can change occasionally the course of a deep river.
MANUEL GONZALES PRADA

Our grand business is undoubtedly not to see what lies dimly at a distance, but to do what lies clearly at hand.
THOMAS CARLYLE

Don't look for the fifth foot of a cat.
SPANISH PROVERB

Sometimes when I considered what tremendous consequences come from little things—a chance word, a tap on the shoulder, or a penny dropped on a newsstand—I am tempted to think . . . there are no little things.
BRUCE BARTON

When one comes down to particular instances, everything becomes more complicated. ALBERT CAMUS

Little drops of water, little grains of sand,
make the mighty ocean and the pleasant land;
so the little minutes humble though they be
make the might ages of eternity.
MRS. JULIA A. FLETCHER CARNEY

To know things well, we must know them in detail, but as that is almost endless, our knowledge is always superficial and imperfect.
FRANCOIS DUC de la ROCHEFOUCAULD

Beware of the man who won't be bothered with details.
WILLIAM FEATHER

The smallest hair throws its shadow.
JOHANN WOLFGANG von GOETHE

Don't be afraid to give your best to what seemingly are small jobs. Every time you conquer one it makes you that much stronger. If you do the little jobs well, the big ones will tend to take care of themselves.
DALE CARNEGIE

No one sees further into a generalization than his own knowledge of details extends.   WILLIAM JAMES

Never cut what you can untie.   JOSEPH JOUBERT

The big things you can see with one eye closed. But keep both eyes wide open for the little things. Little things mark the great dividing line between success and failure.   JACOB M. BRAUDE

A small leak will sink a great ship.
THOMAS FULLER

He who can take no interest in what is small will take false interest in what is great.   JOHN RUSKIN

No matter how trifling the matter on hand, do it with a feeling that it demands the best that is in you, and when done look it over with a critical eye, not sparing a strict judgment of yourself.
SIR WILLIAM OSLER

An ant hole may collapse an embankment.
JAPANESE PROVERB

Do well the little things now; so shall great things come to thee by and by asking them to be done.
PERSIAN PROVERB

Despise not small things, either for evil or good, for a look may work thy ruin, or a word create thy wealth. A spark is a little thing, yet it may kindle the world.
MARTIN FARQUHAR TUPPER

Great battles are really won before they are actually fought. To control our passions we must govern our habits and keep watch over ourselves in the small details of everyday life.   **JOHN LUBBOCK**

To the mean eye all things are trivial, as certainly as to the jaundiced they are yellow.
THOMAS CARLYLE

I like to have a thing suggested rather than told in full, when every detail is given, the mind rests satisfied and the imagination loses the desire to use its own wings.
THOMAS BAILEY ALDRICH

Poor fool! in whose petty estimation all things are little.   **JOHANN WOLFGANG von GOETHE**

Facts

The next best thing to knowing a fact
Is said to be where to find it;
But more than that, it's how to act,
Once you have truly defined it.

The greatest American superstition is belief in facts.
    HERMANN KEYSERLING

If the facts don't fit the theory, change the facts.
    ALBERT EINSTEIN

The telephone book is full of facts, but it doesn't contain a single idea.   MORTIMER J. ADLER

My business is to teach my aspirations to confirm themselves to fact, not to try to make facts harmonize with my aspirations.   THOMAS HENRY HUXLEY

The facts, all we want is the facts.
    SGT. JOE FRIDAY

Comment is free but facts are sacred.   C. P. SCOTT

Value judgments are not to be established on the basis of facts—and that's a fact.
    JOSEPH WOOD KRUTCH

Facts do not cease to exist because they are ignored.
    ALDOUS LEONARD HUXLEY

An ounce of emotion is equal to a ton of facts.

JOHN JUNOR

The man who questions opinions is wise; the man who quarrels with facts is a fool.

FRANK A. GARBUTT

Every man has a right to his opinion, but no man has a right to be wrong in his facts.

BERNARD M. BARUCH

That's the way it is.   WALTER CRONKITE

To get it right, be born with luck or else make it. Never give up. Get the knack of getting people to help you and also pitch in yourself. A little money helps, but what really gets it right is to never—I repeat never —under any condition face the facts.

RUTH GORDON

Facts apart from their relationships are like labels on empty bottles.   SVEN HALLA

Economic distress will teach men, if anything can, that realities are less dangerous than fancies, that fact finding is more effective than fault finding.

CARL BECKER

Facts, when combined with ideas, constitute the greatest force in the world. They are greater than armaments, greater than finance, greater than science, business and law because they are the common denominators of all of them.

CARL W. ACKERMAN

Facts are only the material of thought.
ERNEST DIMNET

To state the facts frankly is not to despair for the future nor indict the past. JOHN F. KENNEDY

Let us take things as we find them: let us not attempt to distort them into what they are not . . . We cannot make facts. All our wishing cannot change them. We must use them.
JOHN HENRY CARDINAL NEWMAN

Now, what I want is Facts . . . Facts alone are wanted in life. CHARLES DICKENS

Facts are apt to alarm us more than the most dangerous principles. JUNIUS

The basic fact is economic insecurity. The correlative fact is the mind's despair.
SAMUEL D. SCHMALHAUSEN

God give me strength to face a fact though it may slay me. THOMAS HENRY HUXLEY

Thought

We have been taught
To use forethought
That is less fraught
Than afterthought.

To think twice in every matter and follow the lead of others is no way to make money.

IHARA SAIKUKU

Whenever I think, I make a mistake.

ROGER STEVENS

If we were all to be judged by our thoughts, the hills would be swarming with outlaws.

JOHANN SIGURJONSSON

Whether you believe you can do a thing or not, you are right. **HENRY FORD**

Today if you're not confused, you're just not thinking clearly. **IRENE PETER**

One gives birth to a thought, a second assists at its baptism, a third produces children with it, a fourth visits it on its death bed, and the fifth buries it.

GEORG CHRISTOPH LICHTENBERG

You would be surprised how hard it often is to translate an action into thought. **KARL KRAUS**

The thoughtless are rarely wordless.

HOWARD W. NEWTON

I was not there to think; I was there to follow orders.

BERNARD L. BAKER

The direction of the mind is more important than its progress. **JOSEPH JOUBERT**

I ought to be rich enough to have a secretary to whom I could dictate as I walk, because my best thoughts always come when I am away from the machine.

HENRY MILLER

Deliberation. The act of examining one's bread to determine which side it is buttered on.

AMBROSE BIERCE

There are boxes in the mind with labels on them: To study on a favorable occasion; Never to be thought about; Useless to go into further; Contents unexamined; Pointless business; Urgent; Dangerous; Delicate; Impossible; Abandoned; Reserved; For others; My forte; etc.

PAUL VALERY

Nothing is harder than to make people think about what they are going to do.

ANDRE MALRAUX

It is a sorry business to inquire into what men think, when we are every day only too uncomfortably confronted with what they do.

MICHAEL ARLEN

The mania of thinking renders one unfit for every activity.

ANATOLE FRANCE

If you make people think they're thinking, they'll love you; but if you really make them think, they'll hate you.

DONALD ROBERT PERRY MARQUIS

Folks that blurt out just what they think wouldn't be so bad if they thought.

FRANK McKINNEY HUBBARD

In a million people there are a thousand thinkers, and in a thousand thinkers there is one self-thinker.
LUDWIG BORNE

Hundreds can talk to one who can think; thousands can think to one who can see.   JOHN RUSKIN

There is no expedient to which man will not resort to avoid the real labor of thinking.
SIR JOSHUA REYNOLDS

When a thought is too weak to be expressed simply, simply drop it.   MARQUIS de VAUVENARGUES

What was once thought can never be unthought.
FRIEDRICH DURRENMATT

It is not much good thinking of a thing unless you think it out.   HERBERT GEORGE WELLS

Everything is simpler than you think and at the same time more complete than you imagine.
JOHANN WOLFGANG von GOETHE

Thinking? . . . Thinking means losing the thread.
PAUL VALERY

A thought must tell at once, or not at all.
WILLIAM HAZLITT

It's all right to have a train of thoughts, if you have a terminal.   BOWKER

A man may dwell so long upon a thought that it may take him prisoner.   LORD HALIFAX

Where all think alike, no one thinks very much.
WALTER LIPPMAN

Thinking is hard work. One can't bear burdens and ideas at the same time.   REMY de GOURMONT

When we deliberate it is about means and not ends.
ARISTOTLE

Men fear thought as they fear nothing else on earth— more than ruin, even more than death.
BERTRAND RUSSELL

A man would do well to carry a pencil in his pocket and write down the thoughts of the moment. Those that come unsought are commonly the most valuable and should be secured, because they seldom return.
FRANCIS BACON

People everywhere enjoy believing things that they know are not true. It spares them the ordeal of thinking for themselves and taking responsibilities for what they know.   BROOKS ATKINSON

High thinking is inconsistent with complicated material life based on high speed imposed on us by Mammon worship.   MOHANDAS K. GANDHI

Thought endangers thought. Place one idea upon paper, another will follow it, and still another, until you have written a page. You cannot fathom your mind. It is a well of thought which has no bottom. The more you draw from it, the more clear and fruitful will it be. If you neglect to think yourself, and use other people's thoughts, giving them utterance only, you will never

know what you are capable of. At first your ideas may come out in lumps, homely and shapeless; but no matter; time and perseverance will arrange and polish them. Learn to think, and you will learn to write, the more you think, the better you will express your ideas.
GEORGE AUGUSTUS SALA

Most men take least notice of what is plain, as if that were of no use; but puzzle their thoughts, and lose themselves in those vast depths and abysses which no human understanding can fathom.
THOMAS SHERLOCK

Thought is always in advance: it can see too far ahead, outstripping our bodies which are in the present.
ALBERT CAMUS

Secret study, silent thought is, after all, the mightiest agent in human affairs.
WILLIAM ELLERY CHANNING

Deliberate with caution, but act with decision and promptness. CHARLES CALEB COLTON

8 · PROFESSIONALS

Professionals

The very worst thing about a profession
Is not the impression we get with discretion;
It's not just the fact,
It's still US that act
But the amount that they charge for each
*   session.*

Professionals built the *Titanic*—amateurs the Ark.
                                                    ANON

Professional men, they have no cares;
whatever happens, they get theirs.   **OGDEN NASH**

Whether four years of strenuous attention to football
and fraternities is the best preparation for professional
work has never been seriously investigated.
                                    ROBERT M. HUTCHINS

A professional is someone who tells you something you already know and makes it sound confusing.

ANON

America is the prize amateur nation of the world. Germany is the prize professional nation.

WOODROW WILSON

The difference between an amateur and a professional is the difference between a general practitioner and a heart specialist. The only similarity is that they're both called doctors.　LEFTY ROSENTHAL

In time a profession is like marriage, we cease to note anything but its inconveniences.

HONORE de BALZAC

A professional is especially careful to make only small mistakes.　ANON

The artistic temperament is a disease that afflict amateurs.　GILBERT KEITH CHESTERTON

The man who knows only one subject is almost as tiresome as the man who knows no subject.

CHARLES DICKENS

A professional is a man who can do his best at a time when he doesn't particularly feel like it.

ALASTAIR COOKE

The professionals exist to fulfil a need;
They're mainly to satisfy pride and greed.

BERTRAM TROY

A sure sign of an amateur is too much detail to compensate for too little life.   ANTHONY BURGESS

A new word ending in "ism," that no-one else knew, was to him a heaven sent gift.   PIO BAROJA

There's no room for amateurs, even in crossing the streets.   GEORGE SEGAL

One of the differences between an amateur and a pro is that an amateur will settle for allowances and a pro won't.   LARRY BLYDEN

The price one pays for pursuing any profession, or calling, is an intimate knowledge of its ugly side.
JAMES BALDWIN

All professions are conspiracies against the laity.
GEORGE BERNARD SHAW

Either there are too few professions conducted honestly, or there are too few honest people in their professions.   DENIS DIDEROT

An egghead is one who stands firmly on both feet in mid-air on both sides of an issue.
SENATOR HOMER FERGUSON

As for doing good, that is one of the professions which are full.   HENRY DAVID THOREAU

Go not for every grief to the physician, for every quarrel to the lawyer, nor for every thirst to the pot.
ENGLISH PROVERB

All professional men are handicapped by not being allowed to ignore things which are useless.
JOHANN WOLFGANG von GOETHE

Of the professions it may be said that soldiers are becoming too popular, parsons too lazy, physicians too mercenary, and lawyers too powerful.
CHARLES CALEB COLTON

Amateurs hope. Professionals work.
GARSON KANIN

No man can be a pure specialist without being in a strict sense an idiot.   GEORGE BERNARD SHAW

The professional mind is so microscopic that it sometimes ceases to be binocular.   BERNARD De VOTO

The priest's friend loses his faith, the doctor's his health.
VENETIAN PROVERB

Lawyers, preachers and tomtit's eggs. There are more of them hatched than come to perfection.
BENJAMIN FRANKLIN

Professions, like nations, are civilized to the degree to which they can satirise themselves.
PETER de VRIES

Men of genius do not excel in any profession because they labour in it, but they labour in it because they excel.
WILLIAM HAZLITT

Just as those who practice the same profession recognize each other instinctively, so do those who practice the same vice.
MARCEL PROUST

It is good for a professional to be reminded that his professionalism is only a husk, that the real person must remain an amateur, a lover of the work.

MAY SARTON

Every man is a revolutionist concerning the thing he understands. For example, every person who has mustered a profession is a skeptic concerning it and, consequently, a revolutionist.

GEORGE BERNARD SHAW

Stockbroking

Blood pressure and the price
Of your stock selections
Will move, to be precise,
In opposite directions.

Fortunes are made by buying low and selling too soon.

BARON ROTHSCHILD

A broker is a man on the right end of the telephone.

GERALD F. LIEBERMAN

Buy on the rumor: sell on the news.

WALL STREET SAYING

I have one client who is neither a bull nor a bear—he's a chicken.

ANON

Select stocks the way porcupines make love—very carefully. ROBERT DINDA

I told my broker that as long as he doesn't tell me where my money should go, I won't tell him where he should go. LEOPOLD FECHTNER

Don't go broke, go public.
WALL STREET SAYING

Don't gamble: buy some good stock, hold it till it goes up and then sell it—if it doesn't go up, don't buy it!
WILL ROGERS

If you hear that "everybody" is buying a certain stock, ask who is selling. JAMES DINES

With my luck, if I ever invested in General Motors, they'd bust it to Corporal! ROBERT ORBEN

They call him 'Broker' because after you deal with him you are. ANON

Never follow the crowd. BERNARD BARUCH

With an evening coat and a white tie, even a stockbroker can gain a reputation for being civilized.
OSCAR WILDE

Last week is the time you should have either bought or sold, depending on which you didn't do.
LEONARD LOUIS LEVINSON

Gentlemen prefer bonds.   ANDREW MELLON

I wasn't affected by the crash of '29. I went broke in '28.   GERALD F. LIEBERMAN

When a company president is ready to buy you lunch, it's time to sell the stock. When he has something really good, you can't get him on the phone.
PHIL STOLLER

May. This is one of the peculiarly dangerous months to speculate in stocks in. The others are July, September, April, November, October, March, June, December, August and February.   MARK TWAIN

Do you realize that 7-Up is down to 4½ percent.
LEOPOLD FECHTNER

A broker is a man who runs your fortune into a shoestring.   ALEXANDER WOOLLCOTT

You have to watch out for the railroad analyst who can tell you the number of ties between New York and Chicago but not when to sell Penn Central.
NICHOLAS THORNDIKE

A janitor is the only one who cleans up in Wall Street and gets away with it.   ANON

The firm is really ahead of the times. It has a stock market ticker that prints its report on thin aspirins.
BOB HOPE

If you're not happy with the price of a particular stock, just wait a minute.   ANON

I'm beginning to wonder about my broker. Yesterday I told him to buy a hundred shares of A.T.&T. He said 'Would you spell that?'   ROBERT ORBEN

I'm 20 percent in oils, 30 percent in utilities, 50 percent in electronics, and 100 percent in hock. ANON

If you are ready to give up everything else—to study the whole history and background of the market and all the principal companies whose stocks are on the board as carefully as a medical student studies anatomy—if you can do all that, and, in addition, you have the cool nerves of a great gambler, the sixth sense of a clairvoyant, and the courage of a lion, you have a ghost of a chance.   BERNARD BARUCH

Don't confuse brains with a bull market.
                              HUMPHREY NEILL

An excellent monument might be erected to the Unknown Stockholder. It might take the form of a solid stone ark of faith apparently floating in a pool of water.   FELIX RIESENBERG

I wish I hadn't acquired respectability. I'd be out selling the market short.   JOE KENNEDY

The more money you have, the harder it is to outperform the market, because the law of averages will mug you in the next alley.   *Business Week*

Committees seem to be as poor in selecting stocks as in composing sonnets.   MURPHY TEIGH BLOOM

Now I'm in real trouble. First my laundry called and said they lost my shirt and then my broker said the same thing.   **LEOPOLD FECHTNER**

Bulls and bears aren't responsible for as many stock losses as bumsteers.   **OLIN MILLER**

A man cannot be a good doctor and keep telephoning his broker between patients nor a good lawyer with his eye on the ticker.   **WALTER LIPPMAN**

My father dealt in stocks and shares and my mother also had a lot of time on her hands.

HERMIONE GINGOLD

It is very vulgar to talk about one's own business. Only people like stockbrokers do that, and then merely at dinner parties.   **OSCAR WILDE**

What boy well raised can compare with your street gamin who has the knowledge and the shrewdness of a grown-up broker.   **ELBERT HUBBARD**

What always impresses me is how much better the relaxed, long-term owners of stocks do with their portfolios than the traders do with their switching of inventory. The relaxed investor is usually better informed and more understanding of essential values; he is more patient and less emotional; he pays smaller annual capital gains taxes; he does not incur unnecessary brokerage commissions; and he avoids behaving like Cassius by "thinking too much."

LUCIEN D. HOOPER

Stockmarket

*I wish that we could always say
About the money that we borrow;
The secure investment of today
Is not the tax loss of tomorrow.*

Wall Street is a thoroughfare that begins in a grave-yard and ends in a river.   ANON

The stock market has called nine of the last five recessions.   PAUL A. SAMUELSON

Let Wall Street have a nightmare and the whole country has to help get them back in bed again.
                    WILL ROGERS

Wall Street is a place where the day begins with good buys.   LEOPOLD FECHTNER

There are old traders around and bold traders around, but there are no old, bold traders around.
                    BOB DINDA

The suckers haven't permanently deserted the stock market. They are merely waiting until the prices get too high again.   ANON

A man is robbed on the Stock Exchange, just as he is killed in a war, by people whom he never sees.
                    ALFRED CAPUS

The stock market has spoiled more appetites than bad cooking.   WILL ROGERS

There is a way to make a lot of money in the market; unfortunately it is the same way to lose a lot of money in the market.
                    PETER PASSELL & LEONARD ROSE

In Wall Street the only thing that's hard to explain is —next week.   LOUIS RUKEYSER

Wall Street is where prophets tell us what will happen and profits tell us what did happen.
                                                    ROBERT ORBEN

Q: Why is the stock market like an oven?
A: They can both be self-cleaning.   ANON

It is wise to remember that too much success in the stock market is in itself an excellent warning.
                                                    GERALD M. LOEB

He made a killing in the Stock Market and shot his broker.   ANON

Wall Street lays an egg.   *Variety*

Men have been swindled by other men on many occasions. The Autumn of 1929 was perhaps the first occasion when men succeeded on a large scale in swindling themselves.   JOHN KENNETH GALBRAITH

Artificial inflation of stocks must be considered a crime as serious as counterfeiting, which it closely resembles.   ANDREW MAUROIS

There is no more mean, stupid, pitiful, selfish, envious, ungrateful animal than the stock speculating public. It is the greatest of cowards, for it is afraid of itself.
WILLIAM HAZLITT

There is nothing like the ticker tape except a woman—nothing that promises hour after hour, day after day, such sudden developments, nothing that disappoints so often or occasionally fulfills with such unbelievable passionate magnificence.
WALTER KNOWLETON GUTMAN

The stock market is only distantly related to economics. It's a function of greed, apprehension, and panic, all superimposed on the business cycle.
RAYMOND F. De VOE

The stock market is but a mirror which, perhaps as in this instance, somewhat belatedly, provides an image of the underlying fundamental economic situation. Cause and effect run from the economy to the stock market, never the reverse. In 1929, the economy was headed for trouble. Eventually that trouble was violently reflected in Wall Street.
JOHN KENNETH GALBRAITH

Buying and selling securities on the Stock Exchange do not start new industries. Big business never starts anything new. It merely absorbs consolidates and profits at the expense of others.
FRANKLIN DELANO ROOSEVELT

The responsibility for . . . soaring "ups" and crashing "downs" belongs not to the Stock Exchange as such, because, after all, that institution is essentially a market, and all that those charged with its administration can do is see to it that the goods dealt in are properly labeled, that no face or otherwise objectionable goods are admitted, and that dealings are conducted honestly and with due and watchfully enforced safeguards for the public.   OTTO KAHN

Architects

So many landmarks,
Tell me why for,
Have all the earmarks
Of an eyesore?

Architecture begins when you place two bricks carefully together.   LUDWIG MIES van der ROHE

Architecture is the art of how to waste space.
          PHILIP JOHNSON

A doctor can bury his mistakes but an architect can only advise his client to plant vines.
          FRANK LLOYD WRIGHT

Too many buildings are designed in the lift going down to lunch.   SIR WILLIAM HOLFORD

Architecture should be dedicated to keeping the outside out and the inside in.   LEONARD BASKIN

I think it is worth remembering, when you look around, that everything that has not been made by God has probably been perpetrated by an architect.
PRINCE PHILIP DUKE of EDINBURGH

Every place I look at I work out the cubic feet, and I say it will make a good warehouse or it won't. Can't help myself. One of the best warehouses I ever saw was the Vatican in Rome.   ARNOLD WESKER

Fools build for wise men to buy.   ANON

To build is to be robbed.   SAMUEL JOHNSON

It is easier to pull down than to build.   PROVERB

It's only air-conditioning which makes my architecture tolerable.   PHILIP JOHNSON

In my experience, if you have to keep the lavatory door shut by extending your left leg, it's modern architecture.   NANCY BANKS-SMITH

Architecture is inhabited sculpture.
CONSTANTIN BRANCUSI

Sir Christopher Wren said, "I am going to dine with some men. If anybody calls, say I am designing St. Paul's."   EDMUND CLERIHEW BENTLEY

The postwar architecture is the accountants' revenge on the prewar businessmen's dreams.
REM KOOLHAAS

Architect: one who drafts a plan of your house and plans a draft of your money.   AMBROSE BIERCE

An arch never sleeps.   HINDU PROVERB

I'm not sure office buildings are even architecture. They're really a mathematical calculation, just three-dimensional investments.   GORDON BUNSHAFT

No person who is not a great sculptor or painter can be an architect. If he is not a sculptor or painter, he can only be a builder.   JOHN RUSKIN

Good architecture lets nature in.   MARIO PEI

Which of you, intending to build a tower, sitteth not down first and counteth the cost, whether he have sufficient to finish it?   *St. Luke*

When your fortune increases, the columns of your house appear to be crooked.   ARMENIAN PROVERB

The larger a man's roof the more snow it collects.   PERSIAN PROVERB

When we build, let us think that we build for ever.   JOHN RUSKIN

A chair is a very difficult object. A skyscraper is almost easier. That is why Chippendale is famous.   LUDWIG MIES van der ROHE

Light, God's eldest daughter, is a principal beauty in a building.   THOMAS FULLER

The challenge for the modern architect is the same as the challenge for all of us in our lives: to make out of the ordinary something out-of-the-ordinary.
                                    PATRICK NUTTGENS

Society needs a good image of itself. That is the job of the architect.   WALTER GROPIUS

No architecture is so haughty as that which is simple.
                                    JOHN RUSKIN

The man who builds, and lacks wherewith to pay, provides a home from which to run away.
                                    OWEN YOUNG

Five lines where three are enough is stupidity. Nine pounds where three are sufficient is stupidity. But to eliminate expressive words that intensify or vivify meaning in speaking or writing is not simplicity; nor is similar elimination in architecture simplicity—it, too, may be stupidity.   FRANK LLOYD WRIGHT

In architecture the pride of man, his triumph over gravitation, his will to power, assume a visible form. Architecture is a sort of oratory of power by means of forms.   FRIEDRICH WILHELM NIETZSCHE

Every man is the architect of his own fortune.
                                    APPIUS CLAUDIUS

Real Estate

Before the deal,
Get it straight;
Is it real,
What's the state?

In the United States there is more space where nobody is than where anybody is. This is what makes America what it is.   **GERTRUDE STEIN**

The best investment on earth is earth.
                                    LOUIS GLICKMAN

Real estate is the closest thing to the proverbial pot of gold.   **ADA LOUISE HUXTABLE**

The money you get from selling land never buys the same land back.   **ANON**

Then one day they opened a Catholic chapel, which was quickly followed by a pub, a block of shops and eventually a school. The school went up last because there was no profit in it.   **DOMINIC BEEHAN**

When the white man came, we had the land and they had the bibles. Now they have the land and we have the bibles.   **CHIEF DAN GEORGE**

When asked by an anthropologist what the Indians called America before the white man came, an Indian said simply, "Ours."   **VINE DELORIA**

The world's best and safest real estate tax shelter—
your own home.   CHRIS WELLES

Property is theft.   PIERRE-JOSEPH PROUDHON

A farm is a hunk of land on which, if you get up early
enough mornings and work late enough nights, you'll
make a fortune—if you strike oil on it.
                                'FIBBER' McGEE

The ultimate question on property . . . who owns it?
                                            ANON

Real estate is the last remaining frontier of tycoon capitalism, where a fortune can still be made by pyramid-
ing borrowed money and taking tax deductions as you
grow.   BOB KUTTNER

If anyone wants to trade a couple of centrally located,
well-cushioned show-girls for an eroded slope ninety
minutes from Broadway, I'll be on this corner tomorrow at eleven with my tongue hanging out.
                                    S. J. PERELMAN

The creativity of real estate brokers when it comes
time to take to the typewriter and compose advertising
has always been a source of amazement.
                                    PAUL GOLDBERGER

The instinct of ownership is fundamental in man's
nature.   WILLIAM JAMES

A monologue is a conversation between a realtor and a
prospect.   ANON

If built in great numbers, motels will be used for nothing but illegal purposes.   J. EDGAR HOOVER

He was nimble in the calling of selling houses for more than people could afford to pay. SINCLAIR LEWIS

Landlords, like all other men, love to reap where they never sowed.   KARL MARX

A Florida land developer with 114 vacant lots for sale advertises his Sunday tours as "The Greatest Earth on Show."   L. M. BOYD

Possession is eleven points in the law.
     COLLEY CIBBER

A feeble man can see the farms that are fenced and tilled, the houses that are built. The strong man sees the possible houses and farms. His eye makes estates as fast as the sun breeds clouds.
     RALPH WALDO EMERSON

Everybody hates house-agents because they have everybody at a disadvantage. All other callings have a certain amount of give and take; the house-agent simply takes.   HERBERT GEORGE WELLS

First time you buy a house you see how pretty the paint is and buy it. The second time you look to see if the basement has termites. It's the same with men.
     LUPE VELEZ

The first man to fence in a piece of land, saying "This is mine," and who found people simple enough to believe him, was the real founder of civil society.
     JEAN-JACQUES ROUSSEAU

Look at every Main Street of every town in America and ask yourself "Who cares?" Nobody cares about community, divinity and humanity, and you can prove it by asking people what they do care about. In terms of shelter they care about downpayment and location. Give me downpayment and location and I'll outsell community, divinity and humanity on any street corner. **VICTOR H. PALMER**

Attend no auctions if thou hast no money.
The Talmud

I never knew an auctioneer to lie, unless it was absolutely necessary. **JOSH BILLINGS**

What we call real estate—the solid ground to build a house on—is the broad foundation on which nearly all the guilt of this world rests.
NATHANIEL HAWTHORNE

Before the cherry orchard was sold everybody was worried and upset, but as soon as it was all settled finally and once for all, everybody calmed down, and felt quite cheerful. **ANTON CHEKHOV**

Politics

*The reason for the circumspection
Is the need for re-election.*

The thought of being President frightens me. I do not think I want the job.   RONALD REAGAN

Politics is the science of how who gets what, when and why.   SIDNEY HILLMAN

It's not the voting that's democracy, it's the counting.
TOM STOPPARD

A politician is one who thinks twice before saying nothing.   ANON

I always wanted to get into politics, but I was never light enough to make the team.   ART BUCHWALD

When the politicians complain that TV turns the proceedings into a circus, it should be made clear that the circus was already there, and that TV has merely demonstrated that not all the performers are well trained.
ED MURROW

Politicians are the same all over. They promise to build a bridge even where there is no river.
NIKITA KHRUSHCHEV

Being in politics is like being a football coach. You have to be smart enough to understand the game and dumb enough to think it's important.
EUGENE McCARTHY

The more you read about politics, you got to admit that each party is worse than the other.
WILL ROGERS

I'm an introvert in an extrovert's profession.
RICHARD NIXON

The essential ingredient of politics is timing.
PIERRE ELLIOTT TRUDEAU

I have no political ambitions for myself or my children.
JOSEPH P. KENNEDY

Suppose you were an idiot and suppose you were a member of Congress; but I repeat myself.
MARK TWAIN

There is an increased demand for codes of ethics in politics, although most office holders are sworn in with their hand resting on one.
BILL VAUGHAN

Our supreme governors, the mob.
HORACE WALPOLE

A politician is one who likes what the majority likes.
EUGENE E. BRUSSELL

A mugwump is one of those boys who always has his mug on the one side of the political fence and his wump on the other.
ALBERT J. ENGEL

Power is a drug on which the politicians are hooked. They buy it from the voters, using the voters' own money.
RICHARD J. NEEDHAM

Politics is the reflex of the business and industrial world.
EMMA GOLDMAN

I would not be truthful if I said I was fully qualified for the office. I do not play the piano, I seldom play golf, and I never play touch football.
BARRY GOLDWATER

It is a pity that more politicians are not bastards by birth instead of vocation.
KATHERINE WHITEHORN

He knows nothing; and he thinks he knows everything. That points clearly to a political career.
GEORGE BERNARD SHAW

That log house did me more good in politics than anything I ever said in a speech.
JOHN NANCE GARNER

I'm not a member of any organized party. I'm a Democrat.
WILL ROGERS

Politicians have stopped passing the buck—now it stays with them.
ANON

I have often been accused of putting my foot in my mouth, but I will never put my hand in your pockets.
SPIRO T. AGNEW

Politician: any citizen with influence enough to get his old mother a job as charwoman in the City Hall.
HENRY LOUIS MENCKEN

Politics is mostly pill-taking.
THOMAS B. REED

One of the luxuries of a politician's life is that you see yourself as others see you.
JOE CLARK

A politician is an arse upon which everyone has sat except a man.
E. E. CUMMINGS

The President spends most of his time kissing people on the cheek in order to get them to do what they ought to do without getting kisses.

HARRY S. TRUMAN

Politics are now nothing more than a means of rising in the world. SAMUEL JOHNSON

Democracy consists of choosing your dictators, after they've told you what you think it is you want to hear.

ALAN COREN

It is now known . . . that men enter local politics solely as a result of being unhappily married.

NORTHCOTE C. PARKINSON

I learned one thing in politics. If you go into it . . . then sooner or later you have to compromise. You either compromise or get out. HUGH SLOAN

Politics has got so expensive that it takes lots of money to even get beat with. WILL ROGERS

An honest politician is one who when he is bought will stay bought. SIMON CAMERON

The longer I am out of office, the more infallible I appear to myself. HENRY KISSINGER

Mothers all want their sons to grow up to be president, but they don't want them to become politicians in the process. JOHN F. KENNEDY

The most successful politician is he who says what everybody is thinking most often and in the loudest voice. THEODORE ROOSEVELT

If you're in politics and you can't tell when you walk into a room who's for you and who's against you, then you're in the wrong line of work.
LYNDON B. JOHNSON

You do not know, you cannot know, the difficulty of life for a politician. It means every minute of the day or night, every ounce of your energy. There is no rest, no relaxation. Enjoyment? A politician does not know the meaning of the word.
NIKITA S. KRUSHCHEV

More men have been elected between Sundown and Sunup than ever were elected between Sunup and Sundown. WILL ROGERS

Bad officials are elected by good citizens who do not vote. GEORGE JEAN NATHAN

Give a politician a free hand and he will put it in your pocket. ANON

Never lose your temper with the Press or the public is a major rule of political life.
CHRISTABEL PANKHURST

All power is vested in the people, public servants are your trustees. . . . We're turkeys for the utilities, and I'm tired of being plucked. HENRY HOWELL

223

A politician divides mankind into two classes: tools and enemies.
FRIEDRICH WILHELM NIETZSCHE

A politician is an animal who can sit on a fence and yet keep both ears to the ground.
AMERICAN PROVERB

Few things are as immutable as the addiction of political groups to the ideas by which they have once won office. JOHN KENNETH GALBRAITH

Lobbyists are the touts of protected industries.
SIR WINSTON CHURCHILL

Politics. The diplomatic name for the law of the jungle. ELY CULBERTSON

Politics makes estranged bedfellows.
GOODMAN ACE

Politics is like roller skating. You go partly where you want to go, and partly where the damned things take you. HENRY FOUNTAIN ASHURST

I'm not an old, experienced hand at politics. But I am now seasoned enough to have learned that the hardest thing about any political campaign is how to win without proving that you are unworthy of winning.
ADLAI STEVENSON

In politics, nothing is contemptible.
BENJAMIN DISRAELI

Democracy is the recurrent suspicion that more than half of the people are right more than half of the time.
ELWYN BROOKS WHITE

When I want to buy up any politicians, I always find the antimonopolists the more purchaseable. They don't come so high.   WILLIAM H. VANDERBILT

Since a politician never believes what he says, he is surprised when others believe him.
GENERAL CHARLES de GAULLE

Politics is like football. If you see daylight, go through the hole.   JOHN F. KENNEDY

I am not made for politics because I am incapable of wishing for or accepting the death of my adversary.
ALBERT CAMUS

Public office is the last refuge of the incompetent.
BOISE PENROSE

Politics are usually the executive expression of human immaturity.   VERA BRITTAIN

Politics is not a good location or a vocation for anyone lazy, thin-skinned or lacking a sense of humour.
JOHN BAILEY

Politics is the art of preventing people from busying themselves with what is their own business.
PAUL VALERY

Politics is the art of the possible.
PRINCE OTTO VON BISMARCK

The ballot is stronger than the bullet.
ABRAHAM LINCOLN

The premises of politics lie in the conclusions of ethics.
HERBERT L. SAMUEL

In politics, a community of hatred is almost always the foundation of friendships.
ALEXIS de TOCQUEVILLE

Whoever could make two ears of corn or two blades of grass to grow upon a spot of ground where only one grew before would deserve better of mankind and do more essential service to his country than the whole race of politicians put together.
JONATHAN SWIFT

It is not easy nowadays to remember anything so contrary to all appearance as that officials are the servants of the public; and the official must try not to foster the illusion that it is the other way round.
SIR ERNEST GOWERS

Politics, as a practice, whatever its professions, has always been the systematic organization of hatreds.
HENRY ADAMS

Engineering

It's bound to go wrong
And disappoint,
If a thing's not as strong
As it's weakest point.

Our national flower is the concrete cloverleaf.
                                    LEWIS MUMFORD

If God had wanted a Panama Canal, he would have
put one here.   **KING PHILIP II of SPAIN**

The buffaloes were the original engineers, as they followed the lay of the land and the run of the water.
These buffalo paths became Indian trails, which always pointed out the easiest way across the mountain
barriers. The white man followed in these footpaths.
The iron trail finished the road. **GRACY HEBARD**

Yesterday I couldn't spell engineer. Now I are one.
                                    GRAFFITI

One has to look out for engineers—they begin with
sewing machines and end up with the atomic bomb.
                                    MARCEL PAGNOL

The wheel that squeaks the loudest
Is the one that gets the grease.   **JOSH BILLINGS**

In the old Met, when an elevator got stuck, a little
man appeared who went bump! bump! bump! And lo,

the elevator worked. Now comes a Harvard engineer
. . . and he investigates.   RUDOLF BING

Did you know that if a beaver two feet long with a tail
a foot and a half long can build a dam twelve feet high
and six feet wide in two days, all you would need to
build the Kariba Dam is a beaver sixty-eight feet long
with a fifty-one-foot tail?   NORTON JUSTER

The first price of intelligent tinkering is to save all the
parts.   PAUL EHRLICH

A little oil may save a deal of friction.   ANON

One trouble with Americans is that we're fixers rather
than preventers.   GENERAL JAMES DOOLITTLE

The reason the Romans built their great paved high-
ways was because they had such inconvenient footwear.   BARON de MONTESQUIEU

Panic Instruction for Industrial Engineers: When you
don't know what to do, walk fast and look worried.
          PAUL DICKSON

Inanimate objects are classified scientifically into three
major categories—those that don't work, those that
break down and those that get lost.
          RUSSELL BAKER

The engineering is secondary to the vision.
          CYNTHIA OZICK

The machine unmakes the man. Now that the machine is so perfect, the engineer is nobody.
RALPH WALDO EMERSON

If you see a man holding a clipboard and looking official, the chances are good that he is supposed to be doing something menial. WAYNE FIELDS

The oil can is mightier than the sword.
EVERETT DIRKSEN

He who does not know the mechanical side of a craft cannot judge it.
JOHANN WOLFGANG von GOETHE

Where the iron goes, there goes also rust.
PORTUGUESE PROVERB

It is the little bits of things that fret and worry us; we can dodge an elephant, but we can't a fly.
JOSH BILLINGS

We shape our tools and thereafter they shape us.
FATHER JOHN CULKIN

Man is a tool-using animal . . . Without tools he is nothing, with tools he is all. THOMAS CARLYLE

Lo! Men have become the tools of their tools.
HENRY DAVID THOREAU

Give us the tools, and we will finish the job.
SIR WINSTON CHURCHILL

I do not believe that you can make a razor blade sharp by Act of Parliament.   JOHN RODGERS

Do not talk to me of Archimedes' lever. He was an absent-minded person with a mathematical imagination. Mathematics command my respect, but I have no use for engines. Give me the right word and the right accent and I will move the world.

JOSEPH CONRAD

Science

Scientists, we must allow,
Are keen to testify,
Where and when and what and how
But cannot tell us why.

A science is any discipline in which the fool of this generation can go beyond the point reached by the genius of the last generation.   MAX GLUCKMAN

A scientist is a man who would rather count than guess.   LEONARD LOUIS LEVINSON

Scientists of over fifty are good for nothing except board meetings and should at all costs be kept out of the laboratory.   ARTHUR C. CLARKE

Science is always wrong: it never solves a problem without creating ten more.
GEORGE BERNARD SHAW

Science has nothing to be ashamed of, even in the ruins of Nagasaki.　JACOB BRONOWSKI

Science has promised us truth . . . It has never promised us either peace or happiness.
GUSTAVE le BON

One humiliating thing about science is that it is gradually filling our homes with appliances smarter than we are.　*Oskaloosa Herald*

Matter . . . a convenient formula for describing what happens where it isn't.　BERTRAND RUSSELL

Science can tell us means to an end, but not about what the ends should be.　LEONARD HODGSON

Scientists should be on tap but not on top.
SIR WINSTON CHURCHILL

Science is a collection of successful recipes.
PAUL VALERY

When a distinguished but elderly scientist states that something is possible, he is almost certainly right. When he states that something is impossible, he is very probably wrong.　ARTHUR C. CLARKE

Scientists are men who prolong life so we can have time to pay for the gadgets they invent.　ANON

There is only one proved method of assisting the advancement of pure science—that of picking men of genius, backing them heavily and leaving them to direct themselves. **DR. JAMES B. CONANT**

Astrology is the only science that does not depend on new discovery. **BERTRAM TROY**

Scientists tend to be very naive on ethical problems. At the drop of a hat scientists are addicted to one of the most dangerous modern diseases—instant wisdom.
MAGNUS PYKE

Science may be described as the art of systematic over-simplification. **KARL POPPER**

The man of science does not discover in order to know; he wants to know in order to discover.
ALFRED NORTH WHITEHEAD

Science has not found a substitute for God.
HENRY DRUMMOND

Science is organized common sense where many a beautiful theory is killed by an ugly fact.
THOMAS H. HUXLEY

Science cannot bear the thought that there is an important natural phenomenon which it cannot hope to explain even with unlimited time and money.
ROBERT JASTROW

In science the credit goes to the man who convinces the world, not to the man to whom the idea first occurs. **WILLIAM OSLER**

Look at those cows and remember that the greatest scientists in the world have never discovered how to make grass into milk. **MICHAEL PUPIN**

A good scientific theory should be explicable to a barmaid. **ERNEST RUTHERFORD**

Science commits suicide when it adopts a creed.
THOMAS HENRY HUXLEY

The stone age may return on the gleaming wings of science. **SIR WINSTON CHURCHILL**

Jesus of Nazareth was the most scientific man that ever trod the globe. He plunged beneath the material surface of things, and found the spiritual cause.
MARY BAKER EDDY

Science increases our power in proportion as it lowers our pride. **CLAUDE BERNARD**

When I find myself in the company of scientists I feel like a shabby curate who has strayed by mistake into a drawing room full of Dukes.
WYSTAN HUGH AUDEN

Though many have tried, no one has ever yet explained away the decisive fact that science, which can do so much, cannot decide what it ought to do.
JOSEPH WOOD KRUTCH

Traditional scientific method has always been at the very best, 20-20 hindsight. It's good for seeing where you've been. **ROBERT M. PERSIG**

I have come to have very profound and deep-rooted doubts whether Science, as practiced at present by the human race, will ever do anything to make the world a better and happier place to live in, or will ever stop contributing to our general misery.

HENDRIK VAN LOON

Art is I; Science is We.   CLAUDE BERNARD

I am tired of all this thing called science . . . We have spent millions in that sort of thing for the last few years, and it is time it should be stopped.

SIMON CAMERON

Whenever science makes a discovery, the devil grabs it while the angels are debating the best way to use it.

ALAN VALENTINE

Anyone who is practically acquainted with scientific work is aware that those who refuse to go beyond fact rarely get as far as fact.

THOMAS HENRY HUXLEY

Why does this magnificent applied science which saves work and makes life easier bring us so little happiness? The simple answer runs: Because we have not yet learned to make sensible use of it.

ALBERT EINSTEIN

Applied Science is a conjuror, whose bottomless hat yields impartially the softest of Angora rabbits and the most petrifying of Medusas.

ALDOUS LEONARD HUXLEY

We shall never get people whose time is money to take much interest in atoms.   SAMUEL BUTCHER

Science cannot stop while ethics catches up—and nobody should expect scientists to do all the thinking for the country.   ELVIN STACKMAN

The sciences are beneficent: they prevent man from thinking.   ANATOLE FRANCE

Science is what you know, philosophy is what you don't know.   BERTRAND RUSSELL

For the scientific acquisition of knowledge is almost as tedious as a routine acquisition of wealth.
                         ERIC LINKLATER

You know very well that unless you're a scientist, it's much more important for a theory to be shapely, than for it to be true.   CHRISTOPHER HAMPTON

Science at best is not wisdom; it is knowledge. Wisdom is knowledge tempered with judgement.
                         LORD RITCHIE-CALDER

One of the most pernicious falsehoods ever to be almost universally accepted is that the scientific method is the only reliable way to truth.
                         RICHARD H. BUBE

In all science error precedes the truth, and it is better it should go first than last.   HORACE WALPOLE

The tragedy of scientific man is that he has found no way to guide his own. He has devised no weapon so terrible that he has not used it. He has guarded none so carefully that his enemies have not eventually obtained it and turned it against him . . . His security today and tomorrow seems to depend on building weapons which will destroy him tomorrow.

CHARLES A. LINDBERGH

Most scientists play to a very narrow constituency of their own peers. It assures the quality of their work, but it does tend to keep them less sensitive to the needs of society as a whole.

BRUCE MURRAY

9 · PROGRESS

Change

Progress is a metaphor
  For benefitting man;
We know exactly what it's for
  But wonder if it can.

The graveyard of business is littered with companies that failed to recognize inevitable changes.   ANON

Careful consideration is the best known defense against change.   JOHN C. BURTON

It is always safe to assume, not that the old way is wrong, but that there may be a better way.
                        HENRY F. HARROWER

Drive your cart and your plough over the bones of the dead.   WILLIAM BLAKE

Let's talk sense to the American people. Let's tell them the truth, that there are no gains without pains.
                        ADLAI STEVENSON

It is a rare enterprise that can assume it will be serving exactly the same market with the same products in ten years time.   JESSE WERNER

You don't have to destroy the city before you can build a new Jerusalem.   LANE KIRKLAND

You've got to do things differently when you get to a certain size or you're going to suffer.
                    H. BREWSTER ATWATER

The longer I live the more keenly I feel that whatever was good enough for our fathers is not good enough for us.   OSCAR WILDE

As a company grows, it changes. To keep pace with the change, the organization must change too. Otherwise, growth stops. The classic pattern is the owner-manager who starts a small business. He causes it to grow by his ability and drive. As it grows, he hires assistants. For a while the business continues to grow. Then it levels off. Try as he will, the owner cannot get it to grow further, no matter how hard he works personally. Why? He has delayed revising his form of organization too long.   H. B. MAYNARD

When it is not necessary to change, it is necessary not to change.
          VISCOUNT LUCIUS CARY FALKLAND

Thinkers prepare the revolution, bandits carry it out.
                    MARIANO AZUELA

Even God cannot change the past.   AGATHON

Most of the companies that rate among the top 100 today were not there 20 or even 10 years ago and some had not even started.   ANON

I cannot say whether things will get better if they change; what I can say is they must change if they are apt to get better.
               GEORG CHRISTOPH LICHTENBERG

The golden age never was the present age.
                    BENJAMIN FRANKLIN

You don't change the course of history by turning the faces of portraits to the walls.
                    JAWAHARLAL NEHRU

When I was a young man we had ten cows and we did very well. When I was thirty we had twenty cows and we did no better. When I was forty we had forty cows and we were barely making it. Now I'm seventy and we have seventy cows, and are not making it at all.
                                   ANON

The men who have changed the universe have never accomplished it by changing officials, but always by inspiring the people.   NAPOLEON BONAPARTE

I will go anywhere, provide it be forward.
                    DAVID LIVINGSTONE

This house, where once a lawyer dwelt
Is now a smith's, alas

How rapidly the iron age
Succeeds the age of brass.　　WILLIAM ERSKINE

Nothing is so dangerous as being too modern: one is
apt to grow old-fashioned quite suddenly.
　　　　　　　　　　　　　OSCAR WILDE

There are two kinds of fools. One says, 'This is old,
therefore it is good.' The other says, 'This is new,
therefore it is better.'
　　　　DEAN WILLIAM RALPH INGE

When people shake their heads because we are living
in a restless age, ask them how they would like to live
in a stationary one and do without change.
　　　　　　　GEORGE BERNARD SHAW

I have my faults, but changing my tune is not one of
them.　　　　　　　　　SAMUEL BECKETT

It is never easy to explain to a later generation the
achievements of an earlier one in shattering an unac-
ceptable status quo, because these achievements in
turn have become a status quo beyond which it wishes
to advance.　　　　　　　FRANK FREIDEL

Man has a limited biological capacity for change.
When this capacity is overwhelmed, the capacity is in
future shock.　　　　　　　ALVIN TOFFLER

The basic fact of today is the tremendous pace of
change in human life.　　JAWAHRALAL NEHRU

No man can be a conservative until he has something
to lose.　　　　　　　　JAMES P. WARBURG

The new ideas of one age become the ideologies of the next, by which time they will in all probability be out of date and inapplicable.   GERALD BRENAN

He that will not apply new remedies must expect new evils.   FRANCIS BACON

Airplanes will be used in sport, but they are not to be thought of as commercial carriers.
                              OCTAVE CHANUTE

All things must change to something new, to something strange.
                    HENRY WADSWORTH LONGFELLOW

There is no way to make people like change. You can only make them feel less threatened by it.
                              FREDERICK O'R. HAYES

An old Dutch farmer, who remarked to a companion once that it was not best to swap horses in mid-stream.
                              ABRAHAM LINCOLN

Men despise great projects when they do not feel themselves capable of great success.
                              MARQUIS de VAUVENARGUES

One must change one's tactics every ten years if one wishes to maintain one's superiority.
                              NAPOLEON BONAPARTE

What is Conservatism? Is it not adherence to the old and tried, against the new and untried?
                              ABRAHAM LINCOLN

To blind oneself to change is not therefore to halt it.
ISAAC GOLDBERG

Such is the state of life that none are happy but by the anticipation of change. The change itself is nothing; when we have made it, the next wish is to change again. SAMUEL JOHNSON

We are entering a very radical world of discontinuities.
EUGENE CAFIERO

One must never lose time in vainly regretting the past nor in complaining about the changes which cause us discomfort, for change is the very essence of life.
ANATOLE FRANCE

This world of ours is a new world, in which the unit of knowledge, the nature of human communities, the order of society, the order of ideas, the very notions of society and culture have changed, and will not return to what they have been in the past. What is new is new, not because it has never been there before, but because it has changed in quality.
J. ROBERT OPPENHEIMER

Innovation

*Innovation's risky work
And often for the good;
When it is, you'll find a jerk,
Who always knew it would.*

If only I had known, I should have become a watchmaker. **ALBERT EINSTEIN**

Innovation is a gamble, but so is standing pat.
ARTHUR B. DOUGALL

Henry Ford was a thinker; he wasn't a repeater.
W. J. CAMERON

America was discovered accidentally by a great seaman who was looking for something else; when discovered, it was not wanted: and most of the exploration for the next 50 years was done in the hope of getting through or round it. America was named after a man who discovered no part of the New World. History is like that, very chancy.
SAMUEL ELIOT MORISON

My favorite thing is to go where I've never been.
DIANE ARBUS

Innovation is the new conservatism.
PETER F. DRUCKER

The 'silly' question is the first intimation of some totally new development.
ALFRED NORTH WHITEHEAD

A conservative is one who does not think that anything should be done for the first time.
JACOB M. BRAUDE

I suppose the one quality in an astronaut more powerful than any other is curiosity. They have to get to some place nobody's ever been before.

JOHN GLENN

Understanding is the beginning of approving.

ANDREW GIDE

One cannot be a part-time nihilist.

ALBERT CAMUS

Innovation is more likely to come from subordinates when the boss expects it.   ANON

A little rebellion now and then is a good thing.

THOMAS JEFFERSON

Innovators are inevitably controversial.

EVA le GALLIENNE

I once knew a chap who had a system of just hanging the baby on the clothes line to dry and he was greatly admired by his fellow citizens for having discovered a wonderful innovation on changing a diaper.

DAMON RUNYON

I think and think for months and years. Ninety-nine times, the conclusion is false. The hundredth time I am right.   ALBERT EINSTEIN

Sometimes it is more important to discover what one cannot do, than what one can do.   LIN YUTANG

It takes genius and courage to originate, not imitate.

ANON

The only thing that should surprise us is that there are still some things that can surprise us.
FRANCOIS DUC de la ROCHEFOUCAULD

That's always the way when you discover something new; everybody thinks you're crazy.
EVELYN E. SMITH

All great discoveries are made by men whose feelings run ahead of their thinking.   C. H. OARKHURST

Everything is connected to everything else.
BARRY COMMONER

Innovation thrives on encouragement and dies with routine.   ANON

Innovation is resisted by individuals who are unwilling to risk the status they have achieved and jealously guard their own job against any change.
WILLIAM T. BRADY

A fool must now and then be right, by chance.
WILLIAM COWPER

He that will not apply new remedies must accept new evils: for time is the greatest innovator.
FRANCIS BACON

If my theory of relativity is proven successful, Germany will claim me as a German and France will declare that I am a citizen of the world. Should my theory prove untrue, France will say that I am a German and Germany will declare that I am a Jew.
ALBERT EINSTEIN

The Great don't innovate, they fertilize seeds planted by lackeys, then leave to others the inhaling of the flowers whose roots they've manured. A deceptive memory may be the key to their originality.

NED ROREM

We must beware of needless innovation, especially when guided by logic.

SIR WINSTON CHURCHILL

Out of every ten innovations attempted, all very splendid, nine will end up in silliness; the tenth and the last, though it escape the preposterous, will show little that is new in the end.

ANTONIO MACHADO

Many things are not believed because their current explanation is not believed.

FRIEDRICH WILHELM NIETZSCHE

An idea, a song, a discovery, an invention, may be born anywhere. But if it is to be communicated, if it is to be tested and compared and appreciated, then someone has always carried it to the city.

MAX WAYS

One doesn't discover new lands without consenting to lose sight of the shore for a very long time.

ANDREW GIDE

The initiator dies—or turns traitor.

HEINRICH HEINE

The intellect has little to do on the road to discovery. There comes a leap in consciousness, call it intuition or what you will, and the solution comes to you and you don't know how or why.   ALBERT EINSTEIN

The sublime and the ridiculous are often so nearly related that it is difficult to class them separately. One step above the sublime makes the ridiculous: and one step above the ridiculous makes the sublime again.

THOMAS PAINE

We ought not to be over-anxious to encourage innovation in cases of doubtful improvement, for an old system must ever have two advantages over a new one; it is established and it is understood.

CHARLES CALEB COLTON

Just as energy is the basis of life itself, and ideas the source of innovation, so is innovation the vital spark of all man-made change, improvement and progress.

THEODORE LEVITT

One way to hasten the development of something new is to experiment with our material in various combinations. The composer of music works with combinations of notes, moving them around on the scale into pleasing harmonies, trying them out on the keyboard of his piano; the inventor works with combinations of substances and mechanisms; the office manager works with combinations of people and records and machines, tuning up his organization by trying this and that change of duty or partnership of workers.

ROYAL BANK OF CANADA

No man can produce great things who is not thoroughly sincere in dealing with himself.

JAMES RUSSELL LOWELL

The great man, that is, the man most imbued with the spirit of the time, is the impressionable man.

RALPH WALDO EMERSON

Creativity

There's many a dumb one,
Who can tell us how it could be;
What we want is someone,
Who will tell us what it should be.

A hunch is creativity trying to tell you something.

FRANK CAPRA

How do I work? I grope.   ALBERT EINSTEIN

Whoever stops creating today is dead the day before yesterday.   NICOLAS REISINI

The freedom to make mistakes provides the best environment for creativity.   ANON

Almost everything comes from almost nothing.

FREDERIC AMIEL

I always said Henry Ford had a twenty-five-track mind. He had a few gadgets in his mind that the rest of us didn't have. He'd see further and see it faster.

W. J. CAMERON

Creativity varies inversely with the number of cooks involved in the broth.   BERNICE FITZ-GIBBON

What we call 'creative work' ought not to be called work at all, because it isn't. I imagine that Thomas Edison never did a day's work in his last fifty years.
STEPHEN LEACOCK

Seeing through is rarely seeing into.
ELIZABETH BIBESCO

Creativity is restricted by overcentralization, too much decision-making at the top, lack of planning, empire building, and poor communications.   ANON

Creation comes before distribution—or there will be nothing to distribute!   AYN RAND

Being creative is having something to sell, or knowing how to sell something, or having sold something. It has been taken over by what we used to mean by being 'wised up,' knowing the tricks, the shortcuts.
PAULINE KAEL

Every time that enterprising spirit is broken down, even a little, every time that little spark of originality is snuffed out, we are choking off the very tap roots of our organization's precious fund of creativity.
WILLIAM T. BRADY

More creativity is the only way to make tomorrow better than today.   ANON

A first-rate soup is more creative than a second rate painting.   ABRAHAM MASLOW

It is intelligent to ask two questions: (1) Is it possible? (2) Can I do it? But it is unintelligent to ask these questions: (1) Is it real? (2) Has my neighbor done it?
SOREN KIERKEGAARD

The executive's loneliest hours are spent in choosing, not between right and wrong, but between two rights or two wrongs. His most creative moments are those in which he successfully integrates values, bringing diverse ideas together into new arrangements.
PROFESSOR DAVID G. MOORE

People support what they help to create.   ANON

In the modern world of business, it is useless to be a creative original thinker unless you can also sell what you create. Management cannot be expected to recognize a good idea unless it is presented to them by a good salesman.   DAVID M. OGILVY

I do much of my creative thinking while golfing. If people know you are working at home they think nothing of walking in for a coffee. But they wouldn't dream of interrupting you on the golf course.
HARPER LEE

The various admirable movements in which I have been engaged have always developed among their numbers a large lunatic fringe.
THEODORE ROOSEVELT

In search of ideas I spent yesterday morning in walking about, and went to the stores and bought things in four departments. A wonderful and delightful way of spending time and money. Better than most theatres

. . . I think this sort of activity does stimulate creative ideas.   ARNOLD BENNETT

There is a correlation between the creative and the screwball. So we must suffer the screwball gladly.
KINGMAN BREWSTER

The essence of the creative act is to see the familiar as strange.   ANON

We often discover what will do, by finding out what will not do, and probably he who never made a mistake never made a discovery.   SAMUEL SMILES

Analysis kills spontaneity. The grain once ground into flour springs and germinates no more.
HENRI FREDERIC AMIEL

The creation of a thousand forests is in one acorn.
RALPH WALDO EMERSON

The only trade at which the novice and apprentice earn nothing while they learn is the creative trade.
W. G. ROGERS

The creative act thrives in an environment of mutual stimulation, feedback and constructive criticism—in a community of creativity.   WILLIAM T. BRADY

The inspirations of today are the shams of tomorrow —the purpose has departed.   ELBERT HUBBARD

The very essence of the creative is its novelty, and hence we have no standard by which to judge it.
CARL R. ROGERS

When Alexander the Great visited Diogenes and asked whether he could do anything for the famed teacher, Diogenes replied: 'Only stand out of my light.' Perhaps some day we shall know how to heighten creativity. Until then, one of the best things we can do for creative men and women is to stand out of their light.   JOHN W. GARDNER

Think before you speak is criticism's motto; speak before you think, creation's.

EDWARD MORGAN FORSTER

Be brave enough to live life creatively. The creative is the place where no one else has ever been. You have to leave the city of your comfort and go into the wilderness of your intuition. You can't get there by bus, only by hard work and risk and by not quite knowing what you're doing. What you'll discover will be wonderful. What you'll discover will be yourself. ALAN ALDA

Our current obsession with creativity is the result of our continued striving for immortality in an era when most people no longer believe in an afterlife.

ARIANNA STASSINOPOULOS

The whole difference between construction and creation is exactly this: that a thing constructed can only be loved after it is constructed, but a thing created is loved before it exists.

GILBERT KEITH CHESTERTON

In creating the only hard thing's to begin
A grass blade's no easier to make than an oak.

JAMES RUSSELL LOWELL

The lash may force men to physical labor: it cannot force them to spiritual creativity.   SHOLEM ASCH

Ideas

The pioneer
With the new idea
Must start it operating.
With this feat
He will beat
Those still contemplating.

Americans have been conditioned to respect newness, whatever it costs them.   JOHN UPDIKE

Ideas are one thing and what happens is another.
JOHN CAGE

New ideas are feared because they change the status quo.   ANON

His quest for something new each month leads to widespread corporate premature ejaculation.
ROBERT TOWNSEND

An idea that is not dangerous is unworthy of being called an idea at all.   OSCAR WILDE

An idea which is six years ahead of its time is a bad idea.   GEORGE LOIS

When I have an idea, I have no pencil.   ANON

The cleverly expressed opposite of any generally accepted idea is worth a fortune to somebody.
                               F. SCOTT FITZGERALD

The half baked ideas of people are better than the ideas of half baked people.
                    PROFESSOR WILLIAM B. SHOCKLEY

Ideas that we thought at one time were a little far out have now become part of our operating procedure.
                                                 ANON

An idea is something that usually comes like firemen —too late.   JEWISH SAYING

Exhilaration is that feeling you get just after a great idea hits you, and just before you realize what's wrong with it.   ANON

To say that an idea is fashionable is to say, I think, that it has been adulterated to a point where it is hardly an idea at all.   MURRAY KEMPTON

I didn't get my ideas from Mao, Lenin, or Ho. I got my ideas from the Lone Ranger.   JERRY RUBIN

We say that education is exposure to new ideas. Yet strangely the typical executive, consciously or unconsciously, builds a Chinese Wall around himself so that he is not exposed to new ideas. He creates a circle of subordinates, of friends, or country club associates who think like he does.   PIERRE MARTINEAU

No grand idea was ever born in a conference, but a lot of foolish ideas have died there.
      F. SCOTT FITZGERALD

The best way to kill an idea is to take it to a meeting.
      ANON

If you want to get across an idea, wrap it up in a person.   RALPH BUNCHE

The harebrained idea may well start discussion that will lead to the perfect improvement.   ANON

In the matter of ideas he who meditates is lost.
      WILLIAM McFEE

A cold in the head causes less suffering than an idea.
      JULES RENARD

New ideas rarely germinate with someone who is scared of being wrong.   ANON

The only sure weapon against bad ideas is better ideas.
      WHITNEY GRISWOLD

There is an element of truth in every idea that lasts long enough to be called corny.   IRVING BERLIN

Every new idea is obscure at first. It is or it wouldn't be new.   ROBERT IRWIN

Serious minded people have few ideas. People with ideas are never serious. PAUL VALERY

Fundamental progress has to do with the reinterpretation of basic ideas.
ALFRED NORTH WHITEHEAD

Unlike company products, ideas cannot be tested in the model stage before placing them on the market.
ANON

New ideas can be good or bad, just the same as old ones. FRANKLIN D. ROOSEVELT

An idea is the most exciting thing there is.
JOHN RUSSELL

One of the most hazardous of human occupations is the transferring of an idea from one mind to another. It's hazardous because you presuppose the existence of a second mind. CHRISTIAN BURCKEL

Many ideas grow better when transplanted into another mind than in the one where they sprang up.
OLIVER WENDELL HOLMES

As soon as an idea is accepted it is time to reject it.
HOLBROOK JACKSON

An idea isn't responsible for the people who believe it.
DONALD ROBERT PERRY MARQUIS

Inspirations never go in for long engagements; they demand immediate marriage to action.
BRENDAN FRANCIS

An idea is a putting truth in checkmate.
JOSE ORTEGA Y GASSET

There is no adequate defense, except stupidity, against the impact of a new idea. PERCY W. BRIDGMAN

The best ideas are common property.
LUCIUS ANNAEUS

An idea is a feat of association.   ROBERT FROST

Man is ready to die for an idea, provided that idea is not quite clear to him.   PAUL ELDRIDGE

If an idea cannot be expressed in terms of people, it is a sure sign it is irrelevant to the real problems of life.
COLIN WILSON

Nothing is more dangerous than an idea, when a man has only one idea. EMILE AUGUSTE CHARTIER

When an idea is too weak to support a simple statement, it is a sign that it should be rejected.
MARQUIS de VAUVENARGUES

Let's remind ourselves that last year's fresh idea is today's cliche.   AUSTEN BRIGGS

Ideas won't keep. Something must be done with them.
ALFRED NORTH WHITEHEAD

Ideas are like beards: men do not have them until they grow up.   FRANCOIS VOLTAIRE

New ideas cannot be administered successfully by men with old ideas, for the first essential of doing a job well is the wish to see the job done at all.

FRANKLIN D. ROOSEVELT

If I have seen further it is by standing on the shoulders of giants.

SIR ISAAC NEWTON

The greatest ideas seem meager enough when they have passed through the sieve of petty minds.

HENRI de LUBAC

Valuable new ideas often prove to be hindrances because of the emphasis given to form over substance.

PROFESSOR RAY E. BROWN

Above all, do not talk yourself out of good ideas by trying to expound them at haphazard gatherings.

JACQUES BARZUN

To die for an idea, if it is right, saves us the labor of an infinity of experiences.

JACQUES MARITAIN

Very simple ideas lie within the reach only of complex minds.

REMY de GOURMONT

One thing that ideas do is to contradict other ideas and keep us from believing them.

WILLIAM JAMES

Results

The adult
Exults
In the cult
Of results.

When your work speaks for itself, don't interrupt.
HENRY J. KAISER

A fellow doesn't last long on what he has done. He's got to keep on delivering as he goes along.
CARL HUBBELL

People forget how fast you did a job—but they remember how well you did it.
HOWARD W. NEWTON

We all like people who do things, even if we only see their faces on a cigar box lid. WILLA CATHER

And yet I told your Holiness that I was no painter.
MICHELANGELO

Funny how people generally can do more than they think they can, and almost always do less than they think they do. ANON

When a thing is thoroughly well done it often has the air of being a miracle. ARNOLD BENNETT

What one has to do usually can be done.
ELEANOR ROOSEVELT

The deed is all, and not the glory.
JOHANN WOLFGANG von GOETHE

A thought which does not result in action is nothing much, and an action which does not proceed from a thought is nothing at all.   GEORGES BERNANOS

You can't get anything done unless you do it yourself. And usually you can't do it very well.
EDWARD WATSON HOWE

By the work one knows the workman.
JEAN de la FONTAINE

If it works, copy it.   TONY SCHWARTZ

The more you do, the more you are.
ANGIE PAPADAKIS

Never use intuition.   OMAR N. BRADLEY

Results! Why, man, I have gotten a lot of results. I know several thousand things that won't work.
THOMAS A. EDISON

Each morning sees some task begun,
Each evening sees it close;
Something attempted, something done,
Has earned a night's repose.
HENRY WADSWORTH LONGFELLOW

Thunder is good, thunder is impressive, but it is the lightning that does the work.   MARK TWAIN

Has God forgotten everything I've done for him?
                                                KING LOUIS XIV

In the arena of human life the honours and rewards fall to those who show their good qualities in action.
                                                ARISTOTLE

What another would have done as well as you, do not do it. What another would have said as well as you, do not say it. What another would have written as well, do not write it. Be faithful to that which exists nowhere but in yourself—and thus make yourself indispensable.   ANDRE GIDE

Seest thou a man diligent in his business? He shall not stand before mean men.   PROVERBS

I never work better than when I am inspired by anger: for when I am angry, I can write, pray, and preach well, for then my whole temperament is quickened, my understanding sharpened, and all mundane vexations and temptations depart.   MARTIN LUTHER

Few men during their lifetime come anywhere near exhausting the resources dwelling within them. There are deep wells of strength that are never used.
                                                RICHARD E. BYRD

Work and thou canst not escape the reward; whether thy work be fine or coarse, planting corn or writing epics, so only it be honest work done to thine own approbation, it shall earn a reward to the senses as well as the thought. No matter how often defeated, you are born to victory. The reward of a thing well done is to have it done.

RALPH WALDO EMERSON

Invention

It's never bad
To make the fad,
That doesn't take
Too long to break.

Anything that won't sell, I don't want to invent.

THOMAS A. EDISON

The optimist invented the aeroplane, the pessimist the parachute.

ANON

What the country needs are a few labor making inventions.

ARNOLD H. GLASGOW

People think of the inventor as a screwball, but no one asks the inventor what he thinks of other people.

CHARLES F. KETTERING

All great discoveries are made by mistake.

HAROLD FABER

The wheel was man's greatest invention until he got behind it.

BILL IRELAND

God hides things by putting them near us.
PRESBYTERIAN CHURCH BULLETIN

The universe is full of magical things patiently waiting for our wits to grow sharper. EDEN PHILLPOTTS

Pasteur discovered a cure for rabbis.
SCHOOL BONER

Most inventions come from making the right discovery, while looking for the wrong thing.   ANON

Name the greatest of all inventors. Accident.
MARK TWAIN

The greatest invention of the nineteenth century was the invention of the method of invention.
ALFRED NORTH WHITEHEAD

One of the advantages of being disorderly is that one is constantly making exciting discoveries.
ALAN ALEXANDER MILNE

I don't think necessity is the mother of invention—invention in my opinion arises directly from the idleness, possibly also from laziness. To save oneself trouble.   AGATHA CHRISTIE

If necessity is the mother of invention, what was papa doing?   RUTH WEEKLEY

Invention is the mother of necessity.
THORSTEIN VEBLEN

Television? The word is half Latin and half Greek. No good can come of it.   C. P. SCOTT

I never did anything worth doing by accident, nor did any of my inventions come by accident.
THOMAS A. EDISON

Thomas Edison did not invent the first talking machine. He invented the first one you could turn off.
HERBERT V. PROCHNOW

Innovation depends on invention and inventors should be treated as the pop stars of industry.
PHILIP, DUKE of EDINBURGH

Have there not been enough inventions?
SACHEVERELL SITWELL

There is always more chance of hitting upon something valuable when you aren't too sure what you want to hit upon.
ALFRED NORTH WHITEHEAD

It is easy to overlook the absence of appreciable advance in an industry. Inventions that are not made, like babies that are not born, are rarely missed.
JOHN KENNETH GALBRAITH

There are things that are known and things that are unknown: in between are doors.
ANON

It is questionable if all the mechanical inventions yet made have lightened the day's toil of any human being.
JOHN STUART MILL

It is a strange fact that the impractical among mankind are remembered.
HANS ZINSSER

Everything that can be invented has been invented.
CHARLES H. DUELL

Inventors and men of genius have almost always been regarded as fools at the beginning (and very often, at the end) of their careers.
FYODOR MIKHAILOVICH DOSTOEVSKY

The fire of invention comes from those who cannot sleep until they have tested their idea. ANON

The very people who have done the breaking through are themselves often the first to try to put a scab on their achievement. IGOR STRAVINSKY

There is little that can be said about most economic goods. A toothbrush does little but clean teeth. Aspirin does little but dull pain. Alcohol is important mostly for making people more or less drunk . . . there being so little to be said, much to be invented.
JOHN KENNETH GALBRAITH

I start where the last man left off.
THOMAS A. EDISON

The moment man cast off his age-long belief in magic, science bestowed upon him the blessings of Electric Current. JEAN GIRADOUX

God forgive those who invent what they need.
LILLIAN HELLMAN

When it seems that a new man or a new school has invented a new thing, it will only be found that the gifted among them have secured a firmer hold than usual of some old thing.　　WALTER SICKERT

Where there is an unknowable there is a promise.
THORNTON WILDER

I invent nothing, I rediscover.　　AUGUSTE RODIN

We are more ready to try the untried when what we do is inconsequential. Hence the remarkable fact that many inventions had their birth as toys.
ERIC HOFFER

When the Paris Exhibition closes, electric light will close with it and no more will be heard of it.
ERASMUS WILSON

In inventing the locomotive, Watt and Stevenson were part inventors of time.
ALDOUS LEONARD HUXLEY

What's the use of inventing a better system as long as there just aren't enough folks with sense to go around!
DOROTHY CANFIELD FISHER

Today every invention is received with a cry of triumph which soon turns into a cry of fear.
BERTOLT BRECHT

The obvious is that which is never seen until someone expresses it simply.　　KAHLIL GIBRAN

The greatest inventions were produced in the times of ignorance, as the use of the compass, gunpowder, and printing.　　JONATHAN SWIFT

Inventions are made by intuition, not intelligence.
GEORGES SIMENON

The Industrial Age had to wait centuries until people
in Scotland watched their kettles boil and so invented
the steam engine.
ALFRED NORTH WHITEHEAD

The greatest milestones in our nation's industrial and
scientific history were achieved by men who did not
shy away from the unconventional, who were not intimidated by fear, whose pride did not rule out the
trial-and-error method. WILLIAM T. BRADY

With all men's marvelous ability to invent things
which are potentially good, he can always be counted
on to make the worst possible use of what he invents,
as witness the radio, printing-press, aeroplane and the
internal-combustion engine. ALBERT JAY NOCK

Every great advance in natural knowledge has involved the absolute rejection of authority.
THOMAS H. HUXLEY

The simple belief in automatic material progress by
means of scientific discovery is a tragic myth of our
age. SIR BERNARD LOVELL

An inventive idea without development is quite
useless. PETER GOLDMARK

It has been said that faith can move mountains but no
one has seen it done, save by faith that man has in
himself in the steam shovels and the dynamite he has
invented in the face of a hostile Nature.
LOUIS BROMFIELD

The average length of time it takes, I think, for any great discovery in the realm of ideas to pass into general currency or to receive any practical effectuation is a thousand years.

ALFRED NORTH WHITEHEAD

The most amazing and effective inventions are not those which do most honour to the human genius.

FRANCOIS VOLTAIRE

Our inventions mirror our secret wishes.

LAWRENCE DURRELL

My dynamite will sooner lead to peace than a thousand world conventions. As soon as men will find that in one instant whole armies can be utterly destroyed, they surely will abide by golden peace.

ALFRED BERNHARD NOBEL

Growth and Development

Whatever you do, don't sit tight,
Waiting till things are just right.
Times are never apt, because
They never will be, is or was.

Success brings growth and growth means change.

ANON

Growth is the only evidence of life.

JOHN HENRY NEWMAN

We have yet to find a significant case where the company did not move in the direction of the chief executive's home.

KEN PATTON

Be not afraid of growing slowly, be afraid only of standing still.

CHINESE PROVERB

In truth, I believe there is no such thing as a growth industry. There are only companies organized and operated to create and capitalize on growth opportunities. Industries that assume themselves to be riding some automatic growth escalator invariably descend into stagnation.

THEODORE LEVITT

He who would learn to fly one day must first learn to stand and walk and run and climb and dance: one cannot fly into flying.

FRIEDRICH WILHELM NIETZSCHE

In the past we have perhaps depended too much on the hope that creating new wealth would automatically provide us a better life. Now we are finding that growth itself causes problems.

CHARLES B. REEDER

Growth, in some curious way, I suspect, depends on being always in motion just a little bit, one way or another.

NORMAN MAILER

When people ask me, "What one factor do you believe has contributed most to the growth and influence of your organization?" I don't have to stop and think about an answer. Unquestionably it has been the emphasis laid from the very beginning upon human relationships—toward the public on the one hand, through careful service, and giving the utmost in values; toward our associates on the other hand.

J. C. PENNEY

If the shoe fits, you're not allowing for growth.

ROBERT N. COONS

Growth for the sake of growth is the ideology of the cancer cell.　　　　　　　　　　EDWARD ABBEY

It is usually wise to let key people have some voice in choosing those with whom they must work. But if you are building for growth, recognize that a weaker man will not willingly choose a stronger man who may soon become a threat to his own position and security.

H. B. MAYNARD

Every one should keep a mental wastepaper basket and the older he grows the more things he will consign to it—torn up to irrecoverable tatters.

SAMUEL BUTLER

Every man's road in life is marked by the graves of his personal likings.　　　ALEXANDER SMITH

Besides resorting to defensive diversification at times, a healthy and self-confident management is always considering whether its total assets can be used as a basis for other profitable enterprises.

JESSE WERNER

The reluctant obedience of distant provinces generally costs more than it is worth.
THOMAS BABINGTON MACAULAY

You must grow like a tree, not like a mushroom.
JANET ERSKINE STUART

Growth itself contains the germ of happiness.
PEARL S. BUCK

There is no fruit which is not bitter before it is ripe.
PUBLILIUS SYRUS

The strongest principle of growth lies in human choice.
GEORGE ELIOT

Improvement makes straight roads; but the crooked roads without improvement are roads of genius.
WILLIAM BLAKE

Live according to what you are and you will grow. To grow in one direction when we should be growing in another is an altogether bogus growth.
HUBERT VAN ZELLER

What grows makes no noise. GERMAN PROVERB

Just as we outgrow a pair of trousers, we outgrow acquaintances, libraries, principles, etc. at times before they've worn out and at times—and this is the worst of all—before we have new ones.
GEORG CHRISTOPH LICHTENBERG

All growth is a leap in the dark, a spontaneous unpremeditated act without benefit of experience.
                                    HENRY MILLER

Whatever is formed for long duration arrives slowly to its maturity.   SAMUEL JOHNSON

There is no growth except in the fulfillment of obligations.   ANTOINE de SAINT-EXUPERY

It is the highest creatures who take the longest to mature, and are the most helpless during their immaturity.   GEORGE BERNARD SHAW

If way to the Better there be, it exacts a full look at the Worst.   THOMAS HARDY

10 · TECHNIQUE

Control

His life was now perfection,
His ambitions all complete;
Never mind which direction?
He was in the driver's seat.

Control circumstances, and do not allow them to control you. THOMAS A. KEMPIS

I will pay more for the ability to deal with people than any other ability under the sun.
JOHN D. ROCKEFELLER

To be a great autocrat you must be a great barbarian.
JOSEPH CONRAD

I like the sayers of no better than the sayers of yes.
RALPH WALDO EMERSON

Almost everybody thought that Marshal Joffre had won the first battle of the Marne, but some refused to agree. One day a newspaper man appealed to Joffre: "Will you tell me who did win the battle of the Marne?" "I can't answer that," said the Marshal. "But I can tell you that if the battle of the Marne had been lost the blame would have been on me."

Newsweek

I am the captain of my soul;
I rule it with stern joy;
And yet I think I had more fun
When I was cabin boy.   KEITH PRESTON

It takes more skill to control others than to do it yourself.   ANON

Watch out for the fellow who talks about putting things in order! Putting things in order always means getting other people under your control.

DENIS DIDEROT

If you command wisely, you'll be obeyed cheerfully.

THOMAS FULLER

One cannot govern with buts.

CHARLES de GAULLE

Greatness does not depend on the size of your command, but on the way you exercise it.

MARSHAL FOCH

Make your business talks as short as your prayers, and you will always be a winner.

EDGAR WATSON HOWE

The common soldier's blood makes the General great.

ITALIAN PROVERB

There is a homely adage which runs: speak softly and carry a big stick; you will go far.
                                    THEODORE ROOSEVELT

The Pentagon is like a log going down the river with 25,000 ants on it, each thinking he's steering.
                                    HENRY ROWAN

Every director bites the hand that lays the golden egg.
                                    SAMUEL GOLDWYN

I don't never have any trouble in regulating my own conduct, but to keep other folks' straight is what bothers me.   JOSH BILLINGS

I have always regarded the forward edge of the battle-field as the most exclusive club in the world.
                                    SIR BRIAN HORROCKS

Command is getting people to go the way you want them to go—enthusiastically.
                        GENERAL WILLIAM WESTMORELAND

To persuade is more trouble than to dominate, and the powerful seldom take this trouble if they can avoid it.
                                    CHARLES HORTON COOLEY

The right divine of kings to govern wrong.
                                    ALEXANDER POPE

Those that are the loudest in their threats are the weakest in the execution of them.
                                    CHARLES CALEB COLTON

Men are of no importance. What counts is who commands. CHARLES de GAULLE

He who rules must humor fully as much as he commands. GEORGE ELIOT

A chief is a man who assumes responsibility. He says 'I was beaten.' He does not say 'My men were beaten.' Thus speaks a real man. ANTOINE de EXUPERY

The big drum sounds well from afar.
PERSIAN PROVERB

To govern is to make choices. DUC de LEVIS

No man is good enough to govern another man without the other's consent. ABRAHAM LINCOLN

Being a general calls for different talents from being a soldier. TITUS LIVY

A bully is always a coward. PROVERB

He that would govern others, first should be
The master of himself. PHILIP MASSINGER

Organization

*Good organization
Is the foundation
Of THE Organization.*

You can take away our factories, take away our trade, our avenues of transportation and our money—leave us with nothing but our organization and in four years we could reestablish ourselves.

ANDREW CARNEGIE

Don't agonize. Organize.

FLORENCE R. KENNEDY

All organizations are at least 50 percent waste—waste people, waste effort, waste space, and waste time.

ROBERT TOWNSEND

Two essential qualities in a good organizer are a thorough and constant perception of the end in view, and a power of dealing with masses of details, never forgetting that they are details, and not becoming their slave.

SIR ARTHUR HELPS

What they could do with round here is a good war. What else can you expect with peace running wild all over the place? You know what the trouble with peace is? No organization.

BERTOLT BRECHT

Specialization and organization are the basis of human progress.

CHARLOTTE PERKINS GILMAN

Look at the John Birch Society. Look at Hitler. The reactionaries are always better organizers.

CESAR CHAVEZ

Routine is not organization, any more than paralysis is order.

SIR ARTHUR HELPS

Keep your eye on the filling station, it is the true agent of decentralization.   FRANK LLOYD WRIGHT

The "organization man" is not merely a slick phrase. He is a growing menace to us all, not because of what he is—a decent and hard-working servant of his organization—but because of what he is not. He is not willing to annoy his organization by any action, and his organization is too easily annoyed.
McGEORGE BUNDY

Reorganization is the permanent condition of a vigorous organization.   ROY L. ASH

Organization can't be beaten without organization.
HEYWOOD BROUN

But where organizing an effect is concerned it is sometimes better to have mediocre talent than a bunch of creative individuals who disturb the situation by questioning everything.   ALAN HARRINGTON

Large organization is loose organization. Nay, it would be almost true to say that organization is always disorganization.
GILBERT KEITH CHESTERTON

We tend to meet any new situation by re-organizing and a wonderful method it can be for creating the illusion of progress while producing confusion, inefficiency and demoralization. PETRONIUS ARBITER

We are half-ruined by conformity: but we should be wholly ruined without it.
CHARLES DUDLEY WARNER

Have a time and place for everything, and do everything in its time and place, and you will not only accomplish more, but have far more leisure than those who are always hurrying, as if vainly attempting to overtake time that had been lost.

TYRON EDWARDS

Let all things be done decently and in order.

Corinthians

Order marches with weighty and measured strides, disorder is always in a hurry.

NAPOLEON BONAPARTE

Everywhere in the world the industrial regime tends to make the unorganized or unorganizable individual, the pauper, into the victim of a kind and human sacrifice offered to the gods of civilization.

JACQUES MARITAIN

The intangible duty of making things run smoothly is apt to be thankless, because people don't realise how much time and trouble it takes and believe it is the result of a natural and effortless unction.

A. C. BENSON

A good organization tends to simplicity: and, when a wise method is proposed, people are ready to say how self-evident it is. But, without the few men who perceive these self-evident things, the business of the world would go on even worse than it does.

SIR ARTHUR HELPS

Tyranny is always better organized than freedom.

CHARLES PIERRE PEGUY

Modern Man is the victim of the very instruments he values most. Every gain in power, every mastery of natural forces, every scientific addition to knowledge, has proved potentially dangerous, because it has not been accompanied by equal gains in self-understanding and self-discipline.　　LEWIS MUMFORD

Structure without life is dead. But life without structure is unseen.　　JOHN CAGE

Decisions

The best of visions
And beyond all price,
That all our decisions
Could be taken twice.

Major decisions usually require predictions about the future.　　HARRY A. BULLIS

Mistrust first impulses; they are nearly always good.
CHARLES MAURICE de TALLEYRAND

All generalizations are dangerous, even this one.
ALEXANDER DUMAS

The desire to remain popular has influenced too many business decisions.　　HERMAN W. STEINKRAUS

The men who run modern international corporations are the first in history with the organization, the technology, the money, and the ideology to make a credible try at managing the world as an integrated unit. By making ordinary business decisions, the managers now have more power than most sovereign governments to determine where people will live; what work they will do, if any; what they will eat, drink and wear; what sorts of knowledge, schools and universities they will encourage; and what kind of society their children will inherit.

RICHARD J. BARNET and RONALD MULLER

I decide. I do. Me. FRANK HAGUE

The percentage of error will multiply the longer you deliberate. ANON

When it is not necessary to make a decision, it is necessary not to make a decision.
LUCIUS, SECOND LORD FALKLAND

Decide, v.t. To succumb to the preponderance of one set of influences over another set.
AMBROSE BIERCE

It is better to err on the side of daring than the side of caution. ALVIN TOFFLER

There will always be someone who will oppose every decision you make. ANON

My way is to divide half a sheet of paper by a line into two columns, writing over one Pro and over the other Con. Then, during three or four days' consideration, I put down under the different heads short hints of the different motives, that at different times occur to me, for or against the measure. When I have thus got them all together in one view, I endeavour to estimate their respective weights; and where I find two, one on each side, that seem equal, I strike them both out.

BENJAMIN FRANKLIN

He is no wise man that will quit a certainty for an uncertainty. SAMUEL JOHNSON

I can think of no blissfuller state than being treated as if I was always right. ROBERT FROST

Take time to deliberate, but when the time for action arrives, stop thinking and go in.

ANDREW JACKSON

I hate people who are wise during the event.

KENNETH TYNAN

Why should it be done at all?
Why should it be done now?
Why should it be done that way?

HERBERT BAYARD SWOPE

Situations are rarely ever black or white; they are usually varying shades of grey.

PROFESSOR RAY E. BROWN

When you think you have obtained a reasonable percentage of the facts, try making a tentative decision and then see whether the evidence supports it.

HARRY A. BULLIS

There never were since the creation of the world, two cases exactly parallel.   EARL of CHESTERFIELD

It is always during a passing state of mind that we make lasting resolutions.   MARCEL PROUST

Make sure you're right, then go ahead.
DAVY CROCKETT

Conclusions are not often reached by talk any more than by private thinking.
ROBERT LOUIS STEVENSON

One resolve is like another—
In one year and out the other.
NOVA TRIMBLE ASHLEY

Now, thank goodness, I've sorted out what matters and what doesn't. And I'm beginning to be intolerant again.   G. B. STERN

Nothing is more difficult, and therefore more precious, than to be able to decide.
NAPOLEON BONAPARTE

Truly, that reason upon which we plume ourselves, though it may answer for little things, yet for great decisions is hardly surer than a toss-up.
CHARLES SANDERS PIERCE

When possible make the decisions now, even if action is in the future. A reviewed decision usually is better than one reached at the last moment.
WILLIAM B. GIVEN

Every truth has two sides, it is well to look at both before we commit ourselves to either.   AESOP

Define the problem. Put it into the clearest language possible. Examine it painstakingly. Get all the facts you can. List the possible choices open to you, and what each choice will lead to. Then make your decision on the basis of values you believe in, and the course of action you honestly conclude the facts lead you to take.   HARRY A. BULLIS

Wretches hang that jurymen may dine.
          ALEXANDER POPE

When once I have made my decision, I go straight to my end, and sweep aside everything with my red cassock.   CARDINAL RICHELIEU

Formulate your feelings as well as your thoughts.
          A. R. ORAGE

In every affair, consider what precedes and what follows and then undertake it.   EPICTETUS

Trust the instinct to the end, though you can render no reason.   RALPH WALDO EMERSON

Trust your heart . . . Never deny it a hearing. It is the kind of house oracle that often foretells the most important.   BALTHASAR GRACIAN

Power

Power is gained
  More with flair
  Than with care,
But is retained
  More with care
  Than with flair.

Power tends to corrupt and absolute power corrupts absolutely.　　　　　　**LORD ACTON**

Power tends to corrupt but absolute power is absolutely delightful.　　　　　　**ANON**

Power is often more important than profit.
　　　　　　BERTRAM TOY

Power is the ability not to have to please.
　　　　　　ELIZABETH JANEWAY

The only prize much cared for by the powerful is power. The prize of the general is not a bigger tent, but command.　　　**OLIVER WENDELL HOLMES**

The men who really wield, retain, and covet power are the kind who answer bedside phones while making love.　　　　　**NICHOLAS PILEGGI**

Power is not revealed by striking hard or often, but by striking true.　　　　**HONORE de BALZAC**

The measure of man is what he does with power.
                                        PITTACUS

People who have power respond simply. They have no minds but their own.   IVY COMPTON-BURNETT

Power is the ultimate aphrodisiac.
                                HENRY KISSINGER

The great secret of power is never to will to do more than you can accomplish.   HENRIK IBSEN

Power corrupts the few, while weakness corrupts the many.   ERIC HOFFER

It is a paradox that every dictator has climbed to power on the ladder of free speech. Immediately on attaining power each dictator has suppressed all free speech except his own.   HERBERT HOOVER

Immense power is acquired by assuring yourself in your secret reveries that you were born to control affairs.   ANDREW CARNEGIE

Power is like a woman you want to stay in bed with forever.   PATRICK ANDERSON

Knowledge! Money! Power!
That's the cycle democracy is built on!
                            TENNESSEE WILLIAMS

No-one can maintain ungoverned power for long, but if it is controlled it will last.
                        LUCIUS ANNAEUS SENECA

If you are a terror to many, then beware of many.
AUSONIUS

Use power to curb power.   **CHINESE PROVERB**

Power abdicates only under stress of counter-power.
MARTIN BUBER

I know of nothing sublime which is not some modification of power.   **EDMUND BURKE**

The reputation of power is power.
THOMAS HODGES

A good indignation brings out all one's powers.
RALPH WALDO EMERSON

What you cannot enforce,
Do not command.   **SOPHOCLES**

Power is much more easily manifested in destroying than in creating.   **WILLIAM WORDSWORTH**

You only have power over people so long as you don't take everything away from them. But when you've robbed a man of everything he's no longer in your power—he's free again.
ALEXANDER SOLZHENITSYN

Power never takes a back step—only in the face of more power.   **MALCOLM X**

If power corrupts, weakness is the seat of power with its constant necessity of deals and bribes and compromising arrangements, corrupts even more.
BARBARA TUCHMAN

Isolation from reality is inseparable from the exercise of power.　　　　GEORGE M. REEDY

Inability to those in power to still the voices of their own consciences is the great force leading to desired changes.　　PRESIDENT KAUNDA of ZAMBIA

They who are in highest places, and have the most power, have the least liberty, because they are most observed.　　　　JOHN TILLOTSON

In all supremacy of power there is inherent a prerogative to pardon.　　BENJAMIN WHICHCOTE

Small tyrants threatened by big, sincerely believe they love Liberty.　　WYSTAN HUGH AUDEN

The secret of all power is—save your force. If you want high pressure you must choke off waste.
　　　　　　　JOSEPH FARRELL

Power acquired by guilt has seldom been directed to any good end or useful purpose.
　　　　　　　CORNELIUS TACITUS

Power is always right, weakness always wrong. Power is always insolent and despotic.　NOAH WEBSTER

The effect of power and publicity on all men is the aggravation of self, a sort of tumor that ends by killing the victim's sympathies.　　HENRY ADAMS

The sole advantage of power is that you can do more good.　　　　BALTASAR GRACIAN

The megalomaniac differs from the narcissist by the fact that he wishes to be powerful rather than charming, and seeks to be feared rather than loved. To this type belong many lunatics and most of the great men of history.   BERTRAND RUSSELL

It is not possible to found a lasting power upon injustice, perjury and treachery.   DEMOSTHENES

Leadership

When conducting the band,
You'll find it's allowed;
You're expected to stand
With your back to the crowd.

If you don't drive your business, you will be driven out of business.   B. C. FORBES

In the simplest terms, a leader is one who knows where he wants to go, and gets up and goes.
                                        JOHN ERSKINE

The leader must know, must know that he knows, and must be able to make it abundantly clear to those around him that he knows.
                              CLARENCE B. RANDALL

Henry Ford could get anything out of men because he just talked and would tell them stories. He'd never say, "I want this done!" He'd say, "I wonder if we can do it."
GEORGE BROWN

Leadership is action, not position.
DONALD H. McGANNON

Leadership appears to be the art of getting others to want to do something you are convinced should be done.
VANCE PACKARD

Never tell people how to do things. Tell them what to do and they will surprise you with their ingenuity.
GEORGE S. PATTON

Leadership does not depend on being right.
IVAN ILLICH

I believe that the Jews have made a contribution to the human condition out of all proportion to their numbers: I believe them to be an immense people. Not only have they supplied the world with two leaders of the stature of Jesus Christ and Karl Marx, but they have even indulged in the luxury of following neither one nor the other.
PETER USTINOV

Leadership is the ability to get men to do what they don't want to do and like it.
HARRY TRUMAN

If you would rule the world quietly, you must keep it amused.
RALPH WALDO EMERSON

Robert Taft's great attribute was that he made decisions. You never had to say, "Well, what are we going to do tomorrow?" He told you. That to me is leadership.   SENATOR BARRY GOLDWATER

The real leader has no need to lead—he is content to point the way.   HENRY MILLER

You don't have to be intellectually bright to be a competent leader.   SIR EDMUND HILLARY

I have an absolute rule. I refuse to make a decision that somebody else can make. The first rule of leadership is to save yourself for the big decision. Don't allow your mind to become cluttered with the trivia. Don't let yourself become the issue.
    RICHARD NIXON

Dictators are rulers who always look good until the last ten minutes.   JAN MASARYK

A leader is best when people barely know that he exists.   WITTER BYNNER

Here's my Golden Rule for a tarnished age: Be fair with others, but then keep after them until they're fair with you.   ALAN ALDA

I cannot commend to a business house any artificial plan for making men producers—any scheme for driving them into business-building. You must lead them through their self-interest. It is this alone that will keep them keyed up to the full capacity of their productiveness.   CHARLES H. STEINWAY

The final test of a leader is that he leaves behind in other men the conviction and the will to carry on.
    WALTER LIPPMAN

The art of leadership consists in consolidating the attention of the people against a single adversary and taking care that nothing will split up that attention.
ADOLF HITLER

I can take no allegiance to a flag if I don't know who's holding it. **PETER USTINOV**

The great leaders have always stage-managed their effects. **CHARLES de GAULLE**

The only real training for leadership is leadership.
ANTONY JAY

If, in order to succeed in an enterprise, I were obliged to choose between fifty deer commanded by a lion, and fifty lions commanded by a deer, I should consider myself more certain of success with the first group than with the second. **SAINT VINCENT de PAUL**

Leaders . . . they grasp nettles. **DAVID OGILVY**

Every despot must have one disloyal subject to keep him sane. **GEORGE BERNARD SHAW**

Churchill? He's a busted flush!
LORD BEAVERBROOK

You've got to lead and not drive, inspire and not dominate, cause respect and not fear, win support and not opposition. **ANON**

He who requires much from himself and little from others, will keep himself from being the object of resentment. **CONFUCIUS**

Personal relationships that inhibit detached evaluation and frank criticism represent a disservice to all concerned.   PROFESSOR RAY A. BROWN

A true leader always keeps an element of surprise up his sleeve, which others cannot grasp but which keeps his public excited and breathless.
                    CHARLES de GAULLE

Kindness. The most unkindest thing of all.
                    EDNA O'BRIEN

Dictators ride to and fro upon tigers from which they dare not dismount.   HINDU PROVERB

Not what they want but what is good for them.
                    OLIVER CROMWELL

There has not been a great leader in this century who wasn't devious at certain times when it was necessary to achieve his goals.   CLINTON ROSSITER

No man is great enough or wise enough for any of us to surrender our destiny to. The only way in which anyone can lead us is to restore to us the belief in our own guidance.   HENRY MILLER

. . . Never harass somebody . . . working at his capacity. A mediocre person I never harass. I believe most people don't know what they can do. Look, what's the difference between Vince Lombardi and a high school football coach? They both know the same plays. It's a question of getting a little more precision.
                    HENRY KISSINGER

Really great men have a curious feeling that the greatness is not in them but through them.
JOHN RUSKIN

I really believe my greatest service is in the many unwise steps I prevent.
WILLIAM LYON MACKENZIE KING

The leader is a stimulus, but he is also a response.
EDWARD C. LINDEMAN

The winds and waves are always on the side of the ablest navigators.   EDWARD GIBBON

A leader or a man of action in a crisis almost always acts subconsciously and then thinks of the reasons for his action.   JAWAHARLAL NEHRU

Strong beliefs win strong men, and then make them stronger.   WALTER BAGEHOT

A superior man may be made to go to the well, but he cannot be made to go down into it. He may be imposed upon, but he cannot be fooled.   CONFUCIUS

11 · COMMUNICATION

Reading

*The person who can read
   And does not
Is no better than those
   Who cannot.*

Reading is sometimes an ingenious device for avoiding
thought.   ARTHUR HELPS

I am part of all that I have read.   JOHN KIERAN

Dyslexia Rules—K.O.?   GRAFFITI

As in the sexual experience, there are never more than
two persons present in the act of reading—the writer
who is the impregnator and the reader who is the
respondent.   ELWYN BROOKS WHITE

He's got a photographic mind. Too bad it never
developed.   LEOPOLD FECHTNER

I read part of it all the way through.
SAMUEL GOLDWYN

I know of no sentence that can induce such immediate and brazen lying as the one that begins, "Have you read—."
WILSON MIZNER

There are times when I think that the reading I have done in the past has had no effect except to cloud my mind and make me indecisive.
ROBERTSON DAVIES

Reading is eye and ass power.   IRWIN van GROVE

I am sitting in the smallest room in my house. I have your review in front of me. Soon it will be behind me.
MAX REGER

Some read to think, these are rare . . . some to unite . . . these are common: and some to talk . . . and these form the great majority.
CHARLES CALEB COLTON

Reading is seeing by proxy.   HERBERT SPENCER

Every man has one thing he can do better than anyone else—and usually it's reading his own handwriting.
G. NORMAN COLLIE

I'm not a speed reader. I'm a speed understander.
ISAAC ASIMOV

The ratio of literacy to illiteracy is constant, but nowadays the illiterates can read and write.
ALBERTO MORAVIA

Some people read because they are too lazy to think.
GEORG CHRISTOPH LICHTENBERG

I have received no more than one or two letters in my life that were worth the postage.
HENRY DAVID THOREAU

All my good reading, you might say, was done in the toilet . . . There are passages of *Ulysses* which can be read only in the toilet—if one wants to extract the full flavour of their content. **HENRY MILLER**

The minute you read something that you can't understand, you can almost be sure it was drawn up by a lawyer. **WILL ROGERS**

Justice Oliver Wendell Holmes was sitting in his library one day when Franklin D. Roosevelt called, a few days after his inauguration in 1933, and found him reading Plato, at the age of ninety-two. "Why do you read Plato, Mr. Justice?" "To improve my mind, Mr. President," Holmes replied. **RUDOLF FLESCH**

If you believe everything you read, better not read.
JAPANESE PROVERB

Reading made Don Quixote a gentleman, but believing what he read made him mad.
GEORGE BERNARD SHAW

If I had read as much as other men, I should have known no more than other men.
THOMAS HOBBES

We read to say that we have read.

CHARLES LAMB

Reading is to the mind what exercise is to the body.

SIR RICHARD STEELE

We read every day, with astonishment, things which we see every day, without surprise.

EARL of CHESTERFIELD

The art of reading is to skip judiciously.

PHILIP G. HAMERTON

My brother cuts the time it takes to read a newspaper by skipping everything in the future tense; and it's amazing what he doesn't miss.

KATHERINE WHITEHORNE

Reading means borrowing.

GEORG CHRISTOPH LICHTENBERG

Integrity is the thing which keeps you from looking ahead to see how the story ends.

JACOB M. BRAUDE

He has only half learned the art of reading who has not added to it the even more refined accomplishments of skipping and skimming. ARTHUR J. BALFOUR

Reading without reflecting is like eating without digesting.

EDMUND BURKE

If you want to discover your true opinion of anybody, observe the impression made on you by the first sight of a letter from him. ARTHUR SCHOPENHAUER

A page digested is better than a volume hurriedly read.   THOMAS BABINGTON MACAULAY

It is well to read everything of something, and something of everything.   LORD BROUGHAM

Reading, after a certain age, diverts the mind too much from its creative pursuits. Any man who reads too much and uses his own brain too little falls into lazy habits of thinking.   ALBERT EINSTEIN

Reading should be in proportion to thinking, and thinking in proportion to reading.
                                        NATHANIEL EMMONS

Resolve to edge in a little reading every day, if it is but a single sentence. If you can gain fifteen minutes a day, it will make itself felt at the end of the year.
                                        HORACE MANN

Reading makes a full man, meditation a profound man, discourse a clear man.
                                        BENJAMIN FRANKLIN

We must form our minds by reading deep rather than wide.   MARCUS FABIUS QUINTILIANUS

I read for three things: first, to know what the world has done during the last twenty-four hours, and is about to do today; second, for the knowledge that I specially want in my work; and third, for what will bring my mind into a proper mood.
                                        HENRY WARD BEECHER

Force yourself to reflect on what you read, paragraph by paragraph.   SAMUEL TAYLOR COLERIDGE

Nothing is worth reading that does not require an alert mind.   CHARLES DUDLEY WARNER

To exchange hours of ennui for hours of delight.
CHARLES de MONTESQUIEU

With half an hour's reading in bed every night as a steady practice, the busiest man can get a fair education before the plasma sets in the periganglionic spaces of his gray cortex.   SIR WILLIAM OSLER

Read every day something no one else is reading. Think every day something no one else is thinking. It is bad for the mind to be always a part of a unanimity.
CHRISTOPHER MORLEY

If I am at all partial, it is to the man who reads rapidly. One of the silliest couplets ever composed is to be found in "The Art of Reading" by one William Walker, a seventeenth-century hollow-head who wrote:

> Learn to read slow; all other graces
> Will follow in their proper places.

This is unmitigated balderdash and if taken seriously can easily result in the wasting of ten or fifteen percent of the few waking hours God has put at our disposal.
CLIFTON FADIMAN

A serious and profitable occupation, reading the papers. It removes everything abnormal from your make-up, everything that doesn't conform to accepted ideas. It teaches you to reason as well as the next person. It gives you irrefutable and generally admitted opinions on all events. MICHEL de CHELDERODE

Let us read with method, and propose to ourselves an end to which our studies may point. The use of reading is to aid us in thinking.   EDWARD GIBBON

To acquire the habit of reading is to construct for yourself a refuge from almost all the miseries of life.
                    W. SOMERSET MAUGHAM

We can never know that a piece of writing is bad unless we have begun by trying to read it as if it was very good and ended by discovering that we were paying the author an undeserved compliment. C. S. LEWIS

A man ought to read, just as inclination leads him, for what he reads as a task will do him little good.
                         SAMUEL JOHNSON

When in reading we meet with any maxim that may be of use, we should take it for our own, and make an immediate application of it, as we would of the advice of a friend whom we have purposely consulted.
                    CHARLES CALEB COLTON

Multifarious reading weakens the mind more than doing nothing, for it becomes a necessity, at last, like smoking; and is an excuse for the mind to lie dormant whilst thought is poured in, and runs through, a clear stream over unproductive gravel, on which not even mosses grow. It is the idlest of all idleness, and leaves more of impotency than any other.
                    FREDERICK WILLIAM ROBERTSON

Books

Give this book the credit due,
It's more than paper and ink;
Not one of those that thinks for you
But one that makes you think.

It is a good thing for an educated man to read books of quotations.　　SIR WINSTON CHURCHILL

To me the charm of an encyclopedia is that it knows— and I needn't.　　FRANCIS YEATS-BROWN

The books we think we ought to read are poky, dull
   and dry;
The books that we would like to read we are
   ashamed to buy;
The books that people talk about we never can
   recall;
And the books that people give us, oh, they're worst of
   all.　　CAROLYN WELLS

A library is thought in cold storage.
　　HERBERT SAMUEL

The worst thing about new books is that they keep us from reading the old ones.　　JOSEPH JOUBERT

The oldest books are still only just out to those who have not read them.　　SAMUEL BUTLER

Due attention to the inside of books, and due contempt for the outside, is the proper relation between a man of sense and his books.

> EARL of CHESTERFIELD

Read the best books first, or you may not have a chance to read them at all.

> HENRY DAVID THOREAU

A best-seller was a book which somehow sold well simply because it was selling well.

> DANIEL J. BOORSTIN

I cannot see that lectures can do so much good as reading the books from which the lectures are taken.

> SAMUEL JOHNSON

If a book is worth reading, it is worth buying.

> JOHN RUSKIN

Never read a book through merely because you have begun it.   JOHN WITHERSPOON

Books think for me.   CHARLES LAMB

I've given up reading books. I find it takes my mind off myself.   OSCAR WILDE

When a book and a head collide, and there is a hollow sound, is it always in the book?

> GEORG CHRISTOPH LICHTENBERG

On how many people's libraries, as on bottles from the drugstore, one might write: "For external use only."

> ALPHONSE DAUDET

Never lend books, for no one ever returns them: the only books I have in my library are books that other folks have lent me.   ANATOLE FRANCE

Where is human nature so weak as in the bookstore?
          HENRY WARD BEECHER

Those who reproach an author for being obscure should first look inside themselves to see how much light there is in them.
          JOHANN WOLFGANG von GOETHE

Readers are of two sorts: one who carefully goes through a book, and the other who as carefully lets the book go through him.   DOUGLAS JERROLD

The real purpose of books is to trap the mind into doing its own thinking. CHRISTOPHER MORLEY

In the case of good books, the point is not to see how many of them you can get through, but rather how many can get through to you.
          MORTIMER J. ADLER

Wear the old coat and buy the new book.
          AUSTIN PHELPS

A man who attempts to read all the new productions must do as the flea does—skip. SAMUEL ROGERS

Much is written of the power of the Press; a power which may last but a day; by comparison, little is heard of the power of books, which may endure for generations.   SIR STANLEY UNWIN

Does a lion tamer enter a cage with a book on how to tame a lion?   DIMITRI MITROPOULOS

Perhaps there are not as many stupid things said as there are set down in print.
    GONCOURT BROTHERS

A book that furnishes no quotations is no book—it is a plaything.   THOMAS LOVE PEACOCK

One always tends to overpraise a long book because one has got through it.
    EDWARD MORGAN FOSTER

He picked something valuable out of everything he read.   PLINY THE YOUNGER

The reading of all good books is like a conversation with the finest men of past centuries.
    RENE DESCARTES

Every little while another man decides what are the best books. Pay no attention to him, and decide yourself.   EDGAR WATSON HOWE

I hate books: they teach us only to talk about what we do not know.   JEAN-JACQUES ROUSSEAU

A few books, well studied, and thoroughly digested, nourish the understanding more than hundreds but gargled in the mouth, as ordinary students use.
    FRANCIS OSBORN

Even with all the leisure in the world and an income large enough to gratify all desires, men will seldom read serious books at the rate of twenty a year.

WALTER B. PITKIN

He that reads and grows no wiser seldom suspects his own deficiency, but complains of hard words and obscure sentences, and asks why books are written which cannot be understood. SAMUEL JOHNSON

'Tis the good reader that makes the good book.

RALPH WALDO EMERSON

Be sure that you go to the author to get at his meaning, not to find yours. JOHN RUSKIN

It was from my own early experience that I decided there was no use to which money could be applied so productive of good to boys and girls who have good within them and ability and ambition to develop it as the founding of a public library.

ANDREW CARNEGIE

A man of ability, for the chief of his reading, should select such works as he feels are beyond his own power to have produced. What can other books do for him but waste his time or augment his vanity?

JOHN FOSTER

One must be rich in thought and character to owe nothing to books, though preparation is necessary to profitable reading; and the less reading is better than more:—book-struck men are of all readers least wise, however knowing or learning.

AMOS BRONSON ALCOTT

Some read books only with a view to find fault, while others read only to be taught; the former are like venomous spiders, extracting a poisonous quality, where the latter, like the bees, sip out a sweet and profitable juice.   SIR ROGER L'ESTRANGE

Speeches

Every speech will often appear
Very short to him who steers it;
But the same speech, it must be clear,
Can be long to him who hears it.

Three things matter in a speech; who says it, how he says it, and what he says—and, of the three, the last matters the least.   JOHN MORLEY

The human brain starts working the moment you are born and never stops until you stand up to speak in public.   SIR GEORGE JESSEL

If you want me to talk for ten minutes, I'll come next week. If you want me to talk for an hour, I'll come tonight.   WOODROW WILSON

There is but one pleasure in life equal to that of being called on to make an after-dinner speech, and that is not being called on to make one.
          CHARLES DUDLEY WARNER

Haven't you learned yet that I put something more than whiskey into my speeches.

SIR WINSTON CHURCHILL

I sometimes marvel at the extraordinary docility with which Americans submit to speeches.

ADLAI STEVENSON

The speaker had a two-second idea, a two minute vocabulary, and a two-hour speech.

ANON

The broad masses of the people can be moved only by the power of speech.

ADOLF HITLER

In many ways, a speaker is faced with the same problem a bridegroom has on his wedding night. Everyone knows what he's there for. The big question is: "Can he deliver?"

ROBERT ORBEN

The recipe for a good speech includes some shortening.

ANON

I do not object to people looking at their watches when I am speaking. But I strongly object when they start shaking them to make sure they are still going.

LORD BIRKETT

There is too much speaking in the world and almost all of it is too long. The Lord's Prayer, the Twenty-Third Psalm, Lincoln's Gettysburg Address are three great literary treasures that will last forever, no one of them is as long as 300 words. With such striking illustrations of the power of brevity it is amazing that speakers never learn to be brief.

BRUCE BARTON

An after-dinner speech should be like a lady's dress—long enough to cover the subject and short enough to be interesting.   R. A. BUTLER

Conclusions are an important part of every speech—especially when they come close to the beginning.
                                         ANON

Speeches are like babies—easy to conceive, hard to deliver.   PAT O'MALLEY

Blessed are they who have nothing to say, and who cannot be persuaded to say it.
                         JAMES RUSSELL LOWELL

He is one of those orators of whom it was well said, "Before they get up they do not know what they are going to say: when they are speaking, they do not know what they are saying; and when they sit down, they do not know what they have said!"
                         SIR WINSTON CHURCHILL

To make a speech immortal you don't have to make it everlasting.   LESLIE HORE-BELISHA

Men can rise to the occasions, but few know when to sit down.   ANON

After-dinner speaking is the art of saying nothing briefly.   EDMUND FULLER

Why doesn't the fellow who says, "I'm no speech-maker," let it go at that instead of giving a demonstration?   FRANK McKINNEY HUBBARD

I never failed to convince an audience that the best thing they could do was to go away.

THOMAS LOVE PEACOCK

A speech that's full of sparkling wit,
Will keep it's hearers grinning,
Provided that the end of it
Is close to the beginning!   ANON

Speech-making is exactly like childbirth. You are so glad to get it over with.   JOHN BARRYMORE

A speech is like a love affair. Any fool can start it, but to end it requires considerable skill.

LORD MANCROFT

Sheridan once said of some speech, in his acute, sarcastic way, that 'It contained a great deal both of what was new and what was true; but that what was new was not true, and what was true was not new.'

WILLIAM HAZLITT

Even when I am reading my lectures I often think to myself, "What a humbug you are," and I wonder the people don't find it out.

WILLIAM MAKEPEACE THACKERAY

It is an inflexible rule of mine not to make impromptu speeches without good warning . . . As Lord Goddard said, they are not worth the paper they are written on.   E. HORSFALL TURNER

A speech is a solemn responsibility. The man who makes a bad 30-minute speech to 200 people wastes only a half-hour of his own time. But he wastes 100

hours of the audience's time—more than four days—
which should be a hanging offense.

JENKIN LLOYD JONES

Lecturer: One with his hand in your pocket, his
tongue in your ear and his faith in your patience.

AMBROSE BIERCE

Speeches cannot be made long enough for the speakers, nor short enough for the hearers.

JAMES PERRY

I've never thought my speeches were too long: I've
enjoyed them.   HUBERT HUMPHREY

The best impromptu speeches are the ones written well
in advance.   RUTH GORDON

People don't seem to realize that it takes time and
effort and preparation to think. Statesmen are far too
busy making speeches to think.

BERTRAND RUSSELL

Accustomed as I am to public speaking, I know the
futility of it.   FRANKLIN P. ADAMS

The relationship of the Toastmaster to the Speaker
should be the same as that of the fan to the fandancer.
It should call attention to the subject without making
any particular effort to cover. ADLAI STEVENSON

A man never becomes an orator if he has anything to
say.   FINLEY PETER DUNNE

A heavy and cautious responsibility of speech is the easiest thing in the world, anybody can do it. That is why so many tired, elderly and wealthy men go in for politics.   GILBERT KEITH CHESTERTON

The difficulty of speeches is that you are perpetually poised between the cliche and the indiscretion.
HAROLD MACMILLAN

Not speech but facts convince.   GREEK PROVERB

A good speech is a good thing, but the verdict is the thing.   DANIEL O'CONNELL

A wise speech sleeps in a foolish ear.   EURIPIDES

If you're offered an honorarium for a speech, you can be sure the money is of no consequencium.
MERLE MILLER

A good talker, even more than a good orator, implies a good audience.   LESLIE STEPHEN

All the skills of speech are of no use if our words are insincerely spoken.   WESLEY WIKSELL

His speeches to an hour-glass
Do some resemblance show;
Because the longer time they run
The shallower they grow.   ANON

There is no inspiration in evil . . . no man ever made a great speech on a mean subject.
EUGENE V. DEBS

Public Speaking

The words they use are nothing new,
I think you will concur;
You often hear both "I" and "you,"
The most popular is "er."

All the great speakers were bad speakers at first.
RALPH WALDO EMERSON

What the country needs is less public speaking and more private thinking.   ROSCOE DRUMMOND

Most speakers feel that 50 percent is what you deliver and 50 percent how you deliver it. Masters and Johnson feel the same way.   ROBERT ORBEN

Be sincere, be brief; be seated.
FRANKLIN D. ROOSEVELT

An orator is the fellow who is always ready to lay down your life for his country.   ANON

Say what you have to say and the first time you come to a sentence with a grammatical ending—sit down.
SIR WINSTON CHURCHILL

I have no time to prepare a profound message.
SPIRO T. AGNEW

Public speakers should speak up so that they can be heard, stand up so that they can be seen and shut up that they can be enjoyed. ANON

I'm going to milk those greedy pauses till they're udderless. RICHARD BURTON

The object of oratory is not truth, but persuasion. THOMAS BABINGTON MACAULAY

Always be shorter than anybody dared to hope. LORD READING

Begin at the beginning and go on till you come to the end; then stop. LEWIS CARROLL

Second wind: what a speaker gets when he says, "In conclusion." ANON

Great talkers are so constituted that they do not know their own thoughts until they hear them issuing from their mouths. THORNTON WILDER

What orators lack in depth they make up to you in length. CHARLES de MONTESQUIEU

Never rise to speak till you have something to say; and when you have said it, cease. JOHN WITHERSPOON

Those who speak "straight from the shoulder" should try from a little higher up. ANON

If you haven't struck oil in the first three minutes— stop boring! GEORGE JESSEL

One must not only believe in what one is saying but also that it matters, especially that it matters to the people to whom one is the king.

NORMAN THOMAS

Once you get people laughing, they're listening and you can tell them almost anything.

HERBERT GARDNER

To sway an audience, you must watch them as you speak.

C. KENT WRIGHT

Oratory: the art of making deep noises from the chest sound like important messages from the brain.

H. I. PHILLIPS

I would lay emphasis above all things, on the speaking voice. People rely far too much on that deceptive gadget, the microphone.

CORNELIA OTIS SKINNER

An orator or author is never successful till he has learned to make his words smaller than his ideas.

RALPH WALDO EMERSON

If you are speaking, forget everything but the subject. Never mind what others are thinking of you or your delivery, just forget yourself and go ahead.

DALE CARNEGIE

Adepts in the speaking trade,
Keep a cough by them ready-made.

CHARLES CHURCHILL

There are three things to aim at in public speaking: first, to get into your subject, then to get your subject into yourself, and lastly, to get your subject into your hearers. ALEXANDER GREGG

An orator is a man who says what he thinks and feels what he says. WILLIAM JENNINGS BRYAN

Never be so brief as to become obscure.
  TYRON EDWARDS

A speech should be made as though you are taking off a pair of long white gloves, which can only be done very slowly . . . You ease into your talk so that by the time you get to what you came to say, your audience is with you. LIZ CARPENTER

Oratory is just like prostitution: you must have little tricks. VITTORIO EMANUELE ORLANDO

You may use different sorts of sentences and illustrations before different sorts of audiences, but you don't —if you are wise—talk down to any audience.
  NORMAN THOMAS

Let it never be said of you, "I thought he would never finish." Follow the advice I was given when singing in supper clubs: "Get off while you're ahead; always leave them wanting more." Make sure you have finished speaking before your audience has finished listening. A talk, as Mrs. Hubert Humphrey reminded her husband, need not be eternal to be immortal.
  DOROTHY SARNOFF

My basic rule is to speak slowly and simply so that my audience has an opportunity to follow and think about what I am saying.   MARGARET CHASE SMITH

There may be other reasons for a man's not speaking in public than want of resolution; he may have nothing to say.   SAMUEL JOHNSON

To be an orator, you have to use your own words and be on fire with them. To be a talker—somebody else can write your words and you can read them.
FULTON J. SHEEN

The right word may be effective but no word was ever as effective as mighty timed pause. MARK TWAIN

Consult a dictionary for proper meanings and pronunciations. Your audience won't know if you're a bad speller, but they will know if you use or pronounce a word improperly. In my first remarks on the dais, I used to thank people for their "fulsome introduction" until I discovered to my dismay that "fulsome" meant offensive and insincere.   GEORGE PLIMPTON

Nothing is more despicable than a professional talker who uses his words as a quack uses his remedies.
FRANCOIS de FENELON

Let they speech be short, comprehending much in few words.   *Ecclesiasticus*

There's plenty of great advice available about the art of making talks, but if you don't adapt it to yourself, none of it is worth much.
JUDY LANGFORD CARTER

Speak properly, and in as few words as you can, but always plainly; for the end of speech is not ostentation, but to be understood.   WILLIAM PENN

Nothing is so unbelievable that oratory cannot make it acceptable.   MARCUS TULLIUS CICERO

The nature of oratory is such that there has always been a tendency among politicians and clergymen to oversimplify complex matters. From a pulpit or a platform even the most conscientious of speakers finds it very difficult to tell the whole truth.
          ALDOUS HUXLEY

Cultivate ease and naturalness. Have all your powers under command. Take possession of yourself, as in this way only can you take possession of your audience. If you are ill at ease, your listeners will be also. Always speak as though there were only one person in the hall whom you had to convince. Plead with him, argue with him, arouse him, touch him, but feel that your audience is one being whose confidence and affection you want to win.   CHARLES READE

In oratory the greatest art is to hide art.
          JONATHAN SWIFT

Great oratory needs not merely the orator, but a great theme and a great occasion.   LORD SAMUEL

Mend your speech a little,
Lest it may mar your fortunes.
          WILLIAM SHAKESPEARE

An orator can hardly get beyond commonplaces: if he does, he gets beyond his hearers.
WILLIAM HAZLITT

As a vessel is known by the sound, whether it be cracked or not, so men are proved by their speeches whether they be wise or foolish.   DEMOSTHENES

The least effect of the oration is on the orator; yet it is something; a faint recoil; a kicking of the gun.
RALPH WALDO EMERSON

I always think a great orator convinces us not by force of reasoning, but because he is visibly enjoying the beliefs, which he wants us to accept.   J. B. YEATS

Bores

It's boring, that's true,
Now don't disagree;
I know it's not you,
So it must be me!

A bore is a man who deprives you of solitude without providing you with company.
GIAN VINCENZO GRAVINA

Some people can stay longer in an hour than others can in a week.   WILLIAM DEAN HOWELLS

A bore is a fellow who opens his mouth and puts his feats in it.　　　　　　　　　HENRY FORD

There's nothing that cannot be made worse by repeating it.　　　　　　　　　ANON

Half the world is composed of people who have something to say and can't, and the other half who have nothing to say and keep on saying it.
　　　　　　　　　ROBERT FROST

Bores can be divided into two classes; those who have their own particular subject, and those who do not need a subject.　　ALAN ALEXANDER MILNE

When somebody says, "I hope you won't mind my telling you this," it's pretty certain that you will.
　　　　　　　　　SYLVIA BREMER

Bore: a person who talks when you wish him to listen.
　　　　　　　　　AMBROSE BIERCE

A bore is a man who, when you ask him how he is, tells you.　　　　　BERT LESTON TAYLOR

When a fellow says, "Well, to make a long story short," it's too late.　　　　DON HERROLD

You shouldn't interrupt my interruptions:
That's really worse than interrupting.
　　　　　　　THOMAS STEARNS ELIOT

He's the kind of a bore who's here today and here tomorrow.　　　　　　　BINNIE BARNES

A bore is someone who follows your joke with a better one.   ANON

Some people are so boring that they make you waste an entire day in five minutes.   JULES RENARD

The best way to be boring is to leave nothing out.
FRANCOIS VOLTAIRE

Blessed are the pure in heart for they have so much more to talk about.   EDITH WHARTON

The more scholastically educated a man is generally, the more he is an emotional boor.
DAVID HERBERT LAWRENCE

We may be willing to tell a story twice but we are never willing to hear it more than once.
WILLIAM HAZLITT

Bore: a guy who wraps up a two-minute idea in a two-hour vocabulary.   WALTER WINCHELL

We often forgive those who bore us, but we cannot forgive those who find us boring.
FRANCOIS DUC de la ROCHEFOUCAULD

As we grow older, our bodies get shorter and our anecdotes longer.   ROBERT QUILLEN

Many bores are so obviously happy that it is a pleasure to watch them.   ROBERT LYND

Rather inclined to collar the conversation and turn it in the direction of his home town's water supply.
                    PELHAM GRENVILLE WODEHOUSE

The problem with telling a good story is that it reminds the other fellow of a dull one.   ANON

Bore: a man who is never unintentionally rude.
                    OSCAR WILDE

A healthy male adult bore consumes each year one and a half times his own weight in other people's patience.   JOHN UPDIKE

Bore: one who makes others take the world seriously.
                    LORD VANSITTART

If at first you do succeed, try, try not to be a bore.
                    FRANKLIN JONES

There is no more conversation more boring than the one where everybody agrees.
                    MICHEL de MONTAIGNE

A never-failing way to get rid of a fellow is to tell him something for his own good.
                    FRANK McKINNEY HUBBARD

Perhaps the world's second worst crime is boredom. The first is being a bore.   CECIL BEATON

It requires no small talent to be a decided bore.
                    SIR WALTER SCOTT

Everyone is a bore to someone. That is unimportant.
The thing to avoid is being a bore to oneself.

GERALD BRENAN

'Tis no extravagant arithmetic to say, that for every
ten jokes . . . thou hast got a hundred enemies.

LAURENCE STERNE

One way to prevent conversation from being boring is
to say the wrong thing.   FRANK SHEED

There is no bore like a clever bore.

SAMUEL BUTLER

12 · KNOWLEDGE

Knowledge

Those who know little
Always repeat it.
Take care committal
Does not complete it!

Knowledge is not knowledge until someone else knows that one knows. **LUCILIUS**

What a man knows at 50 which he didn't know at 20 is, for the most part, incommunicable.
ADLAI STEVENSON

It is not the crook in modern business that we fear, but the honest man who doesn't know what he is doing.
OWEN D. YOUNG

If you don't know what I'm talking about, I share your lack of knowledge. I don't know what I'm talking about. **GENERAL LEWIS B. HERSHEY**

It's what a fellow thinks he knows that hurts him.
                    FRANK McKINNEY HUBBARD

There are some people that if they don't know, you
can't tell 'em.   LOUIS ARMSTRONG

Beware of the man of one book.
                         ST. THOMAS AQUINAS

All that I know I learned after I was thirty.
                         GEORGE CLEMENCEAU

Ours is an excessively conscious age. We know so
much, we feel so little.
                    DAVID HERBERT LAWRENCE

The Law of Raspberry Jam. The wider any culture is
spread, the thinner it gets.   ALVIN TOFFLER

Strange how much you've got to know before you
know how little you know.   ANON

If you understand everything, you must be misin-
formed.   JAPANESE PROVERB

If a little knowledge is dangerous, where is there the
man who has so much as to be out of danger?
                         THOMAS HENRY HUXLEY

Knowledge is the toupee which covers our baldness.
                                    ANON

He was not made for climbing the tree of knowledge.
                              SIGRID UNDSET

To know that we know what we know, and that we do not know what we do not know, that is true knowledge.   HENRY DAVID THOREAU

He half knows everything.
          THOMAS BABINGTON MACAULAY

So much has already been written about everything that you can't find out anything about it.
          JAMES THURBER

All I know is just what I read in the papers.
          WILL ROGERS

He that knows least commonly presumes most.
          THOMAS FULLER

Knowledge is of two kinds. We know a subject ourselves, or we know where we can find information upon it.   SAMUEL JOHNSON

The word knowledge, strictly employed, implies three things, viz., truth, proof and conviction.
          ARCHBISHOP RICHARD WHATELY

Far more crucial than what we know or do not know is what we do not want to know.   ERIC HOFFER

The more one penetrates the realm of knowledge the more puzzling everything becomes.
          HENRY MILLER

Men who know the same things are not long the best company for each other.
          RALPH WALDO EMERSON

Nowhere else can one find so miscellaneous, so various, an amount of knowledge contained as in a good newspaper. HENRY WARD BEECHER

I envy no man that knows more than myself, but pity them that know less. SIR THOMAS BROWNE

We can be knowledgeable with other men's knowledge, but we cannot be wise with other men's wisdom. MICHEL de MONTAIGNE

There is no subject so old that something new cannot be said about it. FYODOR MIKHAILOVICH DOSTOEVSKY

All the business of war, and indeed all the business of life, is to endeavour to find out what you don't know from what you do; that's what I called 'guessing what was at the other side of the hill.' DUKE of WELLINGTON

He who knows only his own side of the case knows little of that. JOHN STUART MILL

We owe almost all our knowledge not to those who have agreed, but to those who have differed. CHARLES CALEB COLTON

He is wise who knows the sources of knowledge—who knows who has written and where it is to be found. ARCHIBALD ALEXANDER HODGE

Our knowledge is the amassed thought and experience of innumerable minds. RALPH WALDO EMERSON

Knowledge rests not upon truth alone, but upon error also.　　　　　　　　　　　　　　CARL G. JUNG

I don't know everything, I just do everything.
　　　　　　　　　　　　　　　TONI MORRISON

To be proud of knowledge is to be blind with light.
　　　　　　　　　　　　　BENJAMIN FRANKLIN

Knowledge is power. Unfortunate dupes of this saying will keep on reading, ambitiously, till they have stunned their native initiative, and made their thoughts weak.　　　　　　　　　CLARENCE DAY

Knowledge is little, to know the right context is much; to know the right spot is everything.
　　　　　　　　　　HUGH von HOFMANNTHAL

You never know what is enough, unless you know what is more than enough.　　　WILLIAM BLAKE

I know by my own pot how the others boil.
　　　　　　　　　　　　　　FRENCH PROVERB

If you know nothing, be pleased to know nothing.
　　　　　　　　　　　　　　JOHN NEWLOVE

If one is master of one thing and understands one thing well, one has at the same time, insight into and understanding of many things.
　　　　　　　　　　　　VINCENT Van GOGH

The most certain way to hide from others the limits of our knowledge is not to go beyond them.
　　　　　　　COUNT GIACOMO LEOPARDI

The more I read, the more I meditate; and the more I acquire, the more I am enabled to affirm that I know nothing.   FRANCOIS VOLTAIRE

We do but learn today what our better advanced judgements will unteach us tomorrow.
        SIR THOMAS BROWNE

Since we cannot be universal and know all that is to be known of everything, we ought to know a little about everything.   BLAISE PASCAL

There is no more merit in being able to attach a correct description to a picture than in being able to find out what is wrong with a stalled motorcar. In each case it is special knowledge.
        WILLIAM SOMERSET MAUGHAM

Culture is "to know the best that has been said and thought in the world."   MATTHEW ARNOLD

Knowledge is a treasure, but practice is the key to it.
        THOMAS FULLER

If you have knowledge, let others light their candles at it.   MARGARET FULLER

All knowledge is of itself of some value. There is nothing so minute or inconsiderable that I would not rather know it than not.   SAMUEL JOHNSON

Knowledge is the true organ of sight, not the eyes.
        Panchatantra

Ignorance

*The fact you don't know
Is enough of a curse;
Not to want to know
Is a fate that's much worse.*

The little I know, I owe to my ignorance.
SACHA GUITRY

A man must have a certain amount of intelligent ignorance to get anywhere. CHARLES F. KETTERING

Where ignorance is bliss,
'Tis folly to be wise. THOMAS GRAY

Ignorance is not bliss—it is oblivion.
PHILIP WYLIE

It is better to know nothing than to know what ain't so. JOSH BILLINGS

Ignorance is the finest and most useful of the arts but one thing that is really and poorly practiced.
LUDWIG BOERNE

Ignoramus, N. A person unacquainted with certain kinds of knowledge familiar to yourself, and having certain other kinds that you know nothing about.
AMBROSE BIERCE

I would rather have my own ignorance than another man's knowledge because I have got so much more of it.　　　　　　　　　　　MARK TWAIN

To be proud of learning is the greatest ignorance.
　　　　　　　　　　　JEREMY TAYLOR

If you think education is expensive, try ignorance.
　　　　　　　　　　　DEREK BOK

The greater our knowledge increases, the greater our ignorance unfolds.　　　JOHN F. KENNEDY

I do not approve of anything which tampers with natural ignorance.　　　　OSCAR WILDE

Wise people are those who can conceal their ignorance.　　　　　　　　　　　ANON

Better an empty purse than an empty head.
　　　　　　　　　　　GERMAN PROVERB

I do not believe in the collective wisdom of individual ignorance.　　　WILLIAM CARLYLE

As for me, all I know is that I know nothing.
　　　　　　　　　　　SOCRATES

The best part of our knowledge is that which teaches us where knowledge leaves off and ignorance begins.
　　　　　　　　　　　OLIVER WENDELL HOLMES

Consistency requires you to be as ignorant today as you were a year ago.　　BERNARD BERENSON

In order to have wisdom we must have ignorance.
THEODORE DREISER

I do not pretend to know what many ignorant men are sure of. CLARENCE DARROW

Naive you are
if you believe
life favors those
who aren't naive. PIET HEIN

The greater the ignorance the greater the dogmatism.
SIR WILLIAM OSLER

Rather know nothing than half-know much.
FRIEDRICH WILHELM NIETZSCHE

When I cannot brag about knowing something, I brag about not knowing it. RALPH WALDO EMERSON

It was a man, and not an ostrich, who invented the dictum that "what you don't know won't hurt you." The truth is the precise opposite. Most of what exists is invisible, and the greatest dangers are those which . . . surprise their victims disarmed as well as ignorant. RALPH BARTON PERRY

Ignorance is the mother of devotion.
JEREMY TAYLOR

Nothing in education is so astonishing as the amount of ignorance it accumulates in the form of inert facts.
HENRY ADAMS

It is and it must in the long run be better for man to see things as they are than to be ignorant of them.

ALFRED EDWARD HOUSEMAN

One of the greatest joys known to man is to take a flight into ignorance in search of knowledge.

ROBERT LYND

Those who are pleased with the fewest things know the least, as those who are pleased with everything know nothing.   WILLIAM HAZLITT

Ignorance is not innocence, but sin.

ROBERT BROWNING

I am not ashamed to confess that I am ignorant of what I do not know. MARCUS TULLIUS CICERO

Our knowledge can only be finite, while our ignorance must necessarily be infinite.   SIR KARL POPPER

Better be unborn than untaught, for ignorance is the root of misfortune.   PLATO

It is impossible to make people understand their ignorance; for it requires knowledge to perceive it, and therefore he that can perceive it hath it not.

JEREMY TAYLOR

Ignorance is preferable to error; and he is less remote from the truth who believes nothing, than he who believes what is wrong.   THOMAS JEFFERSON

He who would be cured of ignorance must confess it.
MICHEL de MONTAIGNE

Mankind have a great aversion to intellectual labor, but even supposing knowledge to be easily attainable, more people would be content to be ignorant than would take even a little trouble to acquire it.

SAMUEL JOHNSON

Learning

The return
From learning
Can concern
More earning.

It's what you learn after you know it all that counts.

JOHN WOODEN

People of quality know everything without learning anything.

JEAN BAPTISTE MOLIERE

A little learning is a dangerous thing, but none at all is fatal.

VISCOUNT SAMUEL

I am always ready to learn but I do not always like being taught.

WINSTON CHURCHILL

Never learn to do anything. If you don't learn you'll always find someone else to do it for you.

MARK TWAIN'S MOTHER

He intended, he said, to devote the rest of his life to learning the remaining twenty-two letters of the alphabet.   GEORGE ORWELL

"Live and Learn" is a fine old bit of advice, but the trouble with it today is that we have time for one or the other but not for both.   HUGH ALLEN

The isness of things is well worth studying; but it is their whyness that makes life worth living.
   WILLIAM BEEBE

After learning the tricks of the trade, many of us think we know the trade.   WILLIAM FEATHER

The finest fruit of serious learning should be the ability to speak the word "God" without reserve or embarrassment.   ANON

It wasn't until quite late in life that I discovered how easy it is to say, "I don't know."
   WILLIAM SOMERSET MAUGHAM

It doesn't make much difference what you study, as long as you don't like it. FINLEY PETER DUNNE

The hardest thing to learn in life is which bridge to cross and which to burn.   DAVID RUSSELL

Do not learn more than you absolutely need to get through life.   KARL KRAUS

No man deeply engaged in serious work has time to learn.   JOSEPH HERGESHEIMER

I have never in my life learned anything from any man who agreed with me.   DUDLEY FIELD MALONE

It is easy to learn something about everything, but difficult to learn everything about anything.
                    NATHANIEL EMMONS

The mind is slow in unlearning what it has been long in learning.   LUCIUS SENECA

We should not ask who is the most learned, but who is the best learned.   MICHEL de MONTAIGNE

You should keep on learning as long as there is something you do not know.
                    LUCIUS ANNAEUS SENECA

Never too old to learn.   PROVERB

What we have to learn to do, we learn by doing.
                    ARISTOTLE

Never seem more learned than the people you are with. Wear your learning like a pocket watch and keep it hidden. Do not pull it out to count the hours, but give the time when you are asked.
                    LORD CHESTERFIELD

The three foundations of learning: seeing much, suffering much, and studying much.   CATHERALL

Let all the learned say what they can,
'Tis ready money makes the man.
                    WILLIAM SOMERVILLE

Don't look for more honor than your learning merits.
JEWISH PROVERB

Whether learning has made more proud men or good men, may be a question.　　　　　ANON

When you stop learning, stop listening, stop looking and asking questions, always new questions, then it is time to die.　　　　　LILLIAN SMITH

A learned man is an idler who kills time by study.
GEORGE BERNARD SHAW

It is the tragedy of the world that no one knows what he doesn't know and the less a man knows, the more sure he is that he knows everything. JOYCE CAREY

Nothing is so firmly believed as that of which we know the least.　　　　　MICHEL de MONTAIGNE

Study to be quiet, and to do your own business.
Thessalonians

The most beautiful thing in the world is, precisely, the conjunction of learning and inspiration.
WANDA LANDOWSKA

It is no profit to have learned well, if you neglect to do well.　　　　　PUBLILIUS SYRUS

A man with little learning is like the frog who thinks its puddle a great sea.　　　　　BURMESE PROVERB

Much as a gardener tends to the soil in order that his plants may grow in their own way and season, so attending to the depths of our own nature tills the soil in which, firmly rooted, we can develop into healthy individuals.   MAGDA PROSKAUER

The finished man of the world must eat of every apple once.   RALPH WALDO EMERSON

Education

Discontinuation
With learning things new
Ends your education
And finishes you!

One of the few things a person is willing to pay for and not get.   WILLIAM L. BRYAN

Education is learning what you didn't even know you didn't know.   RALPH WALDO EMERSON

For the maintenance costs of one horse, you could send two kids to Harvard.   MIKE McGRADY

Education is the ability to listen to almost anything without losing your temper or your self-confidence.
                                          ROBERT FROST

A modern college is a place where 2,000 can be seated in the classrooms and 50,000 in the stadium. ANON

The founding fathers in their wisdom decided that children were an unnatural strain on parents. So they provided jails called schools, equipped with tortures called education. School is where you go between when your parents can't take you and industry can't take you.   JOHN UPDIKE

There is nothing so stupid as an educated man, if you get off the thing that he was educated in.
                                    WILL ROGERS

Television can be very educational. Every time somebody turns on the set I go into the other room and read a book.   JACOB M. BRAUDE

The ultimate goal of the educational system is to shift to the individual the burden of pursuing his education.
                                    JOHN W. GARDNER

Universities are full of knowledge; the freshmen bring a little in and the seniors take none away, and knowledge accumulates.   ABBOTT L. LOWELL

"Whom are you?" he asked, for he had been to night school.   GEORGE ADE

It might be said now that I have the best of both worlds, a Harvard education and a Yale degree.
                                    JOHN F. KENNEDY

Education is a method whereby one acquires a higher grade of prejudices.   LAURENCE J. PETER

The dons are too busy educating the young men to be able to teach them anything.   SAMUEL BUTLER

The schools ain't what they used to be and never was.
WILL ROGERS

I am still of the opinion that only two topics can be of the least interest to a serious and studious mind—sex and the dead. WILLIAM BUTLER YEATS

Education is an admirable thing, but it is well to remember from time to time that nothing that is worth knowing can be taught. OSCAR WILDE

We are students of words: we are shut up in schools, and colleges, and recitation rooms, for ten or fifteen years, and come out at last with a bag of wind, a memory of words, and do not know a thing.
RALPH WALDO EMERSON

The advantage of a classical education is that it enables you to despise the wealth which it prevents you from achieving. RUSSELL GREEN

Education made us what we are.
CLAUDE ADRIEN HELVETIUS

Fathers send their sons to college, either because they went to college, or because they didn't.
L. L. HENDREN

I am entirely certain that twenty years from now we will look back at education as it is practiced in most schools today and wonder that we could have tolerated anything so primitive. JOHN W. GARDNER

The average college student is a very badly programmed computer. JOHN WILKINSON

The greatest innovation in the world is the demand for education, as a right of man: it is a disguised demand for comfort.   JACOB BURCKHARDT

If you work hard and intelligently, you should be able to detect when a man is talking rot, and that, in my view, is the main, if not the sole, purpose of education.
OXFORD PROFESSOR

Perhaps the most valuable result of all education is the ability to make yourself do the thing you have to do, when it ought to be done, whether you like it or not; it is the first lesson that ought to be learned, and however early a man's training begins, it is probably the last lesson that he learns thoroughly.
THOMAS HENRY HUXLEY

Education is the established church of the United States. It is one of the religions that Americans believe in. It has its own orthodoxy, its pontiffs and its noble buildings.   MICHAEL SADLER

Human history becomes more and more a race between education and catastrophe.
HERBERT GEORGE WELLS

A wise system of education will at least teach us how little man yet knows, how much he has still to learn.
SIR JOHN LUBBOCK

Education: that which discloses to the wise and disguises from the foolish their lack of understanding.
AMBROSE BIERCE

Theory

Theories aren't made
To cut out the doubt;
They're to be weighed
And argued about.

A theory is something usually murdered by facts.
ANON

A first-rate theory predicts: a second-rate theory forbids; and a third-rate theory explains after the event.
A. I. KITAIGORODSKII

A young man is a theory, an old man is a fact.
EDGAR WATSON HOWE

On carelessly made or insufficient observations how many fine theories are built up which do not bear examination!
ANDRE GIDE

But I hang onto my prejudices. They are the testicles of my mind.
ERIC HOFFER

Plato . . . the only five-lettered philosopher ending in o.
GILES COOPER

Every real thought on every subject knocks the wind out of somebody or other.
OLIVER WENDELL HOLMES

Do you want your philosophy straight or with a dash of legerdemain?   WILLIAM J. RICHARDSON

Action will remove the doubt that theory cannot solve.   TEHYI HSIEH

No theory is good except on condition that one use it to go beyond.   ANDRE GIDE

First a new theory is attacked as absurd: then it is admitted to be true, but obvious and insignificant: finally, it is seen to be so important that its adversaries claim that they themselves discovered it.
WILLIAM JAMES

Even for practical purposes theory generally turns out the most important thing in the end.
OLIVER WENDELL HOLMES

If facts do not conform to theory, they must be disposed of.   N. R. F. MAIER

What is now proved was once only imagin'd.
WILLIAM BLAKE

There is no sadder sight in the world than to see a beautiful theory killed by a brutal fact.
THOMAS HENRY HUXLEY

If I wished to punish a province, I would have it governed by philosophers.   FREDERICK the GREAT

Generally the theories we believe we call facts and the facts we believe we call theories.   FELIX COHEN

Men are much more apt to agree in what they do than in what they think.
JOHANN WOLFGANG von GOETHE

I prefer thought to action, an idea to an event, reflection to activity.
HONORE de BALZAC

Theory helps us to bear our ignorance of facts.
GEORGE SANTAYANA

We do what we can and then make a theory to prove our performance the best.
RALPH WALDO EMERSON

A theorist without practice is a tree without fruit and a devotee without learning is a house without an entrance.
SA'DI

We call a man a bigot or a slave of dogma because he is a thinker who has thought thoroughly and to a definite end.
GILBERT KEITH CHESTERTON

Let us work without theorizing . . . 'tis the only way to make life endurable.
FRANCOIS VOLTAIRE

It is better to emit a scream in the shape of a theory than to be entirely insensible to the jars and incongruities of life and take everything as it comes in a forlorn stupidity.
ROBERT LOUIS STEVENSON

Dogma does not mean the absence of thought, but the end of thought. GILBERT KEITH CHESTERTON

Every man is encompassed by a cloud of comforting convictions, which move with him like flies on a summer day.
BERTRAND RUSSELL

All eminent sages are as despotic as generals, as discourteous and lacking in delicacy as generals, because they know they are safe from punishment.

ANTON CHEKHOV

The astonishment of life is the absence of any appearances of reconciliation between the theory and the practice of life.   RALPH WALDO EMERSON

13 · ESSENTIALS

Common Sense

*With common sense
You're in the pink;
It's not so common
As you think.*

Common sense is the collection of prejudices by the age of eighteen.   **ALBERT EINSTEIN**

Horse sense is that inestimable quality in a horse that keeps it from betting on a man.
   REV. ERIC P. COCHRAN

Nothing astonishes men so much as common sense and plain dealing.   **RALPH WALDO EMERSON**

It is a thousand times better to have common sense without education than to have education without common sense.   **ROBERT G. INGERSOLL**

Fairyland is nothing but the sunny country of common sense.   GILBERT KEITH CHESTERTON

Men are seldom blessed with good fortune and good sense at the same time.   LIVY

There is nobody so irritating as somebody with less intelligence and more sense than we have.
DON HEROLD

Common sense in an uncommon degree is what the world calls wisdom.
SAMUEL TAYLOR COLERIDGE

Never do anything standing that you can do sitting, or anything sitting that you can do lying down.
CHINESE PROVERB

The wisdom of the wise is an uncommon degree of common sense.   DEAN WILLIAM RALPH INGE

The philosophy of one century is the common sense of the next.   HENRY WARD BEECHER

Some folks get credit for having horse sense that hain't ever had enough money to make fools of themselves.
FRANK McKINNEY HUBBARD

The best prophet is common sense.   EURIPIDES

If a man has common sense, he has all the sense there is.   SAM RAYBURN

Logic is one thing and common sense another.
ELBERT HUBBARD

Everybody gets so much information all day long that they lose their common sense.   GERTRUDE STEIN

Common sense is in spite of, not the result of, education.   VICTOR HUGO

If common sense were as unerring as calculus, as some suggest, I don't understand why so many mistakes are made so often by so many people.
CARY H. WINKEL

One pound of learning requires ten pounds of common sense to apply it.   PERSIAN PROVERB

Common sense is, of all kinds, the most uncommon.
TYRON EDWARDS

Common sense is instinct and enough of it is genius.
HENRY WHEELER SHAW

Good intentions are useless in the absence of common sense.   JAMI

Fine sense and exalted sense are not half so useful as common sense.   ALEXANDER POPE

There is no greater panacea for every kind of folly than common sense.   BALTASAR GRACIAN

Common sense is the wick of the candle.
RALPH WALDO EMERSON

Common sense is the most fairly distributed thing in the world, for each thinks he is so well endowed with it that even those who are hardest to satisfy in all other matters are not in the habit of desiring more of it than they already have.   RENE DESCARTES

Most people die of a sort of creeping common sense, and discover when it is too late that the only things one never regrets are one's mistakes.

OSCAR WILDE

The only sense that is common in the long run is the sense of change and we all instinctively avoid it.

ELWYN BROOKS WHITE

Every hour I live I become an intenser devotee to common sense!   ALICE JAMES

Common sense is the knack of seeing things as they are, and doing things as they ought to be done.

CALVIN ELLIS STOWE

The crown of all faculties is common sense. It is not enough to do the right thing: it must be done at the right time, and place.   WILLIAM MATTHEWS

Common sense, however logical and sound, is after all only one human attitude among many others, and like everything human, it may have its limitations—or negative side.   WILLIAM BARRETT

Common sense is as rare as genius.

RALPH WALDO EMERSON

Common sense suits itself to the ways of the world. Wisdom tries to confirm to the ways of Heaven.

JOSEPH JOUBERT

Pedantry prides herself on being wrong by rules, while common sense is contented to be right without them.
CHARLES CALEB COLTON

Perseverance

The ones we are saluting
Are not so highfaluting.
The very big shots
Are the little shots,
Who only kept on shooting.

Perseverance is another name for success.   ANON

Fight one more round. When your feet are so tired that you have to shuffle back to the center of the ring, fight one more round. When your arms are so tired that you can hardly lift your hands to come on guard, fight one more round. When your nose is bleeding, and your eyes are black and you are so tired that you wish your opponent would crack you in the jaw and put you to sleep, fight one more round—remembering that the man who always fights one more round is never whipped.   JAMES J. CORBETT

When you get to the end of your rope, tie a knot and hang on.   FRANKLIN D. ROOSEVELT

One becomes more interested in a job of work after the first impulse to drop it has been overcome.

FULTON J. SHEEN

The last key in the bunch is often the one to open the lock.

ANON

For when his legs were smitten off,
He fought upon his stumps.   RICHARD SHEALE

Keep on going and chances are you will stumble on something, perhaps when you are least expecting it. I have never heard of anyone stumbling on something sitting down.   CHARLES F. KETTERING

It is not necessary to hope in order to undertake, nor to succeed in order to persevere.

LAURENCE J. PETER

I could never finish anything but now I . . . ANON

Perseverance is not a long race; it is many short races one after another.   WALTER ELLIOTT

When you feel that being persistent is a difficult task, think of the bee. A red clover blossom contains less than one eighth of a grain of sugar; 7,000 grains are required to make a pound of honey. A bee, flitting here and there for sweetness, must visit 56,000 clover heads for a pound of honey: and there are about sixty flower tubes to each clover head. When a bee performs that operation 60 times 56,000 or 3,360,000 times, it secures enough sweetness for only one pound of honey!   *Sunshine Magazine*

One of the first principles of perseverance is to know when to stop persevering.　　CAROLYN WELLS

By perseverance the snail reached the Ark.
　　　　　　　　　　　CHARLES SPURGEON

Perseverance is the most overrated of traits, if it is unaccompanied by talent: beating your head against a wall is more likely to produce a concussion in the head than a hole in the wall.　　SYDNEY HARRIS

Never give up and never give in.
　　　　　　　　　HUBERT H. HUMPHREY

Bear in mind, if you are going to amount to anything, that your success does not depend upon the brilliancy and the impetuosity with which you take hold, but upon the everlasting and sanctified bull-doggedness with which you hang on after you have taken hold.
　　　　　　　　　　DR. A. B. MELDRUM

My downfall raises me to infinite heights.
　　　　　　　　　NAPOLEON BONAPARTE

'Tis a lesson you should heed,
　　Try, try again:
If at first you don't succeed,
　　Try, try, again:
Then your courage should appear,
For, if you will persevere,
You will conquer, never fear:
　　Try, try again.　　　　　W. E. HICKSON

I'm a slow walker, but I never walk back.
　　　　　　　　　　ABRAHAM LINCOLN

When you get into a tight place and everything goes against you, till it seems you could not hold on a minute longer, never give up then, for that is just the place and time that the tide will turn.

HARRIET BEECHER STOWE

One may go a long way after one is tired.

FRENCH PROVERB

Perseverance is a silent power that grows irresistibly greater with time.

JOHANN WOLFGANG von GOETHE

Never shrink from anything which your business calls you to do.

DANIEL DREW

By gnawing through a dyke, even a rat may drown a nation.

EDMUND BURKE

Don't give up whatever you're trying to do—especially if you're convinced that you're botching it up. Giving up reinforces a sense of incompetence, going on gives you a commitment to success.

GEORGE WEINBERG

'Tis known by the name of perseverance in a good cause, and obstinacy is a bad one.

LAURENCE STERNE

The test of a first-rate work, and a test of your sincerity in calling it a first-rate work is that you finish it.

ARNOLD BENNETT

Men are blind in their own cause.   **PROVERB**

Let me tell you the secret that has led me to my goal.
My strength lies solely in my tenacity.
                              LOUIS PASTEUR

The falling drops at last will wear the stone.
                              LUCRETIUS

Great works are performed, not by strength, but by
perseverance. He that shall walk, with vigor, three
hours a day, will pass, in seven years, a space equal to
the circumference of the globe.
                              SAMUEL JOHNSON

Fall seven times, stand up eight.
                              JAPANESE PROVERB

Perseverance. A lowly virtue whereby mediocrity
achieves an inglorious success. **AMBROSE BIERCE**

Even after a bad harvest, there must be sowing.
                              LUCIUS SENECA

To persevere, trusting in what hopes he has is courage
in a man. The coward despairs.   **EURIPIDES**

Little strokes fell great oaks.
                              BENJAMIN FRANKLIN

Pay as little attention to discouragement as possible.
Plough ahead as a steamer does, rough or smooth—
rain or shine. To carry your cargo and make your port
is the point.   **MALTHIE BABCOCK**

Aim at perfection in everything though in most things it is unattainable. However, they who aim at it, and persevere, will come much nearer to it than those whose laziness and despondency make them give it up as unattainable. **LORD CHESTERFIELD**

It is with many enterprises as with striking fire; we do not meet with success except by reiterated efforts, and often at the instant when we despaired of success. **MADAM de MAINTENON**

Some men give up their designs when they have almost reached the goal; while others, on the contrary, obtain a victory by exerting at the last moment, more vigorous efforts than before. **POLYBIUS**

Teamwork

The team is like a clock;
One cog can make it stick.
It's meant to go tick tock,
But then it goes tock tick.

No one can whistle a symphony. It takes an orchestra to play it. **HALFORD E. LUCCOCK**

The power of the waterfall is nothing but a lot of drips working together. **ANON**

A company with internal dissension is drained of energy before it has a chance to devote it to its proper purpose. J. C. PENNEY

A team is a mutual protection society formed to guarantee that no one person can be to blame for a botched committee job that one man could have performed satisfactorily. RUSSELL BAKER

Every great man inevitably resents a partner in greatness. MARCUS ANNAEUS LUCAN

No matter how great a warrior he is, a chief cannot do battle without his indians. ANON

No member of a crew is praised for the rugged individuality of his rowing. RALPH WALDO EMERSON

No matter how much teamwork achieves, the results will be identified with a single name in years to come. ANON

The world is full of willing people, some willing to work, the rest willing to let them. ROBERT FROST

Equality is what does not exist among equals. EDWARD ESTLIN CUMMINGS

Bearing in mind that management is the art of getting things done through people, you can't get things done unless you let your people know what your goals are—what you want to accomplish, why you want to accomplish it, how they will benefit from it and the role they will play in accomplishing it. This is another way of saying that the members of the management team must be able to identify themselves individually with the company's overall goals. No chief executive, no top management committee ever reached these goals by themselves. Unless the entire management team is aboard, the company will never get there.

DON G. MITCHELL

There is nothing in the world I wouldn't do for Hope, and there is nothing he wouldn't do for me . . . We spend our lives doing nothing for each other.

BING CROSBY

The team effort is a lot of people doing what I say.

MICHAEL WINNER

By uniting we stand, by dividing we fall.

JOHN DICKINSON

Bees accomplish nothing save as they work together, and neither do men.   **ELBERT HUBBARD**

That's all one should really ask of anybody—that they attempt to contribute.   **ROD STEIGER**

There is something about a swarm that is damaging to the pride of its individual members.

MERVYN PEAKE

The man who goes alone can start today; but he who travels with another must wait till that other is ready, and it may be a long time before they get off.

HENRY DAVID THOREAU

Even a goat and an ox must keep in step if they are going to plough together.
ERNEST DRAMAH BRAMAH

Never one thing and seldom one person can make for a success. It takes a number of them merging into one perfect whole.
MARIE DRESSLER

There are black sheep in every flock.
PROVERB

Men do not change their characters by uniting with one another, nor does their patience in the presence of obstacles increase with their strength.
ALEXIS de TOCQUEVILLE

A whole bushel of wheat is made up of single grains.
THOMAS FULLER

If a house be divided against itself, that house cannot stand.
St. Mark

The mightiest rivers lost their force when split up into several streams.
PUBLIUS OVID

Opportunity

Opportunities are never found
By looking at the ceiling;
Forget your sense of sight and sound,
You suss them out by feeling.

The reason a lot of people do not recognize an opportunity when they meet it is that it usually goes around wearing overalls and looking like hard work.
Christian Science Monitor

While we stop to think, we often miss our opportunity.
PUBLIUS SYRUS

Opportunity is sometimes hard to recognize if you're only looking for a lucky break.   MONTA CRANE

My folks were immigrants and they fell under the spell of the American legend that the streets were paved with gold. When papa got here he found out three things: (1) The streets were not paved with gold; (2) The streets were not even paved; (3) He was supposed to do the paving.   SAM LEVENSON

Every cloud has its silver lining but it is sometimes a little difficult to get it to the mint.
DONALD ROBERT PERRY MARQUIS

An opportunity is picking the right moment for grasping a disappointment.   ANON

Success in business requires training and discipline and hard work. But if you're not frightened by these things, the opportunities are just as great today as they ever were.   DAVID ROCKEFELLER

The world is an oyster but you don't crack it open on a mattress.   ARTHUR MILLER

Opportunity is closest when everyone is against taking advantage of it.   ANON

Opportunities are usually disguised as hard work, so most people don't recognize them. ANN LANDERS

An opportunist counts his fingers after shaking hands with another opportunist. ANON

The opportunity that God sends does not wake up him who is asleep. SENEGALESE PROVERB

There is no security on this earth; there is only opportunity. DOUGLAS MACARTHUR

The greatest opportunities occur during depressed and discouraging periods, but it is very difficult to recognize them at such times. ANON

There's a sucker born every minute.
PHINEAS T. BARNUM

This is virgin territory for whorehouses.
AL CAPONE

The Chinese use two brush strokes to write the word "crisis." One brush stroke stands for danger: the other for opportunity. In a crisis, beware of the danger—but recognize the opportunity.
RICHARD MILHOUS NIXON

I would like to amend the idea of being in the right place at the right time. There are many people who were in the right place at the right time but didn't know it. You have to recognize when the right place and the right time fuse and take advantage of that opportunity. There are plenty of opportunities out there. You can't sit back and wait.
ELLEN METCALF

There exists limitless opportunity in every industry. Where there is an open mind, there will always be a frontier. CHARLES F. KETTERING

Everything comes to the man who does not need it. FRENCH PROVERB

Do not suppose opportunity will knock twice at your door. SEBASTIAN ROCH NICOLAS

An optimist sees an opportunity in every calamity; a pessimist sees a calamity in every opportunity. SIR WINSTON CHURCHILL

Those who criticize opportunists
Are those who cannot recognize opportunities.
ANON

Equality for women doesn't mean that they have to occupy the same number of factory jobs and office positions as men, but just that all these posts should in principle be equally open to women. ALEXANDER SOLZHENITSYN

A manpower policy should lead us to a society in which every person has full opportunity to develop his —or her—earning powers, where no willing worker lacks a job, and where no useful talent lacks an opportunity. LYNDON B. JOHNSON

One thing life taught me: if you are interested, you never have to look for new interests. They come to you. When you are genuinely interested in one thing, it will always lead to something else. ELEANOR ROOSEVELT

It is no disgrace to start all over. It is usually an opportunity.   GEORGE M. ADAMS

We are confronted with insurmountable opportunities.
                                                  POGO

The secret of success in life, is for a man to be ready for his opportunity when it comes.
                                    BENJAMIN DISRAELI

For the highest task of intelligence is to grasp and recognize genuine opportunity, possibility.
                                          JOHN DEWEY

Opportunity is rare, and a wise man will never let it go by him.   BAYARD TAYLOR

Great minds must be ready not only to take the opportunities, but to make them.
                               CHARLES CALEB COLTON

God's best gift to us is not things, but opportunities.
                                    ALICE W. ROLLINS

Turbulence is life force. It is opportunity. Let's love turbulence and use it for a change.
                                        RAMSAY CLARK

It is common to overlook what is near by keeping the eye fixed on something remote. In the same manner present opportunities are neglected and attainable good is slighted by minds busied in extensive ranges, and intent upon future advantages. Life, however, short, is made shorter by waste of time.
                                      SAMUEL JOHNSON

If we are to establish the secure foundations of equal-opportunity society and master the sensitive arts of building a life encouraging environment, then at this moment in history, we need to realize that: Bigger is not better; slower may be faster; less may well mean more. STEWART L. UDALL

Vigilance is watching opportunity; tact and daring in seizing upon opportunity; force and persistence in crowding opportunity to its utmost of possible achievement—these are the material virtues which must command success. AUSTIN PHELPS

Shrewdness

To know latitude, may be shrewd
And that's to say the least;
But when it comes to longitude,
It's too far west that's east.

We can't cross a bridge until we come to it: but I always like to lay down a pontoon ahead of time. BERNARD BARUCH

It's better to duck than to hurry yourself out of this world by thinking you can roll with the punches. WILLIE "THE LION" SMITH

A dram of discretion is worth a pound of wisdom.
GERMAN PROVERB

No one tests the depth of a river with both feet.
ASHANTI PROVERB

With a relation eat and drink; but conduct no business with him. GREEK PROVERB

Only the game fish swims upstream; but the sensible fish swims down. OGDEN NASH

Better to get up late and be wide awake,
than to get up early and be tired all day? ANON

Tell not all you know, believe not all you hear, do not all you are able. ITALIAN PROVERB

He that fights and runs away
May live to fight another day. ANON

What's the use of wasting dynamite when insect-powder will do? CARTER GLASS

Ending is better than mending.
ALDOUS LEONARD HUXLEY

There is no way to catch a snake that is as safe as not catching him. JACOB M. BRAUDE

Do not climb the hill until you get to it.
ENGLISH PROVERB

What you do not want done to yourself, do not do to others. CONFUCIUS

Never insult an alligator until after you have crossed
the river.   CORDELL HULL

I had rather ride on an ass that carries me than a horse
that throws me.   GEORGE HERBERT

It is best to read the weather forecasts before we pray
for rain.   MARK TWAIN

When you have got an elephant by the hind leg, and
he is trying to run away, it's best to let him run.
                          ABRAHAM LINCOLN

Dig a well before you are thirsty.
                             CHINESE PROVERB

Sell not the bear's skin before you have caught him.
                              THOMAS FULLER

Consider what a canny beast the timid mouse is. He
does not put his trust in just one hole, but has already
made another for use if the first one is blocked.
                        TITUS MACCIUS PLAUTUS

A forewarned man is worth two.
                             SPANISH PROVERB

It is better to light a candle than to curse the darkness.
                                        ANON

Do not put all your eggs in one basket.   PROVERB

Behold, the fool sayeth: "Put not all thine eggs in the
one basket"—which is but a manner of saying, "Scat-
ter your money and your attention." But the wise man

saith, "Put all your eggs in one basket and—WATCH
THAT BASKET." MARK TWAIN

We should lay up in peace what we shall need in war.
PUBLIUS SYRUS

Admire a little ship, but put your cargo in a big one.
HESIOD

Better to turn back than to lose your way.
RUSSIAN PROVERB

A stitch in time saves nine. PROVERB

If thou canst not see the bottom, wade not.
ENGLISH PROVERB

Only the poor man counts his flock. OVID

Better have one plough going than two cradles.
EDMUND FULLER

No wise man stands behind an ass when he kicks.
PUBLIUS TERENCE

In order to try whether a vessel be leaky, we first prove
it with water before we trust it with wine.
CHARLES CALEB COLTON

Leave well—even "pretty well"—alone: that is what I
learn as I get old. EDWARD FITZGERALD

The laundress washeth her own smock first.
ENGLISH PROVERB

Keep a thing for seven years and you'll find use for it.
IRISH PROVERB

Butter spoils no meat and moderation no cause.
DANISH PROVERB

Practice yourself, for heaven's sake, in little things;
and thence proceed to greater. **EPICTETUS**

It is well to moor your bark with two anchors.
PUBLIUS SYRUS

Though you would like to beat the dog, you have to
consider its master's fate as well.
BURMESE PROVERB

Better eat gray bread in your youth than in your age.
SCOTTISH PROVERB

Action

Some do this and some do that
But when all is said and done,
Along comes some smart bureaucrat
Who wants to know why you begun.

Actions speak louder than words—but not so often.
EDMUND FULLER

Act quickly, think slowly.   **GREEK PROVERB**

What's not worth doing is not worth doing well.
DON HEBB

Now, gentlemen, let us do something today which the world may talk of hereafter.
ADMIRAL COLLINGWOOD

Tsze-Kung asked what constituted a superior man. The Master said, "He acts before he speaks, and afterwards speaks according to his actions."
CONFUCIUS

There are three ways to get something done: do it yourself, employ someone or forbid your children to do it.   **MONTA CRANE**

The most decisive actions of our life—I mean those that are most likely to decide the whole course of our future—are, more often than not, unconsidered.
ANDRE GIDE

Never confuse motion with action.
ERNEST HEMINGWAY

Most people do things because they have to.
Those that get ahead do things because they don't have to.   **ANON**

If your spirits are low, do something: if you have been doing something, do something different.   **E. HALL**

Between eighteen and twenty, life is like an exchange where one buys stocks, not with money, but with actions. Most men buy nothing. **ANDRE MALRAUX**

All mankind is divided into three classes. Those that are immovable, those that are movable, and those that move.   ARABIAN PROVERB

What's worth doing is worth doing for money.
                              JOSEPH DONOHUE

Everybody ought to do at least two things each day that he hates to do, just for practice.
                              WILLIAM JAMES

Where we are free to act, we are also free to refrain from acting, and where we are able to say No, we are also able to say Yes.   ARISTOTLE

Take an object. Do something to it. Do something else to it.   JASPER JOHNS

Great actions are not always true sons
   Of great and mighty resolutions.
                              SAMUEL BUTLER

Action springs not from thought, but from a readiness for responsibility.   DIETRICH BONHOEFFER

People may come to do anything almost, by talking of it.   SAMUEL JOHNSON

Is it really so difficult to tell a good action from a bad one? I think one usually knows right away or a moment afterward in a horrid flash of regret.
                              MARY McCARTHY

No action is without its side effects.
                              BARRY COMMONER

To those capable only of ordinary actions everything that is very much out of the ordinary seems possible only after it is accomplished.

CARDINAL de RETZ

A man's most open actions have a secret side to them.
JOSEPH CONRAD

In action, be primitive, in foresight, a strategist.
RENE CHAR

Effective action is always unjust.   JEAN ANOUILH

Life is made up of constant calls to action, and we seldom have time for more than hastily contrived answers.   JUDGE LEARNED HAND

Action is the great business of mankind, and the whole matter about which all laws are conversant.
JOHN LOCKE

The best way to keep good acts in memory is to refresh them with new.   CATO THE ELDER

Our needs determine us, as much as we determine our needs.   GEORGE ELIOT

14 · DANGERS

Indecision

A cluttered desk with lack of precision
Does not always belong to a clerk;
With a manager it is indecision
Much more often than overwork.

Some problems are so complex that it takes high intelligence just to be undecided about them.
                                    LAURENCE J. PETER

According to a study of unsuccessful executives, inability to make decisions is one of the principal reasons of failure.   HERMAN W. STEINKRAUS

The only man who can change his mind is the man who's got one.   EDWARD NOYES WESTCOTT

He who hesitates is last.   MAE WEST

He who hesitates gets bumped from the rear.
                                    HOMER PHILLIPS

The only thing worse than a bad decision is indecision.
PROFESSOR RAY E. BROWN

The decision is maybe and that's final.   **GRAFFITI**

Of all the famous last words in the annals of business, undoubtedly the most famous are these: "He couldn't make up his mind."   **HARRY A. BULLIS**

Do you have trouble making up your mind?
Well—yes and no.   **HERBERT V. PROCHNOW**

I'll give you a definite maybe.
SAMUEL GOLDWYN

Once I make up my mind I'm full of indecision.
OSCAR LEVANT

What the hell—you might be right, you might be wrong . . . but don't just avoid it.
KATHARINE HEPBURN

A man who cannot make up his mind probably has no mind to make.   **ANON**

I must have a prodigious quantity of mind; it takes me as much as a week, sometimes, to make it up.
MARK TWAIN

A Yale undergraduate left on his door a placard for the janitor on which was written, "Call me at seven o'clock: it's absolutely necessary that I get up at seven. Make no mistake. Keep knocking until I answer." Under this he had written, "Try again at ten."
WILLIAM LYONS PHELPS

When ordering lunch, the big executives are just as indecisive as the rest of us.   WILLIAM FEATHER

Some persons are very decisive when it comes to avoiding decisions.   BRENDAN FRANCIS

Like all weak men he laid an exaggerated stress on not changing one's mind.
WILLIAM SOMERSET MAUGHAM

There are men who would even be afraid to commit themselves on the doctrine that castor oil is a laxative.
CAMILLE FLAMMARION

It's no good saying, "Hold it" to a moment of real life.
LORD SNOWDON

I don't know what to do. My heart says yes, my mind says no, and I haven't heard my liver yet.
LEOPOLD FECHTNER

When we are not sure we are alive.
GRAHAM GREENE

Indecision is like the stepchild; if he doesn't want to wash his hands, he is called dirty; if he does, he is wasting the water.   MADAGASCAN PROVERB

Between two stools one falls to the ground.
PROVERB

That is the consolation of a little mind; you have the fun of changing it without impeding the progress of mankind.   FRANK MOORE COLBY

He would come in and say he had changed his mind—
which was a gilded figure of speech, because he hadn't
any.   MARK TWAIN

When I was a boy, they used to say that "only a mule
and a milepost never changed its mind."
                              BERNARD M. BARUCH

When you cannot make up your mind which of two
evenly balanced courses of action you should take—
choose the bolder.   W. J. SLIM

The strong are saying nothing until they see.
                                    ROBERT FROST

Stupidity consists in wanting to come to a conclusion.
                                      EMILE ZOLA

General propositions do not decide concrete cases.
                          OLIVER WENDELL HOLMES

To change one's mind is rather a sign of prudence than
ignorance.   SPANISH PROVERB

The superior man does not set his mind either for anything or against anything.   CONFUCIUS

Nothing is so exhausting as indecision, and nothing is
so futile.   BERTRAND RUSSELL

There is no more miserable human being than one in
whom nothing is habitual but indecision.
                                    WILLIAM JAMES

Indecisive woolliness is the curse of much modern democratic thought.   A. D. LINDSAY

They are decided only to be undecided, resolved to be irresolute, adamant for drift, solid for fluidity, all powerful for impotence. SIR WINSTON CHURCHILL

The man who insists upon seeing with perfect clearness before he decides, never decides. Accept life, and you must accept regret.   FREDERIC AMIEL

Indecision is fatal. It is better to make a wrong decision than build up a habit of indecision. If you're wallowing in indecision, you certainly can't act—and action is the basis of success. MARIE BEYNON RAY

The pretext for indecisiveness is commonly mature deliberation; but in reality indecisive men occupy themselves less in deliberation than others: for to him who fears to decide, deliberation (which has a foretaste of that fear) soon becomes intolerably irksome and the mind escapes from the anxiety of it into alien themes.
SIR HENRY TAYLOR

Pressure

You win the war
The way you make it,
But it's far more
The way you take it.

Let our advance worrying become advance thinking and planning.   SIR WINSTON CHURCHILL

One way to get high blood-pressure is to go mountain-climbing over molehills.   EARL WILSON

A 10,000-aspirin job.
          JAPANESE TERM FOR EXECUTIVE
          RESPONSIBILITY

It is always our inabilities that vex.
                    JOSEPH JOUBERT

I save a lot of time by not unwinding. FRANSCINO

For fast-acting relief, try slowing down.
                         LILY TOMLIN

I'm going to get out of this film business. It's too much for me. I'll never catch on. It's too fast. I can't tell what I'm doing or what anybody wants me to do.
                    CHARLIE CHAPLIN

You'll never have a nervous breakdown, but you sure are a carrier.   FRED FRIENDLY

There is no such thing as talent. There is pressure.
                         ALFRED ADLER

I've got to keep breathing. It'll be my worst business mistake if I don't.   SIR NATHAN ROTHSCHILD

It all depends on how we look at things, and not on how they are in themselves.   CARL G. JUNG

Don't spend ten dollars' worth of energy on a ten-cent problem . . . There are millions of want-to's and have-to's in life. Ultimately, these pressures create stress only when your time and energy-spending decisions aren't consistent with your goals, beliefs and values.   DR. DONALD A. TUBESING

Everyone is running to and fro, pressed by the stomach ache of business.
          FREDERIC AUGUSTE BERTHOLDI

A load of cares lies like a weight of guilt upon the mind: so that a man of business often has all the air, the distraction and restlessness, and hurry of feeling of a criminal.   WILLIAM HAZLITT

When a man has reached a condition in which he believes that a thing must happen because he does not wish it, and that what he wishes to happen can never be, this is really the state called desperation.
          ARTHUR SCHOPENHAUER

Distract your mind when you're under pressure. Do something frivolous, nonstressful and unrelated to "real life." Watch an old movie on TV, play with your dog, do a crossword puzzle, take a long swim.
          SHARON GOLD

The better work men do is always done under stress and at great personal cost.
          WILLIAM CARLOS WILLIAMS

The real world is not easy to live in. It is rough, it is slippery. Without the most clear-eyed adjustments we fall and get crushed. A man must stay sober: not always, but most of the time.   CLARENCE DAY

The bow too tensely strung is easily broken.

PUBLIUS SYRUS

Anxiety is a thin stream of fear trickling through the mind. If encouraged, it cuts a channel into which all other thoughts are drained.

ARTHUR SOMERS ROCHE

Nothing is so fatiguing as the eternal hanging on of an uncompleted task.   WILLIAM JAMES

Don't be afraid to enjoy the stress of a full life nor too naive to think you can do so without some intelligent thinking and planning. Man should not try to avoid stress any more than he should shun food, love, or exercise . . . Trying to remember too many things is certainly one of the major sources of psychologic stress. I make a conscious effort to forget immediately all that is unimportant and to jot down data of possible value. . . . This technique can help anyone to accomplish the greatest simplicity compatible with the degree of complexity of his intellectual life.

DR. HANS SELYE

Start with one thing: that they need you. Without you they have an empty screen. So, when you get on there, just do what you think is right and stay with it. From that point on, you're on your own . . . If you listen to all the clowns around you, you're just dead. Go do what you have to do.   JAMES CAGNEY

No matter how much pressure you feel at work, if you could find ways to relax for at least five minutes every hour, you'd be more productive. Most stress we bring on ourselves through bad habits and bad attitudes.

Take a pencil and paper and write down everything in your day that produces stress, checking the aggravations that create the greatest stress. Analyze all the ways you might change these situations. If you talked with a co-worker, would it ease the stress? If you got up half an hour earlier, could you stop running and take time to walk, or even stroll? Do you exercise at least twenty minutes a day? If you don't, you should, because it will relieve stress and allow you to work and sleep better.   DR. JOYCE BROTHERS

As a rule, what is out of sight disturbs men's minds more seriously than what they see.

JULIUS CAESAR

I find that two days' neglect of business do give more discontent in mind than ten times the pleasure thereof can repair again, be it what it will.

SAMUEL PEPYS

Work and love—these are the basics. Without them, there is neurosis.   THEODOR REIK

To carry care to bed is to sleep with a pack on your back.   THOMAS C. HALIBURTON

In certain trying circumstances, urgent circumstances, desperate circumstances, profanity furnishes a relief denied even to prayer.   MARK TWAIN

Anxiety grows on solitude. Aloneness is the greatest breeding ground for the diffuse, unfocused, pervading uneasiness that makes us vulnerable to chronic worry. Almost anything can become a cause for concern to the solitary person; almost anything can make him fearful.   ALLAN FROMME

Anxiety in human life is what squeaking and grinding are in machinery that is not oiled. In life, trust is the oil.   HENRY WARD BEECHER

Man's highest merit always is, as much as possible, to rule external circumstances and as little as possible to let himself be ruled by them.
    JOHANN WOLFGANG von GOETHE

Weakness

> *It's often that you find,*
> *The cynical observe,*
> *That those who appear kind*
> *Just suffer from weak nerve.*

Of the four wars in my lifetime none came about because the United States was too strong.
    RONALD REAGAN

The meekness of Moses is better than the strength of Samson.   PROVERB

. . . go after a man's weakness, and never, ever, threaten unless you're going to follow through, because if you don't, the next time you won't be taken seriously.   ROY M. COHN

All cruelty springs from weakness.   SENECA

One time it pays to have a firm hand is when it shakes hands with a firmer one.   O. A. BATTISTA

Our strength is often composed of the weakness we're damned if we're going to show.
MIGNON McLAUGHLIN

The greatest weakness of all is the great fear of appearing weak.   JACQUES BENIGNE BOUSSUET

Humility is a strange thing. The minute you think you've got it, you've lost it.   E. D. HULSE

It is as easy for the strong man to be strong as it is for the weak to be weak. RALPH WALDO EMERSON

Let the meek inherit the earth—they have it coming to them.   JAMES THURBER

Probably the meek really will inherit the earth: they won't have the nerve to refuse.   JOHN M. HENRY

The meek shall inherit the earth—if that's all right with you.   GRAFFITI

Some of our weaknesses are born in us, others are the result of education: it is a question which of the two gives us most trouble.
JOHANN WOLFGANG von GOETHE

Our greatest weakness lies in giving up. The most certain way to succeed is always to try just one more time.   THOMAS EDISON

Men are much more unwilling to have their weaknesses and their imperfections known than their crimes. EARL of CHESTERFIELD

There are two kinds of weakness; that which breaks and that which bends. JAMES RUSSELL COWELL

Weak people never give way when they ought to. CARDINAL RETZ

Strong men can always afford to be gentle. Only the weak are intent on "giving as good as they get." ELBERT HUBBARD

Sympathy is never wasted except when you give it to yourself. JOHN W. RAPER

Modesty—the art of drawing attention to whatever it is you're being humble about. *Bits and Pieces*

To feel sorry for oneself is one of the most disintegrating things an individual can do to himself. WINIFRED RHOADES

If we are strong, our strength will speak for itself. If we are weak, words will be no help. JOHN F. KENNEDY

Applause is the spur of noble minds, the end and aim of weak ones. CHARLES CALEB COLTON

Weakness on both sides is, as we know, the motto of all quarrels. FRANCOIS VOLTAIRE

Weak people cannot be sincere. FRANCOIS DUC de la ROCHEFOUCAULD

The greatest men are always linked to their age by some weakness or other.
JOHANN WOLFGANG von GOETHE

It is very disagreeable to seem reserved, and very dangerous not to be.　　EARL of CHESTERFIELD

Weak men are apt to be cruel, because they stick at nothing that may repair the ill effect of their mistakes.
MARQUIS of HALIFAX

A weak man is just by accident. A strong but non-violent man is unjust by accident.
MOHANDAS K. GANDHI

Seriousness is the only refuge of the shallow.
OSCAR WILDE

Do not be too timid and squeamish about your actions. All life is an experiment.
RALPH WALDO EMERSON

In a just case the weak will beat the strong.
SOPHOCLES

Why cannot a man act himself, be himself, and think for himself? It seems to me that naturalness alone is power; that a borrowed word is weaker than our own weakness, however small we may be.
MARIA MITCHELL

Coyness is a rather comically pathetic fault, a miscalculation in which, by trying to veil the ego, we let it appear stark naked.　　LOUIS KRONENBERGER

A realistic assessment of my strengths usually turns up several weaknesses also. Becoming more self-accepting involves not only awareness of strengths but also the acceptance of my weakness not in the sense of not wanting to do something about them, but in the sense of not letting them block the use of my strengths.

DAVID G. JONES

Although men are accused of not knowing their own weakness, yet perhaps few know their own strength. It is in men as in soils, where sometimes there is a vein of gold which the owner knows not of.

JONATHAN SWIFT

Opposition

It's hard to tell how
Which pleasure is greater;
A small victory now
Or real revenge later.

Men are not against you; they are merely for themselves.　　　　　　GENE FOWLER

The best armor is to keep out of range.
　　　　　　ITALIAN PROVERB

If you have no enemies, you are apt to be in the same predicament in regard to friends.

ELBERT HUBBARD

There is no little enemy. BENJAMIN FRANKLIN

We had shown that anyone who slapped us on our cheek would get his head kicked off.
NIKITA KHRUSHCHEV

The first blow is half the battle. PROVERB

We're eyeball to eyeball, and the other fellow just blinked. DEAN RUSK

The art of dealing with one's enemies is an art no less necessary than knowing how to appreciate one's friends. TRUMAN CAPOTE

I respect only those who resist me; but I cannot tolerate them. CHARLES de GAULLE

Pay attention to your enemies, for they are the first to discover your mistakes. ANTISTHENES

There's no point in burying a hatchet if you're going to put up a marker on the site. SYDNEY HARRIS

The true test of a man's mettle is his behavior when his adversary thinks he has him completely at bay.
O. A. BATTISTA

When you appeal to force, there's one thing you must never do—lose. DWIGHT D. EISENHOWER

Treating your adversary with respect is striking soft in battle. ENGLISH PROVERB

There's nothing like the sight of an old enemy down on his luck.   EURIPIDES

If you shoot at a king you must kill him.
                    RALPH WALDO EMERSON

You have undertaken to ruin me. I will not sue you, for law takes too long. I will ruin you.
                    CORNELIUS VANDERBILT

The fight is never about grapes or lettuce. It is always about people.   CESAR CHAVEZ

The ultimate measure of a man is not where he stands in moments of comfort but where he stands at times of challenge and controversy.
                    MARTIN LUTHER KING, JR.

The underdog often starts the fight, and occasionally the upper dog deserves to win.
                    EDGAR WATSON HOWE

Threatened folks live long.   THOMAS FULLER

What is important is food, money and opportunities for scoring off one's enemies. Give a man these things and you won't hear much squawking out of him.
                    BRIAN O'NOLAN

Our worst enemies are often the friends we once talked to as only a friend should.   *Esquire*

You must not fight too often with one enemy, or you will teach him all your art of war.
                    NAPOLEON BONAPARTE

Thank God I've always avoided persecuting my enemies. ADOLF HITLER

We are going to have peace even if we have to fight for it. DWIGHT D. EISENHOWER

Enemy—SP (Suppressive Person) Order. Fair Game. May be deprived of property or injured by any means by any Scientologist without any discipline of the Scientologist. May be tricked, sued or lied to or destroyed. L. RON HUBBARD

Revenge is a much more punctual paymaster than gratitude. CHARLES CALEB COLTON

You can discover what your enemy fears most by observing the means he uses to frighten you. ERIC HOFFER

I don't know what effect these men will have upon the enemy, but, by God, they terrify me. DUKE of WELLINGTON

If you want to make peace, you don't talk to your friends. You talk to your enemies. MOSHE DAYAN

A strong foe is better than a weak friend. EDWARD DAHLBERG

The wise man draws more advantage from his enemies than a fool from his friends. PROVERB

Nothing ever perplexes an adversary so much as an appeal to his honour. BENJAMIN DISRAELI

Don't worry because a rival imitates you. As long as he follows in your tracks he cannot overtake them.
ANON

Treating your adversary with respect is giving him an advantage to which he is not entitled.
SAMUEL JOHNSON

A cunning gamester never plays the card which his adversary expects, and far less that which he desires.
BALTASAR GRACIAN

Better a hundred enemies outside the house than one inside.
ARABIAN PROVERB

The wise man always throws himself on the side of his assailants. It is more his interest than it is theirs to find his weak point.
RALPH WALDO EMERSON

Make no little enemies—people with whom you differ for some petty, insignificant personal reason. Instead, I would urge you to cultivate "mighty opposites"—people with whom you disagree on big issues, with whom you will fight to the end over fundamental convictions. And that fight, I can assure you, will be good for you and your opponent.
THOMAS J. WATSON, JR.

Carry the battle to them. Don't let them bring it to you. Put them on the defensive. And don't ever apologize for anything.
HARRY S. TRUMAN

To refrain from imitation is the best revenge.
MARCUS AURELIUS

By paying our other debts, we are equal with all mankind, but in refusing to pay a debt of revenge, we are superior. CHARLES CALEB COLTON

I'd rather my enemies envied me, than I my enemies. TITUS MACCIUS PLAUTUS

The enemy advances, we retreat; the enemy camps, we harass; the enemy tires, we attack; the enemy retreats, we pursue. MAO TSE-TUNG

Even in a declaration of war one observes the rules of politeness. PRINCE OTTO von BISMARCK

Strong men are made by opposition; like kites they go up against the wind. FRANK HARRIS

One sword keeps another in the sheath. GEORGE HERBERT

Just vengeance does not call for punishment. PIERRE CORNEILLE

Who offends writes on sand, who is offended on marble. ITALIAN PROVERB

Conscience

Conscience tells you what to do
And puts you in a tizzy;
But when it tries to get to you,
The line is sometimes busy.

A business must have a conscience as well as a counting house.　　　SIR MONTAGUE BURTON

Conscience is, in most men, an anticipation of the opinion of others.　　　SIR HENRY TAYLOR

There is something about a cupboard that makes a skeleton terribly restless.　　　ANON

A conscience which has been bought once will be bought twice.　　　NORBERT WIENER

Conscience is the little voice that tells you you shouldn't have done it after you did.　　　ANON

What after all is a halo? It's only one more thing to keep clean.　　　CHRISTOPHER FRY

We always keep God waiting, while we admit more importunate suitors.　　　MALCOLM de CHAZAL

The voice of conscience has a difficult time making connections with the ears.

　　　EDGAR WATSON HOWE

Conscience makes cowboys of us all.　　　SAKI

The devil's boots don't creak.
　　　　　　　SCOTTISH PROVERB

Conscience is a mother-in-law whose visit never ends.
　　　　　　　HENRY LOUIS MENCKEN

Conscience gets a lot of credit that belongs to cold feet.　　　　　　　ANON

Well, I've got as much conscience as any man in business can afford to keep—just a little, you know, to swear by as 'twere . . .
　　　　　　　HARRIET BEECHER STOWE

Conscience is due to yourself, reputation to your neighbour.　　　SAINT AUGUSTINE

So live that you can look any man in the eye and tell him to go to hell.　　　　　　　ANON

Next to Death, the most infallible remedy for a guilty conscience is success.　　　EDMUND FULLER

Mankind had rather suspect something than to know it.　　　　　　　JOSH BILLINGS

Trust that man in nothing who has not a conscience in everything.　　　LAURENCE STERNE

Philanthropist—a rich (and usually bald) old gentleman who has trained himself to grin while his conscience is picking his pocket . . .
　　　　　　　AMBROSE BIERCE

Whatsoever things are true, whatsoever things are honest, whatsoever things are just, whatsoever things are pure, whatsoever things are lovely, whatsoever things are of good report; if there be any virtue, and if there be any praise, think on these things. *Philippians*

INDEX

ABOUT THE AUTHOR

ROLF B. WHITE was born on the first day of Spring,
1932, of a Swedish mother and English father.
He was educated at the 500-year-old Rugby School,
and has been an officer in the British army,
a member of an exploration expedition,
and an international motor racing driver;
he has worked as a lumberjack in Norway,
a continental tractor trailer driver,
and a milkman before becoming managing director
of three large subsidiaries of world-wide companies.
He has spent many years in the United States,
based in Columbus, Ohio, has senior contacts
with many U.S. industrial companies,
and has lectured
at the World Energy Congress.

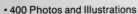